# HEART OF THE
# LILIKO'I

# What Reviewers Said About *Blue Water Dreams*

"…when Lania and Oly set their differences aside and embrace their sexual chemistry, the scenes are graceful, sure, and spicy. This debut shows promise."—*Publishers Weekly*

"It is refreshing to read a love story where there is no jealous triangle, just people working out changes in their individual visions of their futures. …Lania and Oly's sexual encounters are described in detail that goes on for several pages each time. The author uses the reality of what current medical treatment offers trans men to allow her characters to become quite inventive sexually."—*GLBT Reviews*

"Not your typical romance. …It has some extremely hot sex—something I neglected to mention in the original review because I was so blown away by how well-drawn its characters are and how naturally they interact. An absolutely terrific first effort by a novelist I'll enjoy reading even more from in the future."—*Out In Print*.

## By the Author


Blue Water Dreams

Heart of the Liliko‘i

# HEART OF THE LILIKO'I

*by*

Dena Hankins

2015

# HEART OF THE LILIKO'I

ISBN 13: 978-1-62639-556-5

THIS TRADE PAPERBACK ORIGINAL IS PUBLISHED BY
BOLD STROKES BOOKS, INC.
P.O. BOX 249
VALLEY FALLS, NY 12185

FIRST EDITION: OCTOBER 2015

---

**CREDITS**
EDITOR: CINDY CRESAP
PRODUCTION DESIGN: SUSAN RAMUNDO
COVER DESIGN BY SHERI (GRAPHICARTIST2020@HOTMAIL.COM)

# Acknowledgments

This book wouldn't exist without the hard work of a handful of helpful people and resources written by others.

Harold Gary Rhodes provided me with vivid images of working construction in Hawai'i. He inspired me with his decision to leave the industry, with his artistry with wood, and with his stories about how badly a job can go wrong if they found remains.

Kekoa Harman, M.A., is an associate professor of Hawaiian studies in the Ka Haka 'Ula o Ke'elikōlani College of Hawaiian Language School at the University of Hawai'i at Hilo. He checked my usage of Hawaiian words and typography, teaching me about the 'okina and the kahakō and ensuring that I was aware of multiple meanings in the words I chose. He also did me a much greater, though more ephemeral service, in reading the entire book and providing feedback about how Hawaiian culture is represented. He deserves credit for places I get these right, but I take full responsibility for where I may get them wrong. For example, I was unable to get the rhythm of pidgin and so did not use it, though some of my characters certainly would.

Of the many books I read to get a sense of Hawaiian culture beyond what I picked up from living there, two were most helpful to me. *A Nation Rising: Hawaiian Movements for Life, Land, and Sovereignty*, edited by Noelani Goodyear-Ka'ōpua, Ikaika Hussey, and Erin Kahunawaika'ala provided me with a tremendous understanding of the reasons and actions of the independence movement in Hawai'i. *House of Skin: Prize-Winning Stories*, by Kiana Davenport, brought me inside the culture, as only fiction can.

# Dedication

To James, who did the dirty work so I could write this
and who inspires me with love and strength
of conviction. I love you more every day.

## Chapter One

Kerala circled the plot of land, striding from the black beach cliff to the rough lump of exposed pāhoehoe lava that marked the far edge of the construction site. Salt glistened in the bright, tropical sunlight wherever waves had crashed ashore. The Kona side of the Island of Hawai‘i didn't get enough rain to wash it away.

She mounted the hill and turned to look back at the marker flags and check their positions. The litany of next steps flowed in her thoughts, but she focused on the job at hand. She took a step to the left.

The hill disintegrated under her boots.

Surfing the lava rock wave, Kerala dropped ten feet in an instant and thought, oh, shit!

Near the bottom, her feet scraped against the flattening slope and she crumpled, curling and dropping a shoulder faster than thought.

She and the rubble hit the bottom of the grade, and she rolled until she cleared the falling debris.

Momentum spent, she lay on her side and kept her arms around her head for a moment, listening to the ground. Adrenaline sharpened her senses. Tender, tough greenery lay smashed under her. Its freshness complicated the smells of saltwater, dirt, and sun-heated lava rock. She listened closely, tensed to move, but only small spills continued from the top of the new slope. When she confirmed she wouldn't be buried under another rock fall, she rolled onto her back and stretched out flat. She opened her eyes and blinked into the tropical sun, feeling along her bones and muscles from the inside. No real injury.

A burst of fury propelled her to her feet.

Shouts and commotion from the top of the hill cascaded toward her as several men slid-fell to where she stood. By the time they reached her, she had checked the newly exposed rock for clues on why the grade had given way. She would hurt like a bitch later, but she'd use the adrenaline high while it lasted.

When the crew supervisor, Jack Zelinski, stepped forward, he did so with all the care of a handler feeding a tiger.

"Want the first aid kit?"

"What I want are the soils report and the drainage report. I want the survey and the topo. I want them down here where I can compare this motherless mess to the original shelf."

Jack, a thirty-year construction worker, turned to a young man who stood gawking and pushed him away from Kerala. "Stevens, table here…" The growl of Jack's voice faded as he directed the kid to haul a couple of sawhorses down for a makeshift table.

Kerala studied the site in a crystalline state of mind. Deliberating as she turned in a full circle, she scanned the brush and dirt. A cold chill fought another molten eruption of fury when she spotted the track marks.

Sabotage.

A brutal clenching of her sore jaw made her aware of her guy wire tension. She worked her neck muscles as loose as she could while assessing the clues around her. The crew set up a rough plywood-on-sawhorse table, spread out the plans she'd asked for, and weighed down the edges.

Jack tromped over. "Thoughts?"

"Tire tracks."

"Yeah. New?"

"Yeah. The bastards fucked up this time."

"Call the cops?"

"Call Hekili, then the cops. While we wait for them, we need to figure out what happened. Check our notes on the erosion plan. I think we had that hill marked for a problem."

Jack showed her the first aid kit in his hand. "Clean up first. You're gonna scare the children."

"Is it that bad?"

"Head wound." Jack looked into the kit, shrugged, and closed it. "This won't cut it. Better rinse off."

Methodically, she voiced the curses she'd been too busy for when she'd fallen. She scrambled up the hill without pausing in her tirade. She didn't feel any pain, but broken pāhoehoe cut like any sharp blade—the slice happened fast and the blood came first.

She resisted the urge to feel for the wound with her filthy hands. Her baseball cap had come off in the fall and a stickiness pulled the fringe of hair on her neck. She rocked her head. From the skin's pull, the lava had sliced her on or just above her occipital bone.

Blood happens, she thought as she reached the work truck with its five-gallon yellow and orange water cooler. Contractors tried as hard as anyone to avoid injury, but barked knuckles, banged shins, and head knocks were inevitable. She rinsed her hands first, then ducked her head under the flow. She kept the water coming with a thumb on the button.

As the only woman on the crew and its project manager, getting hurt on the job was more than an irritation. She showed off her scars with as much verve as anyone and exaggerated the associated stories, but while scars were tough, wounds were weak.

She drenched her head and grabbed a clean rag to hold against the cut. No pain, just the warmth of fresh blood soaking the rag.

Damn it.

A patrol car pulled into the driveway and Kerala waited where she was. Working with other people's property, she'd been forced to call the cops more than once for vandalism or theft or vagrants sleeping on work sites. It was almost always more trouble than it was worth.

A uniformed officer got out of the driver's side while his partner kept talking on the radio. He sauntered over, looking her up and down. Great, one of those.

"Looks like you got yourself hurt." He may as well have called her little lady.

"Looks can be deceiving. The hill's over here." Kerala led him across the rock and stopped at the top. "This hill must have been undercut by someone. It was stable when we had the survey done and just now it crumbled like feta."

"Uh-huh. And who do you think is stealing dirt from an empty lot?"

This was why she didn't like talking to cops. "I don't think they were stealing dirt. I think they were setting a trap. If you'll come on down, Jack and I can show you—"

"No need. I can see fine from here."

She looked at his shiny shoes and bit her tongue. "There are marks on the hillside that look like excavator bucket teeth and tracks heading into the ʻaʻā over there."

"Can't get tracks from ʻaʻā."

"No, but leading to it." Kerala stopped and took a deep breath. "Would you like me to send you pictures?"

"Sure. Here's my card." She took it in silence. "Why don't you send your guys up here? Anyone who saw what happened."

Jack came at her gesture and took over. While the cop questioned Stevens, she stepped closer to Jack and commanded in an undertone, "No rumors. No chat about the tracks or the cut marks."

"Saw those, did you?"

"Yeah, I saw those. I'm amazed that they're intact." Her slight dizziness felt familiar, like a minor case of dehydration, and she pushed it to the back of her mind to focus on the issue at hand. "Get pictures."

"You're still bleeding, Kel."

"I've been keeping pressure on." She reached back and burrowed her fingers through the hair near the slice until she found the warm suck of blood. She tried to separate the stuck-together hair strands, but the wound gaped under the pressure. Fresh, hot blood covered her fingers, and her stomach floated toward her throat. Her eyesight blurred and she dropped into a crouch to avoid fainting. Still no pain. Head wounds were unpredictable that way.

Focused on breathing, Kerala became aware of Jack's hands under her armpits. She stood with his assistance and shoved him away when she'd gained her feet.

"Hospital."

"Aw, Jack."

"Hospital."

She hissed in frustration. Let some ham-handed ER nurse poke at her head? "Head wounds heal fast."

"Might could use some stitches. Hard hat's gonna hurt until healing's pau." Jack's shadowed eyes seemed worried, but the lag before she remembered that pau meant done in Hawaiian decided her.

"Yeah, yeah. Get me to the hospital, Mother."

"On it." Jack turned to the men standing a respectful distance away. "Stevens, you done with the cop?" At the kid's nod, he said, "Get Kel to the hospital."

When she jumped into the jacked-up work truck, Kerala gritted her teeth, turning a moan into a grunt. She was starting to stiffen. She glanced at Stevens, a kid of twenty-five and a construction veteran of almost ten years, and sighed. He wasn't known for careful driving. The kid hauled himself behind the wheel and started the truck.

On arrival in Kapaau a short time later, Kerala opened the passenger door and jumped to the ground. The instant her old boots hit the ground, a headache exploded in rays from the wound at the back of her head.

She eyed the cascade of blood on the back of the truck's seat. "Back to work. Stick to the speed limit this time. After you're done at the site, clean the truck. I want every speck of blood gone, understand?"

Stevens groaned. He drove off at a normal speed, waiting to gun the engine until he turned the first corner.

Alone at last, she let her head bow to the pain that had finally come and regulated her breathing. The acute care section of the Kohala Hospital awaited her. Reluctance warred with the pain. Home was a few blocks away. Maybe she could clean herself well enough.

The thought of rock fragments in the wound brought her around to push open the door to the antiseptic scent.

When the intake nurse looked up, Kerala turned around in a circle. Unimpressed, the nurse stated the obvious. "Head wound."

"Just a cut."

"We'll be the judges of that, my dear. Auē."

Kerala gave in to the flurry of activity.

❖

At home four hours later, Kerala reclined in her favorite chair with some lemonade. The pills dulled the headache to a low roar. No concussion. Her dog, Bogart, lay beside her chair. He seemed to sense that she was uncomfortable.

Fucking lava shelves. Smooth and ropy until plants anchored themselves in crevices. The roots broke down the sheets of lava and created good soil over time. A couple of feet down, though, the pāhoehoe lingered, sharp as any obsidian blade she'd ever found on the lake in the Cascade Mountains. She had always loved her parents' summer house on the West Coast. The misty Oregon mountain country had been so different from their daily life in Philadelphia.

Kerala, amused by her floating thoughts, sipped her lemonade. She didn't often reminisce, and those idyllic vacations hunkered way back in her memory. Nine months in Hawai'i and she lay there mooning over memories of childhood homes.

Her parents hadn't provided a real home anyway. Tony and the construction crew and the office folk had been her family for eighteen years. Why did Tony's death still feel fresh after a year and a half?

She'd have kept the team together, kept the reputation alive, but Tony's widow sold the construction company to a big developer firm.

Not her company, not her choice.

Fuck it. Reminiscent, now maudlin. She shifted in her beat-up old recliner and resettled her head against the donut shaped pillow she'd purchased when she got her prescription filled.

Her stitches would itch like mad in the sauna under her hard hat. She spent large portions of every day sweating out as much water as she gulped in every free moment. The mix of salt and stray hairs was bound to irritate the short, deep cut. Would it have been better with shoulder-length hair? She had gone short at the back, longer toward the front. It swooped under her jaw when she didn't trap it under a hat. The asymmetrical swing of it was supposed to be dykey. She didn't have to come out as often when she could be IDed as a lesbian on sight.

She pulled her cell phone from its holster on her belt. She set her drink on the table beside her, speed-dialed Jack, and waited with scant patience for him to answer.

"'Lo."

"Jack. Did you get the pictures I wanted?"

"Yep. Get fixed up?"

"Some stitches. Rotten lava must've been damn sharp. Clean little slice."

"Shirt's ruined."

Kerala laughed, the sound echoing in her empty living room. "Yeah, Jack. The shirt is already in the garbage. I don't have time to try out the latest Betty Crocker tips for taking blood out of cotton."

"You eaten?"

"What, are you my mother for real now? I'm fine. I'll pick up some food in a little while. I'm kicking back right now, but I want to get some paperwork done since I won't be back on the job site today."

"Eat something with iron in it."

"Yeah, uh-huh. Do you want to bring the camera to me or e-mail the pictures from home?"

"I'll e-mail 'em. If I have trouble, Danny'll fix me up." Jack sounded both proud and confused at the idea of his ten-year-old son teaching him how to use his laptop.

"I'll have to forward them to the police, not that they'll be any help. That guy as much as patted me on the head and told me I was a crybaby." Kerala gnawed her cheek for a moment, thoughts racing in circles. "Damn. I can't figure out why someone would try to sabotage this job."

"Breakfast meeting?"

"Yeah. Call Nahoa and ask him to meet us there. I know it's out of your way, but pick me up?" Kerala tried to make it sound casual.

"Not driving?" Jack's voice roughened like a revved Harley. "You said you didn't hit your head."

"I didn't!" Kerala cursed herself for the defensiveness. Outrage was a better screen if questioned.

"Why can't you drive?"

"It's nothing. The doctors wanted to keep me overnight in case my brain ruptured while I slept or something. It's ridiculous to pay overnight rates when it's not necessary."

"What kind of a dimwitted halftrack thing was that to do? It's on worker's comp to pay, not you." Jack's vocal Harley was in full growl. "You're as thick as manure and half as useful."

"What do you know? Your brain's as good as new—you've never used it!"

"Hey, I'm busy here. I'll ignore you later." Click.

Kerala hit end on her cell phone. Wait! She leaned the recliner all the way back and closed her eyes while she waited for redial to bring Jack back. "Poor guy, you hung up on accident. I know it takes you longer to rest nowadays than it does to get tired, but maybe it's just narcolepsy. They've got a pill for that, you know." She punched end, satisfied, and jiggled her heel on the footrest of the recliner that dragged her deeper into her exhaustion.

## CHAPTER TWO

Y ou look at the pictures?" Jack's eyes tracked her while Kerala leapt into the truck's crew cab with a boost from her toe on the running board.

Kerala tried to slam her door without aggravating the pain dogging her head. "Yep. And I got all my notes out and went back over everything that has gone wrong on this job. It's a big list." She turned off the shit-kicking country music playing at background volume.

Jack shook his heavy head as he put the truck in gear and backed out of her driveway. "Never been a smooth job in the history of construction."

"It's more than that, Jack." Kerala tapped her fingertips on her knee. "I'll show you the list when we get to the 'Ohana Diner."

"'Kay." Jack idled down the road, easing over bumps and gassing a little between them. Kerala looked over at him, annoyed, studying his heavy jaw and square flattop, his clean-shaven, tidy-gorilla appearance, and his blank face as he asked a delicate question. "Eat last night?"

Kerala tried to slice him with her eyes, but he didn't look at her. "I ate. Why are you driving like a blind grandma?"

"No hurry."

"No reason to be a danger to traffic either. Someone comes around a corner fast and we'll be steel soup." Kerala crossed her arms in front of her, glaring at Jack.

"Whatever you say, boss." Jack increased his speed by a few miles per hour, poker-faced, but Kerala could feel the laughter he swallowed. She looked out the windshield at the road inching toward her. Silence filled the cab like concrete poured into a form.

Jack cracked it. "What did you eat?"

"None of your business."

"Sleep on the recliner again?

"None of your business." Her temper started to slip. "I can take care of myself."

Jack nodded, noncommittal, and signaled for the turn into the diner.

Kerala slammed from the truck and stalked inside. She went to the brown wooden booth in the back corner of the coffee-scented diner, where Nahoa waited. She sat next to him as Jack followed. "This guy won't get off my back. I guess he's defending his mother of the year title."

Jack settled into the red Naugahyde cushion opposite. He turned his coffee mug upright. He looked at them, making them wait another moment. "I'll leave your mothering to the jackal that birthed you."

"Ouch!" Nahoa gave Kerala a consolatory, ungentle pat on the shoulder. "Not going easy on Kel just cause she has a broken head, eh?" Nahoa's laughter ribboned the room, bringing smiles to the customers who heard it.

She grimaced. "It's a relief to be treated normally. He drove fifteen miles an hour the whole way here."

Nahoa radiated good humor. Kerala's lips twisted though she tried to keep a straight face.

"I'm always slow before coffee." Jack turned in his seat and shook his mug at the overworked waitress. She wiggled her head back at him like she was sassing him but sailed to the coffeemaker and grabbed the pot before heading back down the row to take their order.

The waitress filled their mugs, plopped the pot on the tabletop, and raised her eyebrows.

"Yep."

"Yep."

"Yep."

Kerala eyed Jack, considering, but Nahoa beat her to the punch. "You know, that shit's not good for you."

Jack sighed. "I know. Someday, she'll slap me for looking at her like that."

The laugh escaped before she could stop it but turned to a grunt when Nahoa jostled her sore shoulder. He caught her body's automatic reaction. "What the hell, Kel? You said you were fine."

"I am fine." Kerala gritted her teeth. She didn't want to talk about her health all day. "I have a scratch on my scalp and a couple of bruises."

"I heard you filled the cab of the truck with blood from your head. Stevens was still cleaning it and cussing you at eight o'clock last night. I also heard you rolled at the bottom of that hill like a champ, but you looked stiff by the time you reached the hospital. What's bruised? Skin, muscle, ribs?"

Kerala turned sideways on the bench and looked at Nahoa from under her brows. Nahoa, of all people, could expect an answer from her. As the only son of Hekili Kalama, the owner of Mālama Construction, he was the reluctant heir apparent of the company that paid her worker's comp insurance. She waited for the waitress to refill their coffees, and her expression had that poor lady skittering away without a word. "I'll tell you guys this once. I got stitches, but I didn't hit my head and I have authorization to return to duty. I'm stiff in the shoulder I rolled on, and that'll get worked out as I move around. And if anyone asks me about the state of my health again, I will assign that person to wheelbarrowing concrete until Mauna Loa erupts." She cast a sidelong warning at Nahoa. "Spread the word."

Nahoa studied his fingernails while Jack emptied his coffee cup again. Kerala sat in the silence she'd created, comfortable and satisfied that she'd gotten her point across. She sipped the strong Kona coffee, enjoying the scald in her throat.

When she was ready, she opened her portfolio case and pulled out a thick sheaf of paper. "Here are printouts of the pictures."

Nahoa slid the papers closer. "Dad said you cc'ed him on the e-mail you sent the police. What did they say about all this?"

"They said there was no evidence a crime was committed." Kerala shifted in her seat to watch Nahoa. She'd marked the tire tracks and the tooth marks from an excavator bucket where the ground had been undercut, leaving a weak, insubstantial ledge where once had been an abrupt hill. "No one saw the hill crumble and the cop seems to think I'm trying to hide a clumsy fall."

Nahoa looked at her with sympathy. He was Native Hawaiian. Any time she ran into trouble with Hawaiian ways, Nahoa could fix it.

He could get more work from the guys than any other super she'd ever worked with. The Hawaiian construction industry had a bad reputation for slow, inefficient workers, but no one ever wanted to disappoint Nahoa. Before she'd hired on, she hadn't known why Mālama was the best at making their deadlines inside their budgets.

Nahoa was a favorite with everyone he met, twenty-six years old, muscled, and lean from labor and surfing. High cheekbones and a well-defined jaw gave him a clean-chiseled look, but his liquid black eyes fringed with thick lashes and his thin-lipped, mobile mouth made him beautiful. His lips quirked and bowed and spread wide across his face, often creasing his cheeks and eyes with huge grins.

His good-natured expression hid something darker. Kerala was confident of her judgment of people, and she recognized someone who hid an inner pain. Perhaps he didn't date because the injury in his past involved a woman. He might seem wide open, but he wouldn't answer questions on the subject.

As he looked over the documentation, his lips turned upside down. He looked at Jack and over at her. "Kel, this will stop."

The furnace of anger took her aback. "Yeah, that's the plan."

Jack seemed to ask Nahoa a silent question, and Nahoa shook his head in answer.

She studied them both. "What aren't you telling me?" She sat through the ensuing silence, determined to wait out their desire to not speak.

The waitress broke the intensity of the moment, to Kerala's frustration. "Jack gets Portuguese sausage, Spam, scrambled eggs, rice, pancakes, and guava juice. Loco Moco for Nahoa, with brown instead of white rice, hamburger patty well done, over easy eggs, and extra gravy. And Kel's usual." Jack's meal came on two plates the size of serving trays and Nahoa's came in a tureen. They both eyed Kerala's breakfast. It was about half as much food as the Loco Moco and maybe a quarter of Jack's cardiac arrest of a meal.

She shrugged. "I like the Japanese breakfast." She sipped her miso soup from the bowl. Delicious. She smashed her fish into the rice and pickled plums and added soy sauce. "How are we going to make it stop? The cops laughed us off. They won't be any help."

"They're irrelevant anyway. I can get further without them." When Kerala stared at Nahoa, waiting for more, he cut into his hamburger patty and filled his mouth with burger, rice, and gravy. These two men, the only people she trusted on the island, knew something they weren't sharing with her. Her bouncing leg set up a squeak in the booth.

Jack spoke between bites. "Tire marks don't tell us much. Tread's a common off-road style. Tracks disappear in some ʻaʻā that goes all the way to the road. Fact that we got a few feet is surprising, considering."

Nahoa spread the pictures to the side of his bowl and looked them over again. "The cuts in the hillside are fresh, made by an excavator with a small bucket. They trucked it in, unloaded it in this open spot, and did the work." He studied the picture while he ate. "Whoever did this knows a thing or two about soil loading. They managed to create a ledge that would collapse under someone as small as Kel. You're what, 110, 120 pounds?"

Kerala nodded. After close to two decades in construction, she'd lost any sensitivity around her size. At least Nahoa had aimed high.

He whistled. "That's a delicate operation. Getting the roof of the cut thin enough to crumble under you but not under its own weight. Plus getting the angle right so you'd get far enough out on the ledge before realizing the hill didn't exist anymore."

Jack paused in his steady eating. "Dirt."

Nahoa frowned. "Yeah, where's the dirt? That should have made for a heavy load on the way out."

"Look at the pics from my first walk around the property. They didn't take all that much material out. Strategic." Kerala polished off the last of her rice and fish and pushed her plate away. "So the cop doesn't get it, but we agree. It's malicious." She pulled another sheaf of papers from her portfolio. "What about these?"

Jack grabbed the papers this time and thumbed through them, getting sausage grease on the bottom of the stack. He hesitated over the list on the last page.

She asked, "When have you seen so much go wrong?"

Jack glanced at Nahoa. "Burial grounds." He put his fork down.

Nahoa looked skeptical. "You think ʻaumākua are trucking in dozers now?"

Kerala tried to keep up. "Who are ʻaumākua?"

Nahoa said, "Ancestral spirits, family guardians. I'm sure you got this in some sort of orientation, Kel, but it's easy to forget if you've never seen it. Do you remember being told to look out for black sand?"

"Yes." Her headache picked up the beat set by her knee.

Jack said, "Once, a while back, we were using a big dozer, a 375 Komatsu. Exhaust fell off. Mechanic came to work on it and noticed black sand that the operator had almost cut through. Found lots of remains. Covered the bodies with tarps, fenced off the area. Over the next few weeks, tracks fell off both sides of that dozer, engines overheated, hydraulic hoses broke. Equipment wouldn't run for two hours uninterrupted. Something was fighting back. The land or the ʻaumākua."

It sounded too much like a campfire story to put credence in, but Jack epitomized down-to-earth. "What did you do?"

"Relocated all the remains within fifty feet of where we found them in small stone walls. Tomb ended about ten feet square. Landscaper filled the top with soil and planted flowers. I wouldn't spend one night in those condos."

Silence reigned for a moment, until Kerala glanced at her watch. She sighed and asked a plaintive question. "Do you want me to believe that this site is haunted?"

Jack shook his head. "Not haunted. But maybe protected."

Kerala pressed her fingertips to her eyelids and counted to three. In her respectable history in construction, she had never been faced with a project that required her to fight ghosts.

Nahoa took the list from Jack. "All this happened on one job?"

Kerala tapped her fork on her napkin. "Five permit applications lost, the site archaeological survey delayed three times, couldn't get a soils engineer to take the job, topography done in the wrong place, and the state highways department tried to refuse the old road as an existing driveway. I can't get subs to even bid the job. Equipment breakdowns. Then there's the stuff that feels personal."

Nahoa looked up. "Personal?"

"Yeah. Rotor stolen from my car the day of the highways hearing. My hard hat went missing. Something broken off inside the lock on my truck's toolbox." She sighed and stretched her always-tight neck. "What do you think, guys? Is there a way to put it together? This person, or these people, know a lot about construction. Who could do all these things and who would think of them? I can't imagine the same person influencing the state highway department and stealing my rotor."

Jack said, "More than one group."

The generalities were starting to grate on her nerves. "Groups wanting what?"

Jack turned his coffee mug in his rough hands. "A lot of the island is believed to have been used as burial ground. Some places are in old stories; some are guesses."

"Okay, and this site is rumored to be an old burial ground."

Nahoa stared at his gravy. "Not just rumored. Believed. That healthy liliko'i vine is part of it."

"Liliko'i is passion fruit, right? How does the vine play into it? Is the tree important too?"

He looked up. "The tree is koa, more at home higher on the mountains. But the liliko'i vine growing on it is healthy. Unnaturally healthy. They don't grow well in dry, rocky soil. Since the liliko'i started growing there, more people believe that the land is home to ancestors. And I mean believe in the most irrational kind of way."

Jack said, "Not so irrational."

Nahoa shrugged. "There are believers who take it as religious and natural fact that these are burial grounds and must be protected, that 'iwi kūpuna will not rest if they are disturbed." The flat look in Nahoa's eye gave Kerala a cold chill. "Sometimes the sovereignty groups get involved. They go for publicity and try to delay permits, embarrass developers, or make the project prohibitively expensive. Others do whatever comes to mind to protect 'āina, the land. Dumb kids start out messing with things and it gets out of hand. Some people monkey wrench projects, stuff like the nuisances you've had.

I'd say this job has been targeted by the whole range." His grin had a frightening cast to it. "It will stop."

Kerala stilled her leg. "What do we do?"

"I will make it stop." Kerala shook her head, but Nahoa touched her arm. "Don't go to my dad with these details yet. He'll try to throw his weight around, and he doesn't have the credibility for that. He's worked for and gotten the kind of middle-class, assimilated life that wins no friends among these people. I've been on his side for a long time, but I can talk to them better than he can. Let me out and I'll see who's behind this."

Kerala checked her watch again. Against her strong desire to browbeat the whole story from him, she slid from the booth and stood, hands on hips, looking at the top of his head. Nahoa tidied the papers she'd brought and asked as he stashed them in his bag, "Can I keep these?"

When he rose, she got right in his face—he was only a couple inches taller than she was—and spoke softly. "I want it taken care of, but I will not be left in the dark. When you've gone wherever you're going, talked to whoever you're talking to, call me. We hash this out today. Do you hear me?"

Nahoa responded to the authority in her voice like most people did. He straightened and agreed. "I'll tell you what I find out and what I can get done." A grim look flickered over his face. "And hopefully nothing like this will ever happen again."

Kerala stepped back and let Nahoa move away from the table. A couple of steps away, he turned, his usual smile in place. "Aloha."

Jack nodded and Kerala waved as she sat back down. She considered Jack's impassive face. Jack, of all people, could handle the silent treatment, so she didn't even try that tack. "Come on then. If I won't get an explanation from you, at least I can put you to work."

❖

Kerala ignored her stiff shoulder and hefted a case of bottled water from the back of the work truck to a cart. Stevens showed off for the office workers by carrying five stacked cases, biceps rippling as he hefted the weight higher. Joy, Nahoa's cousin and Mālama

Construction's office manager, had called with a summons from Hekili and asked her to stop at Costco.

She leaned against the truck's tailgate and absorbed the dusty smell of a contractor's yard. She missed her friends from Philadelphia, but she had what she loved most right here. Good hard work. The safety-yellow Komatsu dozers, backhoe loaders, and excavators lined the chain link fences.

The scrub desert outside the fence belied the tinge of rain in the air. If all went as usual, the clouds would bunch up behind Mauna Loa and dump their liquid load over Hilo, Puna, and Pahoa. Some would slip between Mauna Loa and Mauna Kea and run up against Hualālai, a much smaller mountain. The rainfall on Hualālai and its surrounding hills succored Kona coffee, prized by aficionados.

Those clouds would be light and dissipated by the time she made it to the work site. Not that it never rained. Storm systems that made it over the mountains raged like hurricanes. The violence surprised her every time.

The sun soaked into her tight neck and shoulders like hot tub jets. Stevens finished unloading and Kerala pulled a shopping list from her zippered nylon portfolio.

"Odds and ends for the trailer."

Stevens took the list without comment, so Kerala hid a smile. He was still working out his punishment for hot-rodding her truck. Sending Stevens to Office Depot was like sending Joy to a lumberyard. Okay, that wasn't fair. Joy knew parts and tools by name and price, even if she didn't know how to use them. Stevens bit his sunburned lip and left. Next time, he'd treat her truck with more respect.

Kerala headed in. Geckos scattered when she reached the shade around the door. The chill inside attacked all her exposed skin.

"Kerala."

"Joy."

Hekili stood in his office with a couple of suits. Mainlanders, since even bankers wore aloha shirts to work in Hawai'i. No need to join that party. She stood at an approximation of parade rest and waited.

A minute later, the men filed past her on their way out and she nodded. Their limp trousers and sweaty shirts mirrored their wilted expressions.

Kerala met Hekili's eyes and allowed her smile to show. His hard black eyes gleamed back. Abundant flesh creased with his satisfied smile. Nahoa would look like him some day, but he was a hundred pounds away from his father's bulk.

Kerala followed him back into his office, closing the door behind her.

"Who was that?" Kerala grabbed a water from the small refrigerator and perched on the edge of a planning table. She twisted off the top and gulped half before sputtering at the icy touch on her teeth.

"Money men. We discussed the payout schedule on the Dietrich job."

"Holding every penny as long as they can?"

"Always." Hekili stood at ease in the middle of the room, facing Kerala. The immovable object, grinning like a shark. "They'll pay. Right now, they feel small and frustrated because they flew out from Honolulu for a ten-minute meeting. I had to cut it short. You are very important."

"Honored."

Hekili sat in a large rolling chair at the planning table and gestured for her to join him. Kerala eased into a chair and set down her portfolio.

"Yesterday, we were staking out the worksite, checking the surveyors' marks, when I walked to the edge of a slope. The edge crumbled under me and I slid, cutting the back of my head on some pāhoehoe but otherwise without injury. The cops showed up pretty fast and took statements. I went to the hospital, got stitches, and went home. This portion of the Dietrich land isn't crucial, but we'll study the photos and the soils data before making a recommendation to Ravi." She slid over her authorization to return to work.

"What happened?"

"I told you. I—"

"You know that land, should have known that ledge."

"Yes. It wasn't a ledge—"

"Then how did it crumble?"

"—when I first saw it. The overhang wasn't on the original topo report." Kerala stopped there. Nahoa had asked that she withhold the full truth for a short while and she'd give him the time he'd requested.

She maintained the cool composure that had been trained into her through years in Philadelphia old money drawing rooms. She worked all day in the heat. He couldn't make her sweat in an air-conditioned office.

Finally, Hekili nodded. "Permits have been slow. Bids aren't coming in. This job is floundering and, as project manager, that's your problem. What are you going to do about it?"

Kerala's composure cracked under this matter-of-fact summation of her first real assignment at Mālama Construction. On one deep inhale and exhale, she released the emotional aspects for later and dealt with the issue at hand.

"I've reworked the schedule to jump once we get the go-ahead on excavation. Since we have the hotel to deconstruct, no one is sitting around. I'd like you to assign Nahoa as liaison with the local subcontractors in hopes we can get some decent bids soon. Once I get this job under my belt, they won't doubt me again." Hekili gave her no reaction, so she continued reluctantly. "And I'll make an effort to be friendlier."

"I can see that this job would benefit from Nahoa's skills. However, it's not just friendliness, Kel. The Hawaiian way is based on relationships. ‘Ohana are extended families, and blood is only one kind of family. I hired you for your experience with the environmental angle, but you're not integrating like I'd hoped."

Great. Another family to push her into a mold she didn't want to fit into. Another set of expectations she would never meet. The hair on her arms rose.

She wanted, more than anything else, the kind of work family she'd lost in Philadelphia. Distant enough to leave her a private life and strong enough to stand for one another. She'd thought the Hawaiian company would respect her for what she respected most in herself while giving her space, outside the main body of the ‘ohana.

She couldn't reject his words. She'd learned that Hawai‘i worked on island time. Her first few months, she'd figured out how to write that into the schedule, plan for it, so that the delays didn't take her by surprise or drive her crazy. Hawai‘i also worked on family ties, and that's what she lacked.

Couldn't blame her for hoping Nahoa could take care of pressing the flesh, but Hekili was as much as telling her she'd have to do it herself.

Whatever the job required. "I'll do better."

"Good. I'll let Joy know to allocate Nahoa to the Dietrich project starting immediately."

"Thank you, sir." Her tension eased. She stood, but she paused before leaving. "Is the company lū'au still on for the day after Christmas?"

"Every year. You'll meet the whole family."

Oh, joy.

# CHAPTER THREE

Kerala strode toward the rental car. "This is a work zone. Do you have business here?"

A familiar-looking guy held out a hand. "Hi, Kerala. Ravi Dietrich."

"Ravi! Good to meet you in person. It's a pleasure to be working on your house." She squinted in the afternoon sun and reached for his hand. His neck, bared by the unbuttoned collar of his dress shirt, changed shades under the hollow of his throat from dark to medium brown. A T-shirt wearer, but one who saw some sunshine. Deep creases bracketed his mouth and lined his forehead. The lines around his eyes deepened when he smiled, the pleased expression settling in like it belonged.

She had enjoyed talking to this client more than most. They'd even veered into personal territory a bit over the months of e-mail contact. He'd come out as genderqueer as part of a conversation about bidets and she'd wondered about his gender flavor since then. Fey man described his manner pretty well, but there were hints that his endocrine system was more about estrogen than testosterone. None of her business, of course.

She might give the crew a head's-up.

When they shook hands, she assessed him. Firm grip, soft skin. The handshake lingered a moment longer than necessary and the softness of his fingers stirred an unexpected response.

Well. Interesting.

Ravi asked, "Have you been to Kerala? The state in India, I mean."

"No. My parents went to India for a meditation retreat in the sixties. And you—have you been to India?" Since he appeared to be a chatty type, Kerala accommodated him. Her childhood training had prepared her for all sorts of social situations, and Tony, back in Philadelphia, had relied on her ability to talk to all types of clients.

"Once, for a conference. My mother's parents were from Kerala."

"I'd like to visit someday. Are you here to watch the hotel come down or do you have something else going?"

"I got an e-mail about the doors and decided to come take a look for myself." Bogart's happy bark rang through the work site and Ravi started toward the sound. "You have a dog here?"

Kerala followed, confused. "I didn't e-mail you about the doors."

He stepped over stacked four-by-eight mahogany beams. "I know, and I wish you had. Joy forwarded your e-mail."

"Okay." Bogart caught sight of them and whined with excitement, his tail shaking his hindquarters so that he danced back and forth as he waited. "You're pretty far away to be a hands-on client, but if that's the way you want to play it."

"I do." He stepped into the invisible boundary of Bogart's roaming area and crouched on his haunches, bringing his head to the level of the mid-sized dog that quivered with repressed desire to jump all over him. "You must be Bogart. Good dog."

When had she told Ravi about Bogart? She had gotten the mutt from the pound several years back and had spent enjoyable hours teaching him manners, plus some good tricks. Bogart had reddish-brown fur, longish on the legs and tidy on his body. His ears cued the spaniel part of his ancestry, soft and silky. His broad forehead and soft mouth signaled lab, though his long nose looked more pointer.

After befriending her dog, Ravi stood and brushed his hands on his pants. "I'm so into this part of the project that I'm staying for a month or two." Kerala raised her eyebrows and he shrugged. "The big yearly board meeting was last week, and it felt like time to get out of the kitchen. Earl's got it under control, but I'll be working remotely too."

"Well, it won't hurt to have you around. We've kept every piece of board and beam and every counter, cabinet, door, and window that looked usable. It'll be good if you can give me your gut reactions as we're warehousing the stuff so we can do a little presorting." She leaned down to scratch Bogart's head when he sat beside her.

"Great. Let's talk about it over dinner tonight. Can I wander around a bit?"

"Just a minute." Kerala said her dog's name and, when he looked up, she made a circle in the air with her finger. "Stay," she said, and he bounded away. "Why do you want to have dinner?"

"We have things to talk about."

"The job?" Caution never hurt.

"Yeah, the job."

"I don't know what time I'll be done."

"We can firm it up later in the day."

There was that CEO tone. Ravi was used to being in charge. "I'll get you a hard hat and a vest, then you can wander anywhere you like except the top floor. It's already come apart enough to be unsafe for visitors."

"I'm not a casual visitor."

"Grab me or Jack and you can go up. But don't go there on your own, got it?"

"Aye, aye." Ravi flashed a mock salute. He watched for a second as Bogart nosed around a hummock of dirt and scrub. "How do you get him to stay?"

"It is a good trick, right? We walk the area first thing in the morning. I say perimeter as we start walking and he gets alert. When we get back to the beginning, I say perimeter again and point inside. Once he's inside the area we walked around, all I have to do is say stay and he'll run around, play, follow animal trails…do all of the normal dog things, but he won't leave that area."

"What made you think of that?"

"A territory thing, I guess. I figured I could give him a territory and he'd stay in it if I asked him to. It doesn't work as well in a busier place, because he gets upset when people walk through it sometimes. He's pretty picky about who he likes and doesn't like."

"I'm honored." He bowed. When he straightened, his gaze tangled with hers. The attraction wasn't one-sided, if she was any judge.

Once she had him settled with the doors and windows they'd removed to date, she headed back to work. On the way, she gave herself an unexpected lecture.

Client. No go.

Liking Ravi was one thing. Feeling attracted to him wasn't going to do either of them any good.

She needed to work off some tension.

Kerala joined her crew on the third floor of the hotel. Cobwebs and piles of rat droppings decorated the old, degraded wooden floor.

She tackled the wainscoting with a crowbar and the screech of old nails shivered up the metal and into her hard hands. She worked up some body heat prying each part away from the wall enough to get a gap for the crowbar in the next section. Not too far, though. Too much at one point splintered the board. Keeping the long boards long was one of the points of the exercise.

Her body misted with sweat in the tropical heat. A lover once called the full-body sheen erotic as hell. Would Ravi agree, or did he prefer his women powdered and languid? Did he even sleep with women? She enjoyed physical activity of all kinds and had discovered sex young, but she couldn't remember the last time she got such a charge from someone she hadn't even touched.

Not really touched.

Kerala grunted as she shrilled the nails from their comfortable beds.

Ravi seemed like the stereotypical scientist, lost in his thoughts to the exclusion of everything around him, but he had looked at her in a way that said he could focus just as hard on her if she'd let him. Long, dark, and shadowed, Ravi's eyes shone quicksilver in shadow and glowed mahogany in the sun. He had a certain softness over strength, a combination that made her think he'd been heavily muscled at some point.

She sighed and stretched. Her shoulder ached, though she'd be damned if anyone would hear that from her. She'd check in with Jack and head back to the office before going home.

Home was a house in Waimea, about twenty-five-hundred feet up in the saddle between Mauna Kea and the Kohala ridge. A continual mist cooled her mornings and evenings, pushed up the island from the Windward side. Still, the Kona and Kohala days cooked her stuffing.

She swung down the scaffold on the outside of the building, a quicker descent than the stairs for someone who'd been up and down scaffolds by the hundreds. On the ground, she took off her hard hat and let herself fold, one vertebra at a time, until her hands hit the dirt. She cursed while she tried to ease the tension from her back and shoulders, neck and arms.

Five years ago, she could have taken that fall without a flinch. Thirty-eight must be that magic age where she hit her prime when it came to ability and the wall when it came to her body's reaction to strain. She worked as hard as anyone still, but she felt it more in the evenings. She couldn't count the number of times she'd woken in her plush recliner with the TV on.

"You won't get out of this conversation by distracting me with the view."

Kerala whipped upright and grimaced when her back pulled tight again. She glared at Ravi with an unreserved, undistracted, fuck-you look. "Shall we start with your implication that I'm afraid to talk to you with your eyes on my ass?"

❖

Ravi's mouth disconnected from his mind while he reeled from the effect of Kerala's eyes. The amber flaked into hints of green around her pupil, but every cell flashed subarctic frostbite at him. He should have been looking at the top of her head, but her energetic presence vibrated to fill a space much larger than her lean body.

He'd been crushing on her mind since she'd taken charge of bidding the project. Now, her physical contradictions fascinated him. She had a youthful body but heavy creases around her eyes and smile lines around her mouth. Regardless of his honest appall at his sexual remark, the image of the strip of pale skin around her lithe waist, bared by her stretch, flashed in his head again and again. A serious amount of mental processor speed compared the red neck, brown face, and lower arms, to the abalone glow of her stretch-revealed upper arms and belly.

He stopped talking when he realized that he didn't know what he'd been saying.

Since Kerala looked at him with grudging acceptance, arms crossed over her chest, he assumed that he'd apologized properly. Derailed, he tossed the conversational ball to her. "What's next for the day?"

"I'm going to check in with Jack and head to the office to do some paperwork."

Ravi swallowed, his thoughts coming back to him as he shoved his fantasies aside. "But we're on for dinner, right?" She looked apt to decline, so he kept talking. "We have to talk about the materials from the hotel, you have to eat sometime, and there's something else I want to discuss." He didn't want to broach the subject in the middle of the work site, but he wasn't letting go of it either.

Kerala acquiesced with scant grace. "Meet me at the Orchid. Seven thirty. Okay?"

"Orchid works. I'll get us a quiet table so we can talk business." Better to have potentially volatile meetings in public.

"Sure. See you then." She took off toward a man wheeling a door and its attached frame out of the hotel. "Whattaya doing? Trying to break your back?" she hollered. "Kekoa, Billy. Come help Superman here get this door down the steps."

Ravi hung back and took off his borrowed hard hat. The four of them swung the solid weight to the ground without jarring the frame. As he turned and walked away, he warmed at the sound of Kerala's continued harangue. "The point is that we don't break shit, man. Remember that. There are plenty of people on this job and you don't have to…"

## CHAPTER FOUR

Ravi sat in the Orchid Café, a restaurant designed to appeal to tourists and anyone else who wanted an upscale meal while casually dressed. The understated décor focused on rich woods, organic colors in the paints, and solid, comfortable chairs and tables. Plenty of room to spread some papers out and a nice separation from other patrons.

He faced the door, watching for her. A smooth, swinging hip passed under the Mylar sign in the front window. Just over the top bobbed a shining cap of brown hair. He'd know that walk after watching her at the old hotel, but he had no idea her ass could look like that. The jeans showed the muscular, springy curve under the pendulum at the base of her spine in an absorbing way. Ravi swallowed.

His crush had never interfered with their work relationship. He enjoyed discussing the house with her because of her amazing focus and ability to laser in on potential problems. She usually had an idea or two on fixing problems as she found them, which made him that much happier.

He'd communicated with her on an enjoyable, if professional, level for months, via phone and e-mail. He loved her e-mails—professional and concise, with a sense of humor that he found lacking in most businesspeople. As if a joke would hurt their reputations.

His house was to be special, a renewable-energy-powered conservationist's dream. His requirements in terms of materials, building methods, and site preparation were strict and out of the ordinary. She'd been in close contact to be sure that she understood the specs. Ravi had researched the construction process so he could judge which contractor would fit his needs. Bidding on jobs was a huge part of the construction industry's process and could mean the difference between making a comfortable profit on a job and having it go down the toilet, resulting in unhappy clients, a bad reputation, and a slim or non-existent profit. Mālama Construction's decision to assign a project manager during the bid phase had impressed him, but Kerala herself had made his decision obvious.

Her size surprised him. Maybe five foot three? Well under average height for construction workers. In her Carhartt work jeans and plain brown T-shirt, she had a delicate frame under her muscle. Narrow but strong shoulders, her chest flattened by a sports bra. She rounded at the hips and ass just enough to make the men's jeans gape at the back of the waist, but skin on bone created that shape rather than padding. He hadn't dreamed that the heavy material of those work pants had hidden such a buoyant ass.

He sipped his liliko'i iced tea and grimaced at the fruity, flowery taste.

Kerala entered and glanced around. He stood and smiled, offering his hand once again, unable to resist the opportunity to touch her, if only for a moment.

"Ravi."

He held her chair and she sat. She'd showered. She smelled of shampoo and nothing else, though Ravi responded to the scent flicked toward him by the ends of her hair as though it were a much more intimate smell.

Maybe this wasn't such a good idea. His plan would require much greater intimacy, and the light touch of her shampoo on his senses undid him.

The server appeared at her shoulder. "Aloha. Anything to drink while you decide on your dinner?"

She nodded. "Plain iced tea, please."

"May I exchange this flavored iced tea for plain?"

The server pretended shock. "I thought for sure you were a passion fruit guy."

"I look gay?" He pantomimed shock.

Amusement popped her eyes open and she giggled. "That's not what I meant." He grinned at her. She huffed at him and flicked her towel at his shoulder. "You're trying to get me in trouble." She pouted with a gleam in her eye.

"No trouble. Just tea."

The server rolled her eyes and walked off.

Kerala smirked. "You're shameless."

"Just having a little fun with the young'un. You have to admit, they're easy to rattle."

She raised an eyebrow. "I'm not sure I like you lumping me in with you and your advanced age."

Ravi pursed his lips. "Thirty...seven?"

"Thirty-eight. And you're forty-four."

"How did you know that?"

"I Googled you."

He laughed. "And remembered the details."

"I like to have a full picture of a client. Excelled in high school; athletic enough to compete, not enough to win. Aimed toward engineering by high school, but didn't get involved in solar until MIT. Trusted by the scientists on staff at Sol Volt. Swam upstream against your inclinations. Not fully satisfied as CEO."

"I didn't know that was online." Not the kind of intimacy he'd been imagining.

"I read between the lines for that part." She picked up her menu. "Are you going to eat?"

"Definitely." Any reason to put off the hard part. Plus, he was hungry.

She perused her menu in silence. He glanced through it. Pretty standard for the island. Lots of fish options, mango and papaya and liliko'i sauces, more sweet options than spicy ones. He sighed for his palate and settled on a yellowtail pesto pasta. Couldn't go wrong with fresh fish.

Once Ravi had his plain tea and they ordered, Kerala asked, "What did you want to discuss?"

"I want to talk about how we can make you and this whole project safer."

"What?" She sat straight and put her hands on the edge of the table. "What have you heard?"

"I get every report you send, Kerala. You may not have realized this, but there's something fishy going on with this project."

Kerala sipped her icy tea. She delayed another moment. "What kind of fishy?"

Ravi listed the so-called accidents plaguing the project, his expression earnest. His understanding and recall impressed her. It had taken the physical proof of tampering for her to put all these things together.

He didn't mention her fall. How would he respond? She didn't know him well enough to guess. "You got all this from the reports?"

"And my instincts for what's left out. Like right now."

He'd hear about it sooner or later. She weighed the risks of bringing another person in on the full story. She studied him as he sat, silent, reading her indecision. He would know if she wasn't forthcoming. And her instincts said to trust him.

She dragged her chair closer to the table and leaned in. "There's been one more incident since you got your last report, and we have evidence of tampering on this one."

"What happened?"

She explained the hill that had been undercut, the marks and the tire tracks. Tension took his broad features. One of his hands flexed around his fresh iced tea, engulfing the pint glass in a white-knuckle grip that highlighted the dark coarse hairs on the back of his hand and fingers.

An octave lower than usual, he asked, "Are you hurt?"

She tried to forestall his inevitable outburst with a dry, matter-of-fact tone. "I slid, tucked, and rolled at the bottom. No real damage done, though the back of my head touched some lava on the way down and got cut."

His lips didn't move. "Did you go to the hospital?"

"Yeah." She grimaced. "And I got a thousand tests that all confirmed what I already knew. No concussion. I wouldn't even know I'd touched anything if it weren't for the stitches."

He stood, abrupt in every motion, and walked around the table. She skewed in her chair to watch him approach. Leaning back under his looming form, Kerala felt small for the first time in a long time.

"Where?"

She waved her hand to indicate the back of her head. When his furious hands reached for her, her natural fight reasserted itself and she drew back with a glare.

A scant second later, he sucked the fight right out of her. As big and angry as he was, he held her head far more gently than the nurse had done. He brushed the hair away from the stitches with his thumbs without pulling on her scalp. His fingertips trembled.

He wouldn't be easy to placate.

"Kerala," he said achingly, and stopped. He pressed a soft kiss to the top of her head.

She trembled in turn, but not in anger or in worry. That tone and that kiss turned her on like a switch, leaving her confused, weakened, impressed. As she retook control of herself, the feeling left in the foreground was the last. She was very, very impressed.

Kerala had been seduced by the best, or had pretended to be. But this intensity over a gentle, platonic kiss? She hadn't been so deeply affected by such a simple gesture in longer than she could remember.

Ravi dropped his hands to her shoulders and down to her upper arms. With a light squeeze, he released her and she heard him sigh. He walked back around and sat heavily.

The server brought their food. Ravi waited for her to leave them alone and took a bite of his fish. Excellent. He cleared his throat and lifted another bite before speaking. "You need protection. Someone wants my house not to be built. It's not a safe situation."

Kerala's eyes crystallized to the amber that presaged a hard time for him. He sighed to see them lose the last of the melted caramel look that had pleased him after his impulsive kiss.

She made him wait. He was supposed to squirm in discomfort under that stare of hers. Well, he wasn't in the wrong here, and he'd been stared at by masters of business intimidation techniques. He stared right back, impassive.

She broke the silence with a calm question. "What do you think I need to do?" She scooted sideways in her chair as though settling in and took a bite.

"Did you go to the police?" He broke a piece of fish loose. It was so fresh that he imagined it had been pulled from the water nearby.

"We called them right after I fell. They blew us off completely. I got one guy's card, but they don't see evidence a crime was committed."

"Well, hell." He forged ahead. "I think you should avoid being alone on the worksite. As a matter of fact, I think the buddy system should be a general rule from here on out."

Kerala unbent enough to acknowledge his idea with a nod of understanding, if not acquiescence. "I don't want the crew to know the whole story. I think it'll be easier to catch the person if they don't know we suspect them." She started putting her food away with serious attention.

She was negotiating. He controlled a sigh of relief. "That's fine. But it should start immediately."

Kerala waved off that detail. "I'll call Jack and coordinate schedules with him before I go to bed tonight." She kept eating.

"And it would be better if you had someone around at other times as well."

Her relaxed pose gained an alert edge. "What other times?"

"When you leave the work site or work at your home office. Before work. In general."

Incredulity wasn't such a surprising response. "Are you suggesting that I get a full-time bodyguard?" She put her fork down.

"I don't think you need some muscle-head with a concealed weapons permit. It would be better if someone else was around to, you know, scare people off or help if something happened."

"I don't need someone to scare people off. I can do a fine job of that myself. And Bogart's no Rottweiler, but he's got a mighty bark." Kerala jiggled her knee against the table, making ripples in her tea. "It's ridiculous that you would imply that I can't take care of myself. Of all people to come out with some caveman bullshit like that."

She'd told him about the sexist baggage of coming up in construction short and female. "I'm not saying you can't take care of yourself. I wouldn't want you coming at me with a crowbar. But you can't deny that a second person more than doubles the danger for an attacker."

"What attacker? You're extrapolating personal danger from a series of impersonally aimed acts of disruption or obstruction."

"Until this fall down the hill."

Kerala drank her iced tea and rolled the glass in her hands.

Ravi continued in the same controlled tone, though he churned inside. "There aren't that many people wandering around my land right now. The surveys and the permits are done. Construction is scheduled to start after New Year's." He paused, no longer controlled, and took a calming breath. "It's getting physical."

"I'll set up a schedule where Jack's not alone in the mornings and I won't stay late in the afternoons. We'll be strict on all safety measures. That's what I can do."

He studied her face. "You can let me stay with you while I'm here."

"Excuse me? Did I just hear you right?"

"Don't give me that, Kerala. You said you had a spare bedroom, right? And an Internet connection?"

"My Internet connection has no bearing on this, since you will not be moving in with me. What are you thinking, Ravi?" She looked him up and down. "You're not the bodyguard type."

Oof. His hackles rose at the reminder of how he'd softened since stopping testosterone therapy. "Don't pretend that six-pack abs are the most important quality for keeping you safe."

"Safe?" She scoffed. "You're a scientist and a desk dweller. It wouldn't frighten the average thug to have you come from the office waving a stapler."

He leaned over the table. "Don't tell me. You know judo."

She sneered. "Kung Fu."

He sneered back. "A bullet will pass as easily through your heart while you're in the crane stance as it will mine while I'm waving a stapler."

She shook her head. "You're assuming a gun, Ravi. That's a condition I can't accept."

He sighed. "Okay, let's back up. If we can stay off the subject of my fat ass, we might get somewhere in this conversation."

She looked like a kid squirming outside the principal's office. "I don't want to insult you. You're sexy. But you're no better equipped to repel a hypothetical household invasion than I am."

"You think I'm sexy?" He chewed on the thought along with his fish.

She pursed her lips. "You're not moving in. I need my privacy. I need some peace and quiet at night."

"I could make it a condition of your employment."

The chill in Kerala's eyes reached new lows. "You even hint at that one more time and I'll resign from this job before you finish the sentence."

Ravi shoved back from the table. He gestured for the server, who'd been avoiding them since the beginning of the fight. "Check, please." She nodded and pulled it from her apron pocket along with a padded holder. She set it in the exact middle of the table facing neither Ravi nor Kerala and skedaddled.

Amusement wormed through him at her clear statement of neutrality. He grabbed the check holder and slid his credit card into the top edge without looking at the total. "Here you go," he called to the server, who took it quickly. "I can't make you invite me to stay with you, but I want you to think of it as an option. I'm staying at the Hilton Waikoloa for now, but I only brought one bag. I can be at your house in an hour if you call."

She accepted his concession speech graciously. "I'll keep your offer in mind in case I feel that the company would make me safer. You'll be here about a month?"

"Until I feel the situation has settled. I can't fly back and forth more than necessary. Flying injects massive amounts of $CO_2$ into the upper atmosphere, the most sensitive part."

"You figure the environment into everything?"

"I try." He went around the table to pull her chair out, took her arm, and wound it around his in the old-fashioned way that his mother enjoyed. On the way out the door, he cursed himself for the self-conscious need to flex his biceps under her hand.

❖

Kerala met Nahoa at the door, alerted to her visitor by Bogart's quick bark. "What did you find out?"

Nahoa went straight through the living room to the kitchen and grabbed a beer. "I couldn't get through to the people I used to know. The sovereignty movement has moved on without me."

"What's next? Call the cops and give them the whole list? I'm in no hurry to get laughed at again."

"Hold off, Kel. I talked to an old uncle. He lives up-mauka, twisting copra into rope and braiding rugs for the ʻohana and to sell at tourist shops. I helped a while and asked him to talk story."

She leaned against the kitchen island. "What's it like up there?"

"Beautiful. Rough. Light rain on the coffee berries, red clusters under green leaves. It sings on the tin roof and drips from the overhanging eaves." He popped the top of the bottle. "Haven't you been to any of the coffee plantations?"

"No time."

"No desire to learn?" He sipped his beer.

Her face warmed.

He moved on. "I got a couple of leads. Give me a few more days. I'll follow up."

"Are you thinking this is a family affair?"

"I don't know. Look, Kel, you got hurt and whatever you say goes. But if someone was pulling a prank and didn't mean to hurt you, I'd hate to see the police arrest them."

"I wouldn't go to the cops on my own behalf. Your dad's going to force my hand, though. This is business, not just personal."

"There's one person I haven't talked to. I was hoping I wouldn't have to."

"Old enemy?"

"The best friend I ever had."

❖

Ravi sweated in a light cotton shirt and cargo shorts outside the Mālama Construction offices.

The sun speared through the yard of heavy equipment. The glare made it hard to look at the bright paint and shining windshields, but he puzzled them out. That one was a bulldozer. Even he knew that. The smaller thing next to it had more complicated...things. He classified the machinery by known use and deduced the use of the others by comparing their components. In the end, there were still several pieces of equipment that had him stumped.

Not his area of expertise.

The geckos were more fun to watch. Could he devise a mounting system that used the same Van Der Waal's bonds that geckos climbed walls with?

Kerala's truck bounced off the road and into the yard, spitting gravel and coming to a dusty halt. She sucked hard on a straw and jumped down.

The curve of her ass was hidden by dirty Carhartt pants. "What do you have there?"

"Iced quad mocha." A guilty look fled across her face. "Guess I should have called to see if you wanted anything."

He waved away the idea. "Do you do that often?"

"What, drink mochas?"

"Drink caffeine in that kind of quantity."

"Yes, Mom, I do." She stalked closer. "Any way I can get it. Energy drinks, coffee, tea, soda. What of it?"

He played straight man to her bad girl guise. "It's not good for you, that's what."

"I like lots of things that aren't good for me."

He stepped closer. "Tell me more."

A flicker, a slick withdrawal. She tossed the empty cup in a trash barrel outside the door and went inside.

"That better be corn plastic." The receptionist looked up at his mutter and he switched on a smile. "Hello, I'm Ravi."

"Aloha. I'm Joy."

Ah, not the receptionist, the office manager. Hekili's niece. They'd e-mailed quite a bit. She stood and picked up a tidy file.

Kerala spoke through the open door. "Come on, Ravi, let's take our seats."

Joy and Kerala settled across from each other at the oval conference table. He could probably get away with taking one end, but he didn't know which Hekili favored.

He made the easy choice and sat next to Kerala.

Hekili entered, shrinking the room, and sat at the end near the door. "Aloha, Ravi. Welcome back to the Big Island."

"Mahalo. Aloha."

Hekili grinned. "One or the other would do."

Ravi smiled back. "I have a lot to learn."

Nahoa arrived, looking even grimier than Kerala. "Aloha, Ravi. Good to see you. How are your parents?"

Talk story. That's what the Hawaiians called the next half hour. Kerala told them about her ride to the hospital and the punishments she'd devised for Stephens. Ravi told them about reading *The Starship and the Canoe*, about an astrophysicist and his canoe-building son, and his plans to build a sailing canoe to keep in his little cove.

Kerala's leg kept a fast rhythm under the table. Her face and hands were composed, but that leg told the truth. She was ready to move on.

Maybe it was his job to move the conversation toward business. When Nahoa finished a story about kids collecting the scrap too small for reuse, Ravi cracked open the door to business. "I hope they're not our only subcontractors."

Nahoa laughed. "Far from it. We weren't getting as many bids as we'd have liked, but that's turned around. It looks like we'll have subs at or below our bid on every piece."

Joy said, "We're not doing as well on the rest of the costs. There have been overruns in several areas, especially labor and parts for small equipment."

Kerala nodded. "There've been a lot of little things missing and tools breaking. We're dealing with them as they come up, but they take time."

Hekili frowned, his eyebrows diving in the middle in melodramatic fashion. Ravi couldn't help but love how it looked. Of course, he wasn't at the receiving end of the displeasure.

Joy cleared her throat. "Recycling material from the old hotel has cost seventeen percent more than budgeted for new material and we're not done yet." Joy glanced at Kerala. "I saw your e-mail about the ledge that crumbled. Adding a retaining wall will require a change order."

Kerala grimaced. "Will we need a full-blown environmental impact study?"

"Shouldn't." Hekili had the air of someone who knew the fix was in.

Kerala glanced over at him, but didn't pursue it. "Damn. We're dipping into the contingency already. I like a meticulous set of plans with no mistakes or surprises."

Nahoa grinned. "That's not the construction field I know."

Kerala shook her head. "Change orders cause nothing but trouble. With owners, with the schedule, and with subs. This retaining wall is a special case."

Ravi didn't want them to misunderstand. "I'm not unhappy, even with some cost increases. Using recycled wood is important to me. Does the need for a retaining wall bring back the possibility of getting a rock wall?"

Nahoa nodded. "That would be a cool way to do it. That'll give you a nice place to sit and look at the ocean."

"And I'll get to hire Tongan masons. I'm in."

Hekili turned to Nahoa. "Get Manase on it."

Kerala opened her notebook. "Have you figured out what you're doing with the brine from desalinating the seawater?"

They hashed through details unique to his project and made quick work of the more common issues.

When the direct questions slowed, he said, "I'd like to hear more about how the job will run for the next month or so."

Kerala shifted in her seat and took the lead. "We'll finish bringing down the hotel, grub and clear the lot, grade it, and excavate for the post and pier foundation. The wood from the hotel will be refinished in a special ventilated shed and installed after all the volatile chemicals have evaporated."

"What about the native vegetation?"

"It's mostly scrub."

"Except the koa tree we talked about."

"And I know you like it."

He narrowed his eyes. "It's a mature tree that deserves to live. Koa trees don't even bear seeds until they're something like five years old. This one is a lot older."

Kerala and Nahoa exchanged looks. She tapped her notebook. "We've looked at it from every angle, and we won't be able to drop the footings for your foundation without bringing the hoist around that direction. The grade is steeper on the other side and complicates access too much. We have to remove the tree so we can build the house."

Ravi pulled his lower lip. "Can it be transplanted?"

Kerala looked at Nahoa again. "We'll start grading the lot after the Christmas break. We could work in the time it would take to dig out around it. Anyone know how big the root ball of a koa tree is?"

Shrugs and looks around the table. Joy sighed. "I'll find out."

"See if you can move the koa tree and the lilikoʻi as well."

Kerala made note of his instructions. "Whatever you say, boss."

Joy opened a new folder. "Speaking of moving things, here's the standard plan for relocating remains. It's the most likely source of delays at this point."

"That's a creepy thought." He shuddered. "The realtor said it was unlikely we'd find any."

"Some are sure you will," Joy said, glancing at Hekili's impassive face.

"What happens? Does someone keep an eye out for bones in the dirt that gets moved?" Shitty job.

Joy leaned across the table as though telling ghost stories. "When buried in the earth, the kūpuna encased the bodies in fine black sand. Much of the soil here in Kohala and Kona is a reddish fine ash like flour."

"Sounds like quite a contrast. Did they do that on purpose?"

Nahoa said, "Their own purpose, sure. It helps us too, though. Cutting with a dozer or excavator, the operator will almost always recognize the change from red ash to black sand and call you. These ʻiwi kūpuna, the bones of the ancestors, are decomposed to the point that even touching them will reduce them to powder."

"Well, that's a cheery note. There's a plan for this?"

Joy handed him a list. "There are a bunch of people we have to contact in that case, and the Burial Council gets their hands all over the job. It always means delays and sometimes means no go on a whole project."

Ravi skimmed the document. "My insurance covers that eventuality. I was told it was a standard clause in Hawai'i. Guess I'll be hoping we're body-free."

Nahoa's mouth twisted. "Here's hoping."

❖

The grass and hills, Bogart's begging, and her good mood seduced Kerala off the Kohala Mountain Road, her usual route, and onto the cinder-cone hills above Waimea. Red and green, the ash and lava rock melted into each other and worked their way toward becoming soil.

She'd finalized the contracts with the subs with Nahoa's help. Add the subs' cooperation to the progress made on deconstructing the hotel, and the week looked good.

On the other front, Nahoa hadn't been able to find his old friend. She'd searched online for similar problems on other construction projects. The little stuff never made the news, and the bigger actions were too dissimilar. She still didn't have a handle on who she was up against.

Four days had passed since her dinner with Ravi and two since their meeting at the office. She hadn't seen him much. He did CEO stuff at the hotel most of each day and went through the cabinetry and trim they had already warehoused with Nahoa the rest of the time. Ravi earmarked a ridiculous amount of it for his house, considering that they were deconstructing a twelve thousand square foot hotel and building a twelve hundred square foot house. They couldn't possibly use all of the materials he liked.

She looked at the mountain. She should take Ravi there. He'd get a kick out of it. Far above Waimea, Mauna Kea wore a crown of planetary and space observatories set in a Martian landscape. The geologically young, red volcanic mountaintop sported younger red cones of volcanic cinder. If one discounted the blue sky, it felt like striding across another planet. In misty fog, it could be mistaken for the moon and had been by the conspiracy theorists who believed the moon landing was faked. At an altitude of fourteen thousand feet, the giddiness of oxygen deprivation enhanced these impressions.

In the hills near Waimea, fresh, bright green growth softened the volcanic cinder cones. Perpetual spring misted the air, a lovely contrast with Kohala's perpetual summer down near the water. Kerala breathed deep of the damp. Light and beguiling soil and plant smells invaded and filled her head. Maybe she'd become a gardener when she retired, in a thousand years or so.

She rambled onward, along the steep sides of Granny-apple-green hills, up miniature peaks and through ravines that she could span with one long step. Bogart ranged as far as the top of the next hill but kept her within sight.

If only she could bottle the way she felt at that moment. Oxygen permeated her system and her muscles moved smoothly, strong and resilient, even after a full day's work. The thinner air sharpened her eyesight, honed her hearing, and filled her with a chest-expanding happiness that made her want to twirl in circles like Julie Andrews in that movie about those Austrian kids.

Humming a song she wouldn't be caught dead singing in front of the men, Kerala turned and looked back across the hills.

The road curved just beyond. No reason to avoid the quicker route home with her stomach demanding dinner.

Kerala whistled for Bogart. He picked his head up and hesitated a moment over whatever absorbing find he'd made. He ran like he'd been born to do nothing else. His long silky ears flew out behind him, his soft lips pulled back along his muzzle, and the longish wispy hair on his legs and tail streamed back like banners. Affection sizzled like a Fourth of July sparkler. He flashed past and churned small clods of dark red dirt in an attempt to turn a tight circle around her. She pivoted as he passed and again as he pranced around her, too excited to hold still.

"Heel," Kerala commanded, and Bogart's whole body danced on the energy created by his thrashing tail as he took his position beside her. She crabbed down a steep grade to the venerable, gnarled jacaranda trees lining the roadside and traversed the deep, gravel-filled ditch. Bogart did his best to stay in position as he slid and bounded along with her.

She and Bogart achieved the road's narrow shoulder. She petted his solid head and crouched beside him. He sat, leaning his heavy torso against her folded legs. "Good dog. You are such a good dog." He let her get away with fawning on him sometimes, but only in private.

She gave him a few more minutes of conversation and scratching before rising to stand. Her long day hit her as she reached her full height but she did not sway. She'd hit the wall so many times in construction that it felt natural to end a day dead on her feet.

"I'm glad we didn't get too far, Bogart. I'm ready for food and bed."

Bogart howled at her. He yawned, licked his chops, and fell into place beside her as she started down the road in the gloaming.

About a quarter of a mile along, a car sat parked on the side of the road, idling and facing the wrong way, headlights off. A tourist, by the model of the car. If someone took that corner fast, they might not be able to get around him. If two cars met there, they'd need the whole road. Probably checking a map. Irritation sputtered. She should set him straight and get him on his way.

The brightest stars muscled through the light from the closest one against a deep blue sky. Under the hovering trees, though, twilight didn't linger.

The driver looked up, perhaps at his rearview mirror. He twisted in his seat to face her. The thought of offering help fled with the attention. She and Bogart had gotten within forty feet and her muscles poised themselves for action in a city-bred instinct for a vulnerable situation.

The car revved and slewed around in a semi-circle. The headlights hit her and flicked to bright. She put a hand up to block the blinding light and the car accelerated straight at her from twenty feet away.

"Bogart!" She yelled in her stiffest command voice and jumped for the ditch.

The fender clipped her hip. Her staples bounced against gravel, making her eyes roll back. Her arm, shoulder, and hip all slid against sharp rocks. She hit the bottom of the ditch with the entire force of her fall, nowhere to roll in the narrow bottom.

Dazed and still, she heard Bogart barking. He sounded scared. Her senses returned in a rush and she shouted for him before pulling herself up the other side of the ditch among the jacaranda roots. Bogart dogged her heels. She limped beyond the sparse trees to hide behind a scrub bush.

Bogart whined and licked her neck and shoulder. She tried to shush him while she listened for the car's return. Had he meant to scare her or hurt her? Hurt or kill her? Would he come back?

After a torturous five minutes by her watch, she slumped, wrapped her arms around her knees, and gave in to the shakes.

Bogart nudged her several times and settled close, canine eyes gleaming into the darkness, guarding his pack of one.

## CHAPTER FIVE

Ravi stood in front of the open window in his over-decorated hotel mini-suite. He had Earl, his executive assistant, on a video call, but he was too restless to stay in front of the camera. The mahogany-stained oak desk held his laptop, open and humming.

A young white couple sat on the manicured grass behind a hedge and kissed in imperfect privacy. "Any news on the graphene PV material?"

"Nothing you haven't seen. The testing is going well enough, but production is years away. It's a good thing the bread and butter side is growing fast, with the leased rooftop solar market booming."

He turned away from the vacationers' pleasure. "How's the staff taking the idea of becoming a benefit corporation?"

"Folks are excited, for the most part. I've heard about some stirrings among the shareholders, though."

"You'd think that investors in a solar power company would understand the concept of long-term returns." He sat in front of his laptop.

Earl looked off to the side, reading something off screen. "Never know about people and their money. Do you want to send another statement?"

He considered. "No, let's wait. I like the board's plan for implementing the change. We won't have any trouble meeting the public purpose requirement. We do plenty of good in the world. And I doubt folks are troubled by the transparency procedures. We'll have to tread carefully with the non-financial accountability pieces."

When his phone played Kerala's ringtone—"Smoking Her Wings" by The Bats—he said, "Let's pick up this conversation later."

Earl waved.

Ravi missed the call fumbling with the charger cord and waited until the voice mail came through.

"Ravi, meet me at my house. Bring your suitcase." His gut heaved in response to the fear, anger, pain, frustration, and command in Kerala's voice. The anger and command reassured him somewhat. She couldn't be so coherent if something terrible had happened.

But the fear. He never imagined he'd hear that tone from her.

He called her back and gripped his phone hard when he got her voice mail. He resisted beating the phone on the desk. "I'll be on my way in ten minutes. I should be able to reach your house by eight. Please call me back if you can."

The word he'd always used as a courtesy came out like a plea. He needed data.

The chirpy receptionist agreed to have his car brought to the side door. He stomped on her offer of more help with a curt thank you and hung up. He zipped his shaving bag and computer into his suitcase.

Should he check out? No, waste of time. What was the cost of one extra night compared to ensuring that Kerala was safe? Besides, she might change her mind about him staying in her guest room once she was back to her usual forward-leaning equilibrium.

A bored looking valet met him outside. After a quick exchange of dollar bills for keys, Ravi tossed his bag to land pell-mell in the passenger seat.

❖

Kerala slumped against the tight-grained white oak island in her kitchen. She sipped a beer in the stove light's yellow pool. Bogart lay at her feet with his head on his paws. Before calling the guys, she had donned jeans and a light sweater with full-length sleeves. The sight of her bruises wouldn't help anyone concentrate.

There was even less evidence this time than last. Not the smallest paint flake, no tire tracks on clean pavement. The cops would call her paranoid and blow her off. If they didn't, what could they do anyway?

Could it have been an accident?

Kerala clenched her teeth. She wasn't going to doubt herself just because she couldn't figure out why someone would attack her with their car. It was ridiculous, but that wasn't her fault.

Bogart rolled his eyes up to her, then sat up with a yawn. If Bogart had been hit...

She shuddered and pulled the top off the cookie jar that held his biscuits and pulled out two. She squatted next to him. "You are the best dog there ever has been. I'm glad you picked me when I came to the pound."

She held her hand out. "Bogart, find it." He snuffled at her closed fist and used his delicate Labrador mouth to peel her fingers back, teeth barely denting her skin, until he could nip the bone-shaped treat from her palm.

That trick had taken a while. For a long time, he had tried to take the biscuit once he had just one or two of her fingers straightened. Still, she didn't try it when he was over-excited or rambunctious. It was a quiet time kind of a thing.

She didn't make him perform for the second one. "That one's because you're wonderful. If it weren't for you, I would be so alone." She swallowed and wrapped her arms around Bogart's neck. He smelled of dust and pollen, but mostly of warm fur. His jaw moved against her shoulder as he chewed.

Adrenaline drop caused self-pity. Chemical crash, blah, blah. Sometimes it helped to be analytical. Sometimes, not so much.

She wasn't alone, anyway. Not really. Though she reserved the word friend for deep connections, she had a dozen acquaintances who would go to bat for her in an instant. She had a loyal crew and a more-or-less respectful boss. Jack would do anything for her except move off the island. Nahoa was more of a friend to her than most, but he didn't open up any easier than she did.

Ravi. She shouldn't move him in. They'd both done a marvelously civilized job of controlling the way they reacted to one another.

He'd estimated that he would spend two to three months at his vacation home per year, three or four weeks at a time. Sounded like the possibility of a good friend and fuck buddy who couldn't get too clingy because he wouldn't be around enough. She had traded in her lesbian gold star in her swinging twenties, but sex with a genderqueer, masculine-of-center guy would be new territory. She'd been willing to think about it.

Strange that she'd dialed him before Jack or Nahoa. When he'd called back, she'd been on the phone with Jack. His message asked that she call him, but she didn't want to explain what had happened on the phone.

Jack had taken the call in front of Danny. He'd responded quietly when she asked for some of his painkillers, because he didn't want to scare the poor kid.

Nahoa had grilled her in a grim tone and she'd gotten sharp with him. She didn't want to hash it out three separate times. She wanted them all together to work it out. The client, the heir, and the buddy: her own league of gentlefolk.

She wandered into her living room. Shit. She didn't have enough seating for four. She dragged back toward the kitchen and grabbed the curved top of one of the bar stools. She tipped it back on two legs and hauled it beside the couch.

With that heroic effort behind her, Kerala gave in and sat in her recliner. Bogart fell to his side next to the chair and heaved a stentorian sigh. She gave her aching body a break and lay back in her broken-in chair.

She should have worn flannel.

Bogart barked once and put his head back down. After a perfunctory knock, Nahoa opened the front door across the room, calling her name. He caught her unprepared and she couldn't rally before he gauged her physical state. She struggled upright to greet him.

"Hey."

"Kel. You have to tell me what happened." Nahoa came to crouch in front of her chair. He took both her hands, surprising her with the contact from a person she thought of as physically reserved.

"Nahoa, I'm okay. I'll tell you everything, but be patient. Ravi and Jack should be here soon."

Nahoa backed up and looked her over. Kerala curled her feet up and tucked them both between the left arm and the seat of the chair. She relaxed against the opposite arm and Nahoa appeared satisfied by her ability to move all her limbs. He mumbled, "I'm gonna get a beer." He tossed Bogart's ears and headed to the kitchen.

"Grab two, I hear another car."

Once again, Bogart woofed and a knock sounded.

At her invitation, Ravi came in and walked across the room to stand in front of her. Unlike Nahoa, he remained upright and his bulk made him a looming presence.

"Ravi, hey. Thanks for coming."

"Thanks for coming? I get a message that sounds like no Kerala I've ever spoken to and you say thanks for coming?"

Uh oh. Maybe she should have called him back. Nahoa returned from the kitchen and stood at the edge of the room, watching Ravi emote all over the place.

"I'm okay. I'm sorry I worried you."

Ravi turned to the couch and fell into it.

Nahoa swaggered over and slapped a cold bottle into Ravi's hand. He leaned on the back of the bar stool and tipped his beer. "It's nice to know you care." He grinned at the emotion Ravi was showing so openly, but a coiled tension remained in his eyes.

Ravi took a pull from the long necked bottle. "That's the best handshake I've ever gotten." He stifled a burp.

When another engine approached, Nahoa disappeared into the kitchen again and returned in time to greet Jack and Danny at the door with another beer. "Aloha."

"Aloha," said Danny, who paused in the doorway with a large, wheeled suitcase. Jack took the beer over Danny's head.

"Jack, what—"

"Hey, you don't need to—"

"Why'd you bring—"

"We're staying." Jack cut through the chatter. He herded Danny farther into the room so he could close the door behind him.

Kerala had to smile at the identical bullheaded looks on two of her favorite men. "Danny, come on in and say hi to Bogart. Jack, take that suitcase from him and put it out of the way. I appreciate your offer, guys, but it won't be necessary."

"Kel—"

"But we're going to—"

"Maybe you should—"

This time, Ravi's voice stopped the pandemonium. "I'm the one who's staying."

Nahoa, Jack, and Danny turned amazed eyes to Kerala. She nodded, amused by the Abbott and Costello routine. Amusement turned defensive when both Jack and Nahoa advanced on her. Bogart stood to attention next to her elbow and she placed a hand on his shoulder.

Jack spoke quietly. "Kel, come in the backyard for a minute."

Kerala answered at normal volume. "Ravi has thick skin. I think it's in the job requirements for a CEO."

Ravi raised an eyebrow and draped his arm along the back of the couch.

Jack turned to him. "I don't bite my tongue when I ought, I've been told. And I'm worried about Kel. That's all the warning you get."

"What are you warning me about?"

Kerala took the reins of the conversation. "Listen up. I'll say this once. Ravi, you own the land and this is your house we're building. You hardly know us, but we're three people you can trust to be working on your behalf and not against you."

She paused, thinking that Nahoa or Jack would react to the implied insult, the suggestion that there was any doubt. When neither responded except with stiff nods, she looked at Ravi.

"I believe that," he said.

She moved on. "Nahoa, Jack. This is our project, our reputations, and our safety at stake here. What you need to know is that Ravi is more passionate about this house than many men are about their wives. He would never sabotage this house. It symbolizes to him the remote possibility that human beings are more smart than stupid."

Ravi seemed surprised to have his confidences summed up like that, but he nodded.

Nahoa said, "Kel, you know that the first person to suspect is the owner. He has our bond for millions of dollars and if we can't finish he gets a ton of money. Ravi, I'm not accusing you of anything."

"Sounds like you are." Ravi remained cool.

Nahoa shook his head. "I know you weren't behind most of the problems we've had."

"Well, let me tell my story and we'll get to the reason I asked the three of you to come here." She shooed Jack and Nahoa back. "Sit down, guys."

Jack handed Danny his backpack. "Can Danny use the computer in your office?"

"Sure. Danny, go right ahead. You know the login and password." Jack ambled over to her side and palmed her two pills. She slammed them fast with an all-bubble pull from her beer. So wrong. She put the rest of her beer aside as Jack took the other end of the couch from Ravi. Nahoa leaned on the bar stool again.

Jack sat on the edge of the cushion with his elbows on his knees and his eyes on the carpet. If he'd had a hat to turn between his hands, he would be the perfect picture of worry. Nahoa rolled his empty beer bottle between his hands and stared at Ravi as though he could penetrate his deepest motivations. Ravi fronted "never let them see you sweat" but the concerned look hadn't left his eyes since his arrival.

Kerala sighed, chilled by the emptiness of her living room. The only furniture she'd shipped to Hawaiʻi from Philly were the recliner and her bed. After months, she had nothing on the walls except an LED television. The couch had graced a yard sale on her block for about five minutes before she snapped it up. White walls, beige carpet, fluorescent lighting, and cheap lightshades formed a depressing environment for talking about what had happened.

"Bogart and I went for our usual evening walk. Our routine takes us up Highway 250 a ways. We delve into fields sometimes, but we're pretty predictable.

"Today we headed out across the hills instead of up the road. When I got hungry, we veered onto the highway and started back." She described her experience second by second from that point on. "I think the guy waited for me to come the other way, toward him. From that direction, he could have gotten some speed and cut the corner just a bit. I don't know that he would have tried to run me down, but he could have." Kerala swallowed in the absolute silence. "Just another bad driver in a rental car. No one would pay attention if I claimed otherwise. But this is twice now that someone went to extreme lengths to scare me."

Time for answers. "Nahoa, do you know who is behind this?"

"The permits were blocked by the usual suspects. I got hints that some of the younger guys pulled your rotor and loosened bolts. The irritating stuff, but not much else. No names, but Tūtū Alapaʻi can hunt them down and make them wish they'd never taken on the Kalama family. I think she'll be with us on this one."

Kerala studied him. "What influence does your grandma have?"

"She's been working with Hawaiian cultural and sovereignty groups since the sixties, when the big revival started. For decades, our language and our religious and cultural practices were banned. We lost a lot of our own history along with our ability to determine the future of our islands, and when our elders tried to bring it back, they did so along a couple different lines. Tūtū Alapaʻi worked on the cultural side, mostly, but others focused on regaining political sovereignty over the islands."

Ravi asked, "You mean secede from the United States?"

Nahoa half-smiled. "I mean kick out the illegal foreign government occupying the Hawaiian homeland."

"Ah, I see." He nodded. "So less like Texas wanting to give the federal government the finger and more like India wanting independence from England."

"Not a bad analogy, though we can talk about settler versus exploitation colonialism some other time. Some in the Hawaiian sovereignty movement want limited self-rule like what Native Americans have on the continent. Others want full de-occupation and a return to independent nation status."

Kerala said, "What do you think?"

"I want sovereignty. My image of a sovereign Hawaiʻi has changed over time, but it's what we need."

Kerala turned it over in her head. "So it's not just a cultural respect issue, or a religious thing, with the burial sites."

"It's all of the above and more. Like I said, Tūtū Alapaʻi worked on cultural issues, like founding Hawaiian language pre-schools called Pūnana Leo and removing bans on our old cultural practices. There's been so much construction on the islands that burials are a sore spot for lots of us. It's where rich white people and development comes into direct conflict with traditional values and culture. She and

Dad have butted heads on this." He hesitated and looked at Ravi. "Stories suggest there's a rather large burial ground on your land."

"The Realtor said that human remains are found all over the islands. You guys brought up moving them in the meeting the other day. I didn't hear any stories."

Kerala said, "There's so much red tape around the Historic Preservation Division that I figured it would be locked down if they could prove anything."

"They can't add the land to the Burial Sites Program unless we find ʻiwi—bones." The corners of Nahoa's mouth flicked up. "But lacking proof never stopped story or tradition. Some of the delays and problems on this job are attempts to make it too expensive, too much trouble, to continue the project. The other reason to hassle us is frustration."

Kerala shook her head. "That succeeded just fine. I've definitely been frustrated."

"No, their own frustration. What do you do when you're angry and you know you can't do anything to fix a situation? Vandalism, theft? For some people, this is what they're doing. Lashing out."

Kerala listened closely, but part of her attention was diverted. "Your grandma is all up in the movement and Mālama is the biggest Hawaiian-owned construction company on the Big Island. Did you have to pick sides? Your grandma or your dad?"

Nahoa froze. His mask hardened and only his eyes showed his turmoil. He looked at Jack for a long moment, then glanced at Ravi before holding Kerala's gaze. He took a deep breath and released his hold on his expression. "I picked sides, yes. My grandma influenced me when I was a kid. I met activists through her who taught me enough history to make me very angry." Nahoa's mouth curved in a humorless imitation of a smile. "I started with petty shit, going out with friends and messing with people's stuff. We were against the tourist and construction industries. As a teenager, the ecological movement inspired me to focus on direct action to stop projects that were bad for the islands. In my opinion, of course."

Kerala sat up in her recliner. "As a teenager? The other stuff started even earlier?"

"I was surrounded by activists from such a young age, I thought that's what I was supposed to do. Anyone who didn't was colluding with the enemy and selling out their own people." He shrugged. "It was the perfect excuse to reject the kind of boring life my dad had. Work, eat, sleep. Always tired and grumpy and for what? Building more hotels, more vacation homes, more condos to rent out, when Hawaiians were homeless or couldn't afford to buy their own places. I completely identified with the sovereignty movement, especially the radicals who wanted to treat the government and non-Hawaiians like invaders. Resist and rebel."

Ravi leaned forward. "What happened?"

"I had a change of heart when I was sixteen and turned my back on direct action. I went to work for Mālama Construction and specialized in building homes and businesses for Hawaiians. I tried to grapple with the situation intellectually. I read a lot, about Hawaiian history and labor history and protest and activism."

Kerala wanted to talk about now. "Am I being attacked by your old buddies?"

Nahoa shook his head. "That's the strange part. I talked to the guys. They won't tell me much, but they swear they wouldn't hurt anyone. The word is out that you're not to be harmed." She wanted to take comfort in the news, but her body knew that someone hadn't gotten that word. She stared at Nahoa. His mobile brows drew low over his dark eyes. "I can't figure why it was necessary to put that word out at all."

"What do you mean?" Kerala asked. It was a mob film all of a sudden, but she didn't know who the rival bosses were or how to stay off their shit lists.

"It's more or less understood that the kids take action where they find the opportunity, but that no one gets hurt unless it's a fair fight."

Jack spoke for the first time in a long time. "You see a lot of picked fights called fair."

Nahoa grimaced but dogged the point. "It's still not running a woman off the road while she walks her dog." He shook his head. "There's no pono in it. And digging out that hillside is beyond the resources of the kids. They're just teenage boys with chips on their shoulders."

His assessment failed to reassure Kerala. "As a group, I don't find anyone more frightening than bored adolescent males with excuses to resent me."

Ravi pulled on his lower lip. "Yeah, but that's how they act. As a group. You don't see one guy in a car on a stakeout when you're dealing with boys that age. You see packs."

Nahoa turned back to Kerala. "You didn't mention the police. Did you report this last attack?"

"No." She clenched her jaw, but it didn't help her focus. The pills were kicking in. "I don't want to get mocked again by assholes with a little power."

Ravi frowned. "They may be able to figure out who attacked you, Kerala. Don't you want the person arrested?"

She shook her head. "I want them stopped, but I wouldn't wish the shit-show we call a justice system on anyone. Let alone prison."

Jack stood and grabbed the beer bottles. "Nahoa, help me clean up." Nahoa's face went blank again, but he followed Jack to the kitchen.

Ravi looked at Kerala and she shrugged. She pushed her recliner back a little and rested her head on the cushion. "Fuck." Nervous energy flowed back into her and she stood. She rubbed her hands over her face. "Fuck."

"I get the feeling they're not telling us something."

Kerala paced. "It's been like that since my fall. So Nahoa was in some direct action group that harassed whitey. It seemed like he was coming clean, but what does Jack know that we don't?"

Ravi's eyes made her conscious of her unsteady steps.

"All right, men, get out of here!" Kerala hollered toward the kitchen. She fought the edge of what had the makings of a real, badass fit. "Out!"

Jack came from the kitchen wiping his damp hands on his loose shirttail. Danny darted from the hallway to the front door. He donned his backpack and mumbled what Kerala assumed was a polite good-bye before he opened the door a bare crack and slipped out. Jack avoided Kerala's eyes but came close enough to say quietly, "I left the pill bottle in the kitchen."

Her irritation lost its edge. "Thanks."

"Bye." He shot Ravi a hopeless look. "Just keep an eye out and call me if there's trouble." Jack gave Ravi the order without regard for their professional relationship. Ravi's face betrayed nothing but dismissal, though Kerala detected a flinch.

Jack walked out the door and headed toward the truck Danny had already jumped into.

"Nahoa!"

"Yeah!"

"What the hell are you doing?"

"Just cleaning up in here."

"Leave it! You're outta here." She stood her ground. If she went into the kitchen, Nahoa would want to talk. She didn't want to talk. She wanted to collapse, but not until after Nahoa left and Ravi was settled...Shit!

Kerala growled deep in her throat and Bogart raised his head. When she put her hand out, he stood, stretched, and ambled over. She bent over to stroke his head but wavered upright after a perfunctory pat. Damn, those pain pills kicked her ass.

"What's wrong?" Ravi kept an even tone.

Good thing someone could hold their shit together.

"Guest bed hasn't made it to the top of my shopping list." She returned her stiff ass to the recliner with as much grace as she could muster. "Nahoa!" Ravi gaped at her work site bellow. A giggle escaped as she sank into the cushions of her faaaavorite chair. Well, not a giggle, exactly. More of a snigger. No, a chortle!

Nahoa stepped into the path of her vision, his mask in place. His eyes weren't hidden, though. The shadows he carried night and day seemed more substantial than usual, closer to the surface.

She nodded once. "Get out."

Nahoa looked at Ravi. "Use Kerala's phone if you need to call us. We're programmed."

Kerala followed Nahoa to the front door so she could lock it behind him. When she turned around, she gave Ravi a hint of an apologetic smile. "They're protective."

His smile back verged on grim. "Yeah, I caught that."

"I'm going to find out what kind of pills Jack gave me."

"Great idea."

Ravi followed her into the kitchen and Bogart followed Ravi. They both stared at her, without shame or manners, while she labored to focus her eyes on the medicine bottle's slightly aged label. The soft light from over the stove didn't make her task easy, but she triumphed. "Oooooh, Norco. I thought Vicodin, like he got last time. Well, that explains the funny feelings. Double the hydrocodone, double the fun..." Ravi watched her more closely than she liked. She leaned her good hip against the butcher block island. "Are you straightedge or something? Dude. You're harshing my mellow."

That wrung a laugh from him. "Did you just call me dude?" He had been so grim since he'd arrived, but he answered her with a grin that looked like trouble. "I haven't been straightedge since I was twelve. But I haven't taken a pill blind since I was thirteen."

Kerala took the bait. "What pill did you take blind when you were thirteen?"

"Phenobarbital. It's a barbiturate used as an anti-convulsive and my buddy James had a cousin who took them for seizures. He swiped a handful. The next time I stayed the night, we took one each."

"What happened?"

He raised an eyebrow. "We slept."

"That's not so bad."

"For two days."

"Oh, your poor parents."

He grinned. "We slept through the excitement. Stomach pumping was off the table by the time his mom realized that she couldn't get us to stir the next morning. They knew what because they found the stash, but they weren't sure how many. Phenobarbital has a half-life of two to seven days and, for a week, I felt like I was the new superhero, Eeeextra-Slooooow Man." He mimicked himself taking one excruciating step while Kerala chortled. Yeah, definitely a chortle.

She relaxed into a slump and a smile. "I can usually handle my opiates pretty well, but the beer...now that was a mistake." Kerala shook her head. "You all arrived so fast. I thought there'd be a gap between the beer and the painkillers."

Ravi intoned, "And so the lucky doth live to frighten friends another day." His body looked bulky, strong and solid, as he leaned against the counter across from her. His arms splayed to each side, braced behind him on the counter. In his light cotton slacks and buttoned-down shirt, he looked comfortable and easy with himself. One ankle draped over the other and one shoulder thrust higher and twisted a little so that he faced her.

His proportions were as queer as his gender. Narrow shoulders buttressed a muscular neck. He carried weight in his hips, but also some in his belly and around his waist. The muscles of his upper arms pressed against the cotton shirt and his darkly furred forearms led her eye to his delicate wrists. Someone had tailored his shirt to straighten his torso, but curves flashed into view when he moved or stretched. His chest was no more than eighteen inches from hers. The stove light washed his face from the side and emphasized the curves and planes.

A melting clench in her midsection made Kerala smile. Oh, yes, her body wanted to be crushed beneath his solid weight, to feel his soft and hard parts. She clenched her PC muscles and kept her pelvic floor taut for a long moment.

"I like your body."

He shifted his weight to stand on both feet and made a little settling motion with his hips. She knew that steely-eyed, stone-jawed reaction. Something rose in her belly and her whole body tensed at the incontrovertible knowledge that Ravi wanted her.

She intuited that he would be skillful with his hands as a lover. Before, she'd figured she could ignore the sizzle of electricity that coursed over her skin. Neither of them were hormone-crazed teenagers. Now she didn't want to ignore a single sensation.

He knew. Neither Kerala nor Ravi played like the reactions didn't exist.

Kerala blew her hair away from her damp lips, only then realizing that she must have licked them at some point. Not remembering that was more unsettling than the heat that suffused her. She'd licked her lips at him. "Wow."

Ravi's lips looked like satiny koa wood, but they moved in a hint of a smile. Though a residual stiffness held his features, his quicksilver eyes expressed his delight. His lips eased into a no-holds-barred grin. "What part do you like best?"

"Of your body?" She rolled her eyes. "What a blatant request for ego stroking."

He cocked his head back. "Your eye-stroking is worth a thousand words."

She laughed with a lightness that came through her rather than from her. She replied with a touch of sass. "Nobody's perfect, Mr. Dietrich."

A warm smile transformed his features back to the softer, easier configuration she was learning to like. He shoved away from the counter. "Got a blanket for my La-Z-bed?"

"Yours? You're the guest. I sleep there a night or two most weeks anyway."

"On the other hand, your body experienced some out-of-the-ordinary stresses. You're not getting any younger."

"Low blow, Ravi." She glared at him, but his resolve looked like a hassle to break. "Fine. There's a blanket on the back of the love seat."

"Good enough."

He led the way to the living room and pulled the folded blanket off the small couch. The way he eyed the recliner almost spurred her to renew her offer, but he turned and said, "Good night, Kerala."

"Night, Ravi."

She went to her bedroom and sloshed through waves of discarded clothing to reach her decadent four-poster bed. She pushed her jeans down her legs and pulled her shirt over her head, squirming more and more weakly as the medication dragged her toward unconsciousness. Almost done.

Kerala unzipped and unhooked her double-trouble sports bra of steel and peeled it away from her breasts. The cool airflow and her hot hands peaked her nipples as soon as she released them. She lifted and massaged them until the blood returned to the tissue and let them rest on her ribs with a sigh. In one of her last semi-conscious thoughts, masturbation crossed her mind, but a brainwave janitor swept that idea gently across into dreamland.

## Chapter Six

Ravi inched his way from his left side to his right. He listened to the plush recliner creak under him with fatalistic attention. If it broke, he'd buy her a new one.

Fuck. The four-letter power word circled his mind with lazy grace, marching across the insides of his eyelids like a nonstop tickertape. He turned onto his back in the recliner and threw his arm behind his head. His muscles recognized one of the few positions in which he'd been able to sleep. They clamored for a break within seconds, and he fought an aching tightness in his shoulder rotator to get his arm back to his side. The love seat had been somewhat worse than the recliner, but he had rotated from one to the other whenever he could no longer hold any position long enough to fall asleep.

He didn't want to open his eyes. If he kept them closed, he would drift off and wake later, alert and refreshed.

His lower back started to spasm in earnest rather than just hinting at it as it had all night. He brought the chair upright, but refused to raise the skin curtains.

He needed to pee.

His lids rasped across the surface of his eyes and he fluttered them, blinking to stimulate his tear ducts. Ow.

Dark windows clued him in on how early it was. He sighed and remained wedged in Kerala's recliner. She'd worn it in enough that a stickler would call it worn out. He pawed at the footrest lever and the chair clanged like a torture device as it folded. He used the armrests to achieve a standing position and swore that he would work on strength and flexibility every day, starting today. He hauled his running pants up at the waist and toed them down at the ankles.

On the way to the bathroom, he noticed that a door stood open that had been closed the night before. As he reached the door, he brushed away the little gnats of compunction that threatened to guilt him out of getting an eyeful.

Her bedroom looked upended, as though it had been searched by vicious foreign agents. Pools of clothing covered the floor, agleam in the small light of early morning. All sorts of materials, velvet and flannel swimming together in the multitude. Dried flowers speared from dusty vases and books lay on the bedside table and the floor beside the bed. Though the oaken four-poster bed murmured New England, the rest of the room blended harem and bordello.

Kerala lay sprawled across the bed.

He traced her shape and lingered on the curves of her butt and back. He took one step into the room to get a better look at the indention of her spine and froze. He exhaled involuntarily.

He inched his way with care through the shoes under satin and books under silk. He moved close enough to get a good look at Kerala's back and stood, sad.

What a liar. She had implied that she'd escaped unharmed from the car by jumping into the ditch.

The sheet covered her ass and right leg, but exposed the multitude of nickel-sized purple, black, and red marks. Scrapes as small as an ant and as large as a snow pea. He imagined the ditch must have been full of large gravel and he could make out some dark bits where he doubted she had been able to wash properly.

A patch of green, red, and yellow blossomed from her shoulder. That would be the healing bruise from her roll when the hill collapsed.

He scooted around for a better look. A dark stain on her left hip disappeared under the sheet, and he resisted the urge to pull the sheet back. He might not be able to look at her any longer without shaking her awake so he could yell at and hold her.

The vivid bald patch around the stitches in her scalp was the last straw.

He took his patient bladder into the bathroom and tried to formulate a plan of action. He leaned his elbow on the sink cabinet beside the toilet and put his weary, aching head on his biceps.

The bits of rock had to come out. He'd need tweezers, bandages, antiseptic, antibiotic. Anti-idiotic, too, if he could find any. Epsom salts for soaking her bruised hip.

None of those things revealed themselves when he checked her cabinets. That meant a trip to town, and he may as well get a bed.

Ravi worked out the kinks in his muscles as he pulled himself together for shopping at six in the morning.

❖

Kerala woke one brain cell at a time. She became aware of a mighty yearning that lingered beyond the dream she couldn't pin down. She tried, and failed, to reject consciousness as her body began to talk to her.

Bitch, bitch, bitch. Aches here and stiffness there. A draft on her arm and a wet heaviness in her pussy. Kerala turned over in bed and came awake abruptly.

Eyes open and aimed at the ceiling, she thought, I didn't. She lifted her head from her pillow and gazed down her bare breasts and barely draped hips, past the posts of her bed and out the open door to the hallway. The silent house felt empty, besides her and Bogart. She dropped her head to the pillow and pulled the satin sheet higher.

Had Ravi looked in at her while she slept? Hell, she would've taken a peek if he'd left himself next to naked like an invitation with the wax seal broken. Well, it was just a body in the end.

He would have seen the bruises from the car's fender and the tumble into the drainage ditch. She'd prepare some tart words for any criticism he might offer. She sat and slid her legs off the bed.

"Whew." What kind of idiot drinks a beer and pops a couple hydrocodone pills? Bogart's nails clicked across the linoleum of the kitchen and went silent when he hit carpet. He appeared in the doorway and stared at her.

She eased upright and looked at her bruises in the mirror that fronted her armoire. She flexed her biceps at her image with a show of disdainful bravado.

It would have been more fun to unveil herself for him and watch his reaction. She liked the idea of her smaller body being the hard one to his big softness. The sensible part asked when that would have happened, since she didn't sleep with clients. Mmmhmm. That part must have been napping the night before when they'd eye-fucked in the kitchen.

She snugged her tits into a sports bra and donned the jeans from the previous evening. The sports bra put pressure on her scrapes and she reconsidered. No, better a little physical discomfort than flopping all over the place. She balanced it out with a light top.

She wandered out of her bedroom, Bogart backing from the doorway with his tail wagging. She'd been right about being alone, but Ravi had left a note on the bar that read, "Have a little shopping to do, hope you'll sleep through it. Call me if you decide to leave for some reason. R"

Very informative. She rolled her eyes. No idea when he'd be back.

Bogart whined at the door and she let him outside with a brief ear scratch.

She dosed herself with one Norco for the worsened ache in her shoulder and a cup of hot instant coffee for the pressurized emptiness in her head. She wiggled her eyebrows and scrunched her nose. Somewhat like a cottony sinus infection.

The coffee crystals dissolved as she swirled the foul faux brew in her mug. Where was Ravi? It was nine, so she'd slept almost five hours past her usual time. She put on some Gillian Welch in deference to her fading headache and paced figure eights. She looked out the picture windows on the living room circuit and watched Bogart sniff around the backyard on the kitchen side.

Sex. Sex sex sex. Would she really hold out? So many good reasons not to mix sex and business.

On the other hand, sex boosted immune response and cardiovascular health.

Maybe Ravi would buy it as a teambuilding activity.

She prepared another mug of coffee and sat at the bar. Where the hell was he? A flash of dream memory involving his hands explained her morning wetness. Shit. She had a sex dream about him.

A volley of barking brought her to attention. She went into the living room and saw Ravi pull grocery bags from the rental car's trunk. She opened the door.

"Need help?"

"I got it." Ravi had four bags in each hand, and he carried them to the kitchen.

"What is all this?" Kerala didn't wait for his answer before poking around in one bag. "Coriander?"

He pulled a carton of eggs from a bag and dumped the rest of the contents onto the counter. "If you have a system of organizing your cupboards, let me know where this stuff goes."

Her mind went blank and Ravi let out a sharp bark of laughter. She leaned against the island while he arranged his purchases in the fridge and cabinets and made a small pile off to one side. The tweezers piqued her interest, but the Band-Aids, antibiotic ointment, and Epsom salts twigged her to his plan.

"I'll run you a bath with these salts while I clean out the wounds on your back. You can soak while I cook breakfast."

"Excuse me?"

"Come on, Kerala, don't be stupid. I saw your back when I got up this morning, and it needs to be cleaned."

So much for him panting over her naked body while she slept. "Peep much, Tom?"

Ravi interrupted his reading of the box of bath salts and sent her a dubious look over his shoulder. "You left the door open. What, I wasn't going to look? Once I got my critical faculties back from the gut punch of your pearly curves splayed across the emerald sheets, I realized that something was wrong, poor light or not."

She raised an eyebrow at this mollifying statement. "Mmmhmm."

"I'll get your bath started. I guess I should clean your back in there too." He gathered the first aid supplies and turned to leave the kitchen. "Off with your shirt. Grab a towel if you want to cover your front while I get your back." He threw the instructions over his shoulder as he left the room and headed down the hall.

Much as she wanted to be irritated with his high-handed treatment, arousal prickled her skin and tightened her confined nipples. She took a spare towel into her bedroom, toed off her shoes, and stripped her shirt and sports bra. She held the towel against her chest. Her jeans confined her, but slip-on pants would feel too easily breached. If she was going to resist her attraction to him, she'd need to be strategic about it.

Ravi had the bath running and his tools laid out on the sink cabinet. He washed his hands with a travel-sized bottle of antibacterial soap, scrubbing his nails and everything. She stepped into the little bathroom. "Where do you want me, doc?"

He flicked a grin at her but answered briskly. "On the toilet seat, facing the wall."

She complied without comment, straddling the porcelain and sitting on the wooden seat. She stared straight at the blank wall and controlled the urge to suck in her gut.

When he had rinsed and dried his hands, he moved behind her and tsked. "Some of these are puffy." He reached out and picked up the tweezers. "I disinfected these too; don't worry."

She felt a pressure and a scratch, then he dropped a tiny stone on the sink cabinet. As he worked a couple more from under her skin, he asked, "Where's the shirt you were wearing?"

"Trash. It was shredded."

"That's what I thought. Turn off the water in the tub, then you'll need to lean forward so I can get some light past your shoulders."

Kerala reached to stop the water flow, pushed her butt back on the seat, and draped herself forward. She held the towel with one arm and put the other forearm across the toilet's tank. She let her head fall onto her arm. He was methodical, moving from left to right and top to bottom. Awareness of his closeness and his smooth hands on her bare skin made her want to arch like a cat being stroked. His hands were gentler than she'd like. If they were going to fuck, she'd have to show him how she wanted it.

The first sharp pain made her flinch a little. Ravi resumed probing when she didn't say anything. At least it was her back—fewer nerve endings in that part of the human body. He did seem to be right on one. Ugh.

The pain distracted her from her sensual haze. He was pulling out a lot of dirt and gravel. Infected scrapes would have meant another hospital visit. Now it wouldn't come to that. Maybe she should be grateful to him, though it chafed a bit.

"I'm finished picking on you. Call me when you're done in here so I can put the ointment on."

She nodded. "Thanks."

After he left the bathroom, she dropped the towel she'd been holding to her chest, stripped off her jeans, and eased herself into the hot water. He had even rolled a hand towel for her to put behind her neck. He was being awfully solicitous. Sex sounded better and better, but he seemed like the type to get emotionally involved.

❖

Ravi focused on the knife, on the whisk. Kerala had good tools for someone who rarely cooked.

The kitchen rocked, with its four-inch-thick butcher-block island in the middle and all the other necessaries laid out intelligently around it. On one end of the room, a bay window framed a small, round, wrought-iron-and-glass café table and three chairs with thick bright-striped cushions tied to the seat and back. A counter half-spanned the opposite end, with a bar on the living room side.

He sang along with Vampire Weekend and popped the biscuits in the oven. The thermostat had better be accurate. He had a routine, but a strange oven could set off his timing. He heated the sauté pan for the vegetable scramble and inhaled the explosion of scents when the chopped garlic and microplaned ginger hit the 250-degree olive oil. Bright yolk swirled through and blended into albumen. Well spiced, the beaten eggs sizzled in the pan with the aromatics. When the biscuits began to brown on time, he started the gravy.

His hard-on subsided well before breakfast finished cooking. He wasn't sixteen anymore, thank you, nor was he the ravening sex hound of his early years on T.

The image of Kerala's stretch to turn the water off flitted through his mind, the grace and power of her back muscles twisting and the crescent of soft breast pulling from the side of the towel. Her lower back had arched when she'd pushed her hips toward him. And dwelling on those memories wouldn't keep him calm.

He shook the soysage links, covered the egg scramble so that the grated cheese would melt on top, and opened the oven. The biscuits needed a couple minutes more. The oven ran a little cool, perhaps five degrees. He should pick up an oven thermometer to make a variation chart.

He wouldn't think about spreading the antibiotic ointment on her wounds, about seeing her semi-topless one more time before eating.

"Ravi?" He spun around. She grinned. "Sorry. Time for the ointment."

He turned the burners and the oven off. The biscuits would finish browning in the leftover heat but shouldn't burn before he got back to them. "Now it is."

Kerala's eyes had widened when he turned. "Wow. Breakfast."

"I like to cook."

"You cook. I'da moved you in earlier if I'd known that." She sniffed over his shoulder as he pushed her backward out of the kitchen. "Smells good."

"It is good." When she turned to walk back to the bathroom, her lithe body moved, skin over muscle over bone. He'd never in his life been that much of a hard body, even when he'd bulked up. It couldn't hurt for him to enjoy the animal grace of her.

Kerala stood in front of the sink and handed the antibiotic ointment over her shoulder. He concentrated on dabbing a bit of ointment on each small puncture, bending for the lower ones. The smell of her drifted to him and he inhaled, slow and deep.

The intensity of the attraction blindsided him. Sex with Kerala might be as mind-blowing as what he'd experienced on T, out of his mind and out of control in response to the feel, taste, and smell of a woman.

He already wanted more, though. He should draw out the courtship, ratchet up the tension until it exploded. He wanted her to fall for him like he was falling for her. He wanted to touch her somewhere deeper than sex alone would get him.

"Come on." He stepped back, away from her, and she turned. The fine brown fringe of her hair rotated from the clean, tight line above her neck to the jagged pieces that let her ear peek through and tipped just under her jawline.

His fingers itched to smooth the long curve away from her cheek, follow the line of her neck to her bare shoulders. He wanted to know all her textures. All her scents.

He didn't touch her.

❖

Kerala dressed and let Bogart in before she joined Ravi at the food-crowded café table in the bay window. "Again, I say wow."

Ravi shrugged. "I love good food. Cooking is like foreplay."

She opened a biscuit and inhaled the yeasty steam. Ravi had made a pyramidal mound on his plate—two opened biscuits, a huge portion of the egg scramble atop them, and an eruption of cream gravy that spilled down the sides of the pile and soaked the four links on one side of the plate.

He cut a hefty bite from his conglomeration. Bogart whined and lay next to the kitchen door. He hesitated. "Do you feed Bogart from the table?" Kerala shook her head. "I'm mostly vegetarian. These links are soy. I didn't think about whether or not dogs can eat them. I saw the old bacon in your fridge, but I don't know anything about cooking meat. If you miss it, you'll have to cook it yourself."

She dished some of everything and took a quick bite. So much flavor! "I think I'll manage for one morning. I'm sure these veggies will keep me going for an hour or two."

He gestured around them. "You keep a clean kitchen." The spotless, aged, green Formica countertop stood testament to her good housekeeping.

"I don't cook much, but I clean the counters after fixing snacks or coffee or the odd meal. It's easy enough since I don't clutter them with knick-knacks."

"Have you always been tidy?"

"No, I spent years living like a bachelor. I had a housekeeper-and-maid childhood and a neat freak of a college dorm roommate at Bryn Mawr, so I got off on kicking my shoes off in the middle of the room. I didn't like it as much when they were there weeks later along with tons of other random shit, but I preferred the mess to lack of privacy. My sociology professor mother called that my backlash period." She steered the conversation away from that particular land mine. "The occasional pizza crust or package of crackers got buried in my apartment, but the one chore I kept up with was taking out the trash. And if a coffee cup sat long enough to grow mold, I boiled the hell out of it to kill any germs."

"Awesome." He looked askance at his mug. "You got over that at some point, I guess."

"Clean kitchen and bathroom. The others rooms slide, but hey." She shrugged and mopped gravy with a bit of biscuit. "The house is as much an investment as a home. I have lots of plans."

"What have you done so far?"

"I come home filthy. I installed a connecting door between the mud room and my bathroom so I can shower without tracking dirt through the house. That improvement cost very little and makes a huge difference."

"So the clothes on your bedroom floor are clean?"

"Oh, you noticed that."

Ravi laughed. "Hard not to. Silk, satin, velvet. I think I even saw flannel."

"Don't knock flannel. It's humble, but it feels damn good."

"No offense intended." He didn't stop grinning, though.

"Well, they aren't muddy or grimy. All of that goes right into its own hamper."

He pointed his fork at her. "You, my dear, are a secret sensualist."

"I don't hide it. My inner sensualist just doesn't get much exercise during the workday."

"Makes sense. Is it all nightwear?"

"I flirted with sleeping nude as a teenager, thinking it was shockingly adult. I changed my tune after my favorite aunt Bridget gave me a calf-length satin spaghetti-strapped ivory nightgown. I blushed when I pulled it out of the box in front of my family, but I flushed for a different reason when I pulled it on that night."

He pushed his plate away and smiled at her. "How do you pick?"

"It's all about the feeling of the material. Scratchy lace and wool are out, though I had a vintage nightgown with delicate hand-tatted silk lace in the deep vee of the neckline. Sometimes I like nightgowns, short, mid-length, or long. Sometimes I like pajamas or top-and-shorts sets. Sometimes I dress for bed early and lounge all evening, reading or watching television. Sometimes I don't dress all weekend."

"Sounds decadent. I wouldn't have guessed that's how you spend your days off."

"To be honest, I can't remember the last time I spent a whole weekend dressed down at home. Getting Bogart changed things some. And maybe I haven't taken the time to be decadent the way I used to." She finished her food. "What's in this, Ravi? I can't believe how good it is."

"Little of this, little of that. My mom taught me to cook, so I use a lot of Indian spices."

"Did you grow up with a lot of Indian culture around the house?"

"Sure. My mom was raised in the US, but my grandparents were immigrants. Mom did a great job of integrating what she learned at home and at school. She's both American and Indian in a way that I admire."

"Is she Hindu? Are you Hindu?" Had she ever asked anyone their religion before? Seemed like a terribly intimate question, but it was too late to take it back.

"Mom's Hindu, with a twist. She raised me as a vegetarian, taught me Hindu stories, celebrated lots of holidays, including some specific to my grandparents' home, like Onam. You may know about it if you've researched your name. Kerala is the Indian state they come from. She left out the caste system and the kind of puja—cleansing ritual—that you have to pay for. I developed a secular Hinduism, kind of like a non-practicing Catholic or Jew. It's part of my identity and I love the stories, but I'm not a believer. My only religion is science."

She didn't know where to go from there, so she called Bogart over. She patted his head and contemplated the rest of the day. "Let's move this party to the living room so we can talk about work. I'll make coffee."

Ravi hesitated. "I'm a bit of a coffee snob."

"Okay."

"So I bought a better coffee machine, a burr grinder, and some Kona coffee."

"Sounds like you're making the coffee." She looked at him. He fiddled with his fork. "What else did you get?"

"A bed."

"And?"

"A lamp and some other odds and ends."

"Bedroom stuff? How long were you gone?"

"I got up about five. I tracked down the name and phone number of the furniture shop's owner on the Internet and called him after I did my grocery shopping. Lucky for me, he's an early riser. Does the books in the morning. He got to the shop right after I did." He looked at her with helpless entreaty. "I can't sleep on that recliner again. I just can't."

"It's being delivered?"

"Yeah."

"When?"

"About three."

"Ah." Well, it was his money. She could understand why he'd done it. On the other hand, it wasn't his place to furnish her guest room. She shook her head. "How about I clean the kitchen and you make that coffee?"

He stood and headed for the door. "I left the big stuff in the car."

❖

A half hour later, Kerala curled in her recliner with Bogart under her left hand. "Was it so bad sleeping here?"

He heaved a long-suffering sigh. She grinned at him and sipped the strong, delicious coffee. Ravi's eclectic mix of music poured from his travel speakers, some artists she knew, some she didn't.

As her energy level started to climb, she bounced her leg against the arm of the chair. The familiar squeak comforted her.

What could she do about this project? When it came down to it, she could take it or leave it. What reason did she have to stick to the project after being injured twice, maliciously? No one would blame her if the job was too hot. She couldn't imagine any reason it would be personal, someone after her and not someone after the project. She'd be safe as soon as word got around that she was off the job.

The bouncing leg gained speed. Ridiculous. She'd never been run off by anyone from anything, if she didn't count avoiding her family.

She'd braved bullies starting with her first boarding school and hadn't let anyone push her around. Her first summer on a construction crew, in college between her freshman and sophomore years, would have been some people's nightmare, a horror story and a trauma never to be overcome. She had known, unshakably, that she could do the work and that the haters were full of fear and confusion. The few who had real anti-female convictions had been easy to spot and avoid. The gay bashing had been occasional but memorable. She'd even fought when she had to, though she'd fought dirty. So dirty that no one had ever tried direct violence on her again.

Physical intimidation hadn't worked then. It wouldn't work now, even two decades older. She was smarter and much more cunning.

Ravi spoke abruptly. "Do you think you'll find remains?"

"On the property?"

"I did some research and there are good deductive reasons for thinking the land was used for burials."

"There's no way to know, Ravi. We could uncover remains the first day. There could be remains two feet from where we dig and you find them years down the road, or never. Does the thought bother you?"

"Some, I guess. I'm less than comfortable about this whole thing."

"Afraid of spirits?"

"No. The ʻaumākua don't scare me, but the people who believe in them do, if they're the ones attacking you." He hesitated. "Have you thought about quitting?"

She smiled faintly. "Not going to happen."

"Maybe it's not such a bad idea."

"I think it is."

"I don't like to see you hurt, Kerala."

"I'm not your responsibility. Any project manager for this job will be in the exact same circumstance. You'd rather see a different person hurt?"

"Of course not. I'd rather see the problems stop. But we don't know how to make that happen."

"You moved in. We've taken a good step there."

"And created a whole new tension."

"I like some tension in my life." For a while.

"There would be some benefits."

"Benefits to quitting?"

"Yeah. Like dissolving the employer/employee barrier."

She stared at him, surprised. She hadn't expected him to bring that up. As if she'd quit a job so she could fuck him. "That's silly."

He had the grace to look embarrassed. "I didn't mean that you would quit just for that. Just that it would be easier for us to, you know…"

"Fuck?"

"Work out the tension between us."

"You mean sex."

"I mean dating! Getting to know each other! And yes," his dark skin darkened further, "I imagine that we'd get around to more intimacy sooner or later."

She couldn't resist a smile. "If we weren't working together on this, we would've already been to bed together."

He came back with an arrogant twitch of his eyebrow. "You don't know me well enough to be sure of that."

"I know myself, and I usually fuck the people who turn me on like you do."

He swallowed but persisted. "And I believe in the potential for more."

"Hell, Ravi, we wouldn't have to not-date if we had sex. Can't you get to know someone outside of bed at the same time you're getting to know them in bed?" How had she gotten into the position of arguing they should have sex?

"Sure, I guess. There's just a dynamic I like to follow. I've never had a good relationship with someone I haven't gotten to know first."

She sobered and real affection welled. "I guess that's why so many people end up dating in their friendship groups. You're not absorbing so much newness all at once."

"And you don't have to worry that she's laying there all sweaty and post-coital, wishing you'd leave."

She grimaced. "I've been that person. Telling someone to leave after sex can be awkward."

"Have you had a lot of one-night stands?"

"Yeah, I was a total slut for years. I had a few relationships that leaned toward serious, but no one who wanted to take me as I was. Keeping it casual avoided expectations." He didn't react visibly and she guessed that he was hiding judgment. "It's been a while now. I toned down my social life when I got into project management ten years ago. More or less switched to the fuck buddy system. I haven't been with anyone since I've been in Hawai'i. Almost a year now." Explaining herself gave her the heebie-jeebies.

"What about community here?"

"What, queer community? I haven't found it. In Philly, queer culture meant bar culture. Spend enough time in bars and it starts looking like a nature documentary."

"When I looked into land, I looked for gay-friendly places. The Big Island seems to have some queer stuff in Puna, but it rains there all the time. Not so good for solar."

"From what I've heard, it's more hippie hipster than my preference, plus it's halfway around the island."

Ravi sipped his coffee, looking thoughtful. "I've been a serial monogamist myself, but I still believe that there might be someone I can make a family with."

"You want kids?"

"No, but two people knit together to the core—that's family too."

"I'm not looking for that. Sounds nice, but it doesn't seem like something that would happen for me." Now she sounded maudlin. She put her coffee cup aside. "But, given that I won't quit, what should we do about the sabotage?"

He went with the change of subject. "We should keep our eyes peeled. Buddy system at home and at work."

"I want more action than that. I've been hoping Nahoa would get us a name or at least a group we could focus on." She stared across the room and tried to find an avenue of approach.

"I wish he'd get something about the attacks on you."

Kerala tuned into a tension in the silence that followed. She looked at him and waited for him to speak.

He shifted, shifted again, and said, "You've known Nahoa a lot longer than I have."

She didn't need to hear the question. "Yes, I trust him. He'll do what's right and he'll tell us what he finds. He might hold back if there's doubt, though. He doesn't trust cops any more than I do."

He balanced his coffee cup on his knee. "What's your thing with cops? They made fun of you and now you're against them?"

The air thickened. Kerala looked at Ravi, searching for his angle. A trans masculine genderqueer person of color, asking her why she had a problem with cops? She gave up trying to figure out what he was after and gave him what she had. "Police forces are the violent arm of government. At best, anyone who signs up to be a cop has a savior complex—already a power issue. At worst they're looking for socially acceptable excuses to be domineering and violent to random-ass people."

"So you have an opinion on this."

"I could go off."

"I'm getting that."

She eyed him, his surprised, middle-class amusement irritating her. "You're not going to tell me they've been on your side."

"Because I'm brown and genderqueer?" He grinned at her. "I'm not saying I've been saved by the cops. I haven't. But I don't think I'd like to live somewhere with no law."

She swirled the last sip of coffee in her cup. "I don't know that it would be worse than the egregious—I love that word—the egregious abuse of power and protection from prosecution we see when cops shoot African Americans with impunity."

"I'm not saying you're wrong. Your passion fascinates me, though. You seem like the demographic most likely to be treated well by the police."

She raised an eyebrow. "I don't have to be the most likely target of mistreatment to be against mistreatment."

"Of course not. To be honest, I've never known a police officer who was the same nice person on the job as off the job. I've been friendly acquaintances with people in law enforcement. Never managed to get close to any of them."

"I wouldn't want to." She stood with gritted teeth.

"More coffee? I can get it."

She waved him off. "I'm better if I keep moving. Sitting still makes me tighten up."

She walked to the kitchen, her hip easing as she walked and proving her right. She yelled. "These problems all circle around your property. Who owned it before you did?"

She touched the pot to make sure it was still hot before pouring. Ravi didn't answer, so she ambled back to the living room. He wasn't on the couch.

She looked around as he came down the hall with his laptop. "I don't know. About the previous owner, I mean. I bought it off the state and there was mention of a long probate or something."

The computer was silent as it booted, but Ravi kept muttering. She sat next to him on the couch and peeked over his arm. He flew through file folders, using keyboard shortcuts and commands for most of his navigation. He already had several windows open, including a couple of documents that looked like purchase agreements.

"What are you looking for?" If he already had the agreement open, why didn't he know who sold him the land?

He popped open a browser window. "The title search gives us a few names. It's changed hands a bit in the last hundred years. The last owner died a few years back—see here?—and it was tied up for quite some time. Why?"

As he spoke, he ran searches on the name of the previous owner, a Mr. Vincent Willoughby, the land title records document number, and the lawyer who handled the sale to him. He bounced between windows so fast Kerala couldn't believe he was reading the results, but he brought up articles and database results in even more windows.

"You're hard on computers," she said. She made sure her tone was joking, but she was impressed. Just when she got used to thinking of him as a nice guy hanging out, this put him back into perspective as the brilliant researcher and scientist, so good on all levels that he tripped and fell into being CEO.

She watched him suck up a ton of information, but even admiration couldn't keep it interesting. She bit her tongue until she couldn't stand it another minute. "What have you found?"

"I'm sending this one to you. Read it on your phone."

As little as she enjoyed that tone, she controlled the urge to buck at his command. "Fine." She heard the message received tone and brought up his text. A touch and she was looking at a news article, a couple years old.

She read aloud. "A mystery from start to finish."

Ravi looked up long enough to glare and she stuck her tongue out. She read the rest in a silence that got colder and colder.

Vincent Willoughby had been an unloved man, rich enough to keep people off his back. He had the sorts of unctuous functionaries who would attend to his business, but he was so isolated that no one noticed for months that he had gone missing.

He'd been seen last leaving his Hawaiian hotel ten years before. No one petitioned to have him declared dead until a few years back. That's when the land had reverted to the state.

"What the hell happened to this guy?"

Ravi looked at her. "I can't find any mention of sabotage, but he was trying to get a house built when he disappeared."

"The police would have any reports he'd filed."

"Your best buddies?" A tense smile broke Ravi's focused expression.

"Shit, Ravi. If they have information we need, let's deal with them." She sighed. "But those jokers blew me off so hard I don't think they'll go back through old records for me."

"I think it's time for me to don my superhero outfit."

She tried to keep her expression impassive, but her lips rebelled. "Your secret identity?"

"CEO Landowner, at your service." He winked and reached for his phone.

His firm-yet-courteous tone got him through several people at the police station, but he was stymied in the end. The officer on Willoughby's case had made detective and was on Oahu for court. "But she sounded certain that this Detective Alakai would have the skinny on the history."

Kerala shrugged off the let-down feeling. "We'll go see him when he's back in town."

Ravi slapped his hands to his knees. "Okay then, we have no choice. We have to go snorkeling."

"Well, that came out of nowhere. I haven't been snorkeling in ages. Let's do it." She grinned. "You're a bad influence on me. I usually do paperwork on the weekends."

He grimaced. "We'll both have to catch up tomorrow. It's a strain on Earl and the team when I'm gone. The best way for me to keep things running is to be responsive to the hundreds of e-mails I get every day. But I don't want to think about that right now. Let's get wet."

## CHAPTER SEVEN

Kerala had second thoughts as soon as she stripped in her bedroom. Her back was sore, itchy, and stiff, with the shoulder she'd hurt a week ago complaining again. The bruises she could see were terrible. One bruise covered her aching hip. Gravity had pulled the blood through the tissues in her leg until the pooling blood had spread far from the original injury—halfway to her knee. The whole thing was tender when she probed it.

Bogart shoved the door open enough to fit through and she closed it behind him.

She'd been hit by a car. On purpose.

As tough as she was, this wasn't business as usual. It wasn't just another injury in the line of duty. A tremor passed through her. Somebody did this to her.

She slid to the floor with her back to her bed. Bogart pushed in close beside her and nuzzled his head under her arm. She pulled her heels close to her butt and leaned her head on Bogart's. Someone was playing with her. Had the same person disappeared Willoughby?

Maybe she'd be safe once they started construction. Anyone protecting the land would give up at that point. Surely.

Or would they move on to Ravi?

She could ask around, track down the contractor on Willoughby's house back in the day. Anything to move toward answers.

She tossed Bogart's soft ears, scratched his back, and held his head so she could look at him and say her silent thanks for his unquestioning company. She stood and forced herself to pull on a swimsuit and clothing.

In the living room, she found Ravi flipping through channels on her TV. "Would you rather stay here?"

"No way. I just wanted to see how the screen looked. It's pretty amazing."

"I watch TV in the evenings to wind down. Sometimes I let it play while I zone out; sometimes I get caught up in stories."

"Well, maybe I can be more interesting than that while I'm here."

He wouldn't be around for long. The reminder gave her an unexpected pang. "Shall we?"

It took a few minutes to grab the snorkels, fins, and other supplies. She drove down the mountain to her favorite spot. Not too busy, kind of hard to get in and out of the water, but brilliant snorkeling once in.

She parked and they stripped to their bathing suits. She pulled the sunscreen out and slapped some onto the backs of her legs. Ravi walked around to her side of the truck and took the sunscreen. He stepped behind her and hesitated.

"Damn. Those shorts look great on you."

"Tell me more." Flirting felt good. The public setting put an automatic limit on it that freed her.

"It's the way the subtle swell of your hips fill the boyish shorts and how the curve of your butt peeks out the bottom." He dabbed sunscreen on her back between her wounds. "I didn't know you had such a great butt until dinner the other night."

She looked at him over her shoulder. "My work pants aren't sexy enough for you?"

He took the teasing with a shrug. "You're hot regardless, but right here…"

Would he touch her ass? She arched the tiniest bit, but he only sighed. His breath feathered over her shoulder and she turned.

He looked at her top, a heavy-duty sports bra type that confined her breasts close to her body, though not as thoroughly as her usual work wear. "Shall we swim?" Her voice came out low, sultry.

"Let's." He rubbed sunscreen across her shoulders. "Salt water might help your wounds."

"I'll be fine in no time. Want me to get your back?"

"No, thanks. I'm dark enough that I don't worry about it."

"Up to you, but this sun is pretty brutal. It's more vertical than at higher latitudes."

He raised an eyebrow. "Are you explaining solar angles to me?"

She laughed. "Right."

"My name is sun."

"Your name is mud."

"No, really. Ravi is sun in Sanskrit."

She eyed him. "You named yourself sun. Was this before or after you went into the solar field?"

"Before. By years. I wanted something simple and Indian. Ravi Shankar, Ravi Varma, Ravi Coltrane."

"You made that last one up."

"Nope. John and Alice Coltrane named their son after Ravi Shankar."

"Huh. Well, I like the name on you."

"Well, thank you. I like it too."

She gathered her snorkel gear and locked the doors to the truck. "And if you get famous, it won't wear you out signing it over and over."

He laughed.

"Let's swim." She put the key into a special pocket in her bottoms and set off barefoot across the water-smoothed black lava rock toward the light colored sand. She took in Ravi's basic boardshorts with a sidelong look. He was big, with more muscle than she'd thought, like the body style common among Pacific Islanders. Plenty of construction workers, herself for example, had less muscle. His top-surgery scars pinched the skin under his chest, with a layer of fat over and under.

She breathed the scent of sea wrack. She didn't get to the water often enough. The salt and seaweed, palm trees and ocean breeze slipped into her, seducing her once again. The labor of walking across soft mounded sand to the harder packed areas burned in her thighs and the hot sand massaged her bare feet. Birds clattered in the palm trees along the waterline.

Two other groups shared the beach. A quiet Saturday, even for a locals' beach like this. Four dark-skinned, dark-haired women lay on their stomachs as though passed out, surfboards stabbed in the sand around them. The other three people dripped on their towels and ate from plastic containers they pulled from a cooler. She lifted a hand to them when they looked and they waved back.

At the first touch of the water on her toes, she responded to the seductive suck with an abandoned run into the glittering blue ocean. She stopped thigh deep and let the intimate grasp and stroke of the water around her body wring a laugh from her throat. She looked back to see Ravi pull on his snorkel and mask a few feet behind her. She did the same, spitting into it and spreading the fog-resistant fluid into a film across the lens. She fit the silicone curtain around her eyes and nose and popped the mouthpiece between her teeth.

She looked over to Ravi, who waded deeper and gave a thumbs up. She turned and dove into the shallow water, fins in one hand. The salt burned in her wounds, but not for long. The cool fluid buoyed her to the surface and she blew to clear the snorkel. After the bottom dropped away, she stopped to put on her flippers and looked around.

Ravi paddled to her, head down and snorkel up. He looked at her, and a distorted smile tried to form around the mouthpiece of his snorkel. She smiled back.

She turned away and struck out for deeper waters where there would be more fish. She experimented with different strokes and settled into a gentle breast stroke as the least painful way to move her shoulder. Ravi kept up, off to one side. Perfect.

More fish congregated around coral outcroppings than swam along flat expanses of sand, so she angled toward the rougher areas. The sand fell away as she went, but the coral grew higher at the same time, and she had a spectacular view of the lobe coral and cauliflower coral and abundant groups of spiny urchins.

One enormous outcropping, at least fifty feet around, hosted something in a hole partway down. She dove and kicked to stay deep enough to scope out the moray eel with its threatening grin.

She finned over the mass and followed a canyon of clear sand with coral in clumps and lines on each side. Ravi watched a turtle maneuver in the tidal surge. She waved to see if she could get his attention and when he looked she gestured along the canyon. He nodded and started toward her.

Kerala folded and stretched back out to change direction. Her abused muscles twanged, but the movement and the salty water felt marvelous. The canyon was a busy fish highway, and she soon stopped and allowed herself to float in the push and pull of the water along with convict tangs, Moorish idols, and Achilles tangs. The tidal motion massaged her soreness away. She followed a spotted puffer for a few minutes, then a lei triggerfish that undulated the long fins on its top and bottom.

She never tired of the bright colors and outrageous configurations of the reef fish. The sun and saltwater wore her out, however. She turned to get Ravi's attention and found him within a few feet of her side, watching the bright traffic flow below.

She brought herself upright and pulled off her mask, a hint of fin action keeping her above water. A backward dunk of her head slicked her hair away from her face, and she resurfaced with a satisfied gasp. She opened her eyes to see Ravi doing the same thing a couple of feet away.

"What do you think?"

"This is a great place." Ravi wiped saltwater from his eyebrows. "I'm so ignorant, though. I don't know what anything is called."

"I have a book of Hawaiian reef fish. You can identify the ones you saw when we get home." That sounded good, getting home with Ravi. Spending the evening with him.

He moved closer and reached out, tiny bubbles lining the hair on his arm. He slipped his hand around her waist to pull low on her back. He had never touched her so intimately. His features were far harder than his gentle hand.

As she swept through the water toward him, the silken caress of the saline water cooled her heated belly. Ravi drew her close and she allowed it. He pulled her until the front of her bathing top touched his chest and flexed her to bring their bellies into contact. Her lips fell open and his eyes heated. A quiver shook her abs when his belly hair tickled her skin and pressed closer.

She brushed the fronts of his thighs with hers and pressed into his chest. She tipped her head and looked at his lips, as much of an order as if she'd yelled kiss me.

The salt on her lips disappeared under the tip of his tongue. When he came back for another taste, she tangled her tongue with his and pulled him so he couldn't back away. She demanded his whole mouth, a slanting lip to lip, open-mouthed kiss that pushed them inside one another. Their tongues moved, rubbing deep and slow, the sea defining their pace. On the ocean swell, she surged into him.

With a gasp and a shiver, she pulled away from the kiss and searched his face. He seemed to feel the same inevitability, the same lack of rush. When she undulated against him, bringing their hips into contact for the first time, his breathing faltered.

An urge welled to wrap her legs around his thigh and grind. She could rub herself to orgasm on him within minutes. She hadn't been so turned on in years. But somehow the ache and anticipation pleased her. She wanted to draw out and feed on this tension, this unbelievable, irresistible, painfully pleasurable tension.

She lifted herself into Ravi for one more kiss. This time, she pressed her lips to his, almost closed, rubbing across to learn his texture, pulling his lower lip between her teeth to learn his shape. She flirted with his tongue when he offered it, but stayed in the shallows.

He stole the momentum from her and brought her into a deeper kiss, another melding of mouths that exploded inside her head. Though she wanted to draw out their seduction of one another, in that moment, she almost broke and fought him for control.

She pushed his chest and drifted off. "I'm done swimming. Let's head in, okay?"

He acquiesced and she donned her mask for the slow swim into the sandy shoreline.

❖

Ravi leaned on the truck and watched Kerala towel herself. The bruise that stretched from her hip halfway to her knee chilled him, though she'd moved easily while swimming.

How could he protect her?

The morass of corporate politics at Sol Volt demanded his return to California before too long. A few shareholders were organizing to pressure the board against becoming a benefit corporation. He was unlikely to get a month in Hawaiʻi, let alone the two he'd hoped for.

He could cancel the contract, not build the house. The more he learned about Hawaiʻi the less confident he was that he should develop the land, even to prove out the possibility of energy independence on the island.

It would force Kerala out of the limelight. She would be safe.

Best case scenario was Nahoa figuring it out soon and getting enough evidence to put the son of a bitch away. Kerala may hate the idea of sending anyone to a cell, but Ravi just wanted her out of danger.

He could follow the money, figure out who had something at stake. If it wasn't about protecting a supposed burial site, maybe they'd been looking in the wrong direction. He pushed this idea to the simmer pot of his thoughts along with the whole question. He'd let the issue cook a while and taste the broth later.

Kerala pulled her shirt back over her wet swimsuit top, and he couldn't resist commenting. "Looking to win a wet T-shirt contest?"

She shot him a steamy look. "If that were the case, I wouldn't be wearing the suit top, now would I?"

He changed the subject for his own comfort. "Are you hungry?"

"Yeah, I'm starving." She rubbed her belly. "The ocean takes it out of you."

"I'll spring for dinner if you'll pick the place."

"No way." Her response was firm but not defensive. "You bought and cooked breakfast. Or brunch. Anyway, the least I can do is buy dinner. You wouldn't thank me if I tried to cook for you. We'll stop by one of my favorite little drive-up restaurants."

They stole a picnic table from a gecko under wide branches heavy with avocados half the size of a human head. He looked along the branch and realized that the tree was growing downslope almost a hundred feet. He looked up. An avocado tree well over a hundred feet tall? He was definitely not in California.

He regretted his agreement the moment his order arrived at the pick-up window. "This isn't food. It's cardboard and Styrofoam."

She laughed and took another bite of her fish burger. "Come on, Ravi. Just take it for what it is."

"It's sad."

"I didn't think you ate meat."

He had ordered a fish burger along with her. "It's a preference and a habit, not a rule. Besides, it sounded more appetizing than Spam musubi, hard-boiled eggs, and white rice."

"I don't get the Hawaiian love for Spam, but I could eat rice every day. Do you eat land animals too?"

"I was raised pure vegetarian, but I tried meat at friends' houses as a kid. I never learned to love it. Since then, it's just been seafood. I got stuck on sushi."

"I love sushi." She ate a fry.

"This makes me sad for the fish." He tried to hold the sandwich together. How a bun could both taste like Styrofoam and come apart in soggy crumbles escaped him.

"This is not good." He ate another handful of crispy, oily crinkle fries. "These are great, though." He pulled the fish from the sandwich and ate it plain. The fillet was good, battered and fried, and probably came from the ocean he'd been swimming in. Much better.

Flowers and trees luxuriated along the road and on the hills. Another area he'd need to research, since he couldn't name anything but the plumeria. He knew that Hawai'i was the most remote land mass in the world, with no other land within twenty-five hundred miles, and that the Big Island had six different biospheres and over three thousand native species of plants and animals. The island continued to surprise him, though.

Kerala demolished her sandwich and fries. Her hair tangled in salty locks along the sides of her face and her skin shone with oceanic cleanliness. The oval imprint of the diving mask circled her eyes. He switched to the coleslaw and ate two bites. Cabbage in mayonnaise. "Ugh."

"Come on, Ravi, don't be such a snob."

He turned to the poke, small chunks of ahi, marinated and chilled. His eyes closed as his defensive tongue relaxed to report soft, melting, sushi-like tuna with a lively chorus singing a seaweed and sesame backup.

Kerala rolled her eyes at him, but he ignored her and took another measured bite. "It's nice to find that something in Hawai'i is neither exorbitantly expensive nor horribly lacking in quality. I can get this anywhere?"

"It's on every menu, pretty much, and the popular places go through it fast enough to guarantee that it's fresh. Price varies." She munched her tasteless coleslaw. "Have you always been so into food?"

"I guess I have. My mom wanted me and my brother to know Indian food as well as the American choices we had around us. She raised us to think about spices—what was used in a dish and what could have made it better. She didn't insist that we cook all of the time, but she wanted us to have educated and flexible palates."

"My parents didn't care about food. If we held a dinner party, they hired a caterer. Our cook had a list of acceptable dishes and rotated through them. We had roast on Sunday. I remember that being a weekly thing when I was home from school. It was about the only meal we shared."

"Your parents didn't eat with you?" Ravi tried not to sound judgmental. He'd known other families that weren't close, but his had been very much in each other's pockets.

"No, not often. When I wasn't at boarding school, they had office hours or evening classes or meetings or dinner dates with friends. Eating with them was a drag anyway. They were always after me about something."

"Your parents are teachers?"

"Yeah. They both taught at University of Pennsylvania. My mother teaches one or two classes per semester, to keep her hand in and stay on the committees she enjoys. My father doesn't teach anymore, but he's active in campus administration."

"Ivy League parents, Ivy League education." He finished the last of the poke.

"I went to Bryn Mawr for undergrad. I did my master's at UP because of the program's excellent reputation."

Ah, defensive. "Even if they didn't teach you anything about food, they passed on an appreciation for a good education."

Her lips twisted. She looked away. "Well, it's true that I went to great schools."

He shelved his curiosity. "Ready to go home?"

Her tension slipped away when he dropped the subject. "Let's go."

A couple of professors rich enough for boarding schools and a cook. She'd already mentioned a housekeeper and a maid. The phrase "poor little rich girl" flitted through his head, but he shook it out. She would hate that description.

But to rarely eat dinner with one's parents? His mom didn't work outside the home when he was young, but his dad had worked hard as the director of public utilities for the small town he'd grown up in. He had always come home for dinner. Gathering the family for meals had been an important part of his childhood.

She put on Miles Davis for the drive home.

"Look—a rainbow." He craned his neck to keep it in view.

"It's one of the nice things around here. This place is so gay there's a rainbow every day."

"It's a double." What a beautiful thing to see every day. He settled into his seat and turned up the volume. "You like jazz?"

She glanced at him. "I love good music. I figure any style of music can be done with creativity and skill. If I listen carefully, I should be able to find something to like about pretty much any genre."

"What do you hear when you listen to this?"

"This version of 'Straight, No Chaser' has one of my favorite bits of piano. During Sahib Shihab's sax solo, Thelonious Monk is on the piano just nudging at the song. Dropping the perfect notes here and there. He hangs back and lets the sax own it, but he doesn't get lazy in the background. I love the confidence in that, giving up the spotlight and still being a crucial part of the song."

He nodded and tuned in to the music. He liked her more and more all the time. His mom enjoyed Miles Davis and Charlie Parker. He preferred the genre filtered through Digable Planets and Us3, groups that blended jazz with hip-hop back in the Nineties.

As she stopped the truck out front, Bogart yipped and danced around. She got out of the truck and took the ball Bogart offered. "I need to wash up." She threw the ball past the house into the backyard and walked to the front door ahead of him.

"I guess I need to rinse the salt off too." The thought of soaping her back made him swallow hard. "Hey, maybe I should put more antibiotic on those wounds."

"Good idea. I'll let you know when I'm done."

Kerala banged around in her bedroom for a few moments and disappeared into the bathroom. He heard the shower start and sank onto the couch. *I am not on T. I do not get fifty hard-ons a day any more. I can control myself. I don't need Kerala like I feel I do.*

At least half of those statements were true.

❖

Waimea was downright chilly. Kerala pulled on a light nightgown of cream silk and a voluminous red velvet robe with huge lapels and deep pockets. She wrapped the velvet around her body and pulled the belt tight. It had been made for a much bigger person, but the excess fabric made her feel that much more comforted.

Ravi's touch lingered on her skin. He had daubed ointment on her wounds and kicked her out of the bathroom.

She walked into the guest room. Spanning one long wall, the mahogany bookcases with their scrolled trim along the top looked old but weren't. The simple oak desk didn't look old and was.

The desk held nothing but her laptop. Metal two-drawer file cabinets stored every scrap of information she had about Ravi's house as well as proposals, pie-in-the-sky ideas, and other work like her personal house plans.

Years ago, she'd labeled the fat folder "Dream House." She disinterred it and pulled out pieces of drawing pad paper, ignoring the scraps of scribbled-on notebook paper, magazine clippings, and other bits and pieces she'd collected over the years.

She'd purchased her house with the idea of building on another room or two and replacing trim, door handles, and drawer pulls to add character. Eighteen years of construction experience and a master's degree in architecture gave her plenty of ideas about what she liked and didn't like. A contractor's home was never complete. She shuffled through papers until she came to the overview drawing.

She chewed her cheek, impatient with her indecision. To flip the house, she would pull down the walls around the dining room and leave it at that. It wouldn't be that much work and it would fix the flow problem.

If she weren't so unsettled, she would plan a bigger change. She'd like the house better with a large bedroom and bath on the opposite side of the house. She hadn't been able to commit herself to the work, though. The idea of moving back to the mainland had been percolating. She could do small projects, one at a time, and plug away until she made a decision.

She put the drawing away and measured the guest room by eye.

A queen bed would fit, but barely. She moved her paperwork into the dining room. It took three trips, and Bogart helped by getting under her feet as she walked. She turned on the dining room chandelier, a drape of five bronze vines tipped by glass foxglove blossoms. It had been the only thing in the room. No reason to furnish a formal dining room when she had her little table in the kitchen.

The shower sound disappeared. She pushed her hands into the deep pockets of her robe.

What was this feeling? If she were younger, she would diagnose it as infatuation. She had experienced the excitement of being pulled to someone, but never so strongly.

There might be more at stake with Ravi than crossing the employer/employee boundary or endangering her dyke cred. Were these the feelings that led to so many mid-life crises, so many marriages that split when things ought to be getting smoother?

The door opened. A thin mist of steam billowed from the room, backlit by the bank of lights over the vanity mirror. Ravi emerged, toweling the back of his head and drying his ears. In the moment of steam and glare, he looked like a knight, broad and thick and strong. The muscles of his shoulders gleamed in the soft light and the shine danced with the motion of his arms. The hair along the top of his chest glowed in the dark hallway and the rest was hidden in the shadow of his body.

He wore boxer shorts and nothing else. From the other end of the hallway, she wanted to touch his thigh muscles, his hips, the spare tire that he seemed unconcerned with. She swallowed.

His motion slowed as he watched her watch him. He reached back into the bathroom and hung the towel. His chest came into view, bulky with muscle and fat, scars underlining his pecs. He smiled at her in a way that let her know she'd been broadcasting her attraction and disappeared into the guest room, closing the door behind him.

She turned away from the hall and moved to the recliner.

He joined her wearing running pants and a light sweater and settled on the couch. "Tell me about your family."

No way. "You first."

"Okay. Once upon a time, there was a beautiful princess…"

The story was a rom com, of course. Sparks flying between the blue-collar electrical worker and the snob, disapproving parents and all. His mom worked in a typing pool to put her husband through a bachelor's degree program. His dad worked overtime to keep her home with the kids after that, and he was promoted eventually to director of the public utilities district. Ravi told a great story and shone with his pride in and love for his parents. Even Kerala's buried heartstrings got plucked.

"My brother and I both got into electrical engineering. I got into solar power early in my master's degree program, but my brother didn't find his niche until he got into computers."

She couldn't hold back the cliché. "Your parents must be proud."

He grinned. "They are, though my mom would say that I've traded too much for my work. Sam married Theresa a few years after college, so she has no one to work on but me. She's a frustrated matchmaker from way back."

"Even my mom did that."

"Tell me about them."

She couldn't figure out how to refuse without sounding ungracious. She didn't have any heartwarming stories about her practical parents.

When the doorbell rang, irritation flitted across Ravi's face and Kerala jumped to her feet. "Just a minute," she said as she kicked the long robe out in front of every step. She opened the door wide enough to talk.

"Delivery for Ravi Dietrich."

She stepped away from the door. "Ravi."

"My bed?"

"A bed, a dresser, a couple of lights. Here's the list." The guy handed Ravi the delivery receipt.

She chewed her cheek. "We need to move my desk."

He turned back to the delivery guy. "Help us make room for this stuff?" The delivery guy looked sour but agreed.

Twenty minutes later, the dining room held her office furniture and a complete set of high-quality bedroom furniture graced her guest room. She stared at it while Ravi tipped the driver handsomely for his help and closed the door behind him. When he walked back down the hall toward the bedroom, she turned and skewered him. "Do I pay you for these things now or when you leave?"

"You don't have to pay me."

"You just spent ten thousand dollars furnishing a guest room I use as an office."

"Why does it matter to you how much I spent?"

"Do you think I need this kind of stuff?"

"Do you think I'm trying to sneak in some kind of present?"

"Aren't you?"

"No!"

She hesitated. "Then what's up with investing so much in temporary furniture?"

"I guess you've forgotten. I'm building a house on this island. I have to furnish it sooner or later, so I thought I'd get some things I liked."

She looked for the catch. There wasn't one. She waited a moment for the embarrassment to pass.

She tried to brush past him in the hallway, but he blocked her way. "What are you doing?" he asked with what sounded like hard-won calm.

"Trying to get back to the living room." She stared at the soft nutmeg cashmere of his sweater woven in cable stitches.

He rotated sideways to allow her past but dogged her steps. She plopped back into her recliner, resigned to the fact that she'd made herself look like an idiot.

Ravi sat on the sofa.

"Once upon a time, there were two people of appropriate background and overlapping interests. Everyone agreed that it was a good match. They married, had one child, and lived in the style they enjoyed."

Her initial discomfort faded. "My parents both come from money. They didn't come across on the Mayflower—too risky. They came later, once the US had proven the economy could be made to perform tricks, sit up, and beg. My mother's side was into deep political control of the economy. They were influential in the federalization of the US government in the eighteen hundreds."

"Hamilton over Burr."

"Right. My father's side developed monopolies in the nineteen hundreds. By the time my parents met, the funds and trusts and investments behaved themselves well. The family members who cared about money took care of the money. My parents act as though it doesn't exist, though it funds their lifestyle."

Ravi listened attentively.

"I have no idea if my parents ever loved one another. I can't imagine them feeling anything that deeply. By the time I was old enough to wonder at it, they were good roommates. They worked as a team in social situations, shared a taste for Domaine Chandon de Briailles Corton Grand Cru, and kissed me with the same amount of pressure on the same spot on my forehead."

"So, not demonstrative people."

She snorted. "To say the least. They worked, but only in the right jobs. They had friends among the working class, but only those who were sufficiently cultured. Their friends rarely understood how rich we were."

"You don't sound like you like them much."

"They return that favor. I fought them the whole time I was growing up. They wanted me to marry the right man and I'm a dyke. When I expressed interest in construction, they pushed me into architecture. When I told them I was going to work for a construction company, starting at the bottom, they were not amused. They said they wouldn't support me while I played in the dirt. I told them I would support myself."

"Did you know what that would mean?" Ravi looked fascinated.

"I had no idea. They continued to pay my tuition and fees as long as I stayed in the architecture program, probably hoping I'd grow out of manual labor, and I got an Ivy League master's degree because of it. They'd given me a credit card, but I didn't think of that as taking money from them." She shook her head at the memory. "I maxed that card out before I realized it was my responsibility to pay it. It took me years before I had my finances under control. Before I even understood them."

Ravi shook his head in patent disbelief. "I can't imagine you letting any part of your life float along outside your control like that."

"Ah, but that's what I learned. A girl has to know where those dollars and cents are. I've made my own way ever since. We've hardly spoken in years and I imagine they don't talk about me much at dinner parties. But I'd be surprised if I was cut out of their wills. Someday I may be a rich woman."

Ravi cocked his head. "Does this have something to do with me buying the furniture?"

She wrinkled her nose. "When my parents first cut me off, I had some well-to-do friends who heard about it. And there were the other branches of the family. They tried for years to give me presents like that. Actually, they tried to give me money too. I got a personal check for my twenty-sixth birthday from a cousin who wrote in the memo line, Buy a nicer place. The check was for three hundred thousand dollars."

Ravi blinked. "I don't have that kind of ready money and I feel like I'm doing really well."

"I'm still habituated to think that it's not that much. But I didn't cash it. I struggled on. I bought this house with my own earnings. Feels good." She patted her recliner.

"So I stepped on some old baggage?"

"To some degree. Then there's the fact that I can't afford to pay you back right now."

"Really? Did you end up in more debt?"

"No, I spent all my savings when I moved here. I put a huge cash down payment on this house. When I started with Mālama, my disposable income went toward paying the house off. I paid it off last month in a big lump sum that was pretty damn stupid." The same buoyancy she'd felt when she'd gone to the bank filled her again. "I was so excited about paying it off that I hardly left myself enough money for fuel and food."

"I just reached the point where I have enough to build this house. Slow-but-steady growth. I can't imagine the financial yo-yo you've been riding since your parents cut you off."

She straightened her legs and flinched. Her hip and leg ached again. Her shoulder didn't hurt unless she thought about it. Jack had given her a whole bottle of pills...

"I think I'm going to take a painkiller." Ravi wouldn't move their physical relationship forward if she was doped and not on her game. But damn. She wanted a pill! Then she groaned for real.

"What is it?" He sounded so concerned.

"I need to walk Bogart. He'll be a complete monster if I don't give him some real exercise." She laid her head back and fought the urge to say fuck it. When she opened her eyes, Ravi stood over her with a glass of water and a single pill.

"I'll walk Bogart. Me and Bogie will be friends, right?" he asked the dog.

"He's a handful. He doesn't respond to Bogie, first of all. And he hates that baby-talk tone."

Ravi eyed the dog with respect. "Well, I think that Bogart and I can get along together. Would you like to get some exercise, sir?"

Bogart looked between them as though he understood the conversation. He popped to his feet and trotted to the door. When he looked over his shoulder at Ravi with his best good-dog expression, Kerala took the medicine.

That dog was a maniac. He led Ravi cross-country and ran literal circles around him. The exercise made him break a sweat under the cashmere, but the loose weave let the breeze through to chill him.

A few leg-noodling hills out, Ravi called Bogart back and lay to watch the stars pop while the dog frolicked in the long grasses. Before it got too dark, he ambled back and let Bogart do all the running around he wanted.

Bogart scratched at the door before Ravi reached it. He opened the door and entered as Kerala pushed upright in her recliner. In the big velvet robe, she looked small and confused. Endearing, if misleading.

Bogart jumped and lunged, but strong training kept his paws off her. Her foggy eyes focused on the bundle of dog energy, delight on her face. "Does he deserve a treat?"

The lines around her eyes looked delicate and the curve of her cheek glowed pink. "Sure. He's a great dog."

She turned and asked the dog as she walked toward the kitchen, "Did you tire the poor guy out? He let you lead, didn't he? Over the hills? Mmmhmm…"

Her voice faded as she turned the corner. He couldn't catch her words, but the tone clearly praised Bogart. She returned to the living room, perched on the edge of her chair, and leaned over to pet her dog. She shrugged her robe off her shoulders and it draped around her hips.

Ravi lost his breath when he saw her backlit by the sunset in the picture windows. Set free under silk, her breasts formed a classic slope from collarbone to nipple, with a heavy undercurve that rested against her delicate-looking ribs.

He acted on instinct.

She looked at his approach and smiled. Her expression grew sultrier at the heat in his face, but she tensed when he knelt in front of her, pushing Bogart aside. He parted her knees and slid between them. She leaned back as he loomed in until again, in a motion similar to the one he'd employed in the water, he slipped an arm behind her and arched her back toward him.

This time, he used his other hand as well. He laid it flat on her belly, fingers up on her ribs. When she arched into him a little bit more, he brought both hands to the front of her ribcage and cradled her breasts.

He lifted them, one in each hand, and pushed them together with a massaging pulse of his fingers and palms. He put his mouth around one attentive nipple and exhaled on it through the silk. The heat of his breath hardened her nipple, and he sucked the damp silk and what it clung to.

She pushed up but held his head close and twisted against his confining hands, adding to the friction and heat. She threw her head back, and his breath left him again at the sight of her brown throat, pale collarbones, and up-thrust breasts.

He trapped her and held her close. He needed to pull off the silk gown and feel her bare nipples against his chest. Her slow writhing was irresistibly sensual, and why the hell try to resist?

Drugged. The memory of the hydrocodone pill jerked at his leash. If the promise of building a relationship couldn't still his hands, the job was done by the knowledge that her memory of the act would be fuzzy. He couldn't risk becoming just another fuck for her.

Oh, shit. He loved Kerala. Whether he broke their acquaintance into the days they'd spent together or he considered the entire year they'd been in contact, the mechanics and numbers of it meant nothing. He loved her.

He stroked her back, soothing her, banking the fires he'd stoked. She hid her face in the crook of his shoulder and, as amazing as the entire rest of the night, allowed him to carry her into her bedroom. She sighed when he set her on the bed and gave her a last quiet kiss.

Kerala watched Ravi leave her room without closing her door. She felt delicate and brutal, vengeful and tender. She lay back against her pillows and put her hand between her legs. Through two layers of fabric and the softness of her labia, her fingers pressed against her clitoris and she bit back a moan. Damn him! She was so worked up. Her fingers moved on her labia, massaging them and pushing her clit in circles at the same time.

She could take at least that much comfort. She pulled the silk of her gown to her belly. One hand remained there and stroked the soft material against her softer skin. The other hand pushed off her panties and slipped back between her legs. She dipped her calloused fingers inside for some of the welling lubrication. She slid them around in her labia, feeling every tiny bit of the soft folds and prolonging the excitement.

Thinking of Ravi, she slid a hand under her silk gown and lifted and squeezed her breast. The soft light from her clock radio let her see her nipple harden and peak against the fabric. She slid two fingers to capture her clit and, keeping them straight, drew them forward and back. As her fingertips and knuckles passed around her clit, she plucked her nipple. The stab of sensation went right to her womb and pushed a moan from her lips.

She didn't have to be quiet. Ravi should know how he made her feel. He should know that she moaned, gasped, and sighed as she touched herself, thinking of him. She circled her clit with two fingertips, but it was too sensitive for such direct touch. She flattened her fingers and rotated three of them over her clit. The quickened breath she drew turned into a repeated oh as she circled that hard knot until it nearly disappeared into its hood. The orgasm drew from her belly into her clenching pubic muscles and to the sharp points of her nipples as she sang her release into the air between her and Ravi.

Ravi lay in his brand-new bed and his fingers pressed his softening clit. He hadn't expected the sounds he'd heard, but even before the shock had faded, he'd dedicated himself to sharing the experience. He'd paced himself and built his orgasm at the speed of her sounds. He'd succeeded, beyond imagining, when the soft wail of her orgasm had spasmed in him to become his own. He turned over, still pulsing, to sleep nude.

## CHAPTER EIGHT

Kerala smelled coffee. Sleep flowed from her mind as water through a sieve, the last bits dripping through and leaving her awake before she was quite ready to move.

"Mmm." She sighed as she tucked farther into her pillow. Now that her body had been consulted, it complained of stiffness and discomfort. Her foggy head cleared some. Drug hangover. She sighed again and rolled onto her back to prepare for opening her eyes.

She usually woke fast. This lazy, thickheaded way of greeting the morning sucked. No more painkillers. She ignored the messages from hip, back, and shoulder and stood. She shook out her nightgown and went to the bathroom.

Again, she smelled coffee. Ravi. What a gem.

She leaned over the sink and bathed her eyes in cool water. He'd gone further than she'd expected with that make-out session while she was drugged, but he'd stopped abruptly.

For the best. She would've passed out on him anyway.

She'd masturbated. She smiled at the saucy expression in the mirror. He had to have heard. She stopped back by her room for a robe and headed to the kitchen.

No one in the house, but a full pot of coffee. She touched the side—still hot—and poured herself a cup. He couldn't have gone far.

Bogart hadn't said good morning. Ravi must have let him out. She opened the back door and laughed. Ravi lay on his back in the grass with Bogart cuddled under his arm.

Bogart jumped up when he saw her. She stepped outside and let the screen door slam behind her. He danced around, begging for attention, and she went through her best "good dog" routine while Ravi lay still, as though he were sleeping.

When Bogart calmed, she knelt beside Ravi. His eyes were closed, but a slight smile curved his lips.

She hovered over him a second before kissing him with soft, closed lips. She kissed his forehead, his eyelid, his cheek, and his lips again. He smiled in earnest and she leaned back. "Good morning. Thanks for the coffee." She raised her mug to him.

"My pleasure." When his long dark eyes swept open, the liquid glow in them ignited a warm spark in her belly. She shook her head at the ease with which he turned her on and gave him a smile.

He pushed up on one elbow and pulled her into another kiss. A little more energetic, though he seemed to recognize her lassitude. When he released her, she sipped her coffee, kneeling back on her heels, grass licking her toes.

"So," she asked with studied casualness, "hear anything funny last night?"

He choked on a laugh. "Funny? No."

"Anything odd?"

"Mmm, no, I wouldn't say odd."

"What would you say?"

"I'd say sexy. Evocative. Arousing. Educational."

Her lips twitched. "Educational? How so?"

"Now I know what you sound like when you come." She held his knowing eyes, shameless. "And I know that you're easy."

A corner of her lips quirked. "I told you that."

"No." He stretched, his arms and legs quivering with extravagant pleasure. "You told me you'd been a slut. That's a matter of quantity." He poked her leg. "Easy is a matter of quality. You came when you wanted to. You paced yourself until you wanted to come and then you just did."

She shrugged a shoulder. "I know what I like."

He put his hands behind his head in the grass. "Tell me what you like."

No neighbors close enough to see or hear. That's what she liked about being at the end of the block, on the edge of the housing development.

"I like squeezing and kneading. I like my nipples plucked and pulled when they're soft and I like them rolled, nibbled, and pinched when they're hard."

Ravi didn't move, but the muscles of his arms bunched. His bulk become taut in response to her words. She mesmerized him and the effects of her words on his body mesmerized her in turn.

"Long strokes on my sides, my belly, my back, my legs. I like firm hands with firm grips. I like wrestling for top." His legs curled. "I like pressure and pulling on my labia. I like pushing and sucking on my clit. I like being penetrated an inch and teased for the rest. Spread wide and fucked hard. What do you like?"

He swallowed. If they were playing chicken, she'd won. He remained silent for a long time.

"Come make me some more coffee." She slapped him on the thigh and scrambled to her feet. She didn't look back as she stalked to the back door and into the kitchen. He'd follow.

❖

Ravi shifted his head in the grass and stared into the bifurcated sky at the point where the clouds of the windward side stacked against the mountains. The emotions roiling inside him felt the same, two different weather patterns created by one huge rock of fact. He loved her and that was dangerous. He didn't want to be project-managed by Kerala, and she was more than capable of it. He couldn't follow her around and accept whatever fleeting affection she offered. She would try to arrange him into her life in a way that was comfortable, unthreatening, and unemotional. She would settle for fondness if she could.

He could appeal to her sexuality. To her sense of romance. To her respect for him. He could woo her with words, with support, admiration, attention.

She seemed so self-sufficient. How was he supposed to get her to fall in love when nothing short of sabotage tripped her up?

He stood and brushed off his clothes. He ignored Bogart and walked toward the house.

He wouldn't make love with her until she hurt for it. He imagined her hands on her breasts, plucking as she'd described, kneading, while she rubbed herself to orgasm. He shook his head to clear those thoughts. Sure, she could get herself off whenever she wanted. But masturbation and sex were two different things. The body might be satisfied with a solo orgasm, but sex between people was communication, not just sensation.

He found her filling the coffee pot with water. He hungered to rip her nightgown to shreds, bend her over the hard counter, and shove his fingers into her softness. He moved to her as she poured it in the coffee maker. Not just that, though.

He wanted tenderness.

She stiffened when he slipped his arms under hers from behind and folded them against her waist, but she leaned back against his chest when he made no move to grope or squeeze her. He dipped his head and tucked it next to her ear. He took a contented breath of her cool, clean hair and rocked her back and forth, a slow and simple motion. When her hands moved to his forearms, the tentative petting made hope sprout, helplessly.

Strong and slender, the curve of her ribs and slight softness of her belly made Ravi want to stand there forever. He couldn't protect her, but he would stand with her to face any danger that threatened.

She was on a different wavelength. She lifted one arm and arched it back to grasp his head. She shifted her round ass against his crotch. He opened his eyes to see her breasts rise and push against the silk he had tasted the night before. He swept his hands from her waist to capture them and lift the weight high. He pressed them to her ribs and caught her nipples in the curve between thumb and forefinger. He tried her suggestions, pulling, plucking. When her nipples hardened, he caught each one deep into the flushed areole and twisted, rolled, and pulled outward. He let his fingers slide off the mesa at the tip. He repeated it again and again to the rhythm of her moans and herded her closer to the kitchen counter. He trapped her there and bit the taut tendon on the side of her neck.

Triumph filled him when her moan dropped an octave and her legs collapsed. Braced between his thighs and the hard counter, she slumped but did not fall. He fought the urge to plunge his hand into the heat between her legs. Kerala and her dispassionate passion had taken round one on the grass, but he had won the match.

❖

Ravi's inbox was stuffed. His most impressive young physicist had demonstrated a mathematical possibility for increasing the light transfer in polycrystalline cells through a new crystallization technique, increasing efficiency without shoving the price of panels through the roof. The math was solid. Ravi was an engineer, not a physicist, but he followed what he could and had the rest combed by other PhDs in the field.

Not everything was going well. A recently-formed shareholder block was giving him indigestion. They were demanding details of the company—within their rights—and then crafting letters of complaint about his decisions. Sol Volt would never become a benefit corporation if these quarterly-profit types had their way.

A tap at the open door diverted his attention. "Still working?" Kerala leaned against the doorjamb.

"Trying to focus."

She cocked her head. "You never talk about leading Sol Volt like it excites you. That online article about you missing the lab made me wonder."

"Admin isn't my favorite."

"How long's it been?"

"I've worked at Sol Volt for seventeen years, in the lab for the first nine. Lab work is torture and reward, daily bread and celebratory cake, water and wine."

"What happened?"

"Eight years ago, I was tapped for a supervisory position. No big deal. But then there was a series of deaths, relocations, and poaching, and the power vacuum sucked me through the ranks."

She came and sat next to him on the bed. "Why you?"

"Co-workers pressured me. 'Come on, Ravi, Derek doesn't know anything about the science of this. Do you want an MBA squeezing your nuts every time you need personnel or equipment? If you take the job, though...' I gave in."

"What was your plan? Just filling in or did you know it was a new career path?"

He stretched his legs out and leaned back against the headboard. "Everyone else believed I was being groomed for the big job, but I fooled myself. I accepted the responsibilities, understanding that I was the best-qualified person, but I figured that I would get out from under the desk-jockey duties. Eventually, there was no question. I laid my hopes of lab work to rest and accepted the position of CEO."

Kerala's opinion was pithy. "Martyr."

"Indeed. I kept the ecological-mindedness that got me focused on solar power in grad school, though. If the board wanted me to lead, my priorities would inform the priorities of the company as a whole."

"So you're guiding company ethics from the driver's seat. Seems like there would be some satisfaction there. Have they adopted your priorities?"

"So far, so good. My idealism has become a part of the company's image and it positions us to stay strong, even with all the new competition springing up."

"But you don't like the work itself?"

"Some of the CEO headaches are huge. I'm trying to get us re-incorporated as a benefit corporation. Basically, it requires that we consider more than profit in our decision making. There's a group of shareholders fighting me tooth and nail. They want the biggest bang for the fastest buck. I don't pick the highest ROI over the shortest time. Alternative power industries are long-term bets."

"Investors never like hearing that kind of thing."

"Mine did. The original shareholders were passionate environmentalists, but their shares have been diluted. I'm fighting for the future of the company." Ravi didn't want to lose the entire day to fussing over that one issue. "I do need to get a little more work done."

Kerala slid off the bed. "Me too." He checked her tone and body language for resentment or irritation, but she looked as casual as she sounded as she strolled out.

Was that what low-maintenance meant? He could get used to that.

Ravi half-cleared his inbox, powered down his laptop and set it on the bedspread. He was too old to be working on a laptop perched on his knees. Why hadn't he bought a desk?

The bed absorbed his falling body and his muscles tried to release their cramped positions. When a wet nose nudged the hand trailing over the edge of the bed, he turned his head and considered the dog from under his drooping eyelids.

"What are you looking at?" This got him a soft woof and a tail shake that made Bogart's whole body wiggle. "Who told you I was going for a walk?" Bogart's ears perked. "Oh, I see. You tricked me, pretending you knew, and now I've confirmed it. So be it."

By the time his shoes were on, he'd stretched the stiffness from his back. He went to the dining room door and knocked. Kerala swung her shining fall of hair toward him and he swallowed a love-struck sigh. "Can I take Bogart on a walk with me?"

"Of course." She looked at her watch. "If you can wait a half hour, I can come with you."

He waved off the idea. "No, I want to call my mother. Let her know about the move out of the hotel and all."

"Cute." She maintained a straight face.

"Thanks." He turned and walked out the door.

Bogart was ecstatic to be out. Ravi let him romp as they walked down the street, but when they reached the larger crossroad, he tried a firm, "Heel." Bogart fell into position at his knee, sniffed the air, and flipped his ears forward and back.

He walked to an empty lot and decided to try Kerala's invisible dog pen trick. He said "Perimeter," feeling silly, and led Bogart around the lot, then said it again, pointing inside their imaginary border. Bogart seemed cool with it. He sniffed all around the dirt mounds and scrub.

Ravi sat on a rock and pulled out his phone. He dialed his mom.

"Ravi! How are you? I haven't seen you on chat the last couple of nights!"

He hadn't thought this through very well. "Hey, Mom, I'm good. How are you? Everything smooth in retirement-land?"

"Don't get me started. Your father is wonderful, but I had no idea the house needed so much work. He gets up and picks a project every day. It's demoralizing to realize how many little things we never do when we're busy with other things."

"There's nothing like owning a house to keep a new retiree busy. If he runs out of things to do, he could come out and help build the house here."

"I think I'll keep him chained in the basement a while longer. This might be a short-term burst of fix-it energy and I want to be sure he finishes recaulking the windows."

"You don't have him on ladders, do you?"

"No, no. He's doing the small ones around the daylight basement. But you didn't call about the windows. What's going on?"

An unfamiliar nervousness twisted his stomach. He'd always been close to his mom. She had listened to his wishes about gender from an early age and let him make his own choices. She'd stood by him in public and, even better, gave him a loving ear whenever he had strong feelings he needed to talk through. He talked to his mom, sharing with her in ways that he believed rare between any parents and their grown children. He knew how lucky he was.

"Ravi? Speak, punnare, you're worrying me."

"I called to tell you that I'm not in the hotel anymore."

"Okay. I wouldn't call you there anyway. Cell phone is easier." A moment passed in silence. "Where are you staying?"

He imagined the growing amusement in his mother's black eyes. In those rare cases when he held something back, she didn't push. She watched him with that amused look that said, you'll tell me eventually, why wait until later?

"I've moved into Kerala's guest room." That covered the situation without giving her the wrong idea.

"Since when?"

"Since Friday night."

"And you like this girl?"

He groaned like an embarrassed teenager. "She's not a girl. She's a woman with a full life, many responsibilities, and a clear picture of where she's headed."

"Well, you'll have to change all that, won't you?"

"What do you mean?"

"If you love her, you'll have to show her how much more her life can contain, be understanding about her responsibilities, and help her create a new vision for the future."

Silence. Some corner of his mind wished for a bad connection, some crackle or hiss to hide his utter speechlessness.

"Nothing to worry about, son. You are a wonderful man. I know that she will grow to love you as strongly as you love her."

He tried. "Mom…"

"Yes?"

He couldn't find a single word. What could he do, deny he loved her? But he couldn't pour his heart out to his mother on this one. He didn't think he could make her understand how special Kerala was by talking about her extensive sexual history or her cold and distant parents.

"I love you, Mom."

"Love you too, sweetie. Now my advice, and you know how I hate to give advice," he rolled his eyes, "is to get her into bed ASAP. You have no time to lose!"

He jerked at the snap of her flip phone. She'd hung up. Of course she had!

He called Bogart and strolled back to Kerala's house.

Kerala finished her analysis of the wood from the hotel. So much for her concern that they wouldn't have enough to work with. They saved so much that she worried storing it would get expensive. Solid stuff, that old growth.

Too much work to sell the excess wood piecemeal. She'd have to gather it together and offer it as a lot.

Back to work tomorrow. Almost done at the old hotel. Christmas break and then Ravi's site. She didn't think of it as the Dietrich land anymore.

She had a little while before Ravi and Bogart would come back, unless Ravi was more of a wimp than she thought. She called Kekoa, one of her best workers.

"Aloha, Kel. How are you?"

"Good, Kekoa. What are you up to?"

"Waiting. Wife is on Hawaiian time."

She laughed. "While you wait, did you know the Dietrich land used to belong to another guy who tried to build a house there?"

"More makai, most on the beach, other end."

She perked up. "So you know about it."

"Mālama job. Got out of there wiki wiki."

Very fast, she translated. "Mālama had the last job too?"

"Eh. Wife's here."

"See you tomorrow. Thanks."

"Aloha."

How was it Mālama had already worked on this land once and no one saw fit to tell her about it? She hadn't studied the entire property, just the house site and its surrounding area, but this was ridiculous.

The sound of the door brought her upright in her chair. "Bogart!" He skittered through the doorway. She dropped to her knees and loved on him.

Ravi followed Bogart to the door and leaned there. She looked at him. Nice. Having him there, spending time together. She liked it.

With so much up in the air, surrounded by danger and uncertainty and uncertainty about how much danger she was even in, she needed to grab hold of the one thing she knew.

She wanted him and she was done playing.

She raised a hand to Ravi and let him haul her to her feet. She couldn't think of anything but the hunger she carried, lower than her belly. "Ravi, I'm done waiting."

He pulled away, full of sudden tension. "I want you so badly that you only have to look at me and I'm hard. I'm trying to remember why we're holding out."

"I don't see any reason for us to keep pushing this moment away." She stood in a drab, undecorated room with bad lighting, head up and shoulders back. "Do you want me washed and wrapped or shall we fall to?"

His eyes gleamed quicksilver. His lips quirked and he took a deep breath. "Washed and wrapped, of course. You haven't learned that I like the whole process?"

"I've learned that you like to control the pace."

"Are you worried I'll go too fast?"

Her lips twitched, the closest to a smile she could achieve. The tension in the air threatened to freeze her muscles. She shivered and turned away without answering.

In the shower, her copious lubrication made a slippery mess of her pussy. She was tempted to touch herself to a different purpose but held back to see how she and Ravi meshed. Once dry, she slipped an amber satin gown over her skin. She pulled a matching robe over it and smoothed her hair.

She left the bathroom glowing warm, and the cool air of the hall rubbed against her toes like a cat just in from a cold night. Ravi leaned in the doorway of the guest room. "My turn."

"Join me in my bedroom when you're ready."

Practical Kerala worried about missing sleep on a work night. Raunchy, hungry Kerala wanted to haul Ravi from the shower and fuck him.

She set the scene. He'd worked hard for this tension. He should get the full impact. She lit candles in wide dishes and placed them around her bedroom. A warm, uneven light bathed her bed.

She heard Ravi leave the bathroom and stood in the middle of her room, back to the door. She tossed her hair to one side but didn't turn. As she'd hoped, his lips on her neck were the first contact between them.

She shed the robe slowly, voluptuously. Why did she play this romance game for him when she had refused it so many times before? She managed her affairs so that the wrong idea could never form. But Ravi drew something more from her.

The thought propelled her around and into his arms. She hid from her erupting emotion in the wave of sensation as her body came into full contact with his. All that nude skin against her gown, against the flesh of her chest and arms. He tossed a strap-on at the bed and wrapped her in his arms. She pulled his head down for a long kiss, ran her hands to his biceps and squeezed. She dug her fingers into him and tried to spur him into jumping the sequence that she anticipated he'd try to follow.

He hauled in a breath and growled. "Can't wait, can you?" He shoved her backward, disorienting her with the unexpected move. She stumbled, feet tangled in her multi-textured litter, and he advanced on her. She fell onto her bed and scrambled backward. Ravi lowered himself onto her. She was trapped on her back with her legs dangling off the bed below her knees. "How many times can you come in a row?"

She panted, equilibrium shaky, but raised her chin. "That depends on you, big guy."

He nodded and did something she never expected. He levered himself back to his feet, took the hem of her ankle-length nightgown, and tore it. The fabric shrieked. Her knees appeared, but the sight dumbfounded her until the cool air hit her thighs. He knotted the fabric in his big hands and rent it high enough to expose her pubic hair and the tender belly above.

Her hunger reasserted itself as she tossed out her expectations. This would be fun.

He picked her up by the hips as he dropped to his knees. He dragged her to the edge of the bed and she braced her heels on his shoulders. He took enormous bites of her tender thighs but did not linger. He opened wide and devoured her, engulfing her for a long weightless moment. Her back arched and she shoved herself higher into his mouth.

He pushed his face into her and spread her labia with his nose, his chin, his cheeks. He rubbed himself in deeper, covering himself with her pungent fluids. She tried to rub herself to orgasm on his face. Then he bit her clit.

She screamed at the intensity and reached for his head. She wanted to scratch him, to mark him as he marked her, but she could only reach his hair. She took firm hold and held his face deep in her pussy while he nibbled and sucked on her clit, hard, so hard. She thrust against his face, her short clit so engorged that she might be able to fill his mouth and gag him. She writhed and pumped her hips, gasps and cries wrung from her throat. He reached around her hips, dislodging her hands. He squeezed and twisted her nipples. A spasm froze her, bow-arched off the bed, the final ratcheting tighter before her torrential orgasm swept through her. Her hands flew to his elbows and she gripped him with all her strength as she rode out the waves of release, set after set until she lost her reason in the storm of sensation.

She lay boneless, on her back, limp hands by her sides, immovable legs draped over his shoulders. His wide, soft tongue eased across her labia and caused continued tremors that swept her from head to toe.

He raised his head. "Do you count extended orgasms as more than one?"

She laughed, diaphragm as weak as the rest of her muscles. He dropped onto the bed beside her and rearranged her. Murmuring lover's words, words of beauty, of value, of need, he nestled close, leaning on one elbow.

"That was off the Richter scale." She stretched under his roaming hand. Her muscles seemed to be coming back under her control. Her appetite seemed to be coming back under his.

She moved to push him back so she could pleasure him, but he forestalled the motion. "Honey, you're tighter than I've felt since high school. That must have been a long year." He nuzzled her neck. "You said you like penetration. A little at first, right? I want you to let me inside."

She expanded and swelled at his words. "I don't think it'll be a problem."

He spoke again, hot in her ear. "I'll make sure of that."

He found the cock and harness and pulled it on. When he snuggled back next to her, the cool head prodded her thigh. He stroked downward and pressed his fingers and palm against her swollen pussy. She moaned to let him know she was too tender, but he reached farther and started to ease a finger into her slick cunt. She shifted to spread her legs for him and he sat up. Her pussy stretched to take him in. "How many fingers is that?"

He sounded breathless when he responded. "Two."

"Your fingers are huge." Her eyes rolled back. "You're sure that's two?"

He thrust a third finger into her, slow and deep, while his thumb pressed and circled her clit. "This is three." She came, calling out in a moan as slow and drawn out as his penetration of her.

His weight settled on her, chest to chest, and she groaned. The strange and unfamiliar tickle of his chest hair dragged her attention to her breasts. Different. Good. Exciting. His body on hers differed from anyone else she'd slept with.

"Yes." She wanted him in her, his cock in her. He pushed up on his elbows and bit her collarbone. His hips pressed her legs apart and she reached to feel his cock. She pushed her hand between their hips and found it angled along her pussy lips. Her slippery lube already slicked the cock and it slid when she stroked it. He lunged against her pressure and she laughed.

She opened her eyes and stared at his tense face. He grabbed the cock from her and thrust it between her labia, nudging her clit. She curled her hips upward.

"Put it in me."

He changed his angle and circled the head against her pulsing opening. She raked her hands up his back and tried to pull him in. His bulk flattened her but her strength gave her a little control. She flexed her belly and curled her hips again, pressing her softness against his hard fingers and his hard cock.

He slid the cock into her, just a bit, and stilled. His knuckles controlled the cock and rubbed her. He withdrew and pushed, withdrew and pushed, giving her no more than a couple inches of his length. He had more to give and she sought it with her restless hips. She'd said she liked a tease, but she was so hungry. A please slipped from her lips.

At that word, he plunged and rocked against her to get deeper. He pulled out, though only to allow him to shove harder and higher into her. He held himself above her with his elbows on the bed over her shoulders and leveraged farther with each measured thrust.

She flexed her abs and raised her hips. The power and rhythm of his thrusts rocked her. He cried out, it sounded like wait. She undulated under him, bringing the speed of their rubbing thrusting pounding to a frenzy, and she yelled again, hoarse with her previous screams, as the weight and pressure and opening and rubbing combined to shove her over that cliff yet again.

The sound shifted him into overdrive and he pounded her, prolonging the orgasm until she could only squeak, a sound that shattered his control and brought him to a clenching, shuddering, shouting orgasm of his own.

Kerala lay under Ravi, short of breath and strength. He groaned and raised himself enough to blow a cool breeze between their chests and bellies. He held the base of the cock while he pulled out of her and the resultant weak tremors from her exhausted muscles brought a satisfied grin to his face. He fell beside her.

She peeked at the clock radio and resettled her head on the pillow, resigned to future pain. "If I go to sleep right now, I'll get three hours and fifty-two minutes of sleep." Ravi pressed a sympathetic kiss to her forehead, and she lifted her chin for one on the mouth. Kissing hadn't figured much in that explosive sex, and they made up for that until Kerala raised her head to look at the clock again and groaned. "If I go to sleep right now..."

## Chapter Nine

Nahoa sat alone on the edge of a lava rock outcrop over the dash of the ocean. Kerala walked toward him, thinking how well he fit there. His hair formed thick twists. He must have been swimming, the salt and his natural curl giving him a style that some would have to spend an hour creating.

She spoke low to alert him to her presence. "Even on the sheltered side, the waves beat the shore. So much power."

He didn't turn. "Maybe Hawaiian violence comes from this constant battering, this fluid enactment of striking over and over something that resists with such resolve."

She sat next to him and pressed her palms into the pits and corrugations of the battered old lava flow. The sunrise mustered its energy behind them. The sky glowed golden and deep blue, with a brighter, lighter blue making its way toward the horizon.

They'd have to get to the old hotel soon, but Nahoa seemed so unsettled. "Didn't expect to see you here." She looked at him. "I was just checking out the old construction site."

Nahoa sat utterly still.

"Why didn't anyone tell me Mālama had built on this land before? There are concrete footings still in the ground over there." She was tired of the game and wanted answers. "When I look at the records from that project, what am I going to find?"

"The Dietrich land. The old Willoughby property, Parker Ranch, and back and back. It's been a hundred years since Hawaiians held it."

"So any burials would be really old."

"I lost a best friend and my own innocence on this patch of land. I did things I don't even want to think about trying to protect the 'āina."

"You did things here? Was this one of your direct actions?"

Nahoa watched the waves disintegrate on the rock, but she couldn't tell if he saw any of it.

"How did you lose your best friend?"

He twisted his head away. When he turned back toward her, he looked so mournful that she reached for his hand, only to stop before touching him. He said, "Pauahi and I battled for the first seat, canoeing. My endurance against his speed. The bow paddler sets the pace. We were inseparable until I stopped."

"Until you stopped paddling?"

He sighed and looked away again. "I stopped everything. I joined my dad, learned the trade. I hardly saw him again, but I heard that he went wild. Ice and alcohol and whatever else."

"Ice, as in meth?"

"Eh. Pauahi turned into another homeless Hawaiian sleeping on beaches and doing petty crimes to feed himself."

Nahoa didn't sound dismissive or disgusted. His voice ached with guilt and mournfulness.

"You can't always save your friends. People go down to drugs all the time and it's not always about what support they did or didn't have."

Nahoa shook his head. "Pauahi and I did things together that haunt us both. We just handle it differently."

"You're not haunted by damaging property. I can tell that you have stronger demons than what you'd get from breaking car windows." She fisted the rough rock and waited, but he didn't speak. "You know that Jack is the worst possible conspirator. He's clear as glass. What does he know that I don't?"

"Jack doesn't know anything."

"About what?" She summoned all her patience. "He implicates himself every time he looks to you for a reaction or tries to protect you. Is it about Pauahi? What is he protecting you from?"

"Prison."

"Nahoa." The warning in her voice had no effect.

He continued speaking in the same hopeless tone. "Prison isn't the right place for me."

"No one belongs in prison."

"My debt can't be paid by marking time in a cell. It requires positive action, creative force."

"What do you owe? Who is trying to collect? Does this have anything to do with the person who ran me down?"

Nahoa turned, his eyes focusing on her for the first time. "If you're being threatened because of me, I can figure it out. I can fix it."

"I'm not going to sit around while you Don Quixote your way around the island. Talk to me, Nahoa." She reached a hand toward him, but he stood and moved away from her. She got up, brushing the rough rock from her work pants, and followed him. He stopped by the koa tree, ancient and gnarled, strangled by the liliko'i vine that used it for support. "If you're protecting someone, you can tell me. What did Pauahi do? Did he get you into trouble? I'm not going to turn you in for something you did when you were a kid."

He shivered and put a hand on the koa. When he turned, his smile was in place. "You're a good friend to me, Kel. I am protecting someone, but it's time I stopped."

He walked across the rubble toward his truck.

She wanted to trust Nahoa, but the secrets were getting heavy. So many people wanted them off Ravi's land and she didn't know any of the players, hadn't assessed them herself. Looking at the visible faces of the sovereignty movement, none of those people looked likely to wait in a car for a chance to take a run at her. Was it a scare tactic or was it attempted murder?

What happened to Willoughby and was Ravi in danger?

Kerala tossed her hard hat on the cramped desk of the trailer. The hotel was down, the pieces logged and stored.

What a miracle, she thought, bitter and angry. In the six days since being run off the road, no one had targeted her personally. But someone hounded her nonetheless.

On Monday, she had been exhausted from her sex fest with Ravi. Work had gone well until lunch, despite the unsettling conversation with Nahoa that morning. Afterward, a slow wave brought the job to a crashing halt. Everything had been fucked with.

Cordless tools missing batteries. A circle saw without the nut to keep the blade in place. On and on.

All the parts were found in a pile out back. No one admitted to seeing anything.

She had gone home that night frustrated and worried, but Ravi distracted her. He hadn't known when she would get home, so he had prepared fillings for make-your-own burritos and warmed the tortillas while she scraped the day from her skin. They walked Bogart and went to bed early, though sleep lagged behind by almost an hour.

Tuesday, she picked a few workers to keep watch, staggering their lunches. Again, Ravi cooked dinner and they walked Bogart together. Detective Alakai got back to town but took a couple days off, stalling their investigation again. Ravi told her more about the issues at Sol Volt and she filled him in on the day's work at the hotel.

On Wednesday, she arrived to a mess. Equipment had been scattered, stacked materials had been shoved into haphazard piles, and the fuel, gear oil, and crankcase oil had been drained from every single engine on site. She scoped out the size of the delay and started yelling.

The whole company closed for the nine days between Christmas Eve and the day after New Year's. She threatened to keep the crews running if they didn't finish the deconstruction before the holidays. Grumbling aside, everyone buckled down to get the machinery working and finish the demo of the hotel.

She arranged overnight security with Nahoa. He could choose the people least likely to be complicit in the problems. Not that any construction worker would ever do shit like that.

Reporting the newest problems got her a first-hand look at Hekili infuriated and the promise of drive-bys by cops who owed him favors. She got home late that night because she took the last of the lumber to the storage unit with a couple of helpers. It was obviously a bad idea to leave anything on the grounds.

She'd called Ravi to let him know she'd be late. It was practical. And courteous. Kind of...intimate, but she preferred a hot meal over a cold one.

Now that Thursday was over, the old hotel site was clean and her crew was out of there. The office trailer had been moved to the side of Ravi's driveway. Everything was ready to go for site clearing after New Year's.

A new year. A new start on a new site. Maybe they'd leave the problems behind, though this was the place with a haunted history.

She wanted to feel satisfied. She wanted to feel like she'd beat them, whoever they were.

Edgy, irritable, nervous—that's how she felt. Worried about the building process. Wary of the eventual inspections on the building's structure, electrical, plumbing. She felt in her bones that this job was already fucked up, and the strain attenuated her usual energy and confidence.

She stood in the tiny space between the desk and the work table, hands on hips. Her jaw was tight, her neck stiff. She tried to relax, but she could feel every hard centimeter of muscle from where they attached at the base of her skull to the spot where they disappeared under her scapulae.

While she stretched her neck, she stared at the paneling's fake wood grain in five shades of shit brown. She had pinned plans and schedules to the wall in the tiny office, but much of the ugly wall was still visible. On this job, as with every other job she'd run, that would change. As the house took shape, her office would grow thick-layered, thumbtacked wallpaper. Plans, drawings, revisions, bids, revisions, purchase orders, revisions, inspections, revisions, and more revisions.

She sniffed the liliko'i she'd picked. Nahoa had taught her to pick the ones with a good smell. She cut it open a little with her pocketknife and sucked at the gap. Sweet, pulpy juice filled her mouth and she licked her lips clean. She cut the fruit the rest of the way through and slurped at each half. The texture was a little weird, but the taste was delicious.

The hard black lines of the architect's plans spread in absolute contrast to the white of the pages. The susurration of the surf on the cliffs over the hill, the breeze through the sparse grasses, and the rustle of the palm trees should have relaxed her, but they stirred a strange tension.

Maybe it was the thought of going home to Ravi. He just…fit. Who wouldn't like coming home to a hot meal, simple conversation, and hot sex? If she could take the situation at face value, it would be like heaven.

He wanted more. She could see it on his face, feel it in his hands, taste it in his mouth. The serial monogamist wanted another relationship. He was looking for that mythical creature, the "one" who would complete him.

It was inevitable that he would start pushing. He would want her to work shorter hours or quit for an office job. He'd need to change her, if only to prove his power over her, and she would need to fight him.

She had to fight him. It's who she always was. Never the malleable little girl, never the easy-going girlfriend.

The wind paused, and the silence infected her with unease. Too quiet.

She could have been killed only days ago. Someone on the island had reached out and hurt her. And could do it again.

Kerala shuddered in the lingering heat of the late afternoon. Her fading bruises thumped with her heart's hard beat.

She was alone, vulnerable.

She left and locked the trailer, climbed into her truck, and took off in a matter of seconds.

As soon as she was moving with the heavy holiday traffic, disgust put a bitter taste in her mouth. Danger, ha! She'd spooked herself right out of her own office.

Whether the problem was her vulnerability or her fear, this had to stop.

❖

In a small pan, Ravi sautéed the ginger and garlic in coconut oil over medium heat, then tipped the oily mixture into a food processor. While the fragrance spread and the paste smoothed under the processor's blades, he stirred the vegetables cooking in the large pan.

He relished the smells of chili powder, tamarind paste, and turmeric rising from the pan to blend with the spiciness of the paste in the processor. When the mixture smoothed out, he added diced tomato to the processor and poured the resulting thick sauce into the pan of vegetables. He stirred it well and added spluttered mustard seeds, curry leaves, and salt. He turned down the heat and allowed the dish to simmer.

The planning meeting for the second quarter's research had gone well, and Sol Volt was rolling along nicely except for the switch to being a benefit corp. He might have to visit some of the agitated shareholders personally if he wanted that to go through.

He'd spent some time looking for the people targeting Kerala. Following the money didn't help. He couldn't see how anyone would get a payout in that case. Not even Mālama would come out of it well, since the cancellation fee would be negated by the bad publicity. Perhaps it would be quiet on that front over the holidays.

Cooking felt good. He had tracked down ingredients for a real Indian masala for Kerala. He'd sneak into her heart through her belly.

He would get done what work he could while Mālama Construction was closed, but their long holiday was a special gift. He and Kerala could get to know each other out of bed as well as in, follow their romantic impulses. He could tip her interest in him toward affection and hopefully toward love.

If she didn't arrive by the time the oil separated, he would allow the base to cool and reheat it before adding the yogurt. It needed to be served quickly after he put the yogurt in or it would get watery.

His program of love and romance started tonight. The meal, candles, and massage oils awaited her arrival.

He glanced at the rice cooker, spewing a thin stream of steam from its vent, stepped back, and glanced around the kitchen. While the food took care of itself, he'd clean some.

She should compost her bio-waste. He tossed the carrot ends and other food trash into the can and made a mental note to pick up a bin. He rinsed the cutting board and his phone warbled a Bollywood song, "Kehna Hi Kya". He dried his hands and fished his phone from his front pocket.

"Mom!"

"Punnare, how are you?"

"Great. I'm cooking a vegetable curry, yogurt and tomato base. I'm waiting for the oil to separate. Smells great in here."

"Mmm, sounds good. You haven't mixed the yogurt in yet?"

"I know better than that. I'm not sure how long Kerala will be. She's usually home by now."

"Cooking for that girl, are you? Very nice." He began to respond to the suggestive tone of his mother's voice but she cut in again. "Don't add the yogurt yet, punnare. I have a surprise for you."

He put the two sentences together and froze. "A surprise, Mom?"

"Yes. I have flown to be with you for Christmas. I am at the Kailua-Kona airport now."

His mother's excitement submerged his sense of impending doom like a breaking wave. He latched onto the only unimportant part of her statement. "For Christmas? But, Amma, we're not Christian." He was in bad shape when he used the Malayali word for mother.

"Yes, yes, but it can be such a quiet, lonely time. These Christians close their businesses and stay home for their family rituals. No one to talk to, nothing to do. I couldn't leave you in a strange place with no friends and no family over this depressing time of year."

Ravi beat his head on the doorjamb. "Mom, I'm not alone, remember? I'm with Kerala."

"Yes, that's right. Does she celebrate Christmas?"

He swallowed his frustration to ask an important question. "Did you arrange a room in a hotel before you came?"

"Oh, no, I think you will know the best place to stay. I don't want to trust a travel agent when you are right there."

The receptionist at his hotel had cheerfully accepted his early checkout, telling him that they had a waiting list for all rooms. There would be no last-minute room over Christmas on the island.

He gave in to the inevitable. "How long are you staying?"

"Just five days."

"Are you renting a car or shall I pick you up?"

"Renting a car, of course. I wouldn't want to be a burden on you, punnare. That's why I called, for directions."

He gave his mother directions, assured her that he was happy she'd come, and hit end. The rice cooker popped into keep-warm mode and he walked over to stir his curry. It bubbled thickly, oil standing on the surface. Had he made enough food?

That was the least of his problems.

He speed-dialed Kerala. She snapped, "I'm pulling in right now."

"Okay." She sounded frazzled and the last of his hopes leaked from his heels. This was not going to be a good night.

❖

Kerala just wanted a shower, but Ravi met her in the driveway and put his hands up as though to surrender. "My mom called."

"And?"

"She's here."

"Here?" He couldn't mean what she thought he meant. She was in no mood to play hostess to a lover's mother.

He scrubbed his hands over his face and sighed. "She thought I'd be lonely over Christmas."

"Seriously."

"Seriously here. She's driving from the airport now and plans to stay for five days."

Frustration boiled and she tried to talk herself down. Maybe it was for the best. Ravi and his mom could go be tourists together. She could pull herself together and figure out what to do about the job. Ravi. Her house. Hawai'i.

"Where's she staying?" She led the way to the mud room entrance.

His lips twisted but his eyes remained flat. "She thought she'd get a room once she was here."

"Over the holidays?" Much as she hated being backed into a corner, she couldn't tell an old woman to go sleep on the beach. She stared hard at Ravi. "You want to offer her your room?"

"If it's not too much of an imposition."

"I'm going to shower."

He took the hint and left. She washed herself clean and tried to rinse away her tension and frustration. Her week called for some deep comfort clothing, guest or no guest. She rummaged through the piles on the floor and couldn't find her favorite flannel pajamas. She looked around. The mess on the floor looked a little thin. She checked her dresser and found her pajamas, along with a bunch more of her favorites, clean and folded.

She rubbed the flannel against her belly and found Ravi in the kitchen. "Does she know why you're here?"

He looked around, surprised. "About the sabotage? No, she doesn't."

"You think she'd freak out if she knew the last owner disappeared ten years ago?"

"Indeed." He sigh. "If we can avoid talking about the problems on the job, I'd appreciate it."

Kerala shrugged. "Fine." She had another thought. "Did you come all over the sheets the other night?"

"Son of a bitch." He started down the hallway to the spare room.

❖

Kerala was raised in a rarified kind of society. She was taught from the time she could walk and talk that there were certain places one did not go and certain ways one did not talk. The rules around proper treatment of guests were immutable.

Decades after she stopped allowing her parents to shape her life, she remained bound in some ways by their strictures.

Irritated, frustrated, and desiring only some brainless TV and a good night's sleep, Kerala graciously welcomed the woman who stepped through her front door.

"Aloha, Mom!" Ravi grabbed her in a big bear hug.

"Ravi, so good to see you. Smells wonderful in here!" She turned to Kerala and reached out both hands. Ambassadorial. Jokes should be tasteful and clever, language refined. Manners ornate, demonstratively respectful.

Kerala accepted the outthrust hands and drew her inside. "I am Kerala Rosemont. Welcome to my home." She bowed her head a slight inch and continued to hold her hands for the reciprocal introduction.

"Maitri Nambudiri-Dietrich. So nice to meet the person behind Ravi's hobby house."

Kerala's smile didn't falter, though she released Maitri's hands. "He is quite excited by the project."

"Ah, yes." Maitri turned to a horrified Ravi. "My Ravi, the dreamer, the believer."

"Ravi." Kerala's calm, firm voice jerked his attention to her. "I'd hate to see your wonderful dinner ruined. Would you like me to get it on the table?"

"No." He glanced between them. "It's not quite ready to serve." He hesitated, obviously wondering if he should leave them alone together. He left the living room, looking back as he walked through the kitchen door.

"Mrs. Nambudiri-Dietrich, please sit." Kerala gestured toward the more uncomfortable end of the broken-down sofa. At the flicker on Ravi's mother's face, Kerala detected surprise that she had gotten the name right on first hearing. She hadn't been raised at international cocktail parties without developing a facility with non-Anglo names.

Maitri responded with an almost-gracious nod. "Thank you."

Kerala cast back for her familiarity with the name Nambudiri. Ah. "I met V.T. Bhattathiripad when he dined at my parent's house in Philadelphia. I was so young he let me call him Paddy. It takes real strength to attack a social system from which one derives power."

Maitri's hands fluttered on her knees. "He was a beacon for the social movements of Kerala."

"He was very old when I met him. He told me that the slogan of his day called for the transformation of 'Brahmans into human beings.' I remember thinking that the Nambudiri must have been terrible people."

Maitri shook her head and shot Kerala a sharp look. "What he advocated was revolutionary and revolting to most other Nambudiri at first. My parents were romantic rebels who loved him. They married in secret and thought their actions would spur a reformation of the rules. But in the death-throws of power and control, the family sent them away with orders never to return. They both spoke English, heavily accented, but they wanted to avoid England. They didn't know that the Asiatic Barred Zone Act had banned Indians from becoming US citizens. They shipped into the Mexican port at Manzanillo and entered the US by land, avoiding the border posts, and lived in the US for almost ten years, until I was born, without documentation."

Kerala softened despite herself. "Sounds intense. Tell me more."

Ravi spoke from the doorway. "Dinner's on the table, ladies."

Kerala bowed Maitri to the kitchen.

Maitri breathed the scent of the curry and kissed Ravi on the cheek. "It looks as good as it smells, Ravi."

A storytelling extravaganza ensued. Ravi contributed stories he'd heard from his grandparents, both still living in California in their nineties.

Better than TV.

Kerala washed up after the meal. Ravi and his mother retreated to the living room and she heard him explain that all the hotels would be full. "The girls will bunk together, then?" Kerala almost laughed out loud at the unsubtle probe for more information about their relationship. Ravi's voice went quiet. She wiped her hair off her steam-damp cheek with her forearm.

See what happened with a furnished guest room? Kerala pulled the plug on the wash water and rinsed the suds down the drain. She lived alone because she preferred it, damn it. Two houseguests were too many. She wouldn't even be able to go to work.

## CHAPTER TEN

A few hours later, Ravi concentrated on the article he'd agreed to review. With Kerala at her desk in the dining room and Maitri fast asleep in the guest room, he worked on the old couch in the living room, laptop on his knees. Not the most comfortable situation.

Ravi scrubbed his hands over his face. His eyes ached and he thought again of the twice-canceled eye appointment for reading glasses.

Old. It made him feel old. The eye strain, the knee that ached when he rode his bicycle too hard, the shoulder that didn't like him doing pull-ups anymore. He couldn't know how much of his bodily change was due to having taken testosterone injections for so many years. How much was deciding not to take T anymore.

He didn't feel the need to emphasize his masculinity, but he missed the easy way he'd bulked on T. His thighs and shoulders, biceps and calves had all grown stronger, even faster than he'd hoped. His body carried muscle well. All it took was biking and weight lifting, and not so much of either that it took over his life, to get him bulging, toned muscles.

Marathon computer sessions seemed easier off T, somehow. Persistence, a longer attention span, a greater ability to brush aside frustration.

Man with holes, man with feminine yearnings. Once, he'd tried to be a man. Just a man, the way he thought his dad was a man. The way men were in movies. Humphrey Bogart and Mickey Rourke. Not handsome, but so damn attractive.

Then he'd tried to redefine manhood. Tried to integrate himself, let himself be warm and soft at the same time he was hot and hard, all under the banner of manliness.

It wasn't a total bust. The models of male behavior, the ways that male privilege policed its boundaries, were opening up, thanks in great part to women demanding more from the men in their lives. There was more room to be metrosexual, to be dapper or even faggy, without losing his man card.

A lot of work had been done by the time he was an adolescent in the late eighties and he'd sprinted off without acknowledging how others had advanced the start line. He and his buddies, his San Francisco support group and Berkeley classmates, had pushed into new gender territory, claiming manhood and then twisting it when it didn't fit as well as they hoped.

Realizing he wasn't a man had hurt. It was harder in some ways than realizing he wasn't a woman. He'd denied others the right to define him as a woman. But he'd decided he was a man, and he'd felt like a quisling at the meetings, knowing that his manhood was not what he'd thought it was.

From butch to trans man. From trans man to what? He'd answered that for himself the way he'd done so much in his life. By living day by day and searching for the words, the rooms, the compatriots that made him feel most himself. He wanted nothing more in life than to be one person, an integrated and complex human being.

As a scientist, he wished there were more long-term studies of hormones for trans folk. He'd never know for sure how much or in what ways his emotional and physical qualities were shaped by the period of time he took testosterone. Human studies were never controlled enough for cause and effect statements anyway. But it would be comforting to have more data.

He shook his head. He wanted the data, but he also wished that the trans experience was less pathologized, not more.

Nothing to do about all that at the moment. Over the years, he'd become less absorbed by the question of gender, his own and others', perception and performance, but it was still a live wire in his life.

Maybe he should go back to T. It had been twelve years on and eight years off. Kerala might like his T body. She appreciated strength.

He shook his head. He wouldn't go back to the shots and the endometriosis. He'd be who he was, mannishly femalesque, without the hormones.

He was just tired. Old and tired. He couldn't contain the small smile. Tired and silly.

Kerala's bed beckoned and he gave in to its pull. He stuck his head into the dining room and told Kerala good night. She mumbled back, head down over her own work.

He slid between her decadent satin sheets, comfortable in her den of iniquity. Four nights they'd slept there together. Three times he'd slept on the right, once on the left. He propped an arm behind his head. His side of the bed. Her side of the bed.

Kerala woke him when she slipped between the sheets, naked, and settled on her side facing him. Ravi slid a hand down her arm and turned over. She cuddled behind him, spooning her legs to his and pressing her breasts into his back. Warmth soaked through him.

A couple of hours later, he woke with her in his arms, face-to-face, his thigh between her legs. She moved, rubbed on him, and he whispered her name. She hummed. He lay still as she coiled and uncoiled on him. Her hair lay under his cheek, her neck at his mouth. Sleep receded as the muscles of her back under his hands and the slick she made on his thigh turned him on. His clit grew and rubbed on her thigh as she moved. She built toward orgasm, undulating, her thigh working him higher until he came with spasming hands and she gasped and followed.

He stroked her back lightly, slowly. He preferred her skin to any of her nightgowns. "Are you asleep?"

"Not yet." Her eyes gleamed in the oblique moonlight.

"Are you mad?"

She didn't move. "A bit."

"Tell me why?"

"You mean other than your mom dropping in unexpectedly?" Now she did move, turning onto her back.

"We don't know each other all that well, Kerala." He turned on his belly so he could look at her. "I know why I would be mad in this situation and I can guess at why you are. Why don't you just tell me instead?"

She stared past his shoulder in silence a moment, chewing her cheek. "You're a whole family of talkers, aren't you? Your mom's a hell of a storyteller."

"My dad's pretty quiet, actually. I think you'll like him."

Her eyes flicked his direction and she sighed. "You moved in for practical reasons, but we ended up in bed as soon as I stopped taking the painkillers. You cook for me, welcome me home at night. You talk like I'm going to become friends with your dad. It's like we've created this instant family."

Her words pierced him. "Do you like it?"

"Yeah, it's great, except that it's not me."

"Why not?" He couldn't keep the plaintive note from his voice, but he could swallow the desire to beg.

Her lips pressed together. "Back in Philly, there was this woman. I couldn't look at anyone else when she was in the room. She was dynamic, sparkling. High femme and practically fetishistic about it. I wanted her so bad and I thought she wanted me too. She called me handsome and I liked it."

"I get that." He wanted to touch her, offer her some kind of support while she talked about what must have been a painful memory. She wasn't opening up so much as explaining, though, her voice clear and thoughtful.

"I hardly noticed when she started pruning my wardrobe. Day by day, I got butcher. I'd fought my parents tooth and nail for the power to define myself, but I slipped away in the gleam of her image of me." She turned onto her side, facing him. "I got obscured somehow. I'm kinda butch, but I'm not a butch. It was too much identity for me to own it all."

"Do you think I want to do that to you?"

"Don't you?" Her lips curved in the shadows. "I rejected my family a long time ago, way before they cut me off. You've said straight out you want home and hearth and that's not me. You want me, but different. And that makes me edgy."

"I don't want to change you. I just want to be with you."

"Relationships are always about adapting to each other. I know that much. As bad as the situation with my ex was, the defensiveness afterward was even worse. I don't want to be defined by what I'm against, what I'm not. It's rough, wondering if I'm being myself or just acting against a controlling influence."

"You think I don't know about that?" Ravi pulled the pillow under his chest to get higher. "I'm genderqueer, Kerala. I wasn't born with a perfectly calibrated understanding of how my masculine and feminine aspects share space and collide inside me. I wish I had a cock and balls, but I also like my clit. I've gotten a shitload of unwelcome feedback on how I did man wrong. I use genderqueer to say that my gender is complicated and won't match your expectations, and that I won't adopt a label that doesn't work just to fit into or rebel against those expectations."

Kerala reached out and it killed him. She stroked his shoulder and laced her fingers in his. He closed his eyes and fought the urge to push her away, to pull her close and hide in her sympathy.

"I always compared my ex to the whole mess of people in my life who've tried to force me to be what I'm not. I'm ashamed to say I never compared myself to someone else on this level. Would you say you feel pressured to provide a clear gender other people can understand?"

"More than pressured. Coerced." She was thinking about it, which was promising, and she had read his gender cues well all along. She followed his lead, using his masculine pronouns but talking about his clit the way he needed to hear it. A lover who didn't understand him could inflict the most intimate wounds. After all these years, it could still make him feel invisible. He'd spent decades working to believe that someone failing to grasp the flavor of his gender didn't make it a figment of his imagination.

He had a document, links to good articles, which he sent people he worked with. He'd asked a few of the women he'd dated to read up on trans history and get grounded in the issues, but it was easier to date inside the community. Maybe it was time to blow the dust off that list.

"How was Maitri about you being trans?"

Ravi turned on his back and looked at the ceiling. His muscles relaxed and exhaustion hit him. "She was great. Always my best friend and my staunchest supporter. Butch, trans man, genderqueer—she's been with me the whole way. I've always known I'm more than my gender, because my gender has evolved, but she has always seen me for who I really am."

"Wow." She was silent a moment and he almost fell asleep. "That's a hell of a thing to be able to say."

"Indeed."

"It's a lot for a lover to live up to."

She sounded so flabbergasted that Ravi fell asleep smiling.

❖

At Kerala's suggestion, Ravi and his mom visited the dolphins, though she grilled him on their living conditions before agreeing to go.

He brought her the iced mocha she'd requested and sipped his cappuccino in the sun, leaning against the bridge's railing. "Have you ever had chai at one of these coffee stands?"

"They are so charming." She ignored his question.

"You can swim with them, if you want."

"I don't need another reminder of how ungraceful I've become. They would have shamed me even at my best. Look at that one. It keeps coming to the side of the tank to wave its head at people."

He leaned over the railing to see. "Maybe he's hungry."

"Maybe she's sociable."

He watched his mom as she drank her mocha. She was aging. As a kid, he'd watched her comb her waterfall hair dry in front of a fire, the long straight strands so black that the fire's glow reflected as in a mirror. Now it was all gray, and it kinked where once it lay smooth.

She laughed at the antics of a trio of dolphin. "They're playing chicken—swimming at the opening between the two pools, but only two can fit at a time. They remind me of you and your brother." He enjoyed seeing her animated. She was loving to him and adventurous in ways that amazed him, but her habitual attitude in the world was blasé. Been there, done that. Not that she'd traveled much. His father's job had been demanding, with little time off for vacations.

Guilt and confusion hit at the same time. "What about Dad?"

"What about him?" She waved a multiple-ringed hand at the creature bobbing below.

"Where is he? Why didn't he come?"

His mom sipped her mocha. "Your father and I disagreed on what we should do while the world closed for the holidays. I wanted to come here; he wanted to go to Las Vegas."

He gave her an incredulous look. "You let Dad go to Vegas alone? What were you thinking?"

She answered with a haughty look. "He's a grown man. He'll gamble and he'll lose, but it won't be too bad." She turned away. "It's the end of the month. Retirement won't be deposited until the first. Everything of value is in both our names. The worst he could do is wipe out our cash. He never did figure out how to withdraw from a credit card at the ATM."

"Did he refuse to come to Hawai'i because you're meddling or did you refuse to go to Vegas because you'd be bored out of your mind? Or shop away what money he didn't lose."

She flicked a chiding look at him, but he held her gaze. "Maybe both. I don't remember which idea came first. We just settled on going our separate ways for a few days."

He took her arm, linked it with his, and led her along the pathway from the dolphin pools along the waterfront to the galleries. Hotel collections held much of the best art on the island. The new work by island artists was available to purchase, and it seemed sensible to him that it would be shown in such places. His discomfort came from the museum pieces—old and ancient masks, tools, terracotta figures, and other anthropological items—being shown to tourists rather than Hawaiians. Better exhibited than stored, but it didn't seem right.

His mom's body clock said it was lunch time, so they stopped at a hotel café for a light meal. They lingered over coffee.

"I'm not sure what to make for dinner." They had potatoes in the cupboard. Maybe baked with chili and other fixings.

"Kerala doesn't cook?" She stirred sugar and cream into her brew.

He gave her a suspicious look. "No. She ate out a lot before I moved in."

"Does she know you love her?" He frowned. "Ravi, she isn't soft like you. I hope you don't get yourself hurt with this one."

He stiffened. "Soft, is it?"

She reached across the table and placed her hand on his. He looked at her skin, thinner and more wrinkled than he remembered. "I apologize for the insult in that, but, punnare, you have a great heart. Your capacity for love is your greatest strength, and I've watched you weaken as you waited for the right person."

Ravi stared at his mother's hand, the hand of an old woman. "I love you."

"And you love your father. And your friends. But there have been fewer of them over the years, haven't there? When someone moved away, left the company, fell out of touch…you didn't make many new friends. You haven't had a new love in a long time."

The litany of loss twisted his gut.

"Kerala seems like a strong, capable woman. She will live out her days going her own way, doing what she sees fit. I am afraid that you will empty yourself out trying to give her enough love that she will give some back."

He shook his head and turned his hand under hers. He grasped the delicate bones under the comfortable layer of padding and rubbed his thumb over the loose skin on the back. "There's no choice here, Amma. You can't tell me it's dangerous to love Kerala and expect me to refuse her my heart. It's too late."

"Far be it from me to offer advice where it isn't wanted…"

He mustered a smile at the old joke.

"You gave up another love a few years back. You left the work you love to fill the needs of the company you love. It was a sensible decision, but not such a good one for your happiness. If you try to make a life with Kerala, you need something outside her that stimulates and satisfies you. To some degree, you're using a lover to fill the hole left by the practice of your science, and she'll sense that. She won't be able to heal what isn't a romantic wound."

He continued to rub his thumb over the back of her hand. "I've been thinking something like that myself. About being unhappy in my work." He gave her a searching look. "Do you really think I'm trying to substitute love for the satisfaction I got as a researcher?"

"It doesn't matter what I think."

This time she got the full grin. The rhythm between them comforted him. "Too bad I never found a woman like you."

"Kerala! What kind of a name is that for a Euro-American? I had hoped for a moment that you had found a nice Indian girl."

"Indian girls aren't that nice, if you're an example."

She smacked his arm and her cackle echoed in the foyer as they walked out of the hotel.

❖

Kerala settled into her recliner and opened her laptop. A sip of beer while it started and she was ready.

They had no suspects, no knowledge of the possible enemies, and only an assumption that the car incident had anything to do with the groups that wanted construction stopped. The sovereignty movement, the folks reinvigorating Hawaiian culture. Since that's all they had, she'd start there.

First, she searched online. The sovereignty movement had some high profile organizations, with glossy websites and fundraising. There'd be nothing useful there, she figured, but scanned through anyway.

A short article provided the jackpot. In distancing themselves from a direct action group, the author used some names and linked to some forums. Searching on the names confirmed that they were fake, or at least not legal names. Combing an independence forum, she started to recognize a pattern that looked significant. It didn't take her long to get familiar with the rudimentary code they used to discuss plans. Odd times and dates, repeated references to places that didn't exist, and arrangements to meet at fake events. She wasn't looking for evidence as much as identities, so she didn't need to know what a particular action planned to achieve.

Then she saw a sideways mention of the scattering of their materials and her skin tightened. She went through the list of problems on the job and started attributing the actions based on the jokes and congratulations, their dates and the little clues that slipped through. Most of the petty sabotage was marked off before she hit the fifth site. She was sure it was the independents.

That left a chunk of the more serious problems unattributed, but her eyes were about to bleed. She took Bogart for a walk and chewed over the problem.

What kind of half-ass conspiracy puts their shit out there like that? Even anonymously?

She tossed a stick for Bogart with half her attention, but he didn't seem to mind. She couldn't stop thinking about the weakness of their veiled references. She barely had to know anything to figure it out. Could she get by their screen names as easily? There were no obvious clues in the names themselves, but people got attached to their online IDs and used them in more than one spot.

Eyes refreshed, she made a sandwich and took it back to the living room to eat while she searched on the screen names. Two words, one word, with punctuation and without. Everything she could think of.

She'd long since finished her sandwich when she sat back and looked at her notes.

Four people on seven sites.

One guy linked to another page of his, under a different screen name, and gave her a new trail to follow.

HI4HIANS got called Mahi'ai by another user. She looked up mahi'ai and found it meant farmer.

She flipped back through her notes. Someone went by Mahi'ai on a different site and his posts had the same tone, the same typos for that matter, as HI4HIANS's.

Not proof, but she felt the tingle of things fitting together. Mahi'ai was a popular screen name, and she followed from forum to forum, looking for similarities.

She read his posts for several hours on a dozen sites. The rhythm and subject matter gave him away, linking him back from the Mahi'ai links to the independence forums. When she struck pay dirt, though, it was on a benign gardening website. He posted a picture of a garden he'd worked on, framed by a kitchen window.

She straightened from her crouch over the keyboard, satisfaction filling her with energy. Find that view and they would have the guy who'd planned most of the sabotage on the job.

Even if he wasn't the man in the car, she wanted to have a few words with him.

Suddenly, she wanted Ravi to come home, until she remembered that Maitri didn't know the story. Okay, no help from Ravi for now.

Maitri would only be there another couple of days. She could put it off that long.

Kerala got herself another beer and thought about finding someone by the view from their kitchen window. Nahoa would be the best person to ask, of course, if he weren't keeping secrets.

She wanted to trust him, but she was starting to wonder.

❖

Ravi woke early the next morning and left Kerala snoring in bed. He cleaned the kitchen and made coffee. His mom and Kerala had gotten companionably drunk the night before, a relief after their cold start. He'd needed a night off from the tension between them.

His mom dragged herself into the kitchen and he handed her a cup of coffee.

"My savior."

He tapped his cheek and she kissed him.

Kerala followed soon after and he poured another cup.

"You're a gem."

He tapped his cheek and got another kiss.

"Who wants breakfast?" From the revolted looks, he gathered he would be eating alone. Kerala and his mom sat across from each other at the café table and stared into their coffee as Ravi ate pancakes alone.

After a quiet Christmas of cards, movies, and light meals for the ladies, Kerala said, "Oh, shit."

Ravi looked over to find a pained look on her face.

"I forgot. Tomorrow is the company lūʻau. The Kalama family puts on this party every year and it's absolutely mandatory. It's my first." She wrinkled her nose. "Want to come?"

"I don't want to be the uninvited guest." His mom said the right thing, but she looked intrigued.

Why not? "I'd be into going. Will a couple extra people be a problem?"

"No, I can bring whoever I want. This is the whole shebang—the kind of party the hotels pretend to throw. We're supposed to bring something. Do you have anything from the mainland?"

He looked at his mom. She blushed. "Seriously?"

She nodded. "Cookie butter."

Kerala looked confused, but Ravi couldn't stop laughing. "Did you think you would go crazy without it for a few days?"

His mom pouted. "You never know."

"What the hell are you two talking about? Cookie butter?" The confounded look on Kerala's face made them both laugh.

His mom took pity on her. "It's a Belgian cookie, not quite like gingerbread, crushed and mixed with oil to make a spread. The texture is like peanut butter."

"I would have used some on my pancakes. It's good stuff." He grinned at Kerala's expression of distaste. "I know, oil and cookies, but just try it."

"I've never seen it around here, so I guess it's a good thing to bring."

"Both jars?" His mom's mournful expression cracked him up again.

Kerala offered, "They're roasting a pig in a pit."

His mom looked daunted. "An imu," he said.

"How do you know?" asked Kerala.

"I've been reading about Hawaiian culture. I should have done the research before I bought the land, but I didn't realize how different it is from the mainland. Which some people call the continent to avoid suggesting that Hawai'i isn't its own main land. So far, my favorite is *A Nation Rising: Hawaiian Movements for Life, Land, and Sovereignty*." It struck him. "You don't use any Hawaiian words."

"Sure I do."

"Place names and types of lava. But you don't say aloha or pau or any of the other words everyone else uses."

"It's not my language."

"But you live here now."

She frowned. "Doesn't it seem like cultural appropriation?"

"Maybe sometimes. But not using it is like refusing to learn the language of any place you live, right?" He looked at his mom for corroboration.

"I think learning the language is a matter of respect."

Kerala frowned. "So it's either cultural appropriation to use it or culturally insensitive not to. Great."

His mom said, "See how many words you can teach me while I'm here, Ravi."

Kerala's avoidance of local words wasn't as simple as she made it out to be. "Jack uses Hawaiian and pidgin."

"He's also lived here a long, long time."

"So he's hānai? Adopted."

"Nahoa says he's ho‘okama. Like, adopted into the family but no one is responsible for him."

"So he's not Hawaiian because he doesn't have indigenous ties to the islands. But he might be kama‘āina, which means local, Mom." He wondered if he would ever qualify.

His mom listened closely. "Is it about whether or not your neighbors accept you?"

Kerala answered. "There may be some of that, but it's also how long you've been here. Locals are either born on the islands or they are similar to other locals. Portuguese people seem to fit in just fine, and people like Jack, who adopt a lot of the Hawaiian ways. He's rooted here."

Rootedness. "And that's the biggest difference between him and you. He went all-in, but you're coexisting with the Hawaiians, at best."

She shrugged, a defensive move. "I don't see how it could be any different. I'm not the kind of person who weaves my way into the fabric of any groups."

Ravi and his mom exchanged a look. Yeah, Mom. She's a bad bet. Too bad he couldn't choose who to fall in love with.

## CHAPTER ELEVEN

K erala wasn't kamaʻāina, but she knew to take off her shoes. Even if she hadn't, the long rack on the front porch would have tipped her off. The lanai. Porch, lanai. Whatever.

She'd worn sandals…um, slippers…to expedite the process. Boots were too much of a hassle to get on and off, and she could see why the workers waited until they got to work to change into theirs.

Energetic music flowed from around back, but she would make nice with the ladies inside before heading out to catch the breeze. The Kalama land was far enough up Hualālai that it was relatively cool.

As the invited guest, she led Ravi and Maitri through the open door to the family room. People sat around, drinking and arguing, but she didn't know any of them. She passed through to the kitchen and found Nahoa sitting at the table with his grandmother.

"Aloha, Kel." He kicked a chair out for her, then stood when he saw her guests. "Aloha, Ravi. And you are?"

Maitri showed every indication of falling for Nahoa's charm. "Ravi's mother. Maitri Nambudiri-Dietrich."

"So wonderful to meet you. Your name is so long it could be Hawaiian."

And they were off. He took her arm and they left for the backyard.

"Hello, Mrs. Kalama. Mahalo nui for inviting me to the lūʻau." She could use Hawaiian words when appropriate.

"Kerala. Sit, please, both of you. Keep me company now that I've been abandoned by my faithless grandson."

"This is Ravi Dietrich. He's the one we're building the house for, down on the Kohala coast."

"Oh, yes. The house that needs no water."

It was easy to get Ravi going. "Or power lines. And the whole place will be non-toxic to the inhabitants."

"To future inhabitants, but what about those who've rested there for over a hundred years?"

He pokered up fast. "I've just started to understand the concept of the ʻaumākua."

Kerala shifted in her seat. Not a religious lecture, please. No one even knew whether there were remains there.

"The ʻaumākua aren't tied only to land, though they will guard places that need it. They are intimate family gods, guardians that can take form in animals, rocks, sometimes even plants. I understand there is a healthy lilikoʻi plant there?"

"We're transplanting it and the koa tree it's growing on. I didn't want to destroy anything about the land, but they can't get the equipment where it needs to go without removing them."

"It's an odd place for lilikoʻi to thrive, which begs the question of how it's being sustained. Perhaps there are ʻaumākua there, from before the land was part of the Parker Ranch, long before Vincent Willoughby bought it."

"I don't know, ma'am. But I think this house is important. It'll be accessible. There won't be expanses of concrete to mess up the flow of water on the land, and even the foundation system was chosen to have the least impact possible. The composting toilet will feed the kitchen garden and gray water will irrigate it. But the most important features use the very things you have in abundance here. Sun, wind, the ocean. I'm sure that traditional Hawaiian life was really, really efficient, but now there's a lot of stuff that's imported and a lot of waste."

She stared at him, impassive, for a long moment. Kerala put her hand on Ravi's knee under the table. His words sounded thoughtful and respectful, but his muscles were tense.

"Please, call me Tūtū Alapaʻi. Tūtū is an honorific for old ladies like me."

"It means she's in charge," said Nahoa on his way back through with Maitri. "We're getting more pūpūs."

Kerala watched them leave with envy, but she wouldn't abandon Ravi.

"Tūtū Alapa'i, do you think the kind of housing I describe could help create a better life on the island?"

"I'm not sure. I've seen the plans." Kerala hadn't realized that. "The house itself sounds intriguing. However, there is more to a good life than a house full of gadgets. Do you know the history between Hawai'i and the US?"

"I remember Clinton apologized for taking the islands by force."

Kerala didn't remember that, but she didn't follow the news much.

"Kamehameha united the islands through battle and assassination. He and his descendants treatied with the Europeans, who encouraged them to reapportion the land, away from the old 'ohana, extended family systems and toward selling large swathes to the Europeans for sugar and pineapple plantations. The plantation owners brought in tremendous numbers of poor people from other parts of the world to work as slaves, though they called it contract labor, because there weren't enough of us to work and die at the rate they demanded. The Hawaiians welcomed the newcomers, intermarried, and had children. By the time the plantation owners overthrew the monarchy using US marines, we were a minority on our own islands."

"I wondered why there were so many people of mixed ancestry when Hawai'i can be unfriendly toward non-locals." Ravi leaned forward on the table and showed every sign of being riveted by the story.

"We have been wounded so deeply that every generation feels it. We need our ea, an enormous word meaning life but also land and sovereignty. Ea is the repeated act of breathing and the state of being that is Hawaiian. Ea is a principle as much as it's a word, and it holds the concepts of both independence and interdependence. It erases the distance between culture and politics."

"Ea," Ravi repeated. "Tell me how you experience ea."

Interesting question. Kerala wouldn't have thought to phrase it like that.

"As an emergence, like the islands themselves, created in and eroded by the ocean, continually born and reborn. We remember ea through caring for wahi pana, the storied places that help us maintain our relationship with the land."

On the woo side, but Kerala rather liked the concept. It helped her understand some things that had bemused her. "So it's not just the stories you need to save, it's the land connected to the stories."

"Exactly. Our moʻolelo are narratives that reflect who we are, so that there's somewhere we can see and recognize ourselves. By social measures, we are the most wretched on the islands, but that is due to losing ea."

Joy appeared next to Tūtū Alapaʻi. "Among other things." They looked like the same person, photographed in youth and old age.

"Like what?" Ravi didn't seem to find it hard to follow Tūtū Alapaʻi's mystical language.

"Cutting us off from productive fishponds and taro fields. Breaking up and selling off the ahupuaʻa."

Kerala spoke without thinking. "Like you can talk shit about construction on the island."

"Kerala." Ravi sounded mortified, but Tūtū Alapaʻi ignored her outburst.

"These things have cut us off from sources of mana. We need to recharge our power from the land. The Pele families in Puna have the only continuous, unbroken ritual history on the islands, worshipping the volcano goddess as their ancestors did, even after it was prohibited."

"We have to read the ethnographic studies done by haole to research our own history." Joy's bitterness made more sense to Kerala, thinking about that. "The Kalama family is Hawaiian and we're not suffering, but we are part of why they say our state bird is the construction crane."

"E ia nei, show respect." Tūtū Alapaʻi turned to Kerala. "My grandchildren, my moʻopuna, can be rude."

"At least I'm no typical hoʻoluhi."

"No, you are always an extraordinary problem." Tūtū Alapaʻi reminded Kerala of a Buddha, rooted, saying she would not be moved. Maybe there was a corresponding Hawaiian myth. She didn't know.

Joy left as suddenly as she'd arrived. Ravi took a deep breath. "Some party."

Tūtū Alapaʻi broke into a huge smile. "This is how we do it. Argue and talk story all day and all night."

"I'm sorry I provoked her." Kerala's apology was as unconsidered as the original barb, but it came from a better instinct.

Tūtū Alapaʻi folded her hands in her lap. "It isn't hard to do. Now go find Nahoa. I need him to help me out to the yard."

Hours later, Kerala left the lūʻau with plates wrapped in tin foil and stacked in the rental car. When the family invited them to "make plate" or "take plate," it wasn't a suggestion. Luckily, they'd seen Jack and Danny before they left, and Jack warned them that it was considered rude to leave the hosts with all the leftover food. Maitri chose to make plate so they wouldn't get more Kālua pig than Kerala could eat. She hadn't had much meat since Ravi moved in and couldn't say she'd missed it. The laulau was good, though, and she'd been pleased to find mochi for dessert.

"What did you think of Tūtū Alapaʻi?" she asked as she drove Maitri's rental car. Maitri didn't like to drive in the dark and got carsick if she didn't sit in the front.

Ravi kept the food from sliding around in the seat next to him while he answered. "She's fascinating. I went back later, when you were talking foundations with Jack and the twins. I didn't catch their names. Anyway, she's like a walking history book but better because she has this amazing feeling for what's most important in a story. I learned more talking to her for an hour than in all my online searches to date."

"About the history of the islands?" She put on the turn signal at the highway and waited for some nice person to let her in. It didn't take long. Go aloha spirit.

"The history of the sovereignty movement, actually. It's been going strong since the sixties and seventies and there was a big Marxist contingent to the original organizers. The whole tone has gone through a lot of changes, from class issues to race issues and settler colonialism theory to occupation theory. It seems like the groups she's tight with try to work it all together to understand how they got here from the olden days."

Maitri said, "Did you know they had a class of people like the untouchables? Alapaʻi said that was one of the things about kapu that she wouldn't want to see come back. She looks forward to a less rigid, more fluid connectedness."

"So everyone got the lecture, I guess."

"I talked to her son, Hekili, too. He's very focused on his work, isn't he? Very different from his mother." Maitri popped a mint in her mouth.

"He's a good boss." Better to be noncommittal. Sometimes she forgot that Ravi was still a client, even if he was more than that now.

"I felt welcome." Ravi sounded thoughtful.

"More welcome than I've been in new places." She could change a lot of things in her life, but she'd always be a WASP. "Maybe they think you're Portuguese."

Maitri laughed. "Do they like the Portuguese so much? They're not as popular in Goa, India."

"I remember that," Kerala said. "Goa was a Portuguese colony until the sixties, right?"

"True. And it's still highly Catholic. Of course, Kochi is as well. Southern Kerala, the Indian state rather than the woman driving"—she winked in the rearview mirror—"is less Christian but the missionaries are persistent."

Ravi said, "That's another thing Tūtū Alapaʻi said. Christianizing the Native Hawaiians messed up the old ʻohana ties. Sounds like this place was a mess for a while there."

"What cleaned it up? Statehood?"

"I wouldn't say that where she could hear you. She says that statehood was just another robbery. But we didn't talk long enough for me to get the details."

As she turned down the street toward her house, she asked, "How do you feel about living here?"

He was silent a moment. Maitri raised a hand to her own shoulder and he took it into his. "If I were moving here, I may be able to contribute and be part of it and do more good than harm. Part-time is weird. I don't know."

Kerala parked behind her truck in the driveway and turned off the rental car. "Something to think about." She opened the door and looked into the cloudy night sky. "Sooner rather than later."

❖

Kerala poured herself a second cup of coffee and leaned against the kitchen counter. She stared across the butcher block at Maitri, who sat fully dressed at the café table, talking nonsense.

"It'll be fun. You'll see. We don't have to stay out long, but I need to get a present for Ravi's dad. Also Sam and Theresa. I'm leaving tomorrow. I can't go back empty-handed."

Ravi appeared from the hallway and she gave him the look. Take this woman off my hands.

"I can take you later, Mom, but I have a video conference this morning."

Kerala glared at him, but he spread his hands in apology.

Somehow, Maitri won. Kerala, an immovable object, had met a truly unstoppable force, and shopping two days after Christmas was no minor defeat.

Maitri had opened up during the course of her visit. The shared hangover had given them sympathy for each other. Losing to Ravi at cards gave them a common enemy. Everything boded well for a good relationship until this.

Once in town, Kerala directed her to the waterfront shops on Ali'i Drive.

Two hours and twenty-five pounds of purchases later, Kerala dropped the shopping bags in the trunk of the car. "You bought every stupid touristy knick-knack and T-shirt they had on sale. I've never seen anything like it."

Maitri set her single bag in the trunk with the others. "I'm so happy about the coffee. Pure Kona coffee, grown by people who've been on the land as long as I've been alive."

Kerala dropped into the passenger seat.

"Now, where are the department stores?"

Kerala groaned. She gave in to the inevitable and directed Maitri to the Big Island's slim pickings. Gottschalks was packed.

"I need to pee."

"Oh, but..." Maitri vibrated at the sale signs.

"You go ahead. I'll find you when I'm done."

Exhausted, Kerala sat on the toilet and put her head in her hand. She needed a plan.

The person in the next stall opened the door, washed her hands, and left.

She stood to pull up her jeans. Someone entered and hesitated by the door for a moment.

The lights went out.

"Hey!" Kerala yelped as she buttoned and zipped. "Turn the lights back on!"

Silence greeted her demand and she heard the unmistakable sound of a deadbolt sliding into its mate. Irritation shifted to alertness.

In the dark, locked in, alone with someone who wasn't talking. Adrenaline and focus sharpened her hearing. A rubber-soled shoe slid across the cheap linoleum, maybe a few inches, not far.

"Kerala Rosemont, I know you're in here. You have to stop. You can't start work on the Kohala land. You're close to the owner. Talk him out of building that house."

The guy's voice was stilted, like he was disguising it. The door of the next stall over swung open. Kerala didn't know what he intended, but this was the same cowardly type of behavior as trying to hit someone with a car.

This time, she would be the one to draw blood.

Retribution or self-defense. She didn't give a fuck.

In complete silence, she slid back the bar on her stall's door. She straddled the toilet and brought up the camera on her phone.

"Someone will suffer if you don't stop. Come out. Talk to me." He stepped in front of her stall. The door flew toward her.

Wham! Kerala punched with her right hand, aiming for his nose, and tapped her phone camera. The flash caught her hand rebounding off thick skull. She yelped and dropped her phone. Now that she had him located, she popped him with a left jab in the dark. The wet spurt and gurgling complaint satisfied her almost as much as having a picture of him.

She tried to follow with a kick to the groin, but he had already faded back. He lunged forward and pushed her off balance.

She fell and knocked her elbow on the toilet seat. "Who are you? Mahi'ai?"

His shoes squeaked on the floor, heading away from her. She disentangled herself from the toilet and grabbed her phone off the floor. "Why are you doing this? Who do you work for?" His steps sped and he was gone before she was standing.

She flew out the door and ran up and down the packed aisles looking for her assailant. Dammit, how hard could it be to spot a bloody mess of a man?

She ignored the shocked looks and small screams until she ran into Maitri. With admirable calm, Maitri barred her way and wiped a businesslike handkerchief across the blood on Kerala's face.

"I don't see where it's coming from, Kerala, so you have to tell me. Are you hurt? Where did this blood come from?"

She'd lost him. "It's not me. It's the fucking bastard that ran me off the road."

Maitri stepped back to give her some breathing room, and Kerala saw the store's security heading over. She couldn't think of anything she wanted less than to hash this over with a bunch of overpaid, undertrained wannabe cops. She grabbed Maitri by the arm. "We're leaving."

"Well, yes, I guess we are."

Kerala dragged an exasperated Maitri to the rental car, glad now that they hadn't driven her truck. She wasn't sure she'd trust it. He could have tampered with it, but all rental cars looked the same.

When Maitri took too long opening the door, Kerala grabbed the keys and did it herself with her left hand. Her right hurt like hell. She slammed the driver's door after Maitri sat and got in the other side. Blood on Maitri's cuff made her gasp. "Did he get you too?"

"No." Maitri started the car and looked at Kerala. "Where are we going?"

He knew where she lived, so they couldn't go home.

Home. Ravi was alone there. Kerala called him and cut off his cheerful greeting. "Leave the house, right away. You have to get out of there. We'll be at the Kailua-Kona police station. Come to us there. Do you know where it is?"

"I'll map it, but what—"

"Don't stay in the house. You have to come to the police station. The guy who ran me off the road just trapped me in a bathroom stall and I punched him."

"Are you okay?"

"Yeah, freaked out but okay."

"How long will it take me to get down there?"

"Maybe as much as an hour. Just get away from the house."

"I'm on my way."

"Thanks, Ravi. Call me if you get lost." She hung up and pulled up her photo gallery. Motion ruined the pic she'd snapped as she got in her first punch. She struggled to make out the guy's features, but her memory was sharper than the image on her phone.

Maitri asked, "Are we going to the police station or the hospital?"

Her hair stuck to her cheek. She pulled the visor down and looked in the vanity mirror. Gross. Maitri waited until Kerala met her eyes. "Police station. I'm fine except my hand. Some guy came into the bathroom and tried to intimidate me. I punched him twice." She picked the hair loose from her cheek. "The blood is from his nose."

Maitri hummed noncommittally. "You'll have to point the way to the station."

"Oh, right." Kerala's eyes wouldn't focus. Adrenaline drop. She directed Maitri to the station and turned to face her. "Thanks."

"For what? I didn't get in any punches."

"For being calm. I needed unflappable just now and you came through."

Anger flashed in Maitri's eyes. "It's not enough for me. I would see this man punished."

Kerala's smile was genuine, though small. "I would too."

❖

"Ravi?"

"Mom, what's going on?" Ravi pulled to the side of the road and parked the rental car.

"I took her to the police station, but they said they'd talk to her at the hospital."

"She's in the hospital? What's wrong? What happened?"

"They think she broke her hand. She's fine otherwise, but her hand swelled while we were waiting on an officer and it's hurting her badly."

"The attacker broke her hand?"

"No." His unflappable mother laughed, the sound shaky. "Sorry, please come to the hospital. I'm giving the phone to this nice medical person and she'll give you directions."

He listened but didn't try to memorize the way. His phone would get him there. He only paid attention to which part of the hospital she'd be in. "Please put my mother back on."

"She went to the restroom," his mom began at once. "She was in there alone, and a man came in and turned the lights out. She waited until he pushed open the door to her stall and she punched him. Her first punch hit him in the forehead and broke her hand. The second punch hit his nose and she got his blood all over herself. She got a blurry picture of him before the blood started flying."

Ravi swallowed hard. "I hope he doesn't know that."

"Me too."

"Why did she want me out of the house?"

"I don't know. She talked a mile a minute for a while, but once the pain kicked in, she got quiet. She said something about getting run off the road. What's going on here, Ravi?"

Ravi put the car in drive. "I'm not too far away. I'll be there soon and I'll explain it all then."

"I love you, punnare. Drive safely."

## CHAPTER TWELVE

K erala sat in a drab chair, awaiting the results of her x-rays.
They'd numbed her hand and splinted it. Local anesthetic
helped.

The cop, a detective, not a uniform, had arranged for them to use
an exam room to talk.

"Detective Thomas Alakai, Ms. Rosemont."

"You've got to be fucking kidding me."

He blinked at her exasperated tone. "No, that's my name."

"I've been trying to get a hold of you for almost a week. I want
to know about Vincent Willoughby."

Alakai's eyes narrowed and he hummed noncommittally. "How
about you tell me what happened first?"

She almost spat her anger at him. Fucking power games. She
didn't have the energy to give him her best, so she complied, starting
with the scene in the bathroom and then jumping back in time to take
him through the problems since starting Ravi's house. She was as
thorough as she could be, but she didn't have any of her notes. She
kept her research about Mahiʻai to herself. She hadn't even shared it
with Ravi yet, and it felt too insubstantial to hand over.

"Okay, Ms. Rosemont, let me summarize. You've been on this
construction job since the Request for Bid came through. You suspect
a conspiracy to keep you from hiring engineers to do the necessary
reports, getting permits, and hiring subcontractors. You began
deconstruction of the old hotel on October ninth, and then you ran
into a series of problems."

"Yeah, little stuff. Could have been accidental."

"These suspicious accidents included disappearing motor brushes, a stripped starter, several cut timing belts, a bent rotor arm." He read the litany, flipping through multiple pages in his notebook. She wasn't sure, but he seemed to be more interested than when he'd arrived. "What else?"

"That's all I remember right now. I can go back to my reports. Then we got some real evidence of sabotage."

Ravi opened the door and rushed over to her. "Are you okay?"

"Did you talk to the doctor?"

"They won't talk. We're not family."

Gulp. "I'm waiting on x-rays."

He looked over at the cop. "And you are?"

"Detective Thomas Alakai."

"Indeed. I've been wanting to talk to you."

"Stand in line." The cop showed a touch of levity, but it wasn't enough to charm her.

Ravi's fingers swept across her cheek. "You sure you're up to talking?"

"It's fine. It doesn't take my mind off the situation, but it helps to tell the story." Simple, factual, and linear. "Sit, Ravi. Don't hover."

Alakai looked between them. "You were saying you got some evidence."

"We were staking the site and I walked to the edge of a steep hill. The ground gave way under me." Kerala recited the story, concise and steady-voiced. "Your coworkers came and took the report. They were less than impressed by my fall. You might even say they were assholes."

"Mmmhmm. The next event?"

"I was walking my dog."

"What day was this?"

"Friday, the eighteenth. Just after sundown." She told the story and continued without pause. "Having just been exposed to the tender mercies of the local police force, I didn't report this one."

Alakai tapped his pencil on his notebook, a blank look on his face. "I'm sorry you didn't feel that you could come to us when you were in danger."

Kerala stared at him, too worn out to challenge his language. "When we got back to work on Monday, they took batteries from cordless tools, nuts off saw blades, and a bunch of other random parts off tools and machinery. They left it all in a pile out back. I can't figure out why. Replacing the parts would have been a much bigger hassle than putting them back on the gear."

"A week ago. Is that the last act of suspected sabotage until today?"

"Yes, but we also instituted a watch schedule." She looked at Ravi. "I already told him about today. I'll catch you up when we're done here."

"My mom gave me the gist."

Alakai flipped through his notes again. "There are some familiar patterns here. Get me the rest of the information as soon as you can. I'll start with today's incident, look for witnesses, anyone who saw something. I am going to look into the big picture, though, Ms. Rosemont."

Kerala nodded when he waited for a reaction. She wanted to go home and sleep through the pain meds.

"Wait!" she said as the detective stood. He looked at her, eyebrows quirked in question. "Can you have someone drive by my house and make sure there's no one around there? I want to go home, but I'm…"

When Kerala didn't finish her sentence, he said, "Of course. I'll make sure the Waimea station sends someone to cruise your house. They'll keep an eye on you."

"I'm at the end of a street. It's not on the way to anything else, so I don't need regular visits, just a sweep before I get there."

"I'm sure the officers know how to do a U-turn. They'll keep an eye out."

Ravi stood to face Alakai. "I'd like to talk to you soon. There's history with this land, with the disappearance of the previous owner, and I'm hoping you can share what you know."

Alakai hesitated. "I'm restricted in what I can share, but I'll check in soon. We'll talk more then."

He left with a nod.

Where were those x-rays? "I hate cops."

"He seems focused and smart."

"Did you hear him? 'I'm sorry you felt…' I wanted to give him chapter and verse on why calling the police is never my best option."

He shook his head. "You keep scaring the shit out of me, Kerala."

"It's not me."

"I know. You don't jump off mountains in a squirrel suit or dive in shark-infested waters. You're just building a house for me."

"Go shop for guilt somewhere else."

He slid his hand from her elbow to her splint. "I can't have even a little bit?"

"This bastard is the only guilty one. If he's been behind all of it, then catching him ends it."

"That's all very goal-oriented, Kerala, but I'm trying to talk about feelings."

"When aren't you?" He stared at her long enough that she gave in. "I feel angry and kinda scared. Is that what you're after? That I'm scared?"

"This isn't how I pictured it, but here goes." He was gearing up for something big and she couldn't figure out how to stop him. "Kerala, I love you. Your safety and well-being are crucial to me, and I'm worried about you."

Well, there it was. The beginning of the end. "Ravi…" She floundered, as always. And as always, resentment followed that feeling of helpless confusion. "What am I supposed to do with that?"

"I won't try talking you out of doing your job. I know it's more than that to you."

"How can you get me so well in some ways, and totally miss the point in others?"

His amusement made her wary. "Kerala, I think you're capable of more than you think."

"Fucking hell, Ravi." She stopped there, at a loss.

"I love you. What are you going to do about it?" The bastard had a great big grin on his face and she couldn't form an intelligible sentence.

She shook her head. "I have no idea."

"Well, if you're not kicking me out, you'll get one eventually."

"Right now, I want to wipe that smug look off your face."

"What can I say? It makes me happy to say it out loud. I love you, Kerala."

"Ravi." She had to slow him down. Something. "I care about you, but you're rushing this way too fast. I'm exhausted and you hit me with this?"

His face softened, just melted right down. "I'm not trying to pin you to anything while you're in a weakened state. Thank you for telling me you care, though."

She shook her head, confused. How had he turned it around into a declaration? "You know what? Fuck it. You love me and I'm glad. I'm glad you're here with me and glad you're living with me right now." Her heart pounded in the mess of emotion. "It doesn't mean we have a future, though."

"It means something. Of course it's confusing and strange and almost as painful as it is wonderful. We'll just take it as it comes." Ravi turned her head toward him. She gave in and met his eyes. "There's hope for us, Kerala. If you care for me at all, there's hope."

She swallowed so hard her ears popped.

Kerala lay in her recliner with the TV on. Maitri had just left for the airport. She'd wanted to stay while Kerala convalesced, but Ravi had seen Kerala's desperation for peace and quiet. He'd told his mom that she was indispensable at home. Maitri wasn't simple enough to fall for it, but she'd picked up on the sincere request that she leave. No pouting even.

Her anger at Ravi for keeping secrets, on the other hand, wasn't going away any time soon. She'd apparently decided that Kerala got a pass, but Ravi was on the hook for hiding the danger Kerala had been in. He seemed resigned to the doghouse.

Now Kerala had nothing to do except lay around and heal. When her phone rang, she snatched it for the distraction. "Hekili, how's it going?"

"Fine here. Just checking on you."

"I'm healing. No big deal."

"Any news from the police?"

"Nope. Nothing. But there haven't been any suspicious people hanging around the neighborhood and they don't have much to go on."

"The blood? Maybe they can get a DNA match?"

"Apparently, there's a backlog. They have more important DNA samples to sequence."

"I see." He hesitated. "Did you submit a worker's comp report?"

"Why? It didn't happen at work." That didn't make any sense.

"But you think it's work related, right?"

She muted the TV. "I think it's related to the project, sure, but I don't think it's work-related in a worker's comp kind of way."

"After the holiday's over, I want you to talk to our lawyer."

So that's what it was. He was covering his ass. "Of course." Her monotone reflected her emptiness.

"We need to keep the situation as free of confusion as possible. All this talk of 'aumākua and sabotage is bad for business. I'll arrange it and let you know when to come into the office."

"Sure, Hekili. Bring it on."

She made it through the small talk, but after hanging up, a wave of sadness passed over her. Suddenly, sharply, she missed her old boss from Philly. That had been a good outfit to work for. They'd cared about each other, taken care of each other.

Whether she was an outsider as a haole or because she hadn't adopted the aloha way, Mālama Construction wouldn't be her new home. She had tried so hard to avoid working for a company she didn't care about. She could have stayed on in Philly if she'd wanted that.

Nothing was playing out like she'd hoped. She was letting Ravi dangerously close for someone who was supposed to be an occasional fuck buddy when he was in town. She was drawn to him companionably as well as sexually and it made her uneasy.

Her house didn't stimulate her, pleasure at Mālama was receding, and the person she wanted to be with lived in California.

Hawai'i wouldn't be home for her, but she resisted thinking about moving. If she did, she'd have to decide whether to figure Ravi into her plans for the future.

She'd been stalked and attacked. Bad as her phone pic was, Ravi had sent it away to be manipulated by a friend of his.

Everything could get back to normal if they found the guy.

❖

Ravi sat next to Nahoa on the ocean wrack, the sun a hot orange glow through his eyelids. Nahoa had been surfing and lay flat on his back. "Is this a good surf spot?"

"The stone and shell keep most people off this stretch of beach and the thousands of wana in the shallows keep the swimmers away. On the board, I'm safe from the spines."

Nahoa had called just before Ravi had waved his mom good-bye at the airport, asking that he come to the beach. "What's the news?"

"I went by your land and the stakes had been pulled. I spent half a day restaking the property from the plans in the trailer before I called you. Good thing Kerala's tidy and the plans were easy to find."

Ravi shook his head. "Why didn't you call her?"

"She's drugged and healing. No reason to tell her about the latest nuisance."

"Nahoa, why is she being attacked? Why not me?"

"Recent transplant, kind of stand-offish. She's in charge of this project."

"But they went after Willoughby last time."

Nahoa pulled a sharp rock out from under his hip without opening his eyes. His muscles quivered when he moved and it hit Ravi that Nahoa was exhausted.

"I don't know what you're up to, but you're wearing yourself out."

Nahoa's eyelids fluttered open. "Did you know that the crew calls Kel a tita? It's a Hawaiian word for a bold, strong, independent woman. Like bitch without the negative connotations. Like butch without the gender part or dyke without the sexual part. English has a ton of ways to insult strong women, but not a single word that praises them."

"Yeah. I'm well aware." Ravi picked up a black rock and turned it between his fingers.

"She'd be down with the tita code."

"Indeed."

"Kel knows her trade. She can weld, do layout, drive a nail in three swings, and cut a two-by-four from her hip. As short as she is, she can wheelbarrow concrete and take her end of a heavy load."

"She's real. No bullshit, no confusion."

"But she's not safe, Ravi."

"I don't know what you think I can do about that. She and I have talked about this over and over, and she flatly refuses to consider quitting."

"I keep talking to folks, but they're not listening to me. If they'd stop the little stuff like the stakes, maybe we could find out who's hurting her." He lay slack as though his exhaustion went deeper than his muscles. "Someone has decided that she's the weak link and they don't know her like we do. She's a tita. She'll scrap until they either give up or kill her."

Ravi shivered in the heat. "Don't say that."

Nahoa opened his eyes and looked at Ravi. "A person can mean well. You think you know where your limits are, your own ethics, your own morality, and you live by it until everything goes to hell and you have no time to consider right and wrong. You suddenly step right past those limits. When things get out of control, there's no telling what might happen."

## CHAPTER THIRTEEN

The next day, Kerala tried to sneak into the kitchen.

"What are you doing? Just yell and I'll get you what you need."

She turned and glared. "I can get my own water, damn it. Your mom was bad enough. Don't hover."

He leaned against the wall. "She made me promise to take care of you. She never would have gone otherwise."

"As much as I ended up liking her, I'd have strangled her if she'd stayed another day."

He grinned. "She can be a bit…oppressive as a caregiver. I'm glad I wasn't a sickly child."

"No more tea, please, no more tea!" She laughed and slumped against the counter. "I'm woozy, but it's my hand that's broken, not my legs."

He came over and pulled her close. "Poor baby, are you feeling petulant?"

"Yes," she said petulantly. She draped her arms around his waist.

"You don't like hurting, do you?"

"No."

"Do you like it when I make you lie there and I just lick and lick and lick?"

"Yeah. I like that."

"You'll let me fuss over you as long as it's sexual."

"Right."

She put her forehead on his shoulder and let him hold her. No one had ever persisted like he did.

"You're glad I'm here, aren't you."

"For cooking and cleaning and massaging my shoulder when the cast feels heavy. And for sex."

He kissed her hair and sighed. He so obviously wanted her to say she loved him.

She needed to get off the opiates. The mood swings could get her in deeper than was safe. "I can't stand the feeling of my head against a pillow. I'm tired of lying down, even in the recliner. I'll scream if I watch another minute of TV."

"Be patient with yourself. You'll heal."

"Easy for you to say."

His next sigh was a little more impatient. "I have to get back to work."

She let go. "Of course. I'll be fine."

"Thanks. Back to it." He kissed her forehead and went back to her desk in the dining room.

She wandered into the living room. Time for another pill. She stared at the bottle.

Nope. No more pills.

Maitri was gone. Her head was clearing.

Time to figure out who was after her. She'd been passive long enough.

She called Jack. "Will you come to my house for another meeting? Around two?"

"Happy to. Been wondering how you're doing."

"I'm fine. I want to talk this through again with you and Nahoa and Ravi."

"Good. Okay to bring the boy?"

"Danny is always welcome. He takes care of himself pretty well. Maybe he'll take Bogart out for some play time."

Jack grunted. Kerala hung up and made the second call, reaching Nahoa's voice mail. She crossed the room and leaned in the doorway. Typing on his laptop rounded Ravi's shoulders. He faced away, three-quarter profile, but there was tension in his back and neck.

Kerala broke his concentration by clearing her throat. "Will you be able to stop for an hour or so around two? I've called the guys over."

Ravi's eyes lost their otherworldly focus and zoomed in on Kerala. "Yes. Yes, of course I can. Should I make a late lunch?"

"No, let's eat at our usual time. I didn't tell them there'd be food."

"Okay. I'm on it."

Ravi turned back to his computer as though mesmerized.

The knock came right on time. Bogart bounced in place until Ravi pulled the door open. Danny threw himself at Bogart and became a giggling, slobbery mess on the floor.

Jack stepped over his son. "Aloha, Ravi. Hey, Kel." He looked her over and nodded. "Kicked some cowardly ass, I hear."

"Sure did. Blood all over the place."

"Just his?"

"Yep."

Jack sat on the couch across from Kerala and they glowed with the exact same satisfaction. Ravi shook his head.

Nahoa drove up before Ravi closed the door.

"Aloha, boxer." Nahoa winked at Kerala.

Ravi couldn't help but stare. "I guess you've been at the beach."

He grinned. "What was your first clue?"

"Let's see. Swim trunks, plastic flip-flops..."

"Slippahs," said Kerala.

When had she started learning local lingo? "And a bare chest. You'll get a chill, kid." Ravi found Nahoa's beauty distracting. His natural smile, his smooth and strong body. And young enough to be his son. What a thought.

Ravi sat on the floor, back against the wall. Nahoa sat next to Jack, grimacing when his bare back hit the cheap upholstery.

Jack patted Danny's head. "Want to play on the computer?" Danny dragged Bogart from the room.

Kerala said, "Okay, let's get to it. We have to figure out who's doing this shit. I'm tired of taking a beating because some guy has a stick up his ass. I did some searches and read a million articles and posts and I think I know who did these things." She handed Jack the list. "The names in the left column are the screen names and nicknames of the people I've tied to certain bits of sabotage."

Jack handed it to Ravi. "Nothing big."

He was right. The attacks on Kerala weren't on the list.

"This photo was taken by the main guy. Find the kitchen with this view and we've got someone, even if they are small-time." She handed the second piece of paper over to make its way around.

Ravi eyed the printout. Even on a regular printer, the image came out pretty clear. Vaguely familiar. "Great work, Kerala."

Nahoa took the second piece of paper from him. "I know where this picture was taken."

"You do?" Kerala sounded so excited.

"Yeah." Nahoa grabbed his beer and took a swig. "This won't make anyone happy."

A cold feeling crept up Ravi's spine.

Nahoa told the bubbles in his bottle, "It's my grandma's house."

## CHAPTER FOURTEEN

Kerala scooted over when Ravi sat on the edge of the bed and took off his watch. She stretched out under the covers and rubbed the flannel across her belly. "Do you think we made the right decision? Not passing this information to the police right away? Alakai is holding back on us. You know he is. He won't even return our calls."

He stripped off his pants and socks, folding them in his bedtime ritual. "Yeah, he is. But he's got the rest of the pieces. How long do we hold back identifying evidence?" He slipped under the covers and snuggled into her side.

"God, Ravi, I don't know. It's his grandma. It's Tūtū Alapa'i." Kerala put her good arm on the one he wrapped over her waist. "If she's involved, she's working against her own son. I knew they weren't on the same page, but..."

"You already waited to tell us. I suggest we give him a week. After that, we have to share this information with Alakai."

"He might think it's worthless. There are a lot of jumps in the logic."

"Not many, once you get down to brass tacks. You did a good job on the documentation. And he can access IP addresses with a warrant."

"Would he have enough for that? It's not even the serious stuff, just the petty shit. Damn it. Every time we get a little more information, Nahoa asks for time. I want to hunt this fucker down, not sit around and wait for him to attack me again."

"One week. Then we pass the information along to Alakai."

"We stirred a shit storm by bringing the cops in. Alakai's been questioning the workers. I bet folks will lay low for a while."

"Let's hope." Ravi sounded fervent, but his hand followed a different track.

She'd been wearing a lot of flannel, the comfort food of clothing, but it didn't seem to turn him off. He slipped his hand between the pajama top and bottoms, exploring from the bottom edge of her tits to the start of her pubic hair. She closed her eyes and let him set the pace.

Her belly clenched, and it must have been the signal he was looking for, because his fingers slipped through her hair and between her swelling labia. Just barely between them. He did like to tease.

She did like to let him.

But not this time. She trapped his hand with her thighs and turned onto her back. "Wait."

"For what?" He stilled. He lay on his side, head in his hand, and looked at her.

"You're great in the sack, Ravi. Technique for days and a gift for tuning in to my body. But I gave you some hints, remember? I want to know how to please you better."

"You do please me, Kerala."

"I know. You get off almost as much as I do, but it's pretty directional. You do things to me that drive me around the bend and you follow. I'd like to lay you down and make you come."

He flexed his hand, just a little. "You sure you wouldn't rather just get fucked tonight?"

She raised an eyebrow.

He pulled free and fell back. She rolled on her side, following him, and pulled on her elbow, reversing their positions.

"You like it when I touch you." She pulled her fingertips across his chest, calluses catching in his hair.

"Indeed."

"What do you like that I've never done?"

He looked at her and opened his mouth. Nothing came out for a moment and she stilled her hand. "I like to feel large. I guess it's a good thing I'm big. Um, but not in a dominance way."

"I get that." She didn't smile. He was having a hard enough time.

"And it's important to me that you get something from whatever you're doing. Before you say it, I get a ton out of going down on you and I know it's not different for you. Or maybe it is, but..."

"I love filling my mouth with tender flesh and feeling it get fat and stiff."

"Oh. Oh, wow." He released a breath. "Right. I haven't gotten a lot of head, some but not, you know, a lot."

"Did you like it?"

"I had a hard time getting out of my head."

She nodded. "I can see where that would be a thing for you." She gazed at him thoughtfully. "What gets you out of your head?"

He flushed and she focused. She was right—he had some kind of turn on he hadn't told her about. "I, um, dated a guy for a while. A cis guy, with such a sweet way about him. He and I clicked on a romantic level, but I wasn't sure how I'd like his bits. I'd dated a few trans guys, but their masculinity made sense to me and they didn't have...testicles."

Again, she controlled a grin. Of course he would default to anatomical language.

"So anyway, we made out for hours before we got to the stage of taking off our clothes. He'd been with one trans guy before and the genitalia thing had confused him a bit, especially with me using the word clit where the other guy called it his cock. We talked about it and he asked how I felt about...butt stuff."

Light bulb. She couldn't keep the smile off her face, so she caressed his belly and said, "Awesome."

"It was amazing, being with a cis guy and skipping the part where I worry about him thinking of me as female. We tried it both ways and I got off on fucking him like that. But I couldn't believe how much I loved...getting...it."

"Tell me what you liked." Her heart was beating heavily. His story turned her on and his body radiated heat with his embarrassment. Oh, yes, he was going to get fucked.

He swallowed and darted a look at her before focusing on the ceiling. "Rimming. A lot." He smiled for the first time since he'd started telling the story. "A lot a lot."

"It's amazing, right?"

"You like it too?" He put his hand on her hip.

"You're not changing the subject that easily. Did you do penetration?"

He'd relaxed quite a bit. "Yeah. His dick was smaller than the one I brought with me, the one we've been using. I guess I thought that made it a reasonable idea. Anyway, I'm glad I agreed to it, because I liked it a lot. We switched at first, but after a while, I mostly bottomed."

"It takes you out of your head?"

"Yeah. I felt so strong and grounded, like a healthy animal, when I was on my hands and knees getting pounded, pounding back. I mean, it took some work to get there, but when it happened..." He rolled his eyes and groaned.

"I'm a hard worker."

He bit his lip and eyed her.

"You're clean, I'm clean. Let me do what you like."

"I'm freaking out here."

"Is that a bad thing?" She stroked his belly again. His muscles tensed.

"Do you mean the whole thing? Do you have a smaller dildo?"

She nodded and held his eyes. "I have a few. Boiled clean and I'll use a condom for easy cleanup. I'm not all about strap-on play, but I like penetration so I have some variety."

He took a deep breath. "Okay."

"Yeah? You'll let me turn you on, get you all hard and soft?"

His muscles tensed again. "Yeah. We can try it."

"Anytime you want to switch to something else or stop, just say the word."

"Safe word?"

She laughed. "If you want, but stop works just as well. Unless you want to play with being forced to let me..."

"One thing at a time, I think."

She grinned at him and he smiled back. She willed him to be comfortable. "It's just you and me and some toys and our bodies enjoying each other. Okay?"

"Let's give it a go."

She bit her cheek, considering. She rolled over him and made him spasm, then laugh. Her toys were in the bedside table on his side. She lay on her belly and opened the bottom drawer with the fingertips of her casted hand. Thick lube, condoms, gloves. She wasn't sure her smaller dildo was in that drawer. It might have been in her toy box.

They had been having great sex, but toys hadn't figured in it much. Her vibrator some. His strap-on, but that seemed more like a prosthesis than a toy.

She found the dildo and sprang up onto her knees. "Found it. What do you think?"

He touched the tip and licked his lips. "I don't know."

"We'll see how it goes." She put the dildo on the bedside table and straddled him. "Do you want to take care of your clit or can I play with that too?"

"I'll do it. I mean, don't worry about touching or whatever, but don't focus there."

"Got it." She draped herself on him and kissed his lips, short, firm presses. She rubbed her nose on his and kissed his cheek and back to his mouth. She sank into a deep, deep kiss and pulled away slowly. "I like eating ass."

Delicious agony screwed up his face. Words had power for him.

"Roll over," she said, rough and quiet, with a pull on his hip.

He opened his eyes and searched her face. Whatever he found, he wiggled under her, turning face down with a sigh.

She hummed and took great big handfuls of the skin and muscle of his shoulders, the skin and muscle and fat down his back and to the roll at his waist. She lay on him, a small trap for a big animal, and scooted until she could bite his neck.

His groan rewarded her and she grabbed his short hair with her good hand. She pulled back a little and used the fingertips of her casted hand to stroke his cheek, his neck, his shoulder. Another deep, slow bite on his neck, then she moved down his body with a kiss for every place that invited her mouth. She took her time, slowing more when his butt nestled into the hollow between her hips. She gripped his hips and tugged upward as though she could fuck him just like that.

Her patience ran out when he helped by pushing toward her. She slid between his legs. He pulled one knee under him, then the other, and his rocking ass rubbed against her belly.

"God, you're so fucking sexy." His thick, dark hair was mussed from her hand, and his arms were folded under the pillow. His arm and shoulder muscles flexed and his spine bowed.

She leaned over him, kissed his back, and ran her good hand up the front of his thigh, then around to his ass. She squeezed his butt cheek hard, then pushed him forward. She dropped to her belly and scooted until the star of his asshole blinked right in front of her. He heaved up just long enough to shove a pillow under his belly, then settled back down.

She held herself on her elbows, cast resting on the bed, and leaned in. He smelled hot like the peak of summer and his dark skin lightened, then darkened as it transitioned to softer tissue. She breathed on him and he clenched. She ignored her instinct to start lower, with his clit, and drew her tongue up his perineum and to his asshole. She licked at it slowly, then pushed her tongue against the ring of muscle on one side, then the other. She flirted with it, going around and around, before pressing his softening opening with her tongue's tip. Gently. Gently.

She set up a slow rhythm, a song with flirtatious verses and a chorus that pushed him open. Back and forth, back and forth, she seduced and fucked, seduced and fucked. When his hand brushed her chin, she adapted her pace to the motion he used on his clit.

She shifted, body tired of its position, and he pushed back toward her. She pulled away and replaced her mouth with her hand. "I'm going to fuck you. You are so ready. You just pull me in, hungry and soft and fuckable. Do you hear me?"

"Yes, yes." The bed muffled his voice, but she could tell he meant yes to more than whether he could hear.

She pressed a hip into him and leaned far over to grab the supplies. She condomed the dildo and put it aside. She pulled a nitrile glove on her good hand, snapping it against her wrist. She associated that sound with sex, though latex had made a louder, different sound back in the day. Hopefully it turned him on too.

It was going to be tricky, handling him and the lube and the dildo with one hand. She'd figure it out.

She kept her hip against his spread butt cheeks so he wouldn't be left hanging in mid-air while she opened the lube. Sitting back on her heels, she squirted lube down his crack and then rubbed her hand in it, spreading it all over the glove and his flesh. She rubbed him with the back of her hand, twisting it and letting it curl so that her knuckles rumbled across his muscular ring. It eased at the attention and she put more lube right where he needed it.

He relaxed under her attention and she propped her casted hand on his lower back. Her questing fingers massaged the ring around his hole and dipped inside as far as the second ring, then massaged from the inside. Up and around, down and around, until the second ring opened like a portal.

Somewhere in the back of her mind, she knew that her pussy was fat and that she kept getting sympathetic clenches in her ass. She shifted to position her heel right under her clit and rocked on it as she explored Ravi deeper and deeper.

He started rolling his hips and she picked up the dildo. She slicked it lengthwise in the copious lube up and down his butt crack. When she placed the tip against his hole, he clenched and released. She pushed on the release and he moaned. A slight inch of the dildo penetrated him and he shifted, back and forth, accommodating it.

"Take it, Ravi. Swallow it up. Fuck yourself back on it."

He shivered at her words and pushed back. She guided the dildo, holding it so that it couldn't flex out of the way. She added a minimal movement to his shallow surge until he pushed up on his hands and knees to thrust back, taking half of it in one surprise gulp.

His groan sounded like it came from his curled toes. Something gave way and she slid the dildo in to the base. Little jerks in his back muscles and flexes of his hips cued her in to his excitement. She was still kneeling back on her heels and his longer limbs put his ass at her chest level. She rose to get a better angle and he pulled partway off the dildo at the same time. His ass clenched around it and he rocketed back just as she braced herself for the shove.

She fucked him and he fucked back at her, setting a slow, drawn out pace with a heavy push at the end. Oh, she wanted to touch herself so badly. His flexing back and shaking head spurred a wild need.

The heat and smell drove her crazy and she braced the outside of her upper arm on the base of the dildo to free her hand. The dildo could only move an inch in and out, but it rotated and rubbed against him, inside and out. She turned her hand to her own clit, demented by the task of fucking herself and him at the same time. He growled, short, low groans that grew with the short, deep thrusts. She had more power, using the strength in her abs and back and legs to thrust her whole body at his. He rubbed up and down, shifting the dildo in his ass and spreading his cunt lips against her arm. His hand on his clit bumped her, but she couldn't focus beyond the enormity of her own clit between her fingers and the wrestling physicality of their fucking.

He condensed suddenly, crouching lower and tightening everywhere, before breaking into a rolling motion echoed by repeated grunts. His scent strengthened and she kept lunging into him. His come pushed her over the edge and she jerked and jerked with an orgasm that didn't want to stop. It circled between them, her shaking and him undulating, her shoving into him and him pushing back at her so hard she almost flew off the bed. She anchored herself to him by wrapping her bad arm around his hips, but he slowed and his motion eased.

Heavy breathing filled the air. Her heart pounded, suffusing all her cells with oxygen like a drug. She could very well float away, simply disappear.

Instead, she pulled the dildo out gently and stripped the condom off. He rolled over and stared at her. "Holy fuck, Kerala."

"I know, right?" She wanted to go for a run, heave herself into the sea, and swim to another island. Or let the high drain away and get some sleep. "Will you pull the glove off?"

"Sure." It was awkward enough to get them both laughing.

She pulled him up and chivvied his lax body into the shower. "Clean up and let's cuddle."

Kerala tapped her beer against Jack's and watched Ravi play in the surf with Danny and Bogart. Danny defended his boogie board from Bogart's soft mouth. Good thing there was no chance of Bogart biting through the lightweight covering on the foam board. It wouldn't take much.

"You and Ravi are a thing now?"

"Whatever that means."

"Are you still a lesbian?"

Kerala gave Jack a cool stare. "I'm a fucking lesbian till the day I die. Got that?"

"Not really."

She sighed. "You've been so good with Ravi's gender."

Jack shrugged.

"I'm a lesbian, because that's my orientation. Just because I'm with a guy doesn't mean I'm walking the streets checking out man-ass now. Ravi's a special case."

Jack sipped his beer. "Okay."

She fidgeted. "Asshole." How much of that kind of shit did she have to look forward to? Time to change the subject. "Have you ever done one of these reconciliation things with Tūtū Alapa'i?"

"Nope."

She watched Danny run into the crashing surf and then fight the sucking retreat to run back to Ravi. Looked like fun, but she had to keep her cast dry. She balanced it on the arm of the low folding chair she'd set on the beach blanket. The palm fronds over her head rustled and the beer cooled her throat.

"Do you know this Walter guy? Mahi'ai?"

"Yup. You do too."

Ravi yelled encouragement when Danny caught the surf just right and rode the board all the way to the sand. Danny turned toward Jack and did a victory dance. Jack pumped his fist in the air and Danny turned away to keep playing.

"How do I know him?"

"Christmas lū'au."

She took another pull from the bottle. She met a lot of people that day, but she didn't remember a Walter or Mahi'ai.

"Don't think so." Pretty sure. Maybe he'd avoided her, the fucker. After Nahoa identified Tūtū Alapa'i's kitchen, he'd gone straight to his grandma with the evidence that one of her friends was the saboteur. Looking at the gardening forum post, she'd recognized the writer. "What I don't get is how Tūtū Alapa'i can be mixed up in this. Or, I don't know, maybe the question is why Hekili is the one person in the Kalama family who doesn't want us out of here."

"Hekili builds. That's what he does."

"He can't just, I don't know, stick to jobs for kama'āina and keep peace in the family?"

Jack looked out to sea. "Hawaiians don't have the money. Money's in hotels, condos, and tourist attractions. If he didn't take these jobs, Mālama Construction would be a handyman business."

"So at some point, Hekili decided he'd go against his principles and take anything he was offered?"

"Don't know about that. He doesn't talk sovereignty."

She pondered that. Ravi rolled Danny's boogie board and Bogart set up a racket barking until he stood up. Lifeguard dog.

"What about remains? He ever say anything about moving someone's ancestors?"

"If everyone refused to dig where there may be bones, there'd be no construction industry here at all."

She scratched under her cast with a palm frond. "Whatever Tūtū Alapa'i found out from this Walter guy, she didn't invite Hekili to the big peace-making meeting."

"Or me. Means there's bad blood to be settled between you and him and Ravi and Nahoa, and Tūtū Alapa'i thinks it can be put to rest by you together."

The glare off the water started getting to her, so she turned to pull sunglasses from her beach bag. Movement caught her eye, someone coming over the rocks separating this beach from the next. A young man with a backpack scrambled down them and started across the sand.

Something bothered her about him. She sat and watched him move, but she couldn't pinpoint it. The shape of his head was familiar and her heart started to beat thickly.

She jumped up. "Hey! Hey, you!" He turned toward her for a brief moment and stiffened. Though his face was partly shadowed, she caught sight of a busted nose and bruised forehead.

"That's him," she shouted. She didn't wait for backup. She jumped to her feet and ran, but the young man recognized her as well and darted away across firm, packed sand. Her thighs burned and she hoarded her breath for the effort of running in deep, dry sand. He jumped the rocks, back the way he'd come, and disappeared. By the time she reached the rocks, she was covered in sweat and he was gone.

"Son of a bitch."

Jack puffed up next to her. "Was that him?"

"I thought he seemed familiar, the shape of his head and the way he moved."

"But you don't know?"

"His nose was broken. It was him."

Jack pulled out his phone. "Nahoa, Kel just saw the guy who attacked her...Yeah...We're at Ho'okena...Yep...I don't know... No...She saw his nose."

Bogart ran up with Ravi and Danny not far behind. "What's going on?"

"I saw the guy who attacked me."

Danny's eyes got big.

Jack kept talking on the phone. "Yep...Big tattoo across his shoulder, down one arm...Polynesian...Couldn't see the details." He looked at her.

She shook her head. She'd been so focused on catching him that she hadn't made note of what she was seeing. She wouldn't even be able to say for certain what color his shorts were.

"Went east...Yep...I don't know." He looked at her again. "Nahoa's getting some people to look for him. You want to stay put?"

"I'm not going to let that fucker ruin my day." She cut her eyes toward the kid and modulated her language. "We came to enjoy the water. Let's enjoy the water."

But Bogart wasn't the only one who stayed close to her for the rest of the day.

❖

Ravi followed Kerala and Nahoa around the side of the house. Tūtū Alapa'i sat in a folding chair on the lanai, the sun bright in her hair. She wore a voluminous mu'umu'u of the sort he thought of as a Hawaiian stereotype. As much time as he'd spent reading about Hawaiian culture and the sovereignty movement, the gaps in his understanding lurked, waiting to suck him into confusion.

He looked at the house and spotted the window to the kitchen. He scanned the yard for the elements Nahoa had recognized in the photo. Healthy hydrangea, liliko'i, and unfamiliar plants grew on and along a high fence. A bird feeder hung from a ten-foot-tall copper pole that looked like plumbing pipe, hammered flat and curled at the top to form a hook. The space looked both hacked from and still the very essence of jungle.

"Aloha, Nahoa. Aloha, Kerala, Ravi. Please sit."

Ravi claimed the wicker love seat and pulled Kerala down with him. He had no idea how this meeting would go, but he would stick close to her.

A person walked from the kitchen, carrying a tray of cold juice and glasses. He put the tray on the small table next to Nahoa and wiped his hands on his boardshorts. He wore slippers and an old T-shirt with an indecipherable logo, something about surfing.

Nahoa rose to greet him with a hug and they touched noses. Ravi hadn't seen that yet, or hadn't noticed, but he'd read it was called honi.

Nahoa turned toward them. "Walter, this is Kerala and Ravi. Guys, this is Walter, a cousin and an old friend of mine. We canoed together back in the day. He posts as Mahi'ai."

Kerala stiffened and Ravi took her hand.

Tūtū Alapa'i waved everyone into seats, poured juice for each, and began. "Thank you all for coming to my house so we can talk."

Walter and Nahoa kept their attention on Tūtū Alapa'i. Ravi sipped his juice. Guava.

"Ho'oponopono is the process of turning our attention to the situation, what has been done, and how it has affected others. In this case, I am the haku, here to guide the process. We are not all 'ohana, but aloha can bring us to a closer understanding of each other. We hope to achieve lōkahi. Harmony."

Kerala's hand was stiff. He gave it a gentle squeeze, but she didn't squeeze back.

"I would ordinarily begin by clearing the channels of communication and emotion with prayer, but I have a feeling, ah, yes, I see it in your faces"—Ravi tried to look impassive—"that prayer would alienate you rather than open you."

"You're not wrong," said Kerala. She relaxed a little. Perhaps it helped that Tūtū Alapaʻi recognized that stumbling block and put it to rest right away.

"This isn't a Christian process, hoʻoponopono, and you would not have recognized the prayers. However, since we're not holding a cultural demonstration, but conducting a good faith effort to bring an end to conflict, we can make the process work for us all. We need to pool our strengths to this shared purpose, bringing truthfulness and sincerity to every stage of the process. We will proceed to mahiki, examination of the many layers of the problem, and examine hihia, or negative entanglements, to find the hala. The initial transgression or the core issue. You will each look inside yourself and express your feelings with honesty, openness, and in such a way as to avoid blame and recrimination. Be humble and be clear. Speak to me."

Kerala said, "How will we straighten this out if we can't talk to each other?"

"In sharing, it's helpful to focus on the person who is least involved. After we identify the hihia and hala, we work for resolution. This is when you will speak to each other directly. Mihi is confession and seeking forgiveness. Kala is the release of the hihia and requires that everyone reach a point where the problem is ʻoki, or cut off. Gone into the past with all its weight and entangled trouble. Pani closes hoʻoponopono.

"We will begin with you, Walter. What has happened?"

"To me, the conflict is between Mālama Construction and the ʻaumākua of the land they're desecrating."

"I understand that you feel there is a large social issue at the heart of this situation and a particular one involving this land. Please focus on your actions, how you have been affected and how you have responded."

He looked at his hands and took a deep breath. "When Vincent Willoughby disappeared, I felt that ʻaumākua had protected ʻāina, my ʻohana ahupuaʻa. Years later, and another haole comes to build in the same place. I wanted to keep the ʻāina from being profaned with a vacation house. It's a slap in the face of every Hawaiian who can't afford a place to live. It erases the history of my ʻohana and separates us from our kūpuna."

"You felt there was spiritual and material danger in the building of this house on that land." Tūtū Alapaʻi nodded as she spoke, pulling more information from him.

"Yes, and so I talked to others who felt like me and we talked to others. Some of us stalled permits. Some did other things."

"Like what, Walter?" Her voice was gentle.

"We will never stop suffering until we have thrown off foreign control of our ʻāina. Political sovereignty is the beginning. But while I'm working on that, I have to protect what hasn't already been taken from us. We broke small things and made machines stop working. I have not hurt one person. We're—I am—nonviolent."

Kerala broke in. "How can you say that?"

Tūtū Alapaʻi stopped her. "Please wait. We need to listen first."

Walter wet his lips with his juice. "I don't have anything else to say."

Tūtū Alapaʻi sat a moment in silence. When she spoke, she searched his face. "You say that you have done property damage in an effort to stall and stop construction of a vacation home on your ahupuaʻa. Is this correct?"

Walter nodded.

Tūtū Alapaʻi turned toward them. "Kerala, Ravi. That is the old way of apportioning land. An ahupuaʻa is a wedge from the mountain to the ocean, giving each ʻohana many types of land and weather, hunting and livestock, and a variety of crops. The system began to unravel when the plantations were set up."

"I read about it a little," Ravi said. Kerala just nodded.

"Kerala, will you please tell us what has happened, what you have done, and how you have felt?"

"Well, sure. I've felt freaking scared, to be honest. This guy says he's nonviolent, but I had a gash in the back of my head and bruises and cuts all over my shoulder, my back, and my hip. Three separate times I've been attacked." She waved her cast at them. "I'm less nonviolent than some, I guess, because when the guy trapped me in a public bathroom and threatened me, he got punched for his trouble."

Tūtū Alapaʻi put a hand up. "Kerala, please. You're angry and I can understand why. Will you wait a moment while I ask Walter a few questions?"

She shrugged. "Sure." She looked over at Ravi and he tried to smile at her. If only she could open to him like that.

"Walter, you didn't say you attacked Kerala. Will you please speak to that?"

He put down his glass of juice with a click. "I have never attacked Kerala. None of us have. We wouldn't do that. Attacking a woman in a bathroom is disgusting. There's no mana in it."

"She was attacked three times. Do you know about the other two?"

Walter looked over at Nahoa and hesitated. "I've heard. Nahoa asked before and we told him the same thing. We didn't cut the hill that collapsed. That's the opposite of what I want for the land there. And we would never run a woman off the road while she was walking her dog. That's terrible. But..."

Tūtū Alapaʻi waited. When Walter didn't continue, she said, "Please, Walter, we need you to be open and honest if this is going to work."

"Look, Nahoa. You disappeared. We were best friends and then you quit school and the crew, went to work for your dad. You come around ten years later and expect us to talk to you like we hung out just the other day?"

"Walter." Tūtū Alapaʻi didn't need to say anything else.

"An old friend has been acting strange, renting equipment without telling anyone why. He keeps disappearing, missing canoe club and ignoring his ʻohana, but he's had a hard time. He's gone missing before and come back skinny and wrecked."

Ravi looked back and forth between Walter and Kerala. He wasn't sure she'd be able to stay silent and let Tūtū Alapaʻi control the pace. Nahoa sat still, his face expressionless.

"Why don't you say his name?"

"I'm worried about him, and the last thing I want to do is get him in trouble if he's just going through a tough time."

Tūtū Alapaʻi nodded. "Kerala, we can come back to the attacks on you. For now, will you focus on the other events?"

Her knee started moving. She had a lot more tension than her face showed. He took her hand again.

"I…" She shook her head. "I can try. You want me to talk about the stuff he says he did and not the stuff he says he didn't do?"

"Please."

"Okay, well, there's a long list of petty shit…pardon me… damage to equipment. Some of it was just a nuisance. Taking the batteries from stuff, taking the nuts and hiding them. But some of it was violent. Stuff smashed and cut and ruined. I have a hard time trusting that it ended there. My reputation and professional pride are at stake here, besides all the rest. This is making me look incompetent and I can't stand for that."

The fervor in her voice didn't get past Tūtū Alapaʻi. Wounded pride. Ravi controlled the desire to roll his eyes.

"It sounds like you have experienced a lot of frustrating and dangerous situations and that Walter's actions have caused you shame."

"Well, shame might be a little strong." She was already backing away from the openness that had left her a little vulnerable.

"Ravi, how have you felt about all this?"

He looked at her in surprise. "I'm part of this?"

She smiled. "Of course you are. You have feelings about it, don't you?"

"Yeah. I guess I do." He tried to pull his thoughts together. He hadn't planned on this. "I feel like my passionate desire to build an impeccably eco-friendly home has turned into a nightmare. My thoughtlessness about the history of the land I bought has played a big part in creating the bad blood here. I still want to see my ideas in the real world, a comfortable house that won't make anyone sick from living in it and won't make the planet sick sustaining it. It's hard to grasp that such a great plan can offend so many people so deeply. I want Kerala to be safe and I want this house to be built and I want it to happen in such a way that it adds mana to the ʻāina, not in a way that desecrates anything."

She smiled again. "You've been studying?"

"Enough to know that power flows through everything and everyone and whatever you do increases or decreases it. You call that mana, right?"

She nodded.

"So, I feel like a good intention has come to a bad end. Work on the house starts in just a few days, after New Year's. I don't have the kind of money it would take to stop construction, pay all the fines for canceling the contract, and go build my dream house somewhere else. If I stop this now, it's the end for me."

Kerala got so rigid that he looked at her. Was the house his only durable tie to her? If he stopped, would he lose her along with the house?

That was the kind of thing he should say out loud to tease out all the emotional ramifications of the issue, but he just couldn't. If they were one 'ohana, maybe he could make himself that vulnerable.

"Some environmental activists blow up trucks and spike trees and ruin oil or fuel with sand or whatever. I read Edward Abbey's *Monkeywrench Gang*. I know what you're doing. There's a strong logical case for property damage being different from and orders of magnitude less horrible than violence to a living creature. Violence is cutting down a redwood, not setting off a bomb in an empty building. It sounds like Walter and his folks draw a similar line and I respect that."

"Seriously?"

"Kerala." Tūtū Alapa'i's admonishment was brief but effective. Kerala subsided with a sideways look at him. He shrugged. Tūtū Alapa'i spoke again. "You are expressing a lot of emotion, Ravi. Thank you for being so honest. You say you have a strong desire to build this house and some shame for how you came to plan it for that location. You want everyone to be happy and safe. And you feel sympathetic toward the actions that Walter has taken."

"That about sums it up." He did feel somewhat better for saying all that out loud. He was no stranger to talk therapy. Now, to see if this was more successful in creating solutions.

Tūtū Alapa'i cocked her head at Nahoa. "Your turn."

Nahoa shook his head. "I thought we were brokering a deal here."

"When you brought this to me, you should have known how I would approach it."

"You said because of Kerala and Ravi that you would do it differently."

"And so I am. Have I recited prayers? I can bend to accommodate them, Nahoa, but you are part of the hihia. Please speak to us."

"I feel what everyone else is feeling. I want that land protected and I want this house to be built and I want to take pride in my work and I want Kerala safe. I want to stop hurting every time I see the liliko'i growing where it shouldn't, strangling the koa. Walter doesn't trust me, and why would he? I left the sovereignty movement years ago and now I'm building a house where I fought one before. The plan is different, though, so much better that I want it for us. It makes me want to get back into the sovereignty movement with some concrete ideas for improving our lives and being independent. I've learned what it is to build something and I love that feeling. I feel like I'm being torn apart in this and that I can only be a loyal friend if my friends stop being enemies."

Tūtū Alapa'i nodded. "You say the struggles are mirrored inside you and that you don't want passion to keep overcoming strength in your life."

"I guess that sums it up." Nahoa wilted.

Tūtū Alapa'i sat in silence for long enough that Ravi looked around at the others. Walter watched the beads of water glisten on the pitcher of guava juice. Nahoa seemed to be looking inward, not focusing on anything around him. Kerala rotated her shoulder. The cast fatigued her muscles and Ravi put his arm around to massage her upper arm and shoulder.

When Tūtū Alapa'i spoke again, she asked Walter more questions about the person he suspected as Kerala's assailant. She didn't insist that he name his source, and Ravi struggled to let her continue with her questions uninterrupted.

She went from person to person again, clarifying and adding detail to the picture they all had of the situation. As she went, it all looked so much sadder and so much less infuriating. They were all good people, acting in good faith. They could come together somehow.

She thought some more and then directed them to talk to each other. "Are you ready to undo this with each other?"

Everyone nodded and Ravi believed them. Strange as it seemed, they had built the mutual understanding necessary to release their bad feelings.

As she led them to apologize and forgive one another, the future impinged. What good would it do to forgive and forget if nothing changed?

"Knowing what matters to one another, how do you intend to move forward?" She wasn't letting anything slide.

Nahoa said, "May I speak first?" She nodded and he continued. "I have the most information about both sides. I see a lot of good in building this house, proving out the way Ravi thinks we could live sustainably without stressing the ʻāina. I also see that the ʻāina and the ʻaumākua must be protected. I can help Kerala plan the construction to do as little harm and as much good as possible. I suggest that we go ahead, but with the idea that Ravi give us access to the house as a test case for Native Hawaiian housing."

"I'm in. It was half experiment from its conception. I'd love to look at the plans again with Hawaiian needs and aesthetics in mind." As a matter of fact, he couldn't have planned it any better. It was exactly what he wanted for the house.

Walter sighed. "I can see how this will go. Even if I could convince Kerala to stop, there would be another owner, and another. Unless the land comes back to ʻohana control, this battle will never end. It's why we need sovereignty. I know you believe the same thing, Nahoa, or you did. I hope you're serious about working with us again. Show us something else we can do, if you don't think we've gone about this the right way. If building this house can help, we will stop getting in the way."

Ravi wanted to clap, but he contained himself. Tūtū Alapaʻi nodded and Kerala relaxed a fraction.

"But there's one condition." He looked at the attentive group. "If ʻiwi kūpuna are found, construction halts. I cannot bargain away the peaceful rest of my ancestors."

Kerala nodded and spoke for the first time since she'd forgiven Walter. "As I understand, that's not just respectful and correct. It's the law."

"We'll be careful while excavating and moving soil. We're transplanting the koa first. I'll brief the operator on what to look for." Nahoa's expression was clearer, more at ease, than at any other point in the conversation. He had settled something for himself, as had they all. Hoʻoponopono was a good kind of mediation, at least with someone as skilled and smart as Tūtū Alapaʻi for a haku.

Kerala shifted in her seat. "This is all well and good. Don't get me wrong. I'm glad we did this. I understand a lot more than I did before, and it feels good to get it all out in the open and get a plan for moving forward. But my body is screaming at me from several points right now and it sounds like nothing we've done is making anybody much safer."

Walter looked her in the eye. "I will keep looking for my friend."

"What if you find him?" she challenged.

"Not sure."

She frowned at him. "We built some trust here, Walter, but I have to know that I'm safe."

"I have to know the truth before I make promises."

Her frown didn't budge, but she let it go.

Tūtū Alapaʻi clapped her hands. "We have found pono through ancient tradition applied in a new way. Will everyone agree that the past is ʻoki, cut off, and that the entanglements that have been released will not be brought up or used again?" An agreeable murmur passed around the circle. "Well then, thank you for the opportunity in this hoʻoponopono, where we have worked through many problems to find what has entangled us in negative relations. Thank you for listening and understanding our impact on others and theirs on us. Thank you for forgiveness and release and for sending our pilikia to the depths of the ocean, never to rise. Now. Let's eat. Nothing seals a deal like meaʻai."

Walter and Nahoa rose. "We'll get the food," Nahoa said, with a pat on her shoulder.

Kerala looked at Ravi. "I think she snuck in a prayer at the end there."

He looked at Tūtū Alapaʻi's sparkling eyes. "Yep."

❖

Kerala took the shit she was dished with good grace. She was happy to be back on the job. She wouldn't swing any hammers for a while, but there was plenty to do.

The temporary fencing was up, the Porta-Potties had been delivered, and they'd constructed a tire wash to keep the vehicles from tracking dirt off the property. They worked on erosion control, and Kerala breathed freely for the first time in a week.

"Can I get you some coffee? Or wipe your nose? Or your ass?" Stevens hovered in a mock-solicitous way that cheered her like nobody's business.

"Are you bored, Stevens? I can find some work for you." She eyeballed him.

"Don't hit me," he yelled, and he skedaddled as though he'd been spanked. Jack cracked a smile at his antics.

Once erosion control measures were in place, they'd spend a week grubbing and clearing and two weeks grading the site. The fast-growing grass and bushes could be hiding old structures, rock walls, foundations. They'd have to clear the whole area to be sure. Grading was where shit could break down, though, with the possibility of finding old collapsed caves, shallow burials.

She breathed the hot dirt and squinted in the bright sun reflecting off the equipment, looking around the work site. It looked different with all the history and emotion laid on it. It had been just a site, with idiosyncratic problems and possibilities, but now it was culture, community, theft, desire. Maybe it wasn't such a good thing to know so much about land she was developing.

Mixed feelings about the land aside, the sounds of people and equipment warmed her as much as the relentless sun did. She fucking loved to build well.

She put so much of her pride and talent into construction that it infuriated her to think of it being destroyed. On the other hand, she kept turning over what it meant to conflate damage to people and damage to property. Calling both of them violence—did that set them up as equally reprehensible?

What the hell. She wasn't getting paid to philosophize. "Jack, meet me in the office in ten."

He nodded and she went in to check on delivery of the light dozer for the koa transplant and main excavation.

❖

Ravi picked up enough groceries for a few meals and headed back to the house with Bogart for company. Bogart ran around the backyard, freed from his decorous work site behavior, and played catch with himself.

It felt good to take care of Kerala, feed her good meals and make sure Bogart got what he needed. She got along fine without him—a glimpse of her favorite vibrator served as a reminder of that when he put the clean laundry away—but maybe a little bit better with him around. He puttered around the house, cooking, straightening, and setting up music on his laptop.

His cell phone beeped with Kerala's heading-home text and he sent back an excited emoji. The stew simmered, scenting the kitchen with cumin and bay leaf, and he set the oven for the garlic bread.

When Bogart barked once and ran to the front door, Ravi peeked out the window. Kerala went through the mud room door and Ravi waited for her with Bogart. She came from the bathroom, energy pumping off her like a steam engine, and greeted Bogart first. Their loving wrestle done, she stood and put her hands on her hips. She looked around, raised an eyebrow, and pursed her lips.

Ravi looked around too and realized what he'd done. A complete and total round of nesting. The pillows on the couch were fluffed. Magazines were tidied in the holder by her recliner. The Afro-Cuban All-Stars played from his wireless speakers. He hadn't gone as far as vacuuming, but he had straightened the fold in the dining room rug. His touch was all over the house.

He raised his chin. "What?" He couldn't help the defensiveness that infused his tone.

She looked around one more time. "Dinner smells good." He relaxed as she walked toward the kitchen and jolted when she grabbed him on the way past. She laughed at his surprise and pulled him around in a quick two-step circle. "It's great in here. You make this dumb house feel like home."

There it went. His heart, flying from his chest and winging its way around the room. He caught her close and continued their dance, spinning her in circles that ended with them in the kitchen.

"Wait right there." He popped the bread in the oven and slipped his arm back around her waist. The music had changed to an Amalia

Rodrigues fado and their dance followed the beat in tight circles. At the end of the song, he leaned in and nipped her lower lip. She shifted against him and he settled in for a long, luxurious welcome home kiss. His insides sparked, aroused by her lips and tongue against his, her nipples against his chest, and the long, slight curve of her back and hips.

Garlic scent reminded him of the bread and he pulled away. She leaned against the kitchen island.

Stew dished, bread cut, meal dispatched, he steered her to the bedroom. She stretched out on the exposed sheets.

He sat on the edge of the bed and looked at his knees. Even in winter and spring, he had a bit of a tan line across his thighs. Bike shorts, swim trunks, whatever. He tanned easily and lost color slowly. Hairy thighs, manly enough, not that he had to be some particular amount manly. His crotch still looked wrong to him, even after all these years. There would always be a little surprise, a little discomfort and aggravation that he didn't have a cock and balls.

And now he was in bed with a dyke who wouldn't be all that interested in a cock and balls she couldn't pick out herself. What a mess. What did she think of him?

"What are you thinking?" Her voice drifted to him.

An attempt at a smile twisted, so he gave it up. He swiveled on the edge of the bed and looked at her. She lay there with one arm behind her head on the pillow, the other on her belly.

"I've never gone for boyish." One of her eyebrows flew up. "With women, it's been plush, lush Venuses. With genderqueer and cis guys, they've all been bulky."

Her hand stroked her belly. "Well, I'm not boyish. This is a woman's body, so it's womanly." The edge in her voice told him this was a sensitive subject.

"So it is." He shook his head. "I guess you've heard that before. Sorry. I didn't think about it."

She shrugged but didn't reply.

"I was thinking about my own body dysmorphia, how I'm still surprised, after all this time, that I don't have a penis. And wondering how much of your attraction to me is contingent on the fact that I don't."

She sat upright. "Not what I thought was coming."

"Kerala, you know that I love you." That wasn't so hard. "But I don't know much about how you feel about me. I don't know what you like and don't like, besides liking my cooking and disliking my need for you."

She rubbed a hand over his bare shoulder, a move more comradely than loverly. "I don't know how I'd react to your penis, if you had one. I started liking you long before I put any thought into what was in your pants. The way you do gender thrills me. You're living proof that masculinity is more than acting tough and rejecting anything remotely soft or giving. Your gender identity and presentation are important parts of what I dig about you. You brought up body dysmorphia and I won't say you're wrong to feel how you feel, but your body is perfect to me. Your textures and smells and responses turn me on so hard, partly because of what feels to me like a complicated blend of male and female. Your mannerisms and how you dress are pretty masculine, overall, and I'm comfortable with men on that level. What you do that thrills me, that's warmed me up and made me give a shit about you past playing around? It's how you act from the heart, from the part of you that's not adopting masculinity or policing femininity. You cook because you like it and you're an engineer because you like it and you switch in bed because you like it all."

Ravi took a deep, careful breath, hoping to control the quiver in his chest. He opened his mouth, but words wouldn't come.

She leaned her head on his shoulder, her hair sliding across his back. She nuzzled him, kissed him. He closed his eyes at the uncharacteristic gentleness, basking in the feeling that she cared for him. He wanted so much more. A declaration of love. A promise of home and family and a fool-proof plan for keeping them together for the rest of their lives.

He swallowed against the thickness in his throat and raised a hand to stroke her bare back. She didn't know how he experienced each moment. He was still guarded, still monitored himself for girly mannerisms. Still thought about how he looked sitting naked on the side of a bed with a short-haired, short-bodied dynamo of a woman curled into him.

Desperate to obliterate that voice, that critical eye, he turned to her, pressed her back on the bed, and reared over her. She put her hand on his chest and locked her elbow to push him away. "Hold on there. I'm not done."

"What?" Her body beckoned, the perfect place to hide.

"Look at me."

He did as she asked and met her eyes across the distance she kept between them. Her hair spread across the pillow and her eyes melted in the glow of the bedside lamp. A little smile played at her lips and her neck looked as relaxed as he'd ever seen it.

It moved when she swallowed and pinked when she spoke. "I want to be with you, Ravi. We can figure out what that means as we go along, but there it is."

His muscles went slack, tension gone in an instant. Her arm folded under his weight and he pressed his face to the curve where her neck met her shoulder. Less than he craved, but more than he'd hoped for.

He'd take what he could get.

❖

Kerala stood on site with no one else around. She'd even beat Jack to work.

She needed the privacy. Ravi was stirring her up, pushing her to change things she thought were just fine. Compost? She didn't garden. Why would she start composting?

Each bit she opened up left her more vulnerable than she expected.

At the same time, he was on that damn laptop constantly. Sitting around with a broken hand while he buried himself in his work had frustrated her no end.

It was good to be back to work.

In all honesty, construction was a thankless profession. She lived for good days or just a good moment here or there. The schedule for workers was restricted for safety and accuracy, but she worked dawn to dusk. She saw the horizon with its golden sunrise necklace and the position of the sun told her how long she'd been working.

The automatic brew function on Ravi's coffee machine sometimes woke her a few minutes early. It clicked on and her eyes sprang open as though that quiet electronic switch ran directly to her body. Other days, the alarm clock would get off a peal before she slapped it. She kissed Ravi's shoulder as she untangled herself from the covers. She wasn't quiet, but Ravi didn't awaken without a brass band to kick his ass. The kiss she gave Ravi was her own, something she did to promise herself that she'd be warm and comfortable in his arms again at day's end.

For a few moments, before the phone started ringing, her head was clear. She tried to stretch those few minutes as long as she could.

There was more to do than fourteen daylight hours would allow. She had to be able to split her attention four, five times in a row and still bring herself back, prioritized interruption by interruption, to the original task. By the end of the day, rapid-fire meals and orders and decisions had all been relegated to the back of her mind, while the next day loomed too close before her.

Then, when that next day waited to start, she could find that moment of peace again. Except that Ravi intruded into her quiet times. She no longer had her old single-minded focus. She needed a time, a place to herself.

She banished Ravi. She banished the work ahead of her. She stood on the west coast of the Island of Hawai'i and let the sun rise over her shoulders to glisten on the salt that rimed the black rock.

It was enough. It had to be.

❖

Kerala shifted her head on Ravi's shoulder, moving her hair from under her cheek. She drew her hand up his belly and caressed the smooth skin of his ribs beyond the hair line. He twitched when she wandered close to his ticklish side and she considered a little cruelty.

Her pleased lassitude didn't lend itself to that sort of romp, so she moved her hand to his hip. Soft, before the rougher hair on his thighs. His big bush started a couple inches down his inner thighs and traveled his abdomen in a treasure trail. She'd seen that hair when they'd gone swimming after her accident.

Not accident. Attack.

When had Ravi become a source of comfort? Whenever it had started, she couldn't deny that he made her feel safer, happier. Better. Her hair moved under his hand and she felt his fingers sift through the light strands. "What are you thinking about?"

The question sounded absent-minded.

"I was thinking about the first time I saw your treasure trail, swimming. And how good you make me feel. Safe and comfortable." He squeezed her shoulder, rubbed her upper arm. "That's nice. Not very sexy, but nice."

She tugged his belly hair. "Hey, what are you saying? You want to go again?"

His shoulder moved under her head in a shrug. "I could go for more."

She pushed herself on her elbow and looked at him. Ravi lay on his back with his eyes closed, cat-cream smile on his sexy lips. She'd thought she was too relaxed for more, but impulse told her to nip at his lower lip. That sculpted, firm flesh between her teeth and on the tip of her tongue put to rest her thoughts of a nap. Her clit stiffened in a sensation that made her groan against his mouth.

She shifted her legs and, sure enough, she turned slippery. "I'm going to fuck your mouth," she said in his ear. His eyes opened and the pleasure in his expression made her harder and softer, squirmy and stretchy. She tossed her leg over him and straddled his belly, knees by his armpits. He loved it when she stroked his neck and shoulders, so she slid her hands up and caressed him, twisting her hips all the while to tease them both. He stroked the curve of her waist from her lower back all the way around to her hipbones.

A push on his shoulders made him wriggle away from the headboard. She knee-walked along his torso and over his arms, pausing a moment with them pinned. He breathed in through his nose and the flush on his cheeks spread across his face. She arched closer so he could smell her salty lubrication. She lost control of her momentum when he raised his arms and tipped her forward.

She caught herself on the headboard and settled over his seeking mouth, encompassing his nose and cheeks and chin. He burrowed between her lips with a few shakes of his head and drew the flat of his tongue up her whole vulva. She groaned and slid back so she could see the glisten on his face and the gleam in his eyes. He stared at her until she brought her pussy back, just within reach if he thrust his tongue out.

Of course, he did and she slid right onto it, his slippery tongue a little coarse on top, just enough to intensify the sensation. His chin hit her behind and her ass flexed. She circled on his tongue, wringing a response from every nerve ending she possessed there, before she gasped. "Make it flat again." Her voice dropped and he obeyed.

She got a good grip on her headboard and rubbed herself on his tongue. All over his face. He lapped as she moved and the rhythm they established made her quiver for uncounted minutes. Too indirect to get her off. Too strong to let her go. Ravi's hands were on her hips, though she couldn't remember when that happened. He changed his tongue somehow, made it different in a way that cupped her clit tighter, bumped it harder, when she tipped her hips back. She cried out and slid forward, where he lapped at her opening, and back again.

She settled on his pulsing tongue and let him get suction. He wanted her to come, but her body was in no hurry for yet another orgasm. She didn't know if she had enough tension left for a great release, but Ravi worked her expertly, wound her tighter than she thought she'd go. He wanted her to come, and she wanted to come for him.

She picked up the pulse of his tongue with a short thrust of her hips, fucking his face seriously now, forgetting to leave his nose free so he could breathe, forgetting everything in her pursuit of the cataclysm he'd built in her. He reached around her hips and plucked her nipples. The squeeze and pull unzipped her from breast to pussy and she flowed, muscles convulsing in liquid pulses.

She rode the orgasms as long as she could stand it, then slapped a hand on the pillow next to his head. He knew her signals and released his suction, left his tongue soft and wet for her to wring out the last shivers against. Torso bowed over him, slack-muscled and gasping, she felt a rush of love fill her. Not just wonder over the amazing sex. The sensation was a complicated heat in her chest and throat made of his desire and thoughtfulness, his knowledge of her and desire to use that knowledge for her pleasure.

❖

Ravi sipped at his smoky scotch and water and enjoyed the spectacle of Kerala at the dark wooden bar, arguing roofs with a woman they'd just met. The woman wore loose, flowing pants that reminded him of Kerala's nightwear, but in a tropical explosion of color that he couldn't imagine Kerala choosing. Her hair flowed down her back, kinked as though braided all day. She worked for another contractor and was officially the competition, but it didn't appear to confound their new friendship. Kerala had lit up at the realization that she wasn't the only female construction worker in Hawai'i.

The bar eschewed grasses and coconut fronds in its decoration. It leaned toward paniolo: scarred floor, dim lighting, rough-hewn wooden tables with bark still on the edges, and plain stools. Nahoa shared the tall table and turned a beer in circles. At twenty-six, he was still growing into his adult body. If Jack was right, his shoulders would keep getting broader and he'd eventually mass as much as Hekili. Ravi could imagine the multiple phases of powerful attractiveness.

Time and familiarity failed to temper his striking beauty. It gained depth with hints of the thoughts behind that gamine grin. Pleasing him held a tug and satisfaction. There was a sexual tinge to it, but the dominant flavor of the attraction and admiration was like a crush on a friend.

The better they got to know each other, the closer they became beyond any shared relationship with Kerala, the stronger grew Ravi's sense that Nahoa was a poetic soul. A person who felt deeply and strongly, who laughed and played in public but who raged and wept in secret. Their conversations about colonialism did nothing to dispel that sense.

He fingered the faceted glass. "Ho'oponopono worked for us, yes. But I wonder how it goes when someone holds ill will and won't let go of it. The US justice system goes too far the other way, with every little disagreement turning someone into a criminal."

"Incarceration is a plague in the US. A targeted epidemic. Ho'oponopono may not turn someone into a nicer person, but it's better to start there. Not that the old ways always did. In kapu, there were things that had set punishments, including death." Nahoa shook his head. "I'm not sorry the punishments are less drastic now, but some good tools got thrown away with the rest."

"India has some of the same problems. The traditional methods were replaced by British colonialism." Ravi sipped his whisky and glanced over at Kerala, still in animated conversation.

"Not in the same way, though."

"What do you mean?"

"Colonialism has had different effects in India, most African nations, Indonesia, and other parts of the South Seas than in the Americas, Hawai'i, and Australia. French Algeria. South Africa. Settler colonialism requires the genocide of all the original inhabitants, clearing the land for the settlers. After centuries of extermination, Native Americans are a tiny minority in their ancestral lands and schools teach about them like they're history. They're erased from reality and kept under the paternalistic thumb of the Bureau for Indian Affairs. They're fighting not to disappear altogether."

"There are a lot more Hawaiians."

Nahoa's voice tightened, as did his hand on his beer bottle. "Because it became unpopular to slaughter natives wholesale. They're waiting for us to die off. Our culture was brutalized along with our people, made illegal, mocked, and replaced. When my parents' generation tried to reinvigorate it in the seventies, when they tried to create a Hawaiian Renaissance, it got commodified and sold to the people who infantilized them and patted them on the head while thanking them for the authentic experience. Your Hindi culture is warped by colonialism, yes, but it has a stronghold in its own home."

Ravi pulled at his lower lip. "Settler colonialism versus, what?"

"Extractive colonialism. But they're not mutually exclusive."

He flashed through his understanding of India's history and compared it to what Nahoa had said. "Hindi appropriation has been going on for centuries."

"Most Hindu people aren't harmed by that in the least." Nahoa watched him as he spoke.

"Hindu is the religion. If you mean Indian citizens or expats, you can say Indian or Desi." He spoke absently while he worked through the implications. "I guess you're right. Maybe. But I grew up in the US, Nahoa. I know what it is to be brown in a white world."

"But you also know what it is to be stereotyped as a good scientist. You also know what it is to have narratives from your history, intact, and a huge country with over a billion people who share your culture."

"My culture is mixed. It's not that simple." The tinge of defensiveness in his own voice alerted Ravi to a touchy point.

"Look up cultural wounding. Read Dr. Maria Yellow Horse Brave Heart on the subject."

"Give me a second. I'm thinking through what you're saying, and I recognize some truth. I'm also feeling kind of attacked, though. We're not competing."

"Of course not. I'm just pointing out some of the ways India and Hawai'i can't be used to understand each other." He sighed. "I'm mad, but not at you."

"I just…I never heard it like this before. Thinking about a billion Indians worldwide."

"Compared to less than three hundred thousand Hawaiians, mostly hapa, mixed, and we lead the US in infant mortality, abuse, drug use, and early death."

"Holy shit."

"No one ever looked at me and assumed I could be an electrical engineer."

Ravi smiled. "Even you, Nahoa? You're kind of a special case around here, it seems. Everybody's favorite, bright, attractive. I have a hard time believing you didn't get some encouraging messages as you were growing up."

Nahoa put his hands up. "Don't put that special case bullshit on me, Ravi. Yeah, I got more encouragement than the classmates who looked like me, but it felt precarious. Since I didn't know what I did to get that treatment, I didn't know how to avoid losing it. Then later, it just seemed gross to differentiate between me and my friends based on, what, looks?"

Ravi tipped his head. "You know it's more than that."

"I don't." Nahoa slipped off his stool and stood at the table, shifting in place. "I just know it's ridiculous. I'm not special or wonderful or whatever you're getting at. Not more than other Hawaiians, who get nothing but messages of worthlessness and hopelessness."

"I'm sorry. You're right. I mean, you are uniquely wonderful, Nahoa, but I know that doesn't mean you were able to skip the experience of racism."

Nahoa's discomfort flattened, but it didn't disappear. It was as though Ravi could see him put it away, hide it behind the mask. He couldn't figure out why Nahoa would back off. He was fierce enough when it came to the systemic mistreatment of Native Hawaiians, but he just twisted with some inner pain when he became the focus.

Ravi let him get away with it. A bar, mixed tourists and locals, wasn't the best place to push a friend to open what must be an agonizing wound. He wondered, though.

Kerala showed up with more beers and another scotch. Her expression was morose. "She's with one of the mainland companies and they leave in a week. Damn it. Where are all the women on this island?"

Nahoa made a big show of looking around at the crowd, more female than male, and started ribbing her. Ravi let the mood change around him, still thinking about Nahoa's Hawai'i.

❖

Ravi slapped the wooden spoon on the counter and sprayed hot sticky tomato sauce on his hand. "Fuck!"

"You okay?" Kerala asked over the phone.

"Yeah, burned my hand a little. About an hour before you get home, then?"

"Yep. I could spend another ten hours here and not get caught up, but that's how it goes."

Ravi bit his tongue on a sharp comment. He'd swallowed more than one critical response to watching Kerala shred herself for this job day after day. The mixture of locked-in scheduling and frantic catch-up-and-wait pacing seemed like a mess compared to the orderly manufacturing processes of the solar panel plant.

Kerala's life was not about long stretches of empty time to fill. She left before he was awake and came back after dark. Whatever it took, he made sure they shared dinner.

It never hurt a pasta sauce to simmer. He put the lid on and turned the gas to low.

The computer drew him, but the pressing issues at Sol Volt needed his presence, not just e-mails and phone calls. He couldn't win over the shareholder block that seemed to hate him by leaving his office unoccupied and letting his assistant take the bulk of the daily work.

He didn't want to think about it. He didn't want to think that he remained in Hawai'i against his best interests, against his duty to Sol Volt, because he wanted to win her love.

He would do anything to have it. And chasing her just drove her away.

He needed to fly back, the sooner the better, and take control of his company. In the meantime, he would plug away at the board of directors and get ahead of any possible complaint. He punished himself with the weekly finance report while he waited for her, again.

Kerala pulled up in front of the house. As always, she entered through the back door. He imagined her stripping in the mud room and walking naked into the bathroom. She would pull the brace off her arm and start the shower.

Frustration roiled in him and he stripped as he walked down the hallway. He joined her in the shower, pulled her tight to his chest with an arm around her waist.

She stretched into him. "Hey."

Her firm ass rubbed against the tops of his thighs. He bent her forward and pushed her under the spray of the nozzle until her neck emerged from the soap. He bit her there, where she was warm and alive under the flow of water. He bit along her neck to her shoulder and pulled the resilient muscle between his lips in a quick suck. She groaned, low.

His hands moved over her breasts, her belly, tangled in her pubic hair and pressed in. One hand settled at her nipple, tugging it as she liked, and the other set a slow pace between her legs. She softened and began to yearn.

He wanted her, but he didn't want her to look at him. His emotions were too close to the surface. She would see his love and pity him for it. So he shoved her over and lifted her hips.

She moaned and arched her back in response. She braced her good hand on the tile wall and wiggled back and forth. He gripped and massaged her hips while her body begged for his.

He slicked a finger into her. The water flowed down her back, fell over her ribs, and ran between her butt cheeks, rinsing his finger as he withdrew it.

Without any more waiting, without teasing either of them, he pushed three fingers into her soft, grasping, moving pussy. He wasted no time, setting a fast rhythm that made her pant and shove back at him. She ground into him with all the considerable strength in her arm and back. He fucked her like they were fighting, like there would be a winner. He fucked her like someone was going to get hurt.

She brought her hand to her clit and he thrust faster. The spray washed over her shoulders and flowed from the ends of her hair. When she came, she locked her knees and shuddered her orgasm.

He saw her reach for the wall, but he didn't want her balanced. He didn't want her invulnerable, independent. He pulled her back on his fingers over and over, keeping her from the wall and pulling her to her toes. She tensed under his hands. He fucked her with such power and fury that her body overcame her surprise. She arched her torso, rising without changing the angle of her hips. She came again, with a sound he'd never heard from her, out of control and primal.

He watched her lose herself and watched her start to come out of the trance, still moving his fingers in her. It pushed him over the edge and he turned his hand to his own clit, coming fast and hard.

After dinner, after Kerala dozed in front of the TV and Ravi read the *Journal of Solar Energy Engineering*, she led him in to bed. She cuddled close and he struggled not to hold on too tightly.

❖

Kerala radioed Nahoa to meet her in the office trailer. He radioed back that he'd be there as soon as he finished instructing Stevens on what to look for while he excavated. Ravi had forwarded an e-mail from his friend, the photo hacker. She stared at it on her computer monitor while she scratched under her brace, a real improvement over the cast. The thing had smelled horrible by the third day, when she'd stalked into the orthopedist's office. She liked the lightweight brace much better, though its pads got a bit rank each day. It held her hand and wrist still, and that's all she needed.

When Nahoa came in, she kept staring. She could feel the breeze off the stall door as it swung by her and the snap of the bone in her hand as she'd tapped the screen to take the shot.

"Take a look at this," she said.

He came around the desk and stiffened. His silence lasted long enough that she looked at him.

"What is it?"

"I know him." He went back around her desk and collapsed in a chair. "Remember, back when this all started and I said I was going to find my old best friend?"

"Yeah, I remember."

"That's him."

She waited for more, glancing between the cleaned-up and stabilized photo and Nahoa's pained face. Finally, she said, "But you couldn't find him."

"No. He's been avoiding me. I thought it was just the history between us. We haven't spoken since we were sixteen."

"Do you think you can track him down?"

"I can try. Now that you have this pic, Walter will help too. He must have figured, but he wouldn't name names because he didn't know for sure."

"Fuck Walter. I'm glad we worked things out, but my broken hand is partly on him if he knew and didn't say."

"I'm going to ask you a huge favor, Kel." She could tell what was coming and pursed her lips. "Will you let me find him before you go to the cops? I need to talk to him, in private. I can find out why he's doing this. I can make him stop."

She let her head fall back against her chair. Thoughts and feelings whirled at hurricane force. Nahoa wouldn't let her come to any more harm, but was that good enough? How did she want this guy punished?

Her hand throbbed, moderating the satisfaction of having broken his nose. She'd paid dearly for that shot.

"What's his name?"

Nahoa didn't hesitate, though she hadn't answered his request. "Pauahi Māhoe. He sleeps on the beach most nights. He doesn't have a home, but someone will spot him, sooner or later."

The feelings shook out more as a need to know than a need to see the guy in jail. "I won't take this to Alakai. I want you to find out why he's been doing this, make sure there's no one else involved, and tell me everything. I don't know if I can forgive him like I did Walter, but I'd rather know why than see him go to jail protesting his innocence with a public defender as a mouthpiece."

"I'll take care of it."

She shook her head slowly. "I don't know if I can let you, Nahoa. I don't know if I can stay out of it. Tell me what you find out and I'll tell you what I want to do about it."

## CHAPTER FIFTEEN

Excavation was like building in reverse. It might seem to the uninitiated that it was destruction, tearing up the land. But excavation built the shape into which one built the house.

Ravi had wanted the koa tree preserved in place, but it made parts of the foundation inaccessible. It might have died from the dirt kicked up during construction. It was better for the tree to just get it out of the way.

Ravi had her thinking like that. For the tree's own good.

He was rubbing off on her. She picked up his less-technical periodicals and flipped through them. There were amazing advances being made in power technologies, some by his company. Solar, wind, water, geothermal. She'd never paid attention to geothermal energy until reading an article by some researchers at MIT, Ravi's alma mater.

Of course, once the idea was planted, she saw references to it everywhere. Some wanted to tap the volcano for geothermal power, but the plan was ridiculously complicated. The power would go to Oahu via multiple underwater and overland stages. Hawaiians who were all about Pele said it was stealing the life from the goddess. The concept of a goddess who could be sapped of strength sounded Greek to her.

So there they were, digging an enormous amount of ground to transplant a tree.

Stevens avoided koa roots and ignored the finer roots belonging to the lilikoʻi vine. He was about two-thirds of the way around when he stopped and turned off his motor. Kerala started his way.

"Shit, Kerala, there wasn't a speck of black sand. I don't know what happened, but I don't think I disturbed it much." Stevens hopped off the excavator and joined her at the edge.

Kerala looked into his trench and saw what had brought Stevens to a halt.

Bones.

There didn't appear to be any in the excavator bucket, but the soil crumbled away from the roots below. The kid had good eyesight. He'd seen through the veil of liliko'i rootlets, a fine mesh that bound the soil, to the wrinkled knob behind. She crouched and squinted into the dark hole, shading her eyes against the tropical sun. The grisly knowledge that there were more bones gave her belly a bounce. It didn't look clean, the rounded edges of the joint showing some kind of clinging tissue. Unless that was all liliko'i?

"It's bones for sure. Not what I'd expected, though."

Stevens moved closer. "What the hell? That doesn't look right." He turned in a circle. "Nahoa!"

She looked at him. "You've found remains before?"

"Yeah. Twice. Not all grown into a plant, though." He turned again and stopped when he saw Nahoa headed their way.

"Shit. I think I see tendons or ligaments or something." She crouched to get a closer look. "Nahoa. We found bones."

"Want me to make the calls?" Nahoa stepped to the edge of the hole and froze.

"I got it." Kerala flipped open her phone and dialed Mālama Construction.

"Kel. I have to go."

She looked over at Nahoa, who still stared at the bones. "You look terrible. Are you sick?"

"Yeah. I…"

"That's fine. Get out of here. As a matter of fact, everyone can go. Jack!"

She stopped all work and sent everyone but Stevens on an early and extended lunch. After talking to Joy, she called the police and Historical Preservation in quick succession.

Then she waited.

The Hawaiian Island Burial Council and the state Historical Preservation officer arrived quickly, and so did the uniformed police officers. Everyone wanted more facts than she had, but she explained in detail what she knew. They questioned Stevens as well, and she kept an eye on how they treated her man.

After two hours, Detective Thomas Alakai appeared over the ridge separating the work site from the road. He stood atop the half-made soil of the old lava flow and scanned the scene. The official types had all been eager to get a close look at the remains.

She turned, hands on hips, and stretched her jaw and neck muscles. Alakai headed her way with an unhesitating stride over the uneven ground and she said, "Long time no see, stranger."

Alakai looked over the operation from behind his dark brown lenses. Squabbling men clumped into several contentious groups around the site. "There won't be a piece of evidence they haven't trampled."

Cop sunglasses, cop posture, even a cop voice. "What are you doing here?"

Alakai turned to face her, his shoulders and hips turning together as though one welded piece. "If the body's been dead less than fifty years, it's mine."

"You think it's new?" She turned to survey the scene with fresh disquiet.

"Won't be able to say for sure until we've had a forensic archaeologist out, but the men believe that it's a more recent death."

"And you're on the job because you're on the other case?"

Alakai's lips quirked, his eyes still hard to see. "Yeah."

Kerala waited for more and didn't get it. "Are you going to question me? Question Stevens?"

"Stevens was running the excavator?"

"Yeah."

"No. I'll read the statements the men have taken and call you in if I have further questions."

"Great." Kerala's flat tone expressed her exasperation.

"It is time to bring some order." The people below had sorted themselves by organization. "They're done fighting for the moment. They'll be ready for someone to pull some facts from this mess."

Kerala scrambled after Alakai, heading downhill to the precise-edged hole that became jagged at the point where the excavator blade was still buried in the dirt. She stopped on the house site.

Alakai passed through the gathered officials like a spoon through batter. The swirls followed him to the edge of the hole and surrounded him with demands. After a quick look at the remains, Alakai reversed the flow by walking back through them and joining Kerala where Ravi's house was to be built.

Everyone focused on Alakai when he stepped onto a small hummock and lifted his hands. "Hear me well, people. This is my crime scene and any person who touches anything will be charged with destruction of evidence." He stripped his sunglasses off and pointed them at the assemblage. "My men will question each of you, and I want independent, accurate statements about every single aspect of this scene when you arrived and everything you've done since then. We might, if we're lucky, be able to separate your contamination of the crime scene from any actual evidence remaining."

A chill hit her warm back. Crime scene.

Murder.

❖

At the sound of Kerala's truck, Ravi leaned back in the office chair at her desk. Kerala was home hours early. She entered from the mud room and started the shower. Whatever it was, it couldn't be too bad.

He'd been practicing how to tell her he was leaving, though he was almost certain she didn't need such delicate handling. Would she even be upset at all?

She appeared in the guest room doorway naked and squeezed her hair in a towel.

"What's up?" he asked.

"Stevens found a body digging up the koa tree."

"Wow. Okay. The guys had me half-convinced they'd find remains. I wonder how Walter and Nahoa will respond. Maybe they're in good enough condition to do DNA testing. Walter would love to have solid evidence that they belong to his ancestors. Well, I don't know if he's that worried about evidence, but I like data."

"It was creepier than I'd expected. They shut down the site for now. They think the body's fresh." She draped the towel over her shoulder and shook her hair out.

"What do you mean fresh? Like someone who died recently?"

"Yeah. Alakai called it a crime scene." She went to the bedroom and he followed.

"Huh." He hung her towel in the bathroom and went back to watch her dress. "Maybe someone flipping the bird at the funeral home industry and doing a natural burial for a loved one? Maybe that's who planted the lilikoʻi." Strange thing to hope for, but it was better than the alternative.

"Does it creep you out?" She pulled on light cotton pajama pants and a ribbed cotton shirt.

"The body itself?" He shrugged and sat on the bed. "Not so much. I don't believe in an essence that hangs around a body after death. Even their last living stem cells die within a couple weeks. I try to be sensitive to the feelings other people have about human remains, but that's a cultural respect issue and nothing to do with the actual people who lived in the body. I'm on the anthropologist's side here."

"Yeah, me too, but I figure anthropologists are doing what most deceased people would want. Renewing their legacy, allowing them to communicate to later generations and pass along whatever knowledge they held. This is different."

"Do they think it was...murder?" There, he said it.

Kerala winced. "The initial estimate was that the person had been in that ground for seven to fourteen years. They're exhuming the body so they can determine cause of death and narrow the timing down."

"Willoughby."

"Right? That was my first thought too." She paced the clean bedroom floor. "Even if it was some natural burial, this will put the job behind."

"I'm not worried about that." He had bigger problems at work.

"Maybe you're not." Kerala's anger cut into his abstraction. "But this is my job and my reputation on the line."

"If it's Willoughby's body, the next question is how did it get there? Did he keel over and get covered over time or did someone bury him there?"

"There's no keeping the cops out of it now. I guess it's up to them to figure that out."

"That's good. I mean, it's probably for the best."

She raised an eyebrow at him. "I thought you'd be a lot more upset."

"I'm sorry, but it's heating up at Sol Volt. I have to go back to California."

❖

Kerala stopped pacing, an unfamiliar panic clanging in her chest. She hadn't noticed how tense Ravi was. "You're leaving? Are you coming back?"

"The board has called an emergency meeting. The new shareholder block is threatening to unseat the board of directors if they don't put my proposal to rest. They want me fired."

"Well hell, Ravi."

"I don't know when I'll be able to get away again. This is big, Kerala. If I can't straighten out the problems in Watsonville, this house will be the least of my worries."

The man who'd attacked her was still out there and the cops were holding up construction because of a dead body that may well belong to the previous owner of Ravi's land. And Ravi was disappearing. "I understand that you have to be there, but it doesn't change that I'm being left with a bag of shit here."

"What do you want me to do about that, Kerala?" He got up and went to the kitchen.

She followed him. "I don't know. I was starting to think of us as a team out here."

He stirred soup in a slow cooker. "A team. Not lovers."

"Well, of course we're lovers."

"Can we keep this up long-distance?"

She studied the taut muscles in his shoulders and the jerkiness of his motions as he leaned over to taste the broth. "Yeah, I guess. We kept in contact through the planning phases of this house and we'll go back to e-mail and phone calls." Impatient with herself for caring, she brushed the discomfort aside. "We built a good working relationship that way. We know each other much better now. It should be even easier to communicate."

He turned and questioned what she had avoided. "But can we have a romantic relationship from two thousand miles away?"

"I'm not romantic at the best of times. I certainly don't know how to be romantic with an ocean between us. We make good friends, stellar sex aside."

He turned the gas off and slumped against the counter. His long, dark eyes were shadowed. "This house will be built—you'll see to that. Everything is on track and you don't need me to be a part of the process anymore. Contact me when you need to and send me regular reports and it'll be fine."

She didn't like the direction he was taking. She cradled her braced hand in her other arm and maintained her silence.

"But friends? I can be close to you or I can be far, far away." He pressed his lips together to steady them. "I love you and you offer me less affection than you show Bogart."

She had no answer to that. She made a reckless wish to be the same person she was before he arrived in her life. Now she wasn't sure that was possible.

Ravi's face hardened over the course of her silence. He stood upright, shoulders back, and pointed the spoon at her. "All right. If that's what you want." He poured soup into a bowl and set it on the table for her. She stood, frozen in her wish that things go back to normal, until he left the room and she heard the zipper.

She dragged her feet to the door of her bedroom. He shoved dirty clothes into the front pocket of his luggage.

She wanted to ignore him.

She wanted to stop him.

She wanted to tear his clothes off and seduce him into staying.

He brushed past her to get his laptop from the dining room and she followed him as far as the door.

She wanted him to throw it all aside for her, and she wanted to follow wherever he went.

When the upright, sturdy center of her being flexed, when she felt the urge to go with him and be the person he wanted, it was the last straw. She couldn't give him that, her core, couldn't turn him into her axis. No matter what else she lost, she couldn't lose herself. She turned away.

She achieved a small distance, enough space between her and her feelings that she could walk him to the door.

Ravi stepped from the bright house into the peek-a-boo stars behind the patchy clouds in the night sky. She drew the crisp air into her lungs and waited to see what would shape that chill. Words blocked her breath as Ravi waited for her to say something, anything that would change his course of action. Finally, silently, he got in the rental car and drove away.

Hot tears dissolved the barrier in her throat.

"I love you."

## Chapter Sixteen

Ravi stretched his neck. He'd paid too much for a mediocre last-minute hotel room and would be flying back coach unless some high roller decided to extend their vacation. He looked around the beige hall of the cop shop and got himself a paper cone of water. He'd spent the last ten minutes getting thirstier and wishing he had a travel mug to drink from.

The police station lent itself to slouching. The atmosphere depressed him, but he figured he should check in with Alakai before leaving. He wanted to know the status of the investigation, but he also needed to know that he wouldn't complicate anything by leaving. Anything further.

He drank a few cones of water. He considered folding the cone to use later but gave in to the ease of crumpling it and tossing it in the trash with a dozen others.

Alakai pushed open the front door and entered with a blast of heat. "Ravi, thanks for coming in, but I don't need to talk to you yet. We're still sorting through the soil and remains and there's no word on when that'll be completed." He waved Ravi along and led the way down the hall.

Ravi trailed him. "I'm checking in because there's a meltdown in California. I have to fly back right away."

Alakai slowed and stopped. He turned, his face impassive. "We find a dead body on your land and you want to leave the island?"

"Come on, Kerala said it was just bones. I haven't owned the land for long enough to bury someone that decayed. Besides, if I were a murderer, I'd be seriously dumb to hire people to dig right in that area."

Alakai narrowed his eyes. "So this is a courtesy visit?"

"Just letting you know how to get in touch with me while I'm gone, in case you need any permissions or have forms or whatever you do." Ravi paused. "Why are you on this case? Do you cover homicides as well as assault and stalking?"

Alakai ignored the questions. "The duty officer called me away from the morgue for this?"

Ravi put his hands up. "I had nothing to do with that. I just asked for you and told them who I was. Have you identified the body?"

"I have no information for you at this time. Leave your contact info at the front desk. I'm going back to the morgue."

Ravi watched Alakai stomp back down the hall and sighed. That hadn't taken long. He wouldn't miss his flight. Maybe he could sleep on the way home.

Home made him think of Kerala and his eyes filled just as he reached the front desk. The duty officer didn't seem surprised. Guess he wasn't the first person to cry at the police station.

❖

Ravi dropped his luggage just inside his office door. As exhausted as he was, work demanded that he get started right away.

He breathed the air of the office he hadn't seen in well over a month. It smelled neutral, cool, and clean. He dropped into the chair behind his desk and fell back into the brooding that had occupied him on the ride from the airport.

He reached out, teetering on the edge of making himself stop. He picked up the phone, though, and listened to the dial tone. Punching in her number was a step he couldn't take.

Damn it. He needed to give up on her. His mom knew Kerala wasn't going to change. He couldn't even blame Kerala for failing to open to him. He hurt, but he knew why. He had anticipated the pain so well that it was familiar when it washed over him.

Rather than put the handset back, he dialed Nahoa.

"Ravi?"

"Hey, Nahoa."

"Where are you?"

"California. I'm in my office, trying to focus, but I'm worried about Kerala. I'm sure she wants to get right back to work. Do you think there will be any fallout?"

"What do you mean?"

"What's wrong, Nahoa?"

"Why? I mean, everything's wrong. His body was mostly bone, with a little bit of shriveled tissue."

"They know who it was?"

"Nobody has said. Why, have you heard something?"

"You said his, so I thought…it doesn't matter. How are you keeping yourself busy?"

"I can't…Ravi, I can't talk. I have to find Pauahi."

"Who?"

"I have to go."

"Okay, Nahoa…" Ravi tried to sound reassuring, but Nahoa had already hung up.

Well. He hadn't expected that. Nahoa was a lot more freaked out about the whole thing than he or Kerala.

Who was Pauahi?

❖

Kerala watched Detective Alakai bump down the driveway and park behind her truck. Five days since they'd found the body, and he'd let them get back to work the day before.

Now what?

She strolled in his direction, in no hurry to make his life easier. She could only hope he had some solid information.

"Can we sit and talk?" He asked politely, but his expression was hard. The guy who'd leaned toward being kind to her in the hospital was back to being his real self. She led the way to her trailer without comment.

She moved behind her desk and sat. "What do you know?"

"I know what happened to Vincent Willoughby."

"Shit." She let her head fall back against her chair and then straightened. "Do you think Ravi's in danger?"

He shrugged. "Not in California. All the signs point to this being local."

"What can you tell me?" She tried to pull the information from him with her will and was surprised when he spilled.

"Willoughby's money separated him from people. The investigation when he disappeared turned up no one who wished him ill but also no one who wished him well. No one stepped forward to lay claim to the man's estate. No one pushed the investigation and it lapsed, never closed. He had no will, so his property reverted to the state."

"You've been studying up."

"I never forgot."

"You had to know, just looking at the skeleton."

"The rough age fit. Of course, nothing is that simple. A forensic anthropologist flew over from Oahu and we untangled the skeleton from the roots of the liliko'i."

"Creepy job." Worry for herself, her crew, and Ravi made her jumpy.

"She was as fussy as a person building a ship in a bottle, but with gravitas. More serious about it than anyone else involved." Alakai shook his head. "The body hadn't been arranged in the hole. The placement of the bones told the anthropologist that it had been rolled in."

Kerala's stomach didn't heave, but something moved. The description was somehow more graphic than seeing it with her own eyes.

"When she got the skull free, cause of death was obvious to anybody who knows what a heavy object does to bone."

She tried to keep her voice steady. "Murder." So much for the hopes of a natural burial. Even with Willoughby's disappearance in the back of her mind, she'd hoped there would be another explanation.

"We confirmed it with dental records. Now I want to announce it to the crew."

"You don't think one of these guys killed Willoughby." Sheer disbelief kept her from being angry.

"I'll take the opportunity to see how they respond."

She stood abruptly. She left the trailer without making sure he followed and rounded up her crew.

Alakai gave them much less information than he'd given her. It didn't take long for the crew to get the point. He scanned the group as he spoke and Kerala did the same.

She would bet she could catch Jack in a lie ninety-nine times out of a hundred. The workers trusted him to tell them straight when something was coming down the pike and they always knew where they stood with him. He had no guile and no tolerance for bullshit, making him a great crew boss. It couldn't have been more obvious that he wasn't surprised about it being Willoughby's body.

He'd been around ten years ago. What had he known?

Nahoa didn't respond visibly, but he was at his most masked. She hadn't gotten ten words from him since Willoughby's body had been found. Jack told her he'd been hunting down an old friend while the job was on hold and she figured he meant Pauahi.

Her thinking slowed. If Pauahi had attacked her to stop her from finding the body, he must have known it was there. How would he have known unless he'd put it there? What had Pauahi gotten Nahoa caught up in?

Alakai finished simply. "I'll be in touch with each of you for separate statements."

Stevens whined. "I already told like six different people about finding him."

"And I have the records of those conversations. I won't call you in if you've already given the information I'm after."

Kerala spoke. "Any possibility these statements could be done after hours? The men don't get paid if they're not at work, and I'd hate for them to lose pay."

Alakai nodded, focused on Jack, who twisted his baseball cap in his hands. What a mess. Alakai left.

"All right, back to work. You know your tasks; get to them." Kerala waved the workers off. "Jack, with me."

She led the way, not looking back. She heard the heavy clomp of Jack's work boots and kept herself to a simmer. Not in front of the others.

She swung into the stifling office trailer and squeezed behind her desk. She threw herself back into the wheeled chair and heard the protesting squeak with some small satisfaction. She wanted to throw the chair, the desk, and her crew boss out the fucking window.

Too bad there was no more demo.

Jack stood just inside the door. When he got a look at her tight face, he closed the door and came to stand in front of her desk like a corporal about to be busted to private. She studied him, the sweat-matted hair, the streak of dirt he'd missed when he wiped his face with his handkerchief. The widespread legs and chest-out stance that looked braced for a punch. The eyes that focused a foot over her head.

"What the fuck do you think you're doing?"

Jack swallowed but didn't reply.

"I'd appreciate you letting me in on whatever had you out there squirming like a little boy who needed to pee." This unflattering description added a little color to Jack's face, but he continued to stare over her head, mouth pinched tight. "If you have information that would aid in this investigation, you'd better spit it out."

Kerala rose from her seat inch by inch, both fists on her desktop. "You can't hold out on me like this and go about your business. You have a responsibility to tell me anything that will affect this job. My job, your job, and the reputation of Mālama Construction depend on me having facts, Zelinski. I need the facts. I cannot be expected to tiptoe around you while you broadcast to every dumbass around that you have a secret. Alakai is not stupid." She shouted into his raised, pained face and wanted to jump on a chair to look at him eye to eye. She could pitch her voice to be heard over loud machinery and through ear plugs and she ripped into Jack with every decibel at her disposal. "What is it? Did you see the murder? Do you know who did it?"

At this last question, Jack's eyes flickered to hers and she drew a long breath at the guilty fear in his expression. She dropped back into her chair and put her head in her hands. Quiet now, she pushed back into a slump and let her head loll against the chair back.

"Sit."

Jack didn't move for a moment. He turned, jerky, to pull a metal folding chair close enough to sit in. He shrank into the seat.

She switched to confidence building mode. "Come on, Jack. This cop's a real ball buster. I can tell. How do you intend to keep your secret from him?"

"Won't answer." He seemed as surprised as Kerala at having spoken.

"Well, that'll only work for so long, Jack. If you refuse to cooperate with the investigation, he can arrest you for it. It's a criminal act." Without compunction, she used the only weapon that fired rounds big enough to make it through the man's hard head. "You can't get arrested. What would Danny do? Of course, I could take him in for a while, but what would he think of you?"

"Kerala." Tight as a compression fitting, Jack's voice expressed the same emotions his face did. "I don't know anything for sure. All I have are suspicions."

"Share them with me."

"It wouldn't be fair to point fingers when I don't have any actual information."

"It wouldn't be fair to hold back the bits of information you have, even if you're not sure you've put them together correctly."

He hung his head. "There's two things that I know that I haven't told you." He looked at her, pained. "People weren't in favor of this job with the other owner either. There was a typewritten note, about the time this guy disappeared, that said they'd salted the cement. And just a little while before, we had a bunch of pumps go down because of sand in the gear oil sumps."

She waited. He sat in silence, head slumped between his shoulders. "So what's the big secret?"

"That's it. Facts, not finger pointing." Jack wouldn't expand on these bits of information and she sent him back out to work.

She worked up a sweat pacing in the hot office, so she opened the door and let the ocean breeze blow the burned-coffee scent out along with much of the claustrophobia. She had planned to see the cement supplier that afternoon. They tended to think of the person in front of them as the first priority, so it paid to visit and kick some ass.

Just perfect. With relish, she planned the siege at the cement works and radioed Jack that she'd be gone for an hour or so.

❖

Kerala lay in bed, smooth skin against soft flannel, draped with satin sheets. She stretched out, spread-eagle, and brought her hands to her belly, folding them over the concavity under her ribs. Some part of her may have been weeping, but her eyes burned, dry, as she stared at the ceiling.

The unfailing comforts of a good shower, comfy sleepwear, and clean sheets had soothed many of the rough edges left by the day. The scene with Detective Alakai. Browbeating Jack and the suppliers. Reporting to Ravi that the body belonged to the land's previous owner.

She had e-mailed her report. Once, she would have called, but she couldn't be casual about hearing his voice. She still hadn't told him that Nahoa knew who'd attacked her. He hadn't been able to find the guy yet and she didn't want to stir Ravi up about it.

Was Ravi in any danger? He hadn't been attacked while living with her, but now that Willoughby had been found...

Maybe it was for the best that he was gone.

Her tension grew into an ache that spread down her thighs, up and down her back, and across her forehead. She missed Ravi, worried about him. She struggled to think about something, anything else. His house was behind schedule, but she'd trim some time. She'd rearranged the schedule a bit and wouldn't have anything arriving too early or, hopefully, too late.

Inhale, hold. Exhale, hold. She tried some half-assed meditative tricks. She managed to unlock her muscles a bit, but she couldn't get her mind off Ravi. As soon as she stopped the controlled breathing, she could feel the tension come back.

Her tried and true method of calming herself to sleep was masturbation—build and release the tension, better than a tranquilizer that would leave her groggy the next morning. She pulled her heels together and tented the covers with her knees. She cradled one breast and pulled its nipple. She used the other to brush her belly, the slight convexity around the funnel-shape of her bellybutton, the canyon-creating mesas of her hip bones. Into fur and farther, Kerala used her hands in her usual ways, producing the expected results.

When she grew still, only a second after the orgasm hit, the easiness of the whole procedure failed to delight her. She'd always been glad that she could enjoy herself, by herself, in a quick and undemanding way. This time, her body took its usual pleasure but whispered about what it lacked. No chest against her ribs and breasts, only the texture of her hand. No weight of hips and thighs pressing her legs wide. No heat, no affection.

She missed the surprise of not knowing what would happen next. She missed tuning in to another body and being turned on by its response to her. And she missed Ravi, how he pushed her to keep coming, to come down the peak just far enough to go back up it.

Kerala lay in bed, flannel and satin doing what they could, eyes burning. Her fingers smelled of seaweed, her pulse still thundered, but she felt cold and sad.

## CHAPTER SEVENTEEN

Kerala waited for a table with Nahoa, Jack, and Danny during the Saturday night rush, a beer in front of each of them except the kid.

Halfway through a Hefeweisen, she looked at Nahoa, hiding behind his smile, and couldn't keep hiding from the facts. Direct action on that land. What had he said? He'd lost his best friend and his innocence there. A construction expert fucking with contractors' jobs. Salted cement on the worksite around the time the previous owner, Willoughby, went missing.

Nahoa must have been involved. Kerala stared deep into the amber gleam of her beer. She grasped at loose ends to find a loophole, to tear apart the fabric she wove with what she knew.

Jack. He couldn't have been involved. No way. He'd get in a fair fight backed into a corner, but not murder. And not the tissue paper of a cover-up she was ripping to shreds at the bar.

He probably figured it out like she did. Sixteen-year-old kid, passionate about Hawai'i for the Hawaiians, got mixed up in more than making signs and chanting in hotel parking lots. Suddenly, he dropped all his old friends, joined his father's construction company doing exactly what he'd fought against. Jack was around then. He must've seen how Nahoa changed after that night. He must've suspected.

Ice seeped along Kerala's veins and she shuddered. Was Nahoa behind the obstructions and violence that had surrounded her for so long? Could he sit with her, pretend to help, if he was mixed up in it?

Kerala stood in an abrupt motion that startled Danny. She passed a hand over his hair as she mumbled, "Bathroom," and walked from the room. She went down the hallway to the women's room and straight out the back door. In the cool evening air, she leaned against the back wall of the restaurant.

Jack wouldn't allow Nahoa so close to Danny if he didn't trust him. The indirect argument calmed her pulse to a small degree.

She sank into a crouch against the weathered cedar siding and stopped thinking. She focused on feeling. She didn't have enough facts to think it through. She needed to decide what to believe based on her instincts.

In rebellion against a sociologist mother, she'd refused to analyze her feelings, a strong point in the contractor world. In the dictionary where feminine meant bad, talking things to death was feminine. Having feelings about things was feminine. For decades, the world of men, the world of construction, had solidified Kerala's distrust of and disdain for feelings.

Where did those abilities go when they weren't exercised? Did they atrophy? Did she even have "women's intuition" anymore or had she given it up when she put on a sports bra? She wrapped her arms around her knees and leaned back hard to feel the roughness of the old wood through her shirt. She needed to know whether she could trust Nahoa, and she wasn't sure how to figure it out.

A breeze lifted a strand of hair and tugged it across her mouth. Feeling, not thinking. The slight tightness in her knees, the roughness of her calluses. The wind in her hair and on the exposed back of her neck filled her awareness and faded into the background when she scrunched and released her shoulders. Her hand ached a little but her bruises had long faded.

A thought popped into her mind. She had already decided. She'd decided long ago. She trusted Nahoa and he had proven himself worthy of that trust. Whatever he may have done in the past, he was now a person she believed in.

Feelings or women's intuition, whatever she wanted to call it, she'd used it the whole time. Everyone did. It wasn't a man/woman thing. Everyone judged the people around them based on more than a strict accounting of their actions. She'd refused to hire people for no good reason, hired others on just as little hard fact, and avoided assignments with people she didn't trust.

Of course. The guys didn't call it the same thing. The people in the real world didn't name each shade of emotion the way her mother did, but everyone used those feeling to make their life decisions. She'd made her decision about Nahoa already, and she trusted that decision, trusted herself, enough to ask him for the story. She deserved an explanation.

❖

"Drink?" Kerala asked.

Nahoa shook his head. "No, I'm too full even for fluids." He had ordered a huge platter of food and finished it all, plus some fries that Danny hadn't eaten. He leaned back, arm draped across the back of the couch in Kerala's living room.

She couldn't figure out how to ease into the conversation. She wanted an intensely private person to tell her about his involvement in a murder cover-up.

She jumped in. "Nahoa, I've been thinking about Willoughby. Based on the things you've told me and something Jack said about sabotage around that time..." She paused, not sure how to end the sentence. "Well, I'd like to know how you were involved. Were you on site the night Willoughby was killed?"

Nahoa sat, frozen. He pulled his arm off the back of the couch and drew himself in.

"Please tell me about it. I'm not here to judge you. I just want to know what happened."

He spoke in a hushed voice. "It's not safe for you to know."

She swallowed, but determination filled her. Nahoa carried some weight around inside, behind the façade of a careless ne'er-do-well. "Please, Nahoa. Don't leave me in the dark on this. It can't be safe for me to stumble around, poking my nose into things."

"I go back and forth like a metronome. Confess, be punished. Or hide forever."

Foreboding stiffened her muscles and brought her forward in her chair. "Nahoa, tell me what happened the night Willoughby died."

After a silent moment, Nahoa sat back against the cushions, limp, and raised his head. His joker's grin had turned into a grimace of such pain that Kerala almost cried out. Could she put him through this?

"I was sixteen years old. I hated school for the way it trained me to be a dark-skinned white man. I hated my father for turning our island into subdivisions and vacation homes for rich men." The wry twist of Nahoa's lips made Kerala's pinch in recognition. Whatever Nahoa had done, it had been done in the fight against projects like Ravi's.

"A sixteen-year-old can hold a lot of emotion. I thought the 'āina demanded nonviolent action to stop haole development. Like Walter's, my dedication to nonviolence extended only to people. Property didn't deserve the same consideration, and fighting the godhood of property became part of our mission." He fell silent.

If he wanted to give her the whole story, there must be a reason. "What was your mission?"

He tried to smile. "I wanted a return to kapu, to the systems before the islands were bound together under a monarchy, before the plantations and the military coup and the occupation. Nā Kānaka lived here in beauty. Physical laws punished gluttony. Water stewards, lunawai, monitored the rivers' flow through kalo fields. We had known how to live with the 'āina. I was influenced by environmental, back-to-the-land philosophies and the surge of resources for Native Hawaiians who wanted to know more about traditional ways.

"I thought we needed to get rid of anyone who wasn't kama'āina, and convince the locals to get back to balanced, self-sufficient lives. We would shred laws that fractured us with blood quanta and put out the call for everyone with ancestral ties to the islands. We could change the islands, if we could change ourselves.

"I'd see my friends in the green room under a wave, then doing ice in a rusted out station wagon parked on the beach under a tarp. The hotels would call the cops to evict them from beaches that were their ancestral lands, so that the guests wouldn't have to see what their theft had created. Then every Tuesday night, I'd see them sneaking up to the hotel with cheap grass skirts and imitation kapa to make pennies pretending to hula. Didn't matter if they were Hawaiian or Samoan or Portuguese as long as their hair was dark enough."

Nahoa spoke as though the pain was old and faded, as though he'd become calloused to the irritation of degradation.

"Bonding kama'āina together and keeping us out of Walmart was hard. How do you fight cheap prices when no one makes good money? Scaring away the tourists sounded more effective and like more fun. My body spoke in favor of action, not talk."

"What did you do?"

"Sugar in a bus's gas tank won't hurt the riders, but it will stop the tour. We'd pull fire alarms in shopping complexes and run away. That put a stop to shopping for a day." Nahoa sat forward. "People kept coming. We couldn't touch the mystique. I got frustrated with tourist baiting at fourteen, maybe fifteen."

He scrubbed his face in his hands. "I used my connections through my father. I went after the electrical, battery, fuels, drive train, and control systems. I put staples through coax cable to short out transmissions. There's more, but…"

"I get the picture. What a nightmare." Kerala's hands gripped the arms of her recliner until she relaxed them finger by finger. Nahoa had been in deeper than she'd known. This wasn't just harassing whitey.

"That was the point." Nahoa looked up and speared Kerala with his gaze. "I never, not once, endangered a single worker. You have to know that. If I made a piece of equipment unsafe to operate, I made sure it was inoperable or I left a note explaining why not to use it. Like marking spiked trees in the Cascade Mountains."

"You go back and forth between 'I did' and 'we did.' How big was your group?"

"Sometimes I worked alone, sometimes one or another of the guys would come to help. Walter sometimes. Mostly Pauahi. The whole canoe club sometimes. Our crew got tight and started getting together outside practice. I don't remember who got us talking about doing something, but the paddling club used a lot of Hawaiian pride rhetoric, so it wasn't far off topic. Of the six guys on the crew, only the steerer avoided messing around outside practice. He was serious about ocean canoeing. The others were up for any wild idea I came up with." He paused. "You know, in the moment I didn't realize I was leading that group, but they followed me into some crazy situations. I didn't trust them to know the machinery, so I didn't bring them along for everything. Especially when I got into messing with stuff on work sites, anyone I brought had specific tasks that wouldn't endanger anyone."

Nahoa paused and braced his forearms on his knees, arms folded in front of him. He spoke with little inflection but with a world of pain in his eyes. "That night"—Kerala didn't have to ask which night—"we were salting the cement mix. I brought Pauahi. Dad had mentioned that the cement supplier was low. They'd had a good laugh about running out of the basics, so I knew it would be a big setback for them. We went out to the work site in the middle of the night. We knocked around, not worrying about noise because there were no more neighbors than there are now."

Nahoa stopped and put his head in his hands. His youth struck her. What happened that night shot him into adulthood, but he was still so young. A decade younger than her. Stevens and Nahoa were the same age, but Stevens was a boy in comparison.

"He came from the black shadow of the excavator. I knew it was Willoughby. Mr. Willoughby, my dad called him. He screamed at us, I don't know what. He came at me with a piece of rebar, stabbing like it was a knife in a horror film. I took it out of his hands. I just reached out and pulled it away from him." Nahoa hesitated and the words came with more of a struggle. "We laughed at him. He was powerless. He fell to the ground, and I laughed. I felt so strong and Pauahi raised his arms like, score. Willoughby lunged at me. I jerked back. I brought the rebar down at an angle and hit him."

Kerala held her breath. And she'd thought that Pauahi had gotten Nahoa into trouble.

"He just crumpled. He fell and the ground was dark, but darker around his head and I knew. I felt for a pulse, but I knew. Pauahi hustled me away from his body, pinned me to a dozer until I stopped screaming. I don't remember how he got me to agree, but he said I needed to leave. He would take care of the body. I left them there. I went to my grandma's house and washed the blood and dirt away." He looked at her. "Tūtū Alapaʻi never saw me that night. She doesn't know anything."

"What happened after that?"

"I couldn't cope. I had no idea how he'd gotten rid of the body. It never occurred to me he'd buried it right there on the land. He tried to see me, but I refused to talk to him. I turned my back on my old friends, the canoe crew, and the sovereignty movement as a whole. I didn't know it at the time, but he did the same. He started doing ice and whatever he could get his hands on. In all this time, he hasn't tried to talk to me since then. I ruined his life and then abandoned him. He...touched him. He buried him so I could get away with murder and it drove him past what he could stand."

"You must have been in shock for a long time."

"Tūtū Alapaʻi took care of me. She hooked me up with a group called Nā Koa, like the tree. It means bravery, courage. They teach a different kind of manhood, where bravery means having the courage to look at your own spirit. Kāne is male, husband, but it's also the procreative energy that's like fresh water, flowing and falling. Manhood is about gaining power and strength through spending your energy."

"Did it help?"

"I learned to direct my energy, physical and mental, toward better aims than destruction. The focus on knowing myself hurt pretty badly, though, and I stopped going. I don't know if I ever would have come out of the guilt and pain without them, but I couldn't think about what I'd done. So I went to work for Dad. I decided that the sovereignty movement was dangerous and maybe even wrong. I became a deserter. My guilt for killing Vincent Willoughby is all tangled with self-loathing for becoming what I used to fight."

Kerala tried to conceive of the mix of feelings. There was a relief in knowing she'd never fully understand what he felt.

"Time went by and I didn't think about it all the time. Every day, many times a day, but not unending loops of guilt. I've spent so much time on the water because it's demanding. Surfing requires concentration. It's occurred to me many times to let the ocean take me, but I can't do it. I can't die with the guilt on me."

She swallowed. "I'm glad you didn't."

"Over and over again, Tūtū Alapaʻi or someone else would puncture my bubble. I started to turn back toward working for some form of sovereignty. Some form of improvement here. Then I'd dive into a depression for even thinking it."

"How did it feel to work on the site of..." She swallowed.

"Working where I…where I killed a man…has brought it all back. Of course. But the koa tree spoke to me. My strength, wrapped in the vine haole called passion fruit. I had been strangled by passion, like the tree by the vine. And then, to find Willoughby's body at the heart of the liliko‘i, feeding the passion fruit that shouldn't have thrived in dry, rocky soil. I've been obsessing on that."

The long silence stretched while Kerala tried to click her mind into gear. She needed to do something. She couldn't hear this story and do nothing.

Nahoa's voice was low, liquid. "What are you thinking?"

She surprised herself by laughing. "I have no fucking clue. I can't just listen to you tell me these things and then go to bed, can I? Don't I have to do something?"

"I've been doing nothing for years. Going to bed with the guilt. Going to work with it." Nahoa sat straight. "I'll do whatever you think I should."

"You can't make me responsible for this."

Nahoa dropped his head into his hand. "Of course not. I'm sorry." He looked at her. "But I'll do what I've done over and over since I was sixteen. I'll head home, go to bed, and get up for work in the morning." He stood.

She reached out a hand and caught his sleeve. "Don't do anything drastic. Hear me?"

His mouth took on the curve she loved. "I learned my lesson about drastic."

"Be safe, and keep looking for Pauahi. We need to tell him what's happened."

"I will." Nahoa turned back at the door. "If you decide to turn me in, please give me a heads up. I won't run. I'd just like to know they're coming."

Kerala's gut tightened. "Sure."

He closed the door behind him. She should have said she wouldn't give him up to the cops. Would she?

She trusted Nahoa. With what? To be whom?

She needed to talk it out with someone. Ravi, of course. He would get it. He'd understand her. The thought made her shiver.

How is it that she could trust someone with her life who'd just admitted to killing someone, but opening up to Ravi seemed an impossible amount of trust? She wanted to live more than she wanted to avoid heartbreak, didn't she?

She wanted to live but she wasn't afraid of death. She was scared shitless of letting Ravi know how much she wanted him, though. How she needed him. Felt about him.

Didn't change the fact that she did. Need him. Right then.

Her intuition continued to say trust Nahoa. She had to admit that it said the same about Ravi.

She looked at the time on her phone before dialing. Late in California, but not too late to call.

❖

"Thanks for calling me back. This isn't something for e-mail." Kerala's voice over the speakerphone in his office warmed Ravi unreasonably. Much as he wanted some distance on his feelings for her, he picked up the handset so he could cradle it at his ear.

He drew his coffee cup closer. "Sorry I couldn't talk earlier."

"You sound tired."

"Yeah. I'm losing this battle. We're losing our company."

"I'm sorry." She sounded tired too. "That's fucked up."

"Yeah." He sat back in his old office chair, the creak of dry-fitted oak a comforting sound. Kerala was uncharacteristically humble. "What did you want to talk about, honey?" The endearment slipped out and he closed his eyes.

"I don't know how to start."

She never sounded so small. "Give me the overview first. We can back up for details if we need to."

Her deep breath came through the phone. "I know who killed Willoughby."

"They solved the murder already?"

"No. The cops don't know. I hope. I just figured it out myself, but I asked Nahoa and he told me the whole story."

Cold streamed down his arms, raising the hairs. "If that was the overview, I'll need more details."

"Fuck." Her voice came through muffled, then cleared and firmed. "Nahoa was on the work site to salt the cement and Willoughby came at him with a piece of rebar. He was killed in the struggle and Nahoa left. His partner in crime buried Willoughby there."

"Nahoa killed him? That doesn't make sense." He couldn't imagine Nahoa killing anyone.

"It was self-defense, kind of. It was an accident for sure. I don't know what to do with this, Ravi. I'm stumped. Prison is a ridiculous way for him to do penance, make restitution…to who? Willoughby had no family. He's been living with this since he was sixteen and I know he's suffered. He's still suffering."

Ravi stopped her. "Back up. You figured it out?"

"Yeah. Jack was trying to keep some sort of secret…"

"Jack knew?"

"He suspected but never asked. The timing is what did it, though. Nahoa was sabotaging development projects one day and quitting school to work for Mālama the next. Right when this guy was murdered."

"How could you even think it? I go blank when I try to picture Nahoa bashing in someone's head."

"I know. It's un-fucking-real. I thought he was covering for his friend, Pauahi, but Pauahi was the one attacking me to protect Nahoa." It sounded like she was pacing.

"You know who attacked you? Did the cops find him?"

"No, Nahoa recognized him from the pic your friend manipulated. I forgot I hadn't told you about that. Nahoa hasn't been able to find him yet. He's living rough and hiding from everyone."

"What the hell?"

"I know, I know. But now he has no reason to hurt anyone. The secret's out."

"I hope that's all there is to it."

"I pushed and Nahoa told me the whole story. He was so careful not to hurt anyone. He said the tree spikers were his model. Do the damage but warn the workers of the danger."

"I get that." Ravi pinched the bridge of his nose.

"But murder. It's the worst, the most horrible thing one person can do to another." She sounded shaky. "He was attacked by an older, larger man."

"In the course of defending himself, the other man died."

"Willoughby didn't just have a heart attack from the excitement. Nahoa hit him, hard enough to crush his skull." Kerala swallowed loud enough for him to hear it. "Salted cement would have been a huge irritant, but I'm not even sure it was wrong, what with Tūtū Alapaʻi and vacation homes and all these ideas about property versus people." He imagined her circling her hands in the air. "I can see why a kid would feel he needed to slow or stop that kind of development."

"He's a friend. It's hard to think of him as being completely in the wrong."

"I can't think that killing someone is ever right." Kerala sighed. "But it can be understandable. If Nahoa had been a different person, one with a stronger desire for violence, this could have been the perfect opportunity to act against Willoughby, the real enemy, with real violence. That person would have used the situation to commit murder and hide it. That person would be guilty."

"What do you do with someone who looks for opportunities to kill their enemies?"

"My ideas about punishment are conflicting and complicated. That murderer, as a person who desired to kill another human being, would create an unsafe environment for others. There would be no way to guarantee that the person would never again desire to kill and act upon that desire. What do they deserve? That's a tough question."

Ravi leaned back in his chair. "We don't have to answer that, anyway. Nahoa's actions can't be characterized like that."

"I believe you're right. I trust my opinion of him." Kerala sounded stronger than before. "He caused a death, but then carefully, with great dedication, avoided any situation that bore the slightest possibility of putting him in the same position where he might harm someone. He worked to control himself, physically and emotionally."

"You trust him, but how can a system made of people, individuals like you and me, be made to recognize the difference in Nahoa's case? I guess that's what a defense attorney is for. Do you think he'll need one?"

"I've been sitting here since I called you earlier, trying to figure out what to do."

"What are your options?"

"I guess the options are turn him in or don't. You know what's creeping me out right now? I ate a piece of fruit that was growing literally in the body of the guy. That liliko'i vine fed on the guy's heart."

He took a deep breath. "Look. It's been a long time since Willoughby died." He stopped. He had to say it. "A long time since Nahoa killed him."

"God. That sounds weird."

He gazed at a vibrant statue of the dancing Shiva, the end of the world held off by a raised foot. "Nothing has to be done tonight. Let's make sure we know all the options. Maybe there's some way it can come out right without just sweeping it under the rug. As long as you're safe from his old friend, we have time to think about it."

She sighed and he heard her recliner squeak. He pictured her curling up, looking so much smaller than she did while moving around.

Kerala sighed again. "Ravi. Thank you for calling me back. Really. You're talking like you're with me in this and that's because I brought you into it. I can't even apologize for it. You've got to help me figure it out so I don't do something half-cocked because I don't have the patience to think it through. I need you on this one."

He squeezed his eyes shut and bit his lip. He couldn't speak.

Her voice came through, strong and certain. "You don't have to say anything. I just want you to know that I'm sorry I let you walk out without telling you how much you matter to me. I was so scared and you were leaving and…Hell. It doesn't matter why. I just wish I had handled myself better. I miss you."

He cleared his throat. "I miss you too. I want to be there for you, honey. I really do, but I can't leave right now. I can't."

"Oh, Ravi. You don't have to. You're here for me right now. If you keep answering my calls, that's a start."

His tight chest strangled his laugh. "You got it."

"You can call me too." Her voice was soft, different.

"I will."

"Good night, then. I'll talk to you soon."

"Soon. Sleep well."

Ravi held the phone another moment before setting it in the cradle. So much for keeping his distance.

## Chapter Eighteen

K erala scanned the crew installing the post and pier foundation for Ravi's house. The job was progressing normally, for a change, since Tūtū Alapaʻi got them all to agree at hoʻoponopono. Walter hadn't taken Willoughby's body as an opportunity to halt construction. He was no one's ancestor.

She stretched her hand, just out of the brace. Gripping made it ache, but her dexterity was good. She couldn't regret hitting the jackass, but she'd been so close to healed. Her head and shoulder didn't even twinge anymore and the bruises and abrasions were gone. A couple marks might end up as scars, but hell, pile 'em on.

Good thing she was almost up to snuff physically. This point in a job stressed her out. Any delay cascaded through the schedule and could require finding new subcontractors if the current ones couldn't push their work back. Nothing smacked of bad project management like ending up with different subs than originally contracted. And nothing gave subs an edge in negotiation like knowing that she had to keep the project moving.

The special stress of knowing that Nahoa had killed Willoughby, whether or not it was murder in the strict sense, put an edge on her usual spring-loaded tension.

She didn't want to take it out on anyone, so she left the supervision to Jack. She, Jack, and Nahoa were cultivating a crew that aimed for perfect, accepted workable, and disdained skating on the tolerances. She usually took an active role in exhorting the workers to greater precision, but it was safer to back off.

Jack gave the hand signal to the crane operator to lower away. The heavy concrete footing settled toward the tamped surface. "Twist," he roared, and two of the crew helped him align it. The motor of the crane rumbled, but the well-maintained rig didn't screech as the taut cable passed over the roller at the top.

A sudden stream of curses from the other side of the site ripped her attention away. She paced along the edge of the foundation and found Nahoa listening to an irate worker. She stayed behind the guy while he blustered about another worker disrespecting his tools. She squinted at Nahoa, who nodded in her direction. He'd handle it.

She turned away, scratching under her hard hat where her hair was growing back, and saw three cars ease down the rough driveway. Two cop cars and a police issue sedan—too many cars. Too many cops.

Nahoa. He could sneak out the back of the plot, leave via the side road below the hill she'd fallen on. She looked over at him. His hand rested on the shoulder of the worker, but the cop cars riveted his gaze.

He wouldn't run. She could see the resignation in his heavy expression, though his shoulders straightened.

The cars pulled up behind the equipment, the crane and tractor striking Kerala as good weapons for demolishing trouble. She scanned Alakai's face as he unfolded from the unmarked car, seeing only the stony blankness of a cop on the job.

"Fuck." She walked toward them and put herself between the growing crowd and Nahoa. Alakai watched her come and looked behind her at Nahoa before checking that his guys were in place. The four uniformed cops spread out to either side, hands on holstered guns, feet shifting on the crunchy ʻaʻā.

"What do you want?" Her growl made the cops' hands twitch.

"I need to see Nahoa Kalama."

"What do you need him for?"

"My business is with him, not you."

"This is my construction site and he's my worker, so you have to go through me first."

Alakai stared at her. "How long have you known?"

Cold spiked through her aggressive anger. "Known what?" She spoke through numb lips, her face aflame.

"If you don't get him over here right now, we'll get him ourselves. And you'll be open to a conspiracy charge."

"You're not entering my work zone without proper headgear."

"Kel, it's okay." Nahoa stepped next to her. She looked at him in agony. "What do you need, Detective?"

"Nahoa Kalama, I need to question you regarding the murder of Vincent Willoughby."

"You brought quite the crowd." Nahoa scanned the semi-circle of uniformed cops as he spoke. They all looked Hawaiian. None wanted to catch his eye.

"Can we use your office?" Alakai spoke to Kerala.

She wanted to deny him any help, wanted to avoid any hint of solidarity with him, but how could it help Nahoa for her to obstruct the investigation? Cop show terms flowed through her thoughts, words for her precarious legal status. Conspirator. Accessory after the fact. She boiled with frustrated desire to save her friend from the system mislabeled justice.

"Can Kel come?" Nahoa's voice steadied her with its calm.

"Sure," Alakai said. "After you."

Kerala joined the parade across the uneven ground to her trailer. Jack's voice rose behind her. "Back to work. Show's over. Get your sorry ass back to the job or I'll kick it right out of here."

She pushed between two cops to unlock the door and led the way inside. She took her customary seat behind her desk, refusing Alakai that position of power. He seemed unbothered by the demotion and sat at the work table about six feet away, sideways to Kerala, his back to the door. He pulled his notebook from his breast pocket and clicked his pen. A uniformed officer entered after Nahoa and took position at Alakai's shoulder.

Alakai waved Nahoa to the seat on Kerala's side, but Nahoa sat opposite, where he could see her. His chair almost touched the plans pinned to the corkboard.

Kerala cleared a spot on her desk, the paperwork crucial an hour ago merely in the way now. She leaned forward on her elbows, alert to any opportunity to help Nahoa stay out of the cars that had surely come to take him away.

She didn't know when she'd decided. She doubted that she had decided, really, to put herself on the line to keep Nahoa from paying for his terrible mistake of so many years ago. It was like she and Ravi had discussed. How could the system, made of people, individuals like Alakai and herself, be made to recognize that Nahoa's case was different?

It would be better to keep him out of their hands altogether.

Alakai scribbled the answers to his initial, routine questions. Name, address, the minutia of citizenry. A flow of information from Nahoa to the paper.

"How did you know Vincent Willoughby?" Alakai's voice maintained its matter-of-fact inflection, but cold washed over her.

"He was a client of my father's. Mālama Construction contracted with him to build a house on this land."

"Did you meet him?"

"Yes, several times."

"When did you first meet him?"

"He came to the house, demanding that the work go faster. He refused all offers of hospitality."

"How did that make you feel?"

Kerala frowned. What was this, therapy?

"Insulted, angry. He came to my father's house and treated him with disrespect. He was rude to my mother and Tūtū Alapaʻi."

"What did you do to pay him back for all that?"

Nahoa's stern look softened a touch. "Nothing. My father took care of his misbehavior. He lectured him on living with aloha. No one does it like Dad. By the end, Willoughby sat next to him with guava juice in hand, confused but agreeable."

Alakai turned the pen in his hand. "Did you two speak on that occasion?"

"I was doing homework in the garden and watched the whole thing from behind the bougainvillea. When my dad caught me peeking, he called me over and introduced us. I got in trouble later for not shaking hands."

"Why didn't you?"

"I was tempted to honi, just to freak him out, but he seemed so confused."

"Confused why?"

"He got steamrolled by my father. He drove up Hualālai to impose his will on the situation and got stuck with aloha."

"Was he angry?"

"No, not then."

Alakai tapped his pen on the notebook. "Tell me about the last time you saw him."

Life leached from Nahoa's expression. "He was angry that time."

Kerala leaned farther forward, hunched over her hands. What was he doing?

"Angry about what?" Alakai sat quietly, as though moving would spook the fish nibbling at his bait.

Nahoa was no ignorant fish. He looked at Kerala, then back to Alakai. Suddenly, his shoulders sagged and he covered his face with his hands. *No, Nahoa.*

"He found me pouring salt in the cement mix. He attacked me and I disarmed him. He attacked me again and I hit him in the head. He dropped to the ground and jerked around. It was horrible. Blood flying all over and I couldn't get a hold on him to check his pulse. He stopped moving after a few minutes. He died. The blood or the convulsions. I don't know why, but he died."

Kerala's stomach surged. He'd spared her some details after all. The image made it much more real, much less philosophical somehow.

Alakai finished writing and folded his hands over his notebook. "We'll finish this at the station. I want to record it." He stood. "Nahoa Kalama, you are under arrest for the murder of Vincent Willoughby."

Kerala sat, elbows on her kitchen table and a cup of strong coffee cradled in her hands. Fog obscured the hills and stars and she fought the chill she'd picked up on her pre-dawn walk with Bogart. She eyed him.

"You're perfectly comfortable, aren't you?"

Bogart stared at her, unblinking.

"Why do I talk to you? It's such a cliché. Single, my family consisting of an admittedly brilliant dog and a couple of coworkers, one arrested for murder and the other a stoic mess."

No response.

"Let's get to work."

Bogart stood and stretched. He padded over to her and sat, leaning with a heavy sigh against her knee. She put her hand on his head, thick fur damp from their walk, and let it rest there.

Calm invaded her in the few minutes it took to drain her coffee and stand. She stretched, the echo of Bogart's motion a reminder of her own animal nature. As complicated as life could be, and today would be a doozy, this was the core of it. Physicality and affection.

She brushed aside the thought of calling Ravi. At three in the morning, even being two hours ahead didn't make it a decent hour in California. She had work to finish before leaving for the arraignment.

She loaded her cooler with sandwich makings and cups of fruit.

Her thoughts turned muddled, balked at what may happen to Nahoa. If they charged him with second-degree murder, the trial would eat his life regardless of the outcome. She didn't want that for him.

If he lost. Well, they couldn't allow that.

Calling Hekili after the cops took Nahoa away had been one of the hardest things she'd ever done. It was all Nahoa had asked of her, and Hekili needed to be told, but what a flood of terrible information. She opened the door of her truck. Bogart jumped in and settled on the passenger side.

Hekili had questioned her about what she knew of Nahoa's ties to the sovereignty movement and who else might have been involved. Maybe he was trying to figure out how exposed Nahoa was. Either way, he'd just found out that his son was arrested for a murder committed years ago. It must have felt like years of lies coming to light.

Lost in thought, she drove without hearing the radio until the DJ said Nahoa's name. She jerked and turned up the volume.

"As the only son of local contractor Hekili Kalama and an employee of Mālama Construction, officials expect a strong defense at the arraignment later today. Nahoa Kalama has no criminal record, but sources say he was a prominent, though secret, member of the sovereignty movement's radical wing. Signs protesting his arrest have begun showing up in front of houses and in business windows. His attorneys will almost certainly focus on reducing the charge, from second-degree murder to manslaughter, because the latter has a ten-year statute of limitations. Stay tuned for the debate between our guests, one from the tourism bureau and the other a leader of the pro-sovereignty group PPC."

"Fuck." Kerala gave the volume knob a vicious twist, turning off the rumor mill masquerading as journalism. She didn't want to listen to a couple of talking heads lob insults over the future of her friend.

She pulled into the work site and jerked to a stop. Bogart stayed close as she walked to the trailer, alternately eyeing her and scanning their surroundings for danger. As soon as she'd unlocked the door, Bogart pushed ahead of her to make a circuit of the small space before heading back out to lie in front of the steps. His ears twitched at sounds she couldn't hear.

Her tension made him nervous.

She left the door open to the beautiful Kohala pre-dawn. It was dry, as usual, and the interior of the trailer held the night's cool. She booted her laptop and shuffled through the papers she'd piled together while Detective Alakai had interrogated Nahoa. Separating them back into their original piles took longer than the computer's startup routine, and she logged on while leaning over the desk.

Frustration pulsed. Anonymous sources and gossip could crucify Nahoa in the public eye before he got a court hearing. What would it do to Mālama to have the company's name tied to an anti-haole murder? They could lose business over this.

She sat for her first duty of the day. Hekili's e-mail address auto-populated when she started typing his name. She pondered a moment before making the subject "Anything I can do." A short note, to the point. She wanted to help.

That sent, she gave in and opened a browser window to read the news about Nahoa. The whole island had been online, expressing a variety of opinions on the subject. Some supported him as a dumb kid who got in trouble. Others held the line that murder was murder and should be punished. It didn't work out exactly along lines of ancestry, but close. A growing thread questioned why he was even being charged after all this time for a crime committed as a minor. Some linked to similar situations where the DA had chosen not to pursue conviction.

The crunch of tires on 'a'ā brought her out of the rabbit hole after she'd clicked links for a half hour.

She put the laptop to sleep, rose, and strode to the door to see Jack parking. He lifted a hand in greeting and turned to pull on his boots. She went back to her desk. She should get to work.

She called Ravi instead.

❖

Frustration filled Ravi. A friend was in jail and there was nothing he could do about it. "Tell me what happened."

She gave him the bare bones. He used his free hand to peck out a Web search as she spoke and skimmed headlines for more. "The family has rallied around him, but no one is making detailed statements. He basically confessed, but they don't know what they'll charge him with. Alakai was talking murder."

"Murder two, according to the news."

"The news." Kerala snorted. "I don't trust a single one of them. They've been quoting anonymous sources in the sovereignty movement, but I bet they make a lot of it up."

"They seem to have some facts right."

"Well, not all of them. They can't hold him, after all this time. They'll have to release him until the preliminary hearing." She sounded determined to make it so.

"What do you know about the criminal process?"

Defensive tension sharpened her tone. "Same as every movie-watching person. Nearly nothing. I've been doing some research, even though it's hard to know what Web sites to trust."

"What happens next?"

"The arraignment is where they inform him of the charges and get his plea. They'll also decide whether to keep him in jail. The preliminary hearing is like a grand jury without the jury. The judge decides whether there's enough evidence to hold a trial."

"So we're hoping that they let him go today and then decide there's not enough evidence for a trial, even with his confession."

"Yeah. Here's hoping." She sighed. "This is exhausting."

Affection moved through him. "You're not used to all this emotional work. Maybe you should get out there and move your body."

"Sounds good. Um, yeah, I have an hour or so until I have to head to Waimea. The courthouse is not far from home. I'll call after and let you know what happens."

"Thanks, Kel. And take care of yourself. Call me anytime."

"Will do. Talk soon."

"Bye."

The empty radiation from the speaker ended with the flash of his phone signaling that she'd disconnected the call. He was starting to hate the company he'd given up so much for. It was turning, he could feel it. It was losing its heart and soul to the profit motive. Meanwhile, he wasn't there for the woman he loved when she needed him.

"The air is different here." Tūtū Alapaʻi settled next to Kerala, her thick haunches perched on the narrow concrete.

Kerala sat on the curb, her arms folded on her knees. The South Kohala Courthouse looked simple for a place that decided the course of a person's life. She suddenly understood the urge to make such places architecturally imposing.

"Different from Kona?" The lush, heavy greenery impinged on her awareness for the first time. Yep, paradise.

"And from Hualālai. We are an island of microclimates and a people with the flexibility to enjoy them all. I love the coffee hills, but the air is mild as a caress here in Waimea." Tūtū Alapaʻi crossed her legs and drew a deep breath.

Nahoa had been arraigned for second-degree murder and pled innocent. They released him into his grandmother's care. He could go to work, but nowhere else.

Kerala looked at her over her shoulder. Thick, wavy hair radiated from Tūtū Alapaʻi's lined face in dark and light rays. "What about Puna?"

Tūtū Alapaʻi waved a hand. "Too ikiiki. Did you know that ʻOlelo Hawaiʻi has a hundred words for rain? The wet coats my skin, invades my nose, fills my chest. Waimea's thin air doesn't hold as much water. See how green and lovely, but still it feels nice." She rubbed her fingers together.

Kerala mimicked the action, her dry fingers sliding easily.

"You would have haole rot living in Puna." Tūtū Alapaʻi's absent tone matched her gaze. She focused on the door Nahoa would exit.

Kerala congratulated herself on recognizing a matter of fact use of the word haole.

Tūtū Alapaʻi looked over at Kerala. "It's good for you here. Cool, somewhat dry. What do you think of paniolo?"

Kerala grimaced. "I haven't thought about it much. I guess Hawaiian cowboys surprised me, but the idea of a white guy showing up and convincing everybody to let him raise cattle isn't all that weird. What do you think?"

Tūtū Alapaʻi sighed. "We can't eat grass, but the cattle can and then we can eat them. The cattle themselves, though. Are they good for the island?"

"Probably not." Kerala felt safe hazarding a guess on that, since waste from feed lots poisoned rivers. Surely an island built of porous lava would be a sieve.

"Why so many? That's what I ask. So many cattle are not good, but if they could be satisfied with less…"

Silence seemed the best choice and they kept quiet company for a while. Tūtū Alapaʻi's next words confused Kerala. "Maybe I should have kept him."

"Kept Nahoa?"

Tūtū Alapaʻi nodded. "It was my fault he grew up angry. I made sure he knew our traditions, learned our language, but I left him with his parents. He had strong tides pulling him in two directions. It's no wonder he was confused."

"I'm sure you did your best for him. I'm sure his parents did too."

"I don't know. He belongs to me, you know. Keiki belong to their grandparents and we decide who raises them. We can raise them or leave them with their parents or adopt them out to another family. I don't know what I should have done."

"You mean legally yours?" Kerala couldn't wrap her head around grandparents with more rights than parents.

Tūtū Alapaʻi scoffed. "Legally. That doesn't matter. ʻOhana is what we decide it is. Who complains if the quiet boy lives with his grandmother? Who complains if the wild girl goes to the house with more aunties so they can keep a better eye on her? Keiki live the way we all wish we could. Free to play, free to roam, free to seek love and learn from everyone."

"Sounds good to me." It did, too. "I'm still surprised parents would let you take their child away."

Tūtū Alapaʻi chuckled. "It's not always easy to remind them of what's best for a child, but if they've been raised right and don't try to live like they see in the movies, it works." She looked over at Kerala. "What do you think parents want for their children?"

"A mirror." The answer flew from her mouth before she could stop it.

Head cocked to the side, Tūtū Alapaʻi considered. "Your parents didn't see you."

Kerala bit her cheek, bitterness and self-consciousness roiling. "It doesn't matter."

"If you want to understand what I'm saying, it matters. Good parents want their children to be healthy and happy. They want their children to feel loved and they want to know the joy that only children share." She shook her head. "Your parents were not good parents."

"Yeah. I know." Kerala lifted her chin, stretching neck muscles gone tight. The glimpse of family, a type of family that was giving and wished the best for each other, birthed an uncomfortable yearning to be part of something like that.

"It's not easy to be a good parent. Keiki are a blessing and they will find their own paths. Nahoa walked his path until it took him somewhere he didn't want to be. He changed, but not all for the better. Now that I know what happened..."

The door opened and an officer stepped through. Tūtū Alapaʻi rocked forward and rose to her feet. Nahoa followed with a few words for the woman in uniform. She touched his upper arm in a gesture that might have been direction but looked instead like comfort. He smiled at her and Kerala caught her breath. He looked so happy.

She followed Tūtū Alapaʻi across the lawn to the courthouse.

Nahoa wrapped his arms around his grandmother's bulk and held tight. She folded him close and rocked back and forth. Kerala stood a respectful distance away, watching them share breath. The intimate greeting called honi separated kama'āina from haole.

Nahoa grinned at Tūtū Alapa'i when she released him to squeeze his cheeks in her hands. "What did you do, silly boy? Why did you tell them all that?"

His eyes swept closed and his mouth flattened. "I can't avoid it anymore, Tūtū. I thought I had to give up the fight, but that's not the answer. You're still connected to the sovereignty movements while I've built haole vacation homes on the 'ohana 'āina. I can do better."

"You can't do anything from inside a cell. Too many of our boys are in prison. You don't need to join them there. It's no good place to plan a revolution."

"Tell that to Bumpy Kanahele."

"Be serious." Tūtū Alapa'i smacked Nahoa's arm with her palm. "Oh, I am."

The intensity on his face worried Kerala. She stepped forward. "I'm so glad to see you."

Nahoa reached out to put his hand on her shoulder, but Kerala walked into his arms for a hug. It's one thing to keep some distance with co-workers. It's another thing to reconnect with a friend who just came out a courthouse.

He squeezed her hard and released her. "You'll see plenty of me."

"I'm glad they're letting you work."

Tūtū Alapa'i sniffed. "I could put him to work around the house."

He looked at Kerala over her head. "Sure, Tūtū, whatever you need."

"That's what you always say."

"And you never come up with stuff for me to do."

"Let's see what I can do about that."

Nahoa paused in the banter that flowed like water in an ancient riverbed. "Kel, mahalo nui for being here. Seeing you in the courtroom helped."

"No problem." She stuck her hands in her jeans pockets.

"Really. I knew 'ohana would come out for me, but I wasn't sure how you would react to all this."

"I know you're not a murderous person. I trust you, Nahoa, when you say you didn't want to hurt that man. I'm behind you."

Nahoa slapped her on the shoulder and gripped the muscle there. "Means a lot to me."

She waved his words away. "Want a couple days off?"

He looked at Tūtū Alapa'i. "Yeah. We'll have a lot of family around for a few days. How about I start again on Monday?"

Kerala nodded. "No problem." She cleared her throat when Tūtū Alapa'i slipped an arm around Nahoa's waist. "All right. I'll see you then. Let me know if you need anything."

"Come by this weekend," said Tūtū Alapa'i. "We'll have food and music. You know the family."

Kerala nodded but didn't answer. A party for a person who had been arrested for murder. She had met the family, but she couldn't say she knew them.

• 260 •

## CHAPTER NINETEEN

R avi paced to the small fridge under the bar. He pulled hard against the strong seal that made it so energy efficient. He should design a suction release of some sort.

He pulled a root beer from the shelf of glass bottles. Affection moved through him at the homemade label. His people at Sol Volt felt strongly about climate change, believing that the earth had been catapulted into a new geological era that many called the Anthropocene. The age of the human.

If they could ameliorate climate change through energy efficiencies and making their own soda, they would.

He held the bottle by the neck in the manly fashion he'd practiced with beer and sipped at the soda. Felt good, tasted good.

He stared out the window, where the Pacific got pummeled by rain. A rare quiet, windless rain that fell straight down, kept off his window by the long overhang of the roof. The horizon was a blurry suggestion in the distance between white-silver rainclouds and silvery-white ocean. They weren't making a speck of solar or wind power, but the tidal turbines never stopped.

He pulled his phone from his pocket and pulled up Nahoa.

"Aloha."

"Aloha, Nahoa. How are you?"

"That question isn't getting any easier to answer. At least I believe you care."

Ravi stared into the indistinct horizon. "I do. I'm worried about you getting justice."

A slow sigh came from the phone. "I'm no more convinced than ever that the courts are the right people to oversee my judgment."

"You sound depressed."

"Yeah. I'm depressed, ashamed, embarrassed, but there's still more to it than that."

He could hear it, behind the flatness of Nahoa's voice. "You're angry."

Ravi waited through the silence until Nahoa replied, almost whispering. "I'm so damn angry."

"Tell me."

"This justice system doesn't know or care about Hawaiian values. I have lawyers trying to control what I say so they can get my charges reduced, but there's no way for me to reconcile with my family and community without mihi and huikala. If I say the right thing and they reduce my charges to manslaughter, I can go free and make a new start. If I say the wrong thing, I'm looking at real prison time. The court could keep me from ho'oponopono. What good is confession without forgiveness and release? And what good is freedom if I can't make an honest confession?"

Ravi shifted on his feet at the window. The rain had eased and barely dimpled the long, calm expanse of the ocean. "What's your best-case scenario here?"

A short laugh preceded a long silence. "Can't say I've been thinking along those lines."

"Try it."

Nahoa hummed. "Best case scenario. I'm allowed to reconcile and regain pono."

"Good start. What about beyond that? What next?"

"Thinking big? Native Hawaiians get to determine our own future and we get serious about the divine in the land and the water and in each other. I don't think we need to go back to the original kapu system, but we need to remember that we had restrictions on overfishing and rules for mālama 'āina. It means taking care of the land. The land was powerful, but we prayed upright and with our eyes open because we had mana too. Spiritual power. You gain or lose mana with everything you do. Maybe it's kind of like karma."

"You want independence, like you always have, but you want Hawaiians to change as well?"

"We can't be independent living like this. Importing enough gas to keep the four-wheel-drive monster trucks on the road would mean selling ourselves right back. Even tourism can't keep exploitative capitalism going if we're on our own. We'd need to grow our own food again. No more monocrops and no more testing bed for new GMOs."

Ravi moved to his desk and started taking notes.

"Deciding who could stay and who would have to go will be tough. Contentious. The Portuguese and Chinese and Japanese are 'ohana, to some degree. There are plenty of locals who belong, even if they don't have our specific indigenous relationship to the 'āina. Some things need to be arranged around that relationship, but others can be more welcoming of non-Hawaiian kama'āina."

Ravi scribbled. "And after people, you have to decide which companies you'll allow to do business."

"Maybe that's the better way, anyway. Reject the businesses, restrict import, and see who wants to stay when life gets really, really simple."

Ravi paused in his writing. "How would you restrict visitors?"

"In my perfect world, all living spaces without permanent residents—vacation houses, rental condos—would be seized and redistributed so everyone had good, sanitary housing."

"Oof."

"I know, Ravi." Nahoa hesitated. "Look, I'm not saying you're evil because you want to be here. I'm not even saying there wouldn't be places left over for visitors. Hotels, though, or rentals that don't leave locals without decent housing."

"This isn't the first time I've heard that I'm doing the wrong thing. Your grandma made it pretty clear that vacation homes are a pox on the islands. I feel more and more unwelcome and less and less certain I even want to be in Hawai'i."

"Why did you want to be here in the beginning?"

Ravi blinked at his notes. "God. That feels like so long ago."

Nahoa laughed and the sound brought a smile to Ravi's face. "It'll come back to you."

"I wanted to get my hands back on what matters to me. Shaping my life to have the least impact I can on the planet. Hawai'i is rich in the resources I use. Sun, wind, water."

"You're right. None of those things are scarce. You aren't even using fresh water from the land."

"Kohala seemed like the perfect place to retreat to when my compromises started to hurt. Driving a car, using grid power from coal or nuclear plants."

"You're making the biggest mistake of the environmental movement. Considering the planet and not the people."

Heat hit Ravi's cheeks.

"Your house won't have a big impact on the land or its resources, but building on a suspected burial ground is what started this revolution in the cycles of violence. You didn't consider your impact on the people. Not those who believe that their 'aumākua would be angered by the construction. Not the social situation for the locals who can't afford a simple house, let alone one like yours, but have to watch yours sit empty for most of the year."

Ravi swallowed. "I get the point."

"We're building an amazing house for you, Ravi. Your planning and our execution will turn that piece of contested land into a model of how we could be independent on the islands. I don't hate your house. I hate that it spits in the faces of the people who believe it's a burial ground. I hate that it's yours and you don't even want to live in it. You want to use it for those times when you can't handle the legacy of bad decisions on the continent."

Ravi let Nahoa's words soak in. His plans shifted. "You think it's a good model?"

Exasperation sharpened Nahoa's voice. "Of course I do. I recognize that you've done brilliant design work. There's just no upside for Hawaiians."

Ravi tapped his pen on his notes. "Let's see if we can't change that."

❖

Kerala whistled Bogart back when Nahoa called. "What's up?"

"I found Pauahi and talked him into coming to my grandma's house. She's with him in the garden now."

Her arm hair stood on end in the cool air of her backyard. "What does he have to say for himself?"

"Can you come talk to him?"

Could she? Did she want to? She still couldn't pinpoint what she wanted. Punishment? Retribution? To even the scales? What would that even look like?

"I was about to walk Bogart."

Nahoa waited in silence. He was letting her think it through, but thinking wasn't getting her anywhere.

"I'm on my way."

She drove without coming up with any answers. Tūtū Alapaʻi met her at the car and took her hands while Bogart went nosing around the yard.

"How are you feeling, Kerala?"

She couldn't help but smile. "Confused."

Tūtū Alapaʻi smiled back. "Best possible answer. I'm glad your mind isn't made up."

Her amusement faded fast. "I don't know if I can do it. Hoʻoponopono. I don't know if I can let go, even if we can manage all the rest."

"I'm not afraid of trying. Are you?"

She raised an eyebrow. "Pushing my buttons already?"

Tūtū Alapaʻi just laughed.

Kerala followed her around to the back garden. She'd put aside frustrations there before and the flowers, the stones, the birds and bugs weaved their magic. Her chaotic mind settled and she let it, after the obligatory kick against being manipulated.

If the environment could help her figure out what was right, she'd let it.

She studied the young man who stood nervously as she came closer. Nahoa sat nearby, not close enough to have ranged himself alongside his old friend but not so distant as to disclaim him altogether.

Her hand still ached, but the bruising on his forehead was gone. On the other hand, it looked like she'd put a permanent bend in his nose.

Her satisfaction didn't fill her with pride, but she wouldn't hide from it.

Tūtū Alapaʻi poured Kerala a glass of juice and took her seat. "Please sit. We need to talk about what we hope to accomplish."

Nahoa sat straight. "First things first. Kerala Rosemont, meet Pauahi Māhoe."

"We're already acquainted."

"No, you don't know each other at all. If you both hold onto the pictures in your head, the specter of the person who attacked you or the representative of all desecration of the ʻāina, you won't be able to really listen."

Kerala smirked. "You bucking for Tūtū Alapaʻi's role here?"

"Just hoping for the best."

Heaviness settled over her. So much was at stake, but almost none of it for her.

Tūtū Alapaʻi said, "European law is like standard physics. It simplifies things as far as possible and derives some general rules, then tries to apply those rules across the board. Appending mediation to the law attempts to account for what lies beyond. Hoʻoponopono, mediation, arbitration, these are the quantum physics of justice, where it can be recognized that a thing can be in multiple states at the same time. Where we can see that measuring something changes it."

Kerala frowned. She'd like to hear Ravi's reaction to this.

"Before we can proceed, I want to know. Kerala, do you want legal remedies here? Do you want someone to determine what happened"—she could practically see the air quotes—"and apply a scale of severity to decide how to proceed? Or do you want to understand what happened, to know it won't happen again, and to release the negative entanglements that bind you to your pain?"

Kerala held Tūtū Alapaʻi's eyes. "I get it. I do. Maybe more than you know. The stitches for my head are long gone, my shoulder's fine, my scrapes are healed. What worries me is that I'm not just aching in the hand I broke on this guy's forehead. I may be able to sit here and make peace intellectually, understand what he did and why. But my skin tightens when I look at him. My heart beats faster and aggression feels like a natural response." She gripped her juice in both hands and looked at Pauahi. "When I see you, I see danger."

Pauahi's neck bobbed when he swallowed. He was young to be so weathered and beaten. His voice was low but he held her gaze. "I stole a car and sat on your road. I wanted to scare you off. I needed to make you leave Willoughby's land alone. I swear to you, while I sat there, I was sweating so hard I couldn't hold the wheel. My vision blurred and my hands were numb. I didn't want to hurt you, but you wouldn't go away."

"If you try to turn this on me, I'm walking away."

"No, I'm sorry. That's not what I meant. I just…I saw you in the rearview mirror and I panicked. You took me by surprise. You saw me. I freaked out and hit the gas. When the car shook, when it hit you, I…I burst into tears. I was doing the same thing Nahoa had done. I was getting myself into situations where things went wrong."

She considered. "What did you mean to do?"

"I had a mask. I was going to flash my lights at you, put the mask on, and tell you it had to stop. I just wanted to scare you away."

Nahoa shook his head. "It never would have worked. She wouldn't have quit."

"I followed you all day when you took the old lady shopping. You went to the bathroom. It was my last chance to stop you before you started working there. Why there? Why right where I'd buried the body?"

She grimaced. "It's a beautiful spot. You must have known. You must have picked it for the same reason."

Pauahi looked at his hands on his knees.

Kerala lost her patience. "You were going to threaten me some more. I thought you were trying to kill me, Pauahi. Can you imagine how that felt? Trapped in a dark room with someone who wanted me dead?"

Pauahi crumbled, weeping. "I didn't. I don't. I had to protect Nahoa. I've always loved him. He could do anything. He could make anything possible for me. Even when he wouldn't see me anymore, I kept an eye out for him."

Nahoa's mouth twisted. "I never wanted this. I would never have asked you to do this for me."

"I had to protect you."

"No. You didn't."

Kerala looked at the two young men, both anguished, both guilty and paying for their wrongs. She looked at Tūtū Alapaʻi. "I'm done here."

She nodded, lips tight. "I'll take care of them. They have much to discuss without you." She paused. "If you want to try again, let me know."

"We'll see." Kerala took her full glass of juice into the kitchen and rinsed it down the drain. She stood at the sink, hands cool under the running water, and watched Nahoa and Pauahi turn toward one another.

Nahoa needed his friend back. Perhaps he'd never forgive himself until Pauahi got his life back on track. He had to let go of that feeling of responsibility, though. Pauahi's decisions had been his own.

She watched them talk, Tūtū Alapaʻi beside them. They would work it out. She wasn't as sure she could be a part of that peace. She might be able to forgive, but she would never forget.

❖

Kerala walked straight through the wooden piers perched on their concrete blocks. As she approached, conversation stopped and work began, but it wouldn't last.

She put a bare palm on the dense wood, shipped to the Big Island by a cattle baron a century ago. The wood deserved better, but the work was barely within tolerances. Borderline work, shoddy by her standards, and on this, of all projects. Ravi deserved better.

"Jack!" Her voice carried over the hydraulic hammer drills, bringing his head around. She waved him over. He walked through the site, eyes on the move. "What the fuck, Jack?"

"I know. Shitty work, all over the place."

"Is it more sabotage, but subtle this time?"

"No. Just distraction."

"What can I do to help? I can't look over their shoulders every moment."

"Kel, I know. Half would walk if we sent Nahoa home. The other half wants to walk every time he comes around. He's due back any minute now and you'll see."

"How is he dealing with this?"

"He's not saying much to me."

"Me either."

She contemplated the shoddy workmanship in silence. Awareness of the telephoto lenses itched at her. The press camped on the Queen Kaahumanu Highway took pictures of everyone who came or went. They mingled with the protestors who'd taken position opposite each other, some supporting Nahoa and a smaller group outraged by the support.

The sound changed, wheezing tools falling silent. Jack and Kerala both looked around like hounds sniffing the air.

Shouts from the highway carried down the long driveway and the cordon of media cars and vans broke for Nahoa's truck. An eager reporter was blocked from following by the lone cop stationed to keep them off the work site.

Kerala met Nahoa in the parking area. "Private property laws are helping you out this time."

He grimaced.

"How'd the meeting go?"

"Fine."

"What's that mean?"

"Fine. I told them what happened a hundred thousand times and they tried to talk me into saying things differently."

"Lawyers."

"Yeah. Coaching me to downplay my responsibility, they say."

"You're already on record. They want you to change your story?"

"Murder two means prison time. If they can get it reduced to manslaughter, I walk. Because of the high profile of my case, they're being allowed to mount a defense at the preliminary trial to get the charges reduced. Bringing evidence and witnesses. They're not sure it would help to get Pauahi up there, with his history. Usually it's just killer cops who get to defend themselves at this stage, but since it's the difference between trial and no trial..." He shrugged.

"Well, get to work. At least that still makes sense." Kerala whacked him on the shoulder in comradely fashion, forcing good cheer.

"On it."

They walked around the vehicles shoulder to shoulder, falling into step with each other. Kerala picked up her pace and reached the excavated area first. Work stumbled to a halt as Nahoa joined her on the edge.

Jack hollered at the crew. "What is it, break time?" They shuffled dirty boots, passed their tools from hand to hand, but their focus on Nahoa seared Kerala with its intensity. "Get to work," he roared.

Kerala braved Jack's wrath by chopping her hand through the air. "Wait a minute. Let's clear the air. Gather up."

"Gather up! You heard the boss. Get your asses over there."

The group that formed in front of her sorted itself along complicated Hawaiian lines. A couple haole with sunburns. Some Portuguese locals. Native Hawaiian, hapa. A lone hapa with Japanese ancestry.

The two-foot excavation gave her the advantage of height.

"What are we doing here?" She didn't hesitate long enough for anyone to answer. "Building a house, that's what. That's the job. Everything else is outside the job."

So many eyes focused on the ground. How could she bring them together again? Nahoa stood stock-still beside her.

"We're a crew, people. You've all done good, solid work for me in the months I've been here. Jack has vouched for you and I trust him when he tells me you're good workers." That got a flinch. "You've all agreed that this crew is better than the rest. We work together and get shit done, right?"

Murmurs from the assembled group threatened to deflate her, but Jack said, "What? I can't hear you." Several feet below her, he crossed his arms, anger condensed into unyielding demand.

"Yeah." "Sure." "Eh." "Uh-huh."

"I'm proud to work with you. I trust you and I hope you trust me. I know that you trust Jack."

She paused. Kekoa looked over at Jack and up at her. He stood straighter, lips tight.

"Jack and I trust Nahoa."

A worker scratched the back of his head. Another shifted from foot to foot while a third crossed his arms in front of his chest.

Kerala sighed. "Look. We know things about him now that we didn't before. It's bound to affect the way we see him, but it doesn't mean we were wrong about him."

She looked around. They wanted to believe her, but she would have to give them the arguments to counterbalance finding out they knew a killer. They'd worked side by side with, ate and drank with, maybe surfed and partied with him.

"You've read the statement his lawyers released for the papers or someone's told you about it. When Nahoa was a kid, he fucked up bad. He killed a man and panicked. What I know, what you all need to know so we can get on with the job, is that Nahoa doesn't have the heart of a murderer. You wouldn't be working with him if he did."

Heads came up. Posture softened. They were interested.

"The kid that fucked up beyond all fuck-ups knew one thing. That he would never, ever do anything like that again. He gave up everything he gave a shit about, stopped putting himself in situations that could go sideways. Stopped looking for opportunities to salt cement or break tools." Kerala took a deep breath. Fuck. She was still mad about him doing that.

Bring it home. "He changed his life when he was sixteen. You know." She pointed to a local who'd gone to high school with him. "He dropped out of high school and came to work for Mālama. He did an about-face and threw himself into erasing what he'd done." The crew looked at her, glanced at Nahoa, Jack, and each other.

"I don't know if you can erase murder. But I know that you can get the hell out of the situation that put you in that position. He did. Nahoa changed. And I respect that."

She stopped. Nothing else to say. Either they'd come around or they wouldn't.

"All right. Back to work, and I want total focus from here on out. Got it?"

Jack's voice led the loud chorus of agreement, and the crew splintered back into work groups. Jack followed and made the rounds.

Kerala inhaled deeply. Salt flavored the back of her tongue and the sun's heat crept through her light long-sleeved shirt.

A slight headache made her aware of her tension and she stretched her neck while turning toward Nahoa.

"Well, um." It occurred to her, belatedly, how excruciating that must have been for him. "Maybe that'll help."

She could see hints of a much older Nahoa in the heaviness of his expression. Then his lips began to move, forming the gamine grin that charmed everyone who knew him. His shoulders relaxed. "It already has."

"Well, good." His bearing grew lighter and his smile spread to his eyes. Kerala watched warily. "Let's give them a few minutes to settle in."

She and Nahoa walked away from the house site toward the ocean. The ground changed under her feet, soil giving way to more rubbly lava.

Nahoa spoke as they walked. "The lawyers had me see a counselor. They wanted me to be sure in my own head that I was not at fault, or I'd never convince a judge to reduce the charges, they said. She's smart and attentive, but she hasn't given me a scrap of what you did just now."

"That's good to hear." Her words echoed back and she laughed. "Not that she wasn't helpful." She crunched to a stop in sight of the breakers smashing themselves against the shallows a couple hundred feet out.

Nahoa laughed with her. "I know what you mean." He turned serious. "I am different now, you know. But not in every way."

She cocked her head.

"I turned away from the sovereignty movement because I couldn't deal with what I'd done. You're right. I thought I had to get out of the effort to be sure it would never happen again."

"It worked."

"I haven't killed again." He grimaced and his shoulders shook as if he had a chill. "I've been talking to Ravi…"

"Always trouble."

"…and I've got some ideas on what we can do to focus all this energy, all this anger and frustration that derails kids like me. Move them toward construction rather than destruction. Change the future for them, and for adults like me and Pauahi, people with big mistakes in their past. I've learned about building, making a house or a store or a library or a theater. And I've found a conceptual pathway between the kind of construction we do at Mālama and the creation of a culture. I'm starting to see a way forward."

"So you won't focus on sovereignty?"

The hard sun beat straight down, glossing his wavy hair and gilding his eyelashes. It occurred to her again how beautiful he was. Inside and out. His passion and excitement were gorgeous, all the more so with the addition of some strange hope.

"I have to help find a way to be independent. We have to put together energy systems, agricultural systems, and social systems that use the natural gifts of the islands and our culture to make us strong. Once we're standing tall, we'll be able to kick out the occupying forces and move into our own future."

Kerala bit her cheek. "I wish you all the luck in the world. That's a big job."

"We'll need lots of help."

She shook her head. "I'm almost done here. This is your island, not mine. Those assholes out there protesting that you're not being lynched think they have a right to anything they want. They're so used to being first that they can't handle the idea they're the foreigners here. That's what haole means to me now." She stared across the lava.

"I'll miss you." Nahoa meant it, but he also agreed with what she'd said. She could see it all over his face.

"I'd rather be a guest in your house on occasion than an invader." She shook it off. "First, let's get this house built."

## Chapter Twenty

T he courthouse parking lot was jammed. Ravi rounded a switchback before joining the cars lining the narrow road.

The car behind him parked just beyond and several young people got out. They all looked Hawaiian and chattered excitedly. As he turned, they unrolled a banner and marched toward the courthouse. He tried to make out the words on the other side of the white fabric. "Restore Hawaiian Independence," it read.

He followed the protestors to the courthouse, a chant getting louder and louder as he rounded the dark green leaves of the bright hibiscus. The marchers joined the chant and surged forward. They broke through the gathered crowds and Ravi used the opening to get closer to the courthouse.

When they stopped moving, he was in the middle of an energetic gathering. He turned in a circle, taking a survey of the signs. Some were in Hawaiian, impenetrable to him. Others called for an end to the US occupation of Hawai'i or recognition as Hawaiian nationals. He recognized words like pono and 'āina. Some folks were wrapped in red fabric, holding the Hawaiian flag, and others wore garments of grass and leaf. The chanting and dancing was accompanied by drums, a powerful beat that stirred his blood.

Most people were dressed as though heading to the beach, but many had leis of palm leaves or what looked like chrysanthemums. He pushed through the crowd, murmuring his excuses to people who ignored him. He reached the police guarding the courthouse and showed a cop his driver's license. Kerala had texted him to say he'd need it to get in.

The cop nodded him through and he broke free of the crowd. He tugged his suit coat back into place and looked out over the crowd. He could see two general sentiments expressed on the signs. Most were pro-sovereignty, though only a few mentioned Nahoa directly. The remainder decried Nahoa's actions with statements like "Stop Anti-Haole Violence" and "Bad for Business."

Ravi tore himself away from the vivid outpouring of emotion and entered the courthouse. The chill air tightened the skin on his face after the warmth outside and he found the right door. The courtroom throbbed, almost under the level of hearing, with the drums from out front. It underlay the solemn quiet while a lawyer paced before the judge. A witness appeared calm and answered in a strong voice as Ravi scanned the audience.

Kerala's cropped hair came into view when a large guy shifted in his seat. Ravi took a seat next to her on the otherwise crowded bench. She looked over at him and whispered, "You missed the prosecution's case. Grisly."

Jack and Danny sat just beyond Kerala. Nahoa's father, his mother, and his grandmother, all dressed in aloha formal, were lined behind him. The whole court buzzed with stiff, new aloha shirts.

The witness had moved on to explaining how she knew Nahoa and Ravi settled in to listen.

The judge drummed his fingers on the leather blotter in front of him. He was dark-skinned, about as dark as Ravi himself, but with a European cast to his eyes and bone structure. Portuguese, perhaps, though most positions of power on the island were held by people with Anglo and Japanese backgrounds. Ravi didn't know enough about race relations in Hawai'i to know how the judge's background would affect things.

The defense called witness after witness to attest to Nahoa's good character. People spoke of his youth and his passionate adoption of non-violent direct action. Others addressed the time around his conversion, when he changed so abruptly, giving a clear image of how Willoughby's death had affected him.

The defense spoke. "We call one last witness, Your Honor. Pauahi Māhoe, please take the stand."

Ravi and Kerala exchanged a look. He'd wondered about this. The friend who'd buried the body was the person most able to speak to what happened that night.

"Mr. Māhoe, please tell the court what happened the night you went to salt the cement on Mr. Willoughby's property."

Pauahi swallowed. He looked at the judge and back at Nahoa. "We were best friends. We did everything together. We planned to salt the cement and we got the salt, drove it to the site, and did the job. Nahoa put out one of his little notes." He looked over at the judge. "He always made sure that no one would get hurt. He left warnings behind, telling the workers what we'd done."

The judge nodded his understanding and Pauahi continued. "The man came from nowhere. He just appeared and attacked Nahoa with a metal rod. I ran toward them, but Nahoa took the metal away and he fell. I thought it was funny to see this guy sprawled out. He weighed a lot more than Nahoa, but we were strong from canoeing. We were amped from just being out there and the guy screamed like a little girl. He came at Nahoa again and Nahoa tried to dodge. The guy kept coming and Nahoa hit him."

The courtroom was silent. After all the sideways testimony, all the information about Nahoa's state of mind, the story boiled down to this. The moment when Nahoa struck Vincent Willoughby and caused his death.

Pauahi leaned forward. "I loved Nahoa. I wanted to be him. He could do anything and everybody loved him. He even tried to save the guy, held onto him and tried to stop the bleeding with his hands. When the guy stopped moving, Nahoa screamed. He kept screaming. There wasn't usually anyone around there in the middle of the night, but I was afraid someone would hear and come find us. I pushed him against a truck and held him there until he stopped. I made him leave and then I dragged the body across the ground and buried it under a koa. I did that."

The defense attorney nodded, solemn. "What happened after that?"

"Nahoa never talked to me again. I tried to see him but his grandma turned me away. She said he wasn't well. He never came back to school. He stopped canoeing with us. He changed completely.

I went back and planted a liliko'i. Vincent Willoughby would have wanted a marker. I couldn't give that to him, but I could mark his resting spot that way. I spread stories of 'aumākua protecting the land to keep people away."

Kerala took Ravi's hand, tension radiating from her.

"I couldn't let the body be found. Nahoa couldn't be arrested, he had to be left alone. I always knew he would come back to the sovereignty movement. He wouldn't abandon us forever and I couldn't abandon him."

Nahoa put his hands to his face. Ravi couldn't see his expression, but he imagined the pain.

"Why did they have to pick that spot?" The anguish in Pauahi's voice rang in the silent room. "They didn't need to build there. Anywhere else would have been fine."

Kerala's hand relaxed in Ravi's. He looked at her, only to see the strangest expression move across her face. Relief, pity, aggravation. All played across her face until she looked at him and smiled. He searched her eyes, but she just smiled wider. He raised his eyebrows and she shrugged.

"No further questions." The defense attorney seemed anxious to stop Pauahi's testimony. Ravi imagined he knew what Pauahi had done to stop the construction.

Pauahi left the witness seat and walked straight from the room.

The defense attorney stood. "I'd like to make a motion to vacate."

"Grounds?" The judge's eyes flickered to the prosecutor. Ravi watched the back of the prosecutor's head, wishing he could see his expression.

"My client was not a violent child. He did not plan a murder, nor did he take advantage of an opportunity to kill. Striking Vincent Willoughby was an act of self-defense. Yes, he was the younger and stronger, but he was also the smaller of the two. His wild strength was a product of fear and passion. This is a clear case of impaired judgment and the weight of case law bears on the side of reducing the charge here to manslaughter."

The prosecutor heaved a sigh.

The judge didn't look toward the prosecutor. "We don't need to do this in stages, son. Spit it out."

"The damage done by my client to the cement would have been a Class C felony, not Class A, giving the manslaughter charge a ten-year statute of limitations. Unless the court chooses to try for a murder two conviction, I believe my client must walk free."

The gallery exploded around Ravi. Kerala jumped to her feet and put two fingers in her mouth for a quick whistle. The judge struck his gavel and his jowls shook. "Quiet. I will have quiet."

Ravi sat, frozen. Could this be it?

"What do you have to say, son?"

The prosecutor shrugged. "May I approach?"

"Come ahead," the judge said with an impatient wave. His frown turned fierce as the lawyers joined him at the bench. A sotto voce conversation raged for a few short minutes while the gallery vibrated with renewed tension.

The conference came to an end and the judge cleared his throat. A quivering attention waited on his words and he added to the tension by sipping at a glass of water.

"The court believes that the state lacks probable cause for second degree murder and accepts the defense's argument that the case is beyond the statute of limitations as manslaughter."

The air left Ravi's lungs as though pulled by a vacuum. He put his face in his hand, unable to comprehend that Nahoa would be free. When he looked up, Nahoa held his grandmother's hand.

"I have a strong suggestion. Not an order, mind you. The resolution of these proceedings leaves me without the authority." Ravi searched the judge's face for rancor but only found hints of satisfaction. "Nahoa Kalama. You will not be charged with murder, but you killed a man."

A shiver passed over Nahoa, and he nodded.

"Given your ties to Native Hawaiian ideals, it's past time for hoʻoponopono. If you need a recommendation for a kūpuna, I would like to point you to a new organization that is partnering with us at the courts to bring Hawaiian reconciliation techniques into our sentencing options."

"Thank you, sir." Nahoa's voice sounded full of tears.

"You will need to be out-processed and then you are free to go."

Nahoa's grandmother cried out in joy and he turned into her arms, where he belonged.

❖

Kerala walked Ravi to his car. She thought about taking his hand. "I wonder if Alakai will follow up on Pauahi."

"I don't know."

She tried to slow their pace, but Ravi walked ahead. "Pauahi seems so beaten already. I'm leaning toward asking Tūtū Alapaʻi to run another hoʻoponopono. Maybe I can let go, maybe I can't."

He turned around and stopped. "He hurt you, Kerala. I don't know if I can forgive that."

She tried to smile, but it didn't work. "I know better, Ravi. You have a huge heart."

He walked away.

She'd hoped reconnecting with him would go smoother. He reached the rental car, opened the door, and stood there, eyes steady on her but shadowed. He looked tired. Wasn't he taking care of himself?

"Need a place to stay? I have plenty of room." His hands tensed on the door's weather stripping. He released the door and shook his head.

He was going to make this hard.

Before he could reply, she grabbed his hand through the open window. "Please, come home with me." She let go of his hand and stepped around the door. "Come home with me," she repeated as she twined her arms around his neck and lay her body along his. Rising to her toes slid her suit coat along his, silk on silk, and brought her lips to his.

The long, slow pull in her belly fought with an edgy awareness that he had yet to wrap her up the way she wanted. "Don't be difficult," she said against his lips, looking into his eyes from millimeters away. She'd rather irritate him than hurt him.

His eyes narrowed and his lips firmed under hers. He started to speak and she took the opening of his lips as an opportunity. The slide of her tongue inside made him groan. She filtered her fingers through the thick hair at his nape, warm from the sun, tickling his neck while she continued to deepen the kiss in slow, teasing thrusts.

His hands grabbed her hips in the thin slacks. His shoulders bunched when he pulled her harder into him and she ran her hands across them. She lowered herself back into the heels of her men's dress shoes and slid her hands down his lapels.

"Nice suit."

"I like yours too. The nipped in waist makes me think of Marlene Dietrich."

"That was a tux in *Monaco*."

"I know." He smiled for the first time. "Still."

Kerala's heart kicked and she tried to hold his eyes. Instinct and training told her to turn away, to hide her emotion until she could get it under control.

She pulled back far enough to give him a smacking kiss on the lips. She framed his face in her hands. She knew what she needed to say. "I've missed you."

"I've missed you, too." He leaned closer.

"You feel so good." She stroked his back. "Do you know how long you'll be staying?"

"About a week, this time."

"Well, we'd better make it count. There will be a party for Nahoa's release. Tomorrow, maybe."

"I thought about hanging out with him tonight."

"Tonight's for family. Let's get home." Home with Ravi. Perfection.

"I'll follow you there."

"Or we could return the rental car, stick together this week."

Ravi looked wary. "I'm in."

Ravi pulled his sunglasses from his pocket as he left the rental car office. Eyes protected, he crossed to Kerala's truck and slipped out of his suit coat. He opened the passenger door and draped the coat across the back of the seat.

Kerala had also taken the formality down a level.

Her breasts hovered under the soft, thin layer of cream silk, more revealed than hidden by the wedge-shaped lace panels. Spaghetti straps lay lax on her muscular shoulders next to bra straps that dug in. The material bunched in loose folds at her waist and disappeared into her slim slacks. Ravi swallowed hard and reached out for her across the bench seat.

"Get in, horndog. We already made out at the courthouse. We're not repeating the scene here."

A hop got him onto the seat and a bounce brought her within reach. The long, lean shape of her hip drew one of his hands, but he cupped her breast through the silk chemise and bra with the other, finding her nipple and teasing it hard in seconds. "Why don't you take us home?"

She blinked and blew at her hair. "Yeah, good idea." She glanced over at him and he leaned in to kiss her cheek, her hairline at her temple, her jaw where it angled toward her chin. When her eyelashes fell and flickered, his chest tightened.

He didn't want to love her. But he did.

When she pulled into her driveway, he got out and slammed the truck door behind him. He reached her open door as she turned, took her by the waist, and pulled her from the truck.

She tried to turn around, perhaps to grab her suit coat or his luggage.

"Later," he growled. A nudge closed the door, and he bundled her to the front door.

She groped for her house key, but he couldn't let her be. He wrapped himself around her from the back and slid his fingers into the waist of her slacks. Her belly flexed, the instinctive muscular reaction sending him into a frenzy. He bit her shoulder and grabbed her breasts, his arms under hers. Her skin was milk against the cream of the chemise.

The keys in her hand rattled, useless, against the door when she braced herself against his shove. She moaned long and low, her hips seeking backward, bending to take the thrust. He sought her nipples through the bra and snarled in frustration. He pushed one leg between hers and she shoved back against it.

They were as near to fucking as he'd ever been on a front stoop, in a populated neighborhood, in full daylight. He grabbed her keys and stabbed at the lock. One hand still pulled her breast tight to her ribs, lifting and squeezing, but he managed the bolt-lock and door knob.

They fell through the door and landed on the carpet beyond, scrabbling at each other's clothes. Ravi's undershirt came over his head and his belt slackened while he unclipped Kerala's bra. She kicked out and the door slammed.

He pinned her to the floor, hands on her wrists and his full weight on her torso. Her legs twisted around his and she lurched. He refused to be flipped and bit at her chin, her lips, her neck, until she went lax beneath him.

He released her wrists and her hands speared into his hair, pulling him in for a deep kiss. She rocked under him and swept her tongue against his feverishly. He spread his legs, depriving her of something to push her pussy against, and slowed the kiss. Braced on his elbows, he stroked her hair and forced her to accept slow, drugging kisses that went on and on. His weight seemed to anchor her and she let her legs fall.

Her compliance cracked the veneer of control he'd formed. His mouth raced down her throat to her shoulder. He straddled her hips and sat up far enough to pull the chemise's straps off her arms. He pulled off the loose bra and tossed it aside.

She licked her lips. Her slitted eyes showed only a gleam. The flush across her chest and shoulders gave way to the tan that started at her biceps. He'd never seen anyone look so complicated, so sexy and multifarious, with silk draped across her stiff nipples and pure strength in the arms that rose to his shoulders. Knowing that she could pull him in or push him away, gratitude filled him when she simply held on, letting him lead.

He drew his hands along her arms and brought her hands up for a kiss, one at a time. He would glut himself on her, give himself permission to take what he wanted, whether that be more time or less. She always wanted to rush, to chase the orgasm. She would just have to wait this time.

"What?" she asked, voice low.

He breathed the skin of her knuckles, damped one with the tip of his tongue, rubbed it on his cheek. Crack, crumble, crash. The last of the walls he'd built around his heart blew away under the power of his love for her.

"Tell me what you want," she demanded. Her body began a sinuous motion that made him want to feel her waist flex. As soon as he became aware of the desire, he gave into it. He released her hands and stroked her sides while she moved. The muscularity of her torso amazed him and he held tight.

"Talk to me," she begged.

"I'll show you, instead."

Ravi sat on her thighs, knees against her hips, and brought his mouth to the silk over her nipple. It tightened in his mouth and he sucked, hard. His hands slid the silk over her ribs. Up and down, up and down, while his teeth bit and pulled, while he sucked and gnawed at her. Her abdomen flexed and eased, telegraphing his effect, making him want more.

He parted her legs with a knee and released her wet nipple. He slid the silk down with his hands and followed with his mouth. Her ribcage flowed with her breath, in and out, hot even in the slight chill of the closed-up house.

Her hands on his shoulders urged him down, but he slowed further. The faint, simple scent of her skin soaked into him, made him linger with his lips and nose in the hollow under her diaphragm. She arched into him and he wrapped his arms around her.

He moved to her side, but when she tried to roll with him, he draped his upper body over hers. Her stiff nipples poked at his side and he looked down her body, away from her face. She arched once but subsided when he didn't budge. The lanky, subtle curves of her flowed away across the floor and he explored with his hand.

He could smell her now, the rich loam of her inside the silk underwear. He grazed his fingers just under, along the liminal zone where smooth skin turned to soft hair, softer than most. He loved her pussy, puffed with desire. He slipped his fingers inside, between silk and satiny skin, between silk and hair, along the curve to the part he couldn't see from his position. He pulled her lips, squeezed them together, and pressed them against bone.

He took an unsteady breath at the unequivocal signs of her arousal. Heat, damp, and the insistent press of her clit. He rocked it, oh so gently, from side to side. From one side and then the other, he explored the edges of her from outside the protective pillow of her labia.

When she writhed, a slow, dreamy flex of hips and thighs, his throat tightened.

He moved lower, between her legs. He met her eyes, soft and calm, stroked her waist. Her thighs spread wide and drew her lips apart like ripe fruit bursting.

Before his moan ended, his breath stirred the light hair framing her deep rose center. He breathed deeply and her scent was on his tongue when he touched her with it. Soft, flat tongue to sweep up as much of her taste as he could reach. One side and the other, as deep as he could reach and up over the top of her proud clit, back down and back up. He moved the shaft of her clit from side to side, until she groaned and grasped at his ears.

He pulled free and moved lower. Her hips rose off the floor and he braced them on his palms. His nose nudged her clit and he licked around her pussy, gathering her wetness where it pooled. She shivered when his tongue passed over her urethra and arched harder when it flicked over her clit once, twice. He returned to her opening, lapped at it, and swirled around just inside. She pulsed around his tongue and he trembled. Her hips danced in his hands, swiping her clit across his forehead, wetting his entire face. He gasped and dove to capture her clit in his mouth.

The tiny hard-on scraped against his teeth when she jerked and shook. He used the flat of his tongue again, curled to the shape of her clit, and lapped with agonizing slowness at the raw flesh. The taste of her lubrication faded into the metallic flavor of skin that isn't skin, of the body's interior made accessible, and he shuddered.

He pulled a hand free and she braced her own hips high enough for him to slip two fingers into her. The arch of her back, the tension of her thighs and ass, whipped the frenzy in him. He pushed deep and pulled back out partway. Setting complimentary rhythms, he sucked while pulsing his tongue, pushing on her clit when his fingers pulled down from the inside. He visualized her whole clit, from the head in his mouth, inside her body, branching along the sides of her pussy. He twisted his hand to massage the clit legs inside while his mouth courted the most tender, most sensitive bit.

Low moans flowed between them. From his mouth into her clit and from her mouth into the air, they vibrated together until she jerked, harder and harder, her clit pulling back and her pussy tightening around his questing fingers. He nuzzled hard, chasing her clit in its retreat and switching from sucking to fast rubbing.

She gasped over and over, short wails that matched the contractions of her thick walls. His body did the same, to his great surprise, orgasm sneaking up from his utter preoccupation with her body's response.

When her breaths became pants and began to steady, he thrust his fingers, the flesh of her sliding against his knuckles, and made fast circles with his lips smashed hard into her clit. She screamed, convulsed, hips falling to the floor and rolling from side to side. He followed her, too hungry to give her a moment to recover. When her hips tipped down and his mouth couldn't follow, he gripped her hard in his hand, like a bowling ball, and kept fucking her with his fingers while the base of his thumb did what she needed on her clit.

Her hands scrabbled at his shoulders and he rose over her, his hand still in her pussy. He caught her weeping cries in his mouth and fucked her with his tongue and fingers, sucked at her lips, met her crazed eyes from centimeters away. She rolled and twitched, writhed and sobbed until her hand gripped his. She continued to quake as he pulled his fingers from her. He pet her pussy and rested his hand on it soothingly.

Her eyes focused and the hectic flush eased from her skin. Ravi made himself comfortable on one elbow next to her and watched the process. She was so beautiful, contrasts and all. If only he could keep her like this forever. Soft. Accepting.

Her face took on its more familiar lines, tighter, stronger lines and she looked over at him. He loved this part of her too, no matter what words were about to come from her opening mouth.

"Wow."

He laughed, relief and joy. He'd been so sure she would look for distance right away.

"I'm a selfish pig, but you'll just have to wait to get yours." The last word wavered, caught in the final shudder of a full-body stretch.

"Don't worry about it. I came a little too, just from feeling you go over like that."

Her eyes popped all the way open. "No way."

"Way." He lay back and closed his eyes, satisfaction pulsing from him in waves. Maybe he should try to devise an instrument that could measure the emanations of serious pleasure.

"Seriously?"

"Seriously." He chuckled when he felt her lean over him and opened his eyes to see her searching his face. Apparently satisfied, she lay back on the carpet.

"Wow."

"Never had a sympathetic orgasm?"

"I had no idea that was even possible."

Amused, Ravi tipped his head toward her. She'd raised her arms over her head. The hard line of her farmer's tan drew his fingers.

She jerked. "Hey! That tickled."

"Sorry." Mostly.

He looked at the ceiling, hands on his belly. The softness felt good, as did his loosened belt and undone trouser button.

"Sympathetic orgasm, eh?"

Everything felt good. "Yep."

"Do you think you have to, to love someone to get that?"

Ice pierced his lungs, his ease gone in an instant.

"Hey, shhh. It's okay."

He hadn't made a sound. The textured plaster on her ceiling held deep shadows, reminding him both that it was getting late and that he'd started his day in a different time zone. Exhaustion flooded him and he closed his eyes.

"I'm sorry, Ravi. I wasn't trying to make light of your feelings. Come on, man. Look at me."

It seemed so much easier to just float away. Sleep would make things better.

An irritable edge crept into her voice. "Ravi. Look at me."

She wouldn't leave him alone, so he opened his eyes. He tried to blank his expression, tried to maintain a little privacy with his pain. He should have known better than to hope. He'd left and he'd accepted. Then she called him, needed him, and he'd been there for her. He'd rationalized it. He didn't hate her. He could be a friend.

But she knew. She knew he loved her and still she made a crack like that? He hadn't thought her cruel.

He sat, stiff after the flight, sitting around in court, sex on the floor. The goddamn floor for fuck's sake. He rolled to one knee and gained his feet. His pants sagged at his waist and he buttoned them. His hands went to his belt, but Kerala's were there first.

She held on and he let go.

"Ravi, I'm sorry for the way things went. I don't know that it could have gone any other way, given who you are and who I am. I learned a lot about my feelings when you left, though, and I know now that you're important to me."

He met her eyes. She wore her most sincere expression, but it was the hint of temper that got through to him. She was saying the words, but she wasn't happy about it. "Is that so?"

Lines formed on her forehead. "What are you looking for here?"

He sighed and glanced down. Her slacks and underwear were pooled around her ankles and she was otherwise nude. Unwelcome humor flowed through him. Whatever happened, she would always be the woman who could have a relationship fight with her pants around her ankles.

A weary smile spread across his face and he waved at the couch. "Would you like to put your clothes back on so we can talk?"

She chewed her cheek and nodded once like she'd made a decision. "Nope. I want to get you naked and talk in bed."

He raised his hands and let them fall. "That's your answer? Fuck some more?"

"I said talk, didn't I?" She looked calm, like her mind was settled. She reached out and undid his button. Tug of war with a single trouser button.

She stepped out of her clothes and closer to him. She ran his zipper down and slid his pants off his hips. He shook to help them fall and stripped his shorts.

"There. We're both naked. Now what?"

"Come on." She led him into the bedroom and sat. He was so tired that he spread out across the bed flat on his back. She took one of his hands and put it to her cheek. She swallowed once, and again, before she spoke.

"I never knew that there was a love that pulsed in fingers and toes. I feel suffused with love for you right now, Ravi. It must be radiating from me everywhere." She shrugged helplessly. "It's beautiful and exciting and I've never been so scared in my life."

Energy flooded back into him. "I can't believe what I'm hearing."

She touched his face. "I'm trying to be brave here. Help me out."

"I love you too, Kerala. I don't want to scare you, but I agree that it is beautiful and exciting."

"You don't scare me. My feelings scare me. The possibility of hurting you scares me."

"I can take care of myself." He pushed up to lean against the headboard. It was truer than it used to be. He'd come a long way too. She'd overcome some of her fear and he'd gained a lot of strength.

Kerala searched his face, looking for more reaction. She found hope and love and decided that was good enough. "Well, then. I should tell you that I've been making some big life decisions in the last few weeks."

His eyebrows rose. "Have you."

She sat facing him, cross-legged on the bed. "Hawai'i isn't working for me." She gave him a moment, but he just looked at her. "I was looking for a no-strings work family and jumped headfirst into a place where family is never casual. Developing the island chafes at me, and I have more sympathy now for people who don't want their ancestors' remains messed with. But mostly, I just think that Hawai'i belongs to the Hawaiians."

"What will you do?"

She eyed him suspiciously. His tone was mild, but he'd crossed his arms on his chest. "Find work on the mainland. Move back. This house is in pretty good shape. I put some work into it and it shouldn't be hard to sell it for what I've got in it, at least."

"That's all very practical."

Stung by his tone, she said, "Why wouldn't I be?"

A strange smile passed over his face and disappeared. "Well, I've been having the same thoughts. Nahoa and I have talked a lot since he was arrested and I can't see my way clear to being an absentee landowner in a place so heavily marked by colonialism. We're working on plans to turn the house you're building me into a community center and sort of demo house for the technologies that might help Hawaiians gain real independence. Not just from the political hand of the US, but from the resources that have to be shipped in for practically everything."

She sat ramrod straight. "You're changing the building plans and just telling me now?"

"You're changing your life plans and just telling me now?"

She brushed his argument aside. "We've already started framing in the rooms. If you're making significant changes, we have to nail them down right away."

"We can do that later. So where do you think you'll end up?"

Irritated by the distraction, she said, "I don't want to go back to the East Coast and don't want to get too far from the ocean. I don't know how the market sits right now, but I'm planning to start checking it out. I won't be leaving before your project is done, of course."

"Yeah. You'll do what you've committed to."

"Don't make it sound like that's a bad thing."

"It's not. Of course it's not." He sighed. "We've talked about it some, this feeling that Hawai'i just isn't for us, but I didn't know you were serious about leaving."

"I won't say that I made the decision on impulse, but it wasn't something I felt the need to talk through either. You and Nahoa hashed it all out, I bet. The structural and interpersonal inequities and racism and colonialism and its long-term effects on people. That's not how I make most of my big decisions, Ravi. I get as clear a picture as I can and let it slosh around a while. The right choice makes itself known before too long, for the most part."

"Your method intimidates me, Kerala. Do you see how it could be nerve-wracking, knowing that you may be sloshing around ideas that affect me without talking to me about them?"

"Sure." She twisted the sheet in her hands. "I've been told before that I'm unpredictable and cruel and hardheaded and all sorts of things. When I left the ex, it was sudden. To her, at least. We weren't happy together and it took a little while for me to realize that the answer wasn't try harder. Be more butch. Let her have her head. It was to reject her need to shape me into someone I wasn't."

"I see why you had to leave her. I get it. But I'm worried that there's something stewing in you right now, or there will be sometime later, that will be the end of us. And I won't see it coming."

"I told you I love you just ten minutes ago. Why worry about all that now?"

Ravi cocked his head. "No, you didn't."

"Yes, I did." Disbelief and irritation edged her voice.

"You said you felt full of love. Suffused with love."

"How is that different?"

"I love you, Kerala. It is an enduring connection that I feel in different ways in different moments. Sometimes it suffuses me too and I'm overwhelmed by it. Sometimes it leaves room for being pissed off at you or busy working or whatever else. You spoke to the momentary sensation, not to the connection that created it. I've learned to cherish the moments you are close to me and not try to rope you into connection and commitment. I've done a pretty good job, but I'll be damned if I'll let you think it's not hard, knowing that you may decide at any moment that you're done. That something sloshed around and spit out the end of us."

Kerala looked at her hands. She looked at his gentle, understanding face. She rubbed her hand on her chest, where a knot seemed to have formed.

"Okay, back up." She looked at him, eye to eye, and put all the strength of her self-knowledge behind what she had to say. "I love you, Ravi. I won't wander off or casually wave good-bye. Promises are a big deal and I don't know what I can promise you along the lines of forever."

"I don't want you to say things you don't mean."

She raised an eyebrow. "I don't." She shook her head. "Look, we're at so many crossroads that I can't see six months into the future, let alone into the deep long term. But I can make you a promise that might help. Even if it's hard, even if it goes against my inclinations, I won't let anything stew without coming to you about it. I can promise you that, if I leave you, it won't be a surprise."

His eyes crinkled. "I've never heard anything so romantic."

She threw a pillow at him. "You're going to make fun of me, after I open up like that?"

He reared up and pinned her back on the bed. "I'm not making fun." She glared at him until the sincerity in his voice penetrated. "You are the most amazing person and I love you so much. That's a generous promise and it makes me feel so much better. You heard what I needed and offered it. That is romance to me."

She softened, suspicion fading, replaced by a warmth she'd never felt before. Love and trust and the prospect of hard work in tough times. She could do this.

## CHAPTER TWENTY-ONE

Hekili sat at the head of the table and Ravi decided that, this time, he would take the foot. Though Mālama Construction hosted the meeting, Ravi and Nahoa would run it.

In that spirit, Ravi tapped the table with his knuckles. "Let's get started, folks."

The conference room air conditioner labored to process the combined body heat of better than a dozen people. A handful of Nahoa's old friends fidgeted in chairs along one wall, while the main players sat at the table.

Joy sat close to Hekili, Nahoa next to her. Ravi had pulled Kerala down beside him. Opposite, Tūtū Alapaʻi sat surrounded by Walter and the other guys from the canoe club.

Ravi said, "This is a meeting to rough out a plan for an organization that will take over the house Mālama started for me. We're going to try to leave here with some concrete steps for the next couple of months. Big questions include the type of organization you want to form, the steps for assuming ownership of the land and the building, and conditions or considerations in the meantime."

Nahoa put his hands on the table. "I'd like to start by thanking Ravi for coming to me with his concerns about the house. He had the will and the resources to plan it as a sustainable dwelling. When he began learning about the island, he had the wisdom and empathy to change that plan for the good of the Hawaiians who have kuleana, or the privilege of responsibility, for the ʻāina."

"Thanks, Ravi." A chorus of voices repeated the sentiment, and Ravi tried to wave away their gratitude. His face warmed at being acknowledged for doing the right thing.

"I wish I could donate it to you directly. The loan is a problem, though. I planned to document the performance of the technology we install and tweak the systems. The data would have made the payments and taxes worthwhile to me in my position at Sol Volt."

Nahoa nodded. "I don't see why that can't happen anyway. I'm thinking about the building and the land as laboratories for Hawaiians to experiment with the best blends of tradition and new tech. Though our metrics might be different from yours, we could commit to taking whatever measurements you need along with our own."

"Excellent. Even though I'm leaving Sol Volt and returning to the lab, the data will be immensely helpful. Especially if we can hammer out ways of using and improving the systems without getting in each other's way."

Nahoa sat forward and leaned his elbows on the table. "We need to talk about ownership. Even if we register as a nonprofit tomorrow, no bank is going to let us assume Ravi's loan. We can dedicate ourselves to raising enough money to pay the taxes through programs and donations, but I don't think we can count on taking over the loan payments right away. We should write the agreement so that when we can make loan payments, that counts toward eventual purchase."

Hekili spoke. "Mālama Construction has to change. We should assume the loan and take a lead in this new type of construction. Our company was known for being a Hawaiian-owned company that worked well with outsiders, inspectors, and workers. With all the publicity around Nahoa's trial"—Nahoa flinched—"we've had several prospective jobs pulled. With new room in our schedule and a shared desire to do better for our 'ohana, I want to become the island's experts on building Native Hawaiian houses on Hawaiian Home Lands. Mālama can be the number one name in construction on these homestead lots with grants from the Office of Hawaiian Affairs."

"Yes!" It burst from Ravi before he could think. How perfect!

Nahoa breathed out slowly. "I never thought I'd be able to keep working construction after all that's happened. I can do that, though. I can specialize in getting the approvals and finding the clients. We can incorporate what works for the community center in the houses we build."

"You're going to be busy, if you plan to run a community center, work a full time job, and get up to speed on the requirements from the

OHA." Hekili seemed pleased by Nahoa's reaction, but worry tinged his voice.

Joy touched Nahoa's arm. "We can work on it together."

"All of it." Nahoa took her hand.

Hekili held his mother's eyes and Tūtū Alapaʻi reached down the table to grab his hand.

Kerala shot Ravi a smile and he grinned back. The group seemed to knit itself tighter and tighter. If anyone could change life for Hawaiians, it would be these people, this ʻohana, working with like-minded folks. "I wasn't expecting that when I walked in here today. I'm excited that the community center might open under Native Hawaiian ownership from the beginning. I have to admit that I was looking forward to having a part in it, though."

Nahoa raised his eyebrows, his signature grin wide and happy. "There is so much of you in the design of the building and the systems that you'll always be a part of it. Besides, I think we should write into any contract that we'll continue to measure and share the data you wanted to gather from the systems."

Walter pounded his fists on the table. "Hell yeah! The only problem is this community center language. We need a name, something that doesn't smell like dirty socks and look like cheap vinyl tile."

Kerala spoke for the first time. "I've been thinking about that."

Everyone turned to her in surprise. Nahoa said, "You don't know any Hawaiian."

She pursed her lips. "Be that as it may, I flipped through some Hawaiian dictionaries and lists of common words. I thought it might be nice to name it after what you want it to be. A workshop."

Nahoa cocked his head. "A workshop. A place where things are brought to be fixed or restored. We can honor the work we do there and recognize that it's a process at the same time." He savored the words. "Hale ʻOihana. The place where we work on ourselves and our culture."

A murmur swept the room, one voice after another repeating the name. As the repetitions got louder, they also regularized and turned into a chant. One of the canoe team tapped on the table, drumming the beat, and the decision was made.

Walter turned to Kerala. "Good insight, Kerala. Good name."

"Thanks." She looked pleased with the reaction to her suggestion.

❖

Kerala sat cross-legged on the bed. She folded Ravi's socks while he took care of his shirts. They'd gotten pretty damn domestic, but it worked for her.

"What made you look into names for the community center?"

She shrugged and picked up two more matching socks. "I don't know. I read it somewhere and the name struck a chord with me."

He tucked the stack of shirts next to the pants in his suitcase. Tidy as he was, even he couldn't live out of a suitcase without having to repack before leaving. Thinking about that, she said, "Next time you visit, you should hang your stuff in the closet." She pushed the small pile of socks toward him.

He didn't answer, so she looked at him.

Fuck. What had she said this time?

His flush and the tension in his neck both faded. "You are something else, Kerala. Stand up."

Wary, she unfolded her legs and stood next to the bed. He wrapped her in a tight hug and swayed. She hugged him back. "I love you, Ravi. I'll miss you."

"Not for long." He squeezed tight enough to make her squeak and released her with a laugh. "Haven't you learned that I'm a milestones kind of guy?"

"That's it? You got verklempt because I said you should use the closet?"

"Of course I did." He turned away to zip his suitcase closed. "It's the kind of thing most people do earlier. Well, I don't know about most people, but it usually comes earlier in my relationships."

"Yeah, you bring the toaster on the second date. Or have furniture delivered."

"You don't know." He winked at her and she laughed. "I love you too, Kerala. I've worked hard to keep from putting too many expectations on you, but I've done such a good job that you can take me by surprise with the smallest things."

She felt it again. The welling fullness in the breast that she hoped never to lose. "I want you to be comfortable with me, Ravi. I think it's time you stop worrying about pushing for too much and start telling me what you need."

He gazed at her intently. "Okay. I will." He laughed again, this time more freely. "I will."

She leaned in and kissed him. Just a meeting of mouths, lips soft and easy.

"I can't wait to show you around Santa Cruz and Capitola and Monterrey. And we're invited to dinner at my parents'."

She pulled back. "In for a penny, in for a pound."

"You already know my mom."

"And you're convinced I'll love your dad. I remember. Of course. It'll be great."

"Everything's up in the air. Sol Volt is gone for me. It doesn't matter that there's still a company by that name. It's not the place I loved. But, when it comes right down to it, I belong in the lab. I'm putting feelers out with universities and colleges, though not with other companies, for professional courtesy."

"And because of those pesky NDA and non-compete agreements."

He grinned at her. "Sol Volt's are liberal compared with most, but there are some lines I can't cross. Regardless. It doesn't matter. I'm trying to say something else right now." He kissed her forehead, her cheek, and her lips. "I don't know where I'll be, but I want to be with you."

"Me too." Kerala hugged him hard.

"Will you sell your house and move in with me?" Nerves prickled, though he figured he knew her answer.

"Well, sure, handsome. Or we can get a new place and move in together. How long do you think it'll take to wrap up the CEO thing? Wonder where we'll end up."

Ravi inhaled Kerala's scent. Leave it to her to go straight to practicalities. He pulled back and looked into her eyes. "I love you."

She grinned, eyes sparkling like she knew what she'd done. "I love you too."

❖

Months later, the party flowed around the tables of food. Kerala ate wakame, the seaweed and sesame flavors making her want more and more. Better with sake, but needs must. Whatever the hell that meant.

The speeches had lasted awhile. Hawaiians knew how to talk story, though, and she'd never been to a more interesting ribbon cutting. Nahoa had poured himself into making sure that the community understood what they were trying to do at Hale 'Oihana. He explained how the plan that went along with it could put the islands on an independent footing, whether political sovereignty came quickly or took longer to achieve.

Kids brought people water and the older folks sat under awnings.

Walter brought dozens of people to the event. Detective Alakai showed up with a huge family she didn't know he had. Tūtū Alapa'i was around somewhere, along with Hekili and the rest of the Mālama Construction crew.

Even Pauahi was present. He'd requested permission through Nahoa, asking whether it would ruin her enjoyment of the day if he attended. Kerala had been surprised to realize that she was okay with him being there. Really, truly okay with it.

Ravi broke off his conversation with one of the solar retailers on the island and walked over to her. She offered him the seaweed-laden chopsticks and he nipped the wakame right off the end.

They finished it together and he put the dishes in a bin. "Come see the house."

"I know the place. I helped build it."

"Yeah, but see what they've done."

Her house had sold before she'd completed construction on the Hale. A few weeks in a motel had been a rough transition from her house in Hawai'i to the house she and Ravi had chosen together. Their first month of living together had been hectic, with both of them starting new jobs and getting used to each other on a new level.

They approached the Hale. She could see from the outside that they'd decorated the place gorgeously. Flowers and palm leaves covered everything, and no surface looked industrial.

Ravi led her inside and they listened in on the mini-tour Joy was giving.

"Some green-specific building standards are natural here. With the walk-off matt and shoe storage area at the entrance, we preserve the floors and keep the building cleaner. Also, taking off our shoes can make us feel at home, welcome, and more relaxed. It's an invitation, though, not a requirement, so folks with orthotics don't need special permission to leave theirs on.

"Speaking of accessibility, the entire building and grounds far exceed ADA requirements, including the use of materials safe for people with chemical sensitivities. So far, we've chosen to have lots of plants and we're measuring the effect of various species on our visitors.

"Some of our energy efficient features are the clerestory windows for natural lighting, light tubes in side rooms, and all-LED lighting controlled with dimmers, photo cells, timers, and motion detectors. We measure how much each fixture uses and rotate through controllers so that we can choose the best for each room.

"The solar on the roof and past the hill provide much of the energy we need. Add the wind generator, and we should be able to make power in most weather. We've applied for permits to build a wave generator that would use regular ocean movement to make more power. That's one force that never stops."

Kerala turned to Ravi. "They're doing it?"

He grinned. "Maybe. They have a better chance of being approved than I did."

Joy continued. "Our power draws are mostly twelve-volt. We have an inverter, small for a place this size, for the remaining needs. With all this, we have watched our battery banks fill and empty like lungs, soaking up natural power and providing us enough to run computers, kitchen appliances, and much more."

Kerala looked at Ravi. Sure enough, he was beaming.

Joy led the group through an open archway and stopped at the kitchen sink. "Food waste goes through a chute built into the counter here and becomes compost out back. The water comes from a cave about fifty feet down. The cold seawater travels one of two routes. When the air inside the Hale 'Oihana is hot, it travels through pipes in the walls, cooling each room. Otherwise, it bypasses those pipes and goes to the desalinator, which separates the salt out. The brine goes to the secondary workshop across the way so we can turn it into health and beauty products without the scented ones causing trouble. Some of the water goes to holding tanks and the rest is pumped to the rooftop solar heating system. Hot and cold fresh water at each tap from the ocean right out there." She waved a hand at the horizon.

A stranger said, "I'm surprised there's no view of the ocean."

Joy pointed back to the main room. "The only ocean views are through the periscope in there."

Two teenaged boys dashed toward it and the group laughed at their eagerness.

"There are good reasons for that," she continued. "This land is delicate. The Hale is far enough from the shoreline to protect the beach and cliffs, which also makes the house disappear from the water and keeps the view clear."

The talkative stranger said, "I thought I'd see more of the house driving up, too. From the road, it just looks like this shining cantilevered arch in the middle of lava rock."

Joy focused on him. "The shine comes from the solar panels. The arch is the roof of the lanai."

"I get that now, but you have to admit that it seems more like art than architecture."

Kerala wanted to clap and Ravi looked like he was about to burst his buttons. She'd seen that arch so many times in her imagination as the construction had progressed. As an architect, she had fallen in love with that feature.

Joy nodded. "We can't all squeeze into the bathrooms, but you'll see that we have a collection of composting toilets. Since that's not my favorite subject to talk about, anyone who would like more information can ask Nahoa."

That got a general laugh as Joy stepped out the back door. "The Hale 'Oihana is built on a low-impact post and pier foundation, but construction is rough on land. Grading was limited to fifteen feet all around the Hale and no part of the disturbed site has been left uncovered or unstabilized. As a matter of fact, there are no impervious surfaces outside the house footprint, meaning that water can flow nearly as easily through the ground now as it could before construction began."

Joy led the group around the house, pointing out that all the walkways were made with recycled wood or stone. She started down a path to show the group how gray water and rainwater runoff from the roof panels were sent to a catchment and piped to the garden in drip irrigation systems.

Ravi and Kerala lingered on the lanai.

Kerala leaned against his arm. "I've seen the rest."

"Me too." He looked after the group a moment. "I have to admit, they've done more with this place than I could have. With the new housing Mālama is building, I have more data than I'd expected. UC Solar is thrilled. They get me and all the information from this new hotbed of eco construction."

"We're making our own hotbed in the Bay Area." She didn't need to soothe him, but she had found that she enjoyed it sometimes. Of course, she did it her own way.

"I'm glad we started the ball rolling here, even though we can't stay. You wouldn't be the new kid here anymore."

"They're not treating me as the new kid at my new job. You'd think they'd built their entire company around me, the way they want me around for everything." She loved the company so far. They had a new initiative to do more green building, greener building, beyond the rubber stamps and green codes and into experimental and ancient technologies for temperature maintenance and lighting and all sorts of things. She was hot property with the Hale ʻOihana under her tool belt.

"We should get going so we don't miss our flight."

Kerala turned and walked toward the truck with him. "I can't wait to get off this island."

"Beautiful as it is, I'm with you."

"Better be."

Ravi faced her and took her hands. "I love you, Kerala."

"I love you, Ravi." She walked with him to the rental car.

"I hate driving," he said. "What do you think of commuting by bike?"

"I think you're going to have an uphill battle if you want me to bike to work."

He grinned at her. "I'm in."

# About the Author

Dena Hankins writes aboard her boat, preferably in a quiet anchorage. Being a military brat, wanderlust is deep in her, and she has been sailing since 1999, covering waters from Seattle to San Francisco, across to Hawai'i, and from Virginia to Maine. She spent eight years as a sexpert at Babeland, soaking up the most stimulating stories of human sexuality, and is honored to provide some tales in return. She is a queer, poly, kinky, adventurous sailor with so much left to learn!

Her queer/trans romance novel, *Blue Water Dreams*, was named one of the Best of 2014 by Out in Print, and the sex scenes are called "graceful, sure, and spicy" by *Publishers Weekly*. She started as a short story erotica writer and has well-reviewed stories in seven anthologies. Find out more at www.denahankins.net. She would love to hear from you at dena@denahankins.net.

Whether traveling in the physical world or ranging far in her imagination, she is happiest accompanied by her partner since 1996, James Lane.

# Books Available from Bold Strokes Books

**Break Point** by Yolanda Wallace. In a world readying for war, can love find a way? (978-1-62639-5-688)

**Countdown** by Julie Cannon. Can two strong-willed, powerful women overcome their differences to save the lives of seven others and begin a life they never imagined together? (978-1-62639-4-711)

**Heart of the Liliko'i** by Dena Hankins. Secrets, sabotage, and grisly human remains stall construction on an ancient Hawaiian burial ground, but the sexual connection between Kerala and Ravi keeps building toward a volcanic explosion. (978-1-62639-5-565)

**Keep Hold** by Michelle Grubb. Claire knew some things should be left alone and some rules should never be broken, but the most forbidden, well, they are the most tempting. (978-1-62639-5-022)

**The Courage to Try** by C.A. Popovich. Finding love is worth getting past the fear of trying. (978-1-62639-5-282)

**The Time Before Now** by Missouri Vaun. Vivian flees a disastrous affair, embarking on an epic, transformative journey to escape her past, until destiny introduces her to Ida, who helps her rediscover trust, love and hope. (978-1-62639-4-469)

**Twisted Whispers** by Sheri Lewis Wohl. Betrayal, lies, and secrets—whispers of a friend lost to darkness. Can a reluctant psychic set things right or will an evil soul destroy those she loves? (978-1-62639-4-391)

**Deadly Medicine** by Jaime Maddox. Dr. Ward Thrasher's life is in turmoil. Her partner Jess has left her, and her job puts her in the path of a murderous physician who has Jess in his sights. (978-1-62639-4-247)

**New Beginnings** by KC Richardson. Can the connection and attraction between Jordan Roberts and Kirsten Murphy be enough for Jordan to trust Kirsten with her heart? (978-1-62639-4-506)

**Officer Down** by Erin Dutton. Can two women who've made careers out of being there for others in crisis find the strength to need each other? (978-1-62639-4-230)

**Reasonable Doubt** by Carsen Taite. Just when Sarah and Ellery think they've left dangerous careers behind, a new case sets them—and their hearts—on a collision course. (978-1-62639-4-421)

**Tarnished Gold** by Ann Aptaker. Cantor Gold must outsmart the Law, outrun New York's dockside gangsters, outplay a shady art dealer, his lover, and a beautiful curator, and stay out of a killer's gun sights. (978-1-62639-4-261)

**The Renegade** by Amy Dunne. Post-apocalyptic survivors Alex and Evelyn secretly find love while held captive by a deranged cult, but when their relationship is discovered, they must fight for their freedom—or die trying. (978-1-62639-4-278)

**Thrall** by Barbara Ann Wright. Four women in a warrior society must work together to lift an insidious curse while caught between their own desires, the will of their peoples, and an ancient evil. (978-1-62639-4-377)

**White Horse in Winter** by Franci McMahon. Love between two women collides with the inner poison of a closeted horse trainer in the green hills of Vermont. (978-1-62639-4-292)

**The Chameleon** by Andrea Bramhall. Two old friends must work through a web of lies and deceit to find themselves again, but in the search they discover far more than they ever went looking for. (978-1-62639-363-9)

**Side Effects** by VK Powell. Detective Jordan Bishop and Dr. Neela Sahjani must decide if it's easier to trust someone with your heart or your life as they face threatening protestors, corrupt politicians, and their increasing attraction. (978-1-62639-364-6)

**Autumn Spring** by Shelley Thrasher. Can Bree and Linda, two women in the autumn of their lives, put their hearts first and find the love they've never dared seize? (978-1-62639-365-3)

**Warm November** by Kathleen Knowles. What do you do if the one woman you want is the only one you can't have? (978-1-62639-366-0)

**In Every Cloud** by Tina Michele. When she finally leaves her shattered life behind, is Bree strong enough to salvage the remaining pieces of her heart and find the place where it truly fits? (978-1-62639-413-1)

**Rise of the Gorgon** by Tanai Walker. When independent Internet journalist Elle Pharell goes to Kuwait to investigate a veteran's mysterious suicide, she hires Cassandra Hunt, an interpreter with a covert agenda. (978-1-62639-367-7)

**Crossed** by Meredith Doench. Agent Luce Hansen returns home to catch a killer and risks everything to revisit the unsolved murder of her first girlfriend and confront the demons of her youth. (978-1-62639-361-5)

**Making a Comeback** by Julie Blair. Music and love take center stage when jazz pianist Liz Randall tries to make a comeback with the help of her reclusive, blind neighbor, Jac Winters. (978-1-62639-357-8)

**Soul Unique** by Gun Brooke. Self-proclaimed cynic Greer Landon falls for Hayden Rowe's paintings and the young woman shortly after, but will Hayden, who lives with Asperger syndrome, trust her and reciprocate her feelings? (978-1-62639-358-5)

**The Price of Honor** by Radclyffe. Honor and duty are not always black and white—and when self-styled patriots take up arms against the government, the price of honor may be a life. (978-1-62639-359-2)

**Mounting Evidence** by Karis Walsh. Lieutenant Abigail Hargrove and her mounted police unit need to solve a murder and protect wetland biologist Kira Lovell during the Washington State Fair. (978-1-62639-343-1)

**Threads of the Heart** by Jeannie Levig. Maggie and Addison Rae-McInnis share a love and a life, but are the threads that bind them together strong enough to withstand Addison's restlessness and the seductive Victoria Fontaine? (978-1-62639-410-0)

**Sheltered Love** by MJ Williamz. Boone Fairway and Grey Dawson—two women touched by abuse—overcome their pasts to find happiness in each other. (978-1-62639-362-2)

**Asher's Out** by Elizabeth Wheeler. Asher Price's candid photographs capture the truth, but when his success requires exposing an enemy, Asher discovers his only shot at happiness involves revealing secrets of his own. (978-1-62639-411-7)

**The Ground Beneath** by Missouri Vaun. An improbable barter deal involving a hope chest and dinners for a month places lovely Jessica Walker distractingly in the way of Sam Casey's bachelor lifestyle. (978-1-62639-606-7)

**Hardwired** by C.P. Rowlands. Award-winning teacher Clary Stone, and Leefe Ellis, manager of the homeless shelter for small children, stand together in a part of Clary's hometown that she never knew existed. (978-1-62639-351-6)

**No Good Reason** by Cari Hunter. A violent kidnapping in a Peak District village pushes Detective Sanne Jensen and lifelong friend Dr. Meg Fielding closer, just as it threatens to tear everything apart. (978-1-62639-352-3)

**Romance by the Book** by Jo Victor. If Cam didn't keep disrupting her life, maybe Alex could uncover the secret of a century-old love story, and solve the greatest mystery of all—her own heart. (978-1-62639-353-0)

**Death's Doorway** by Crin Claxton. Helping the dead can be deadly: Tony may be listening to the dead, but she needs to learn to listen to the living. (978-1-62639-354-7)

**Searching for Celia** by Elizabeth Ridley. As American spy novelist Dayle Salvesen investigates the mysterious disappearance of her ex-lover, Celia, in London, she begins questioning how well she knew Celia—and how well she knows herself. (978-1-62639-356-1)

**The 45th Parallel** by Lisa Girolami. Burying her mother isn't the worst thing that can happen to Val Montague when she returns to the woodsy but peculiar town of Hemlock, Oregon. (978-1-62639-342-4)

**A Royal Romance** by Jenny Frame. In a country where class still divides, can love topple the last social taboo and allow Queen Georgina and Beatrice Elliot, a working class girl, their happy ever after? (978-1-62639-360-8)

**Bouncing** by Jaime Maddox. Basketball Coach Alex Dalton has been bouncing from woman to woman, because no one ever held her interest, until she meets her new assistant, Britain Dodge. (978-1-62639-344-8)

**Same Time Next Week** by Emily Smith. A chance encounter between Alex Harris and the beautiful Michelle Masters leads to a whirlwind friendship, and causes Alex to question everything she's ever known—including her own marriage. (978-1-62639-345-5)

**All Things Rise** by Missouri Vaun. Cole rescues a striking pilot who crash-lands near her family's farm, setting in motion a chain of events that will forever alter the course of her life. (978-1-62639-346-2)

**Riding Passion** by D. Jackson Leigh. Mount up for the ride through a sizzling anthology of chance encounters, buried desires, romantic surprises, and blazing passion. (978-1-62639-349-3)

**Love's Bounty** by Yolanda Wallace. Lobster boat captain Jake Myers stopped living the day she cheated death, but meeting greenhorn Shy Silva stirs her back to life. (978-1-62639-334-9)

**Just Three Words** by Melissa Brayden. Sometimes the one you want is the one you least suspect. Accountant Samantha Ennis has her ordered life disrupted when heartbreaker Hunter Blair moves into her trendy Soho loft. (978-1-62639-335-6)

**Lay Down the Law** by Carsen Taite. Attorney Peyton Davis returns to her Texas roots to take on big oil and the Mexican Mafia, but will her investigation thwart her chance at true love? (978-1-62639-336-3)

**Playing in Shadow** by Lesley Davis. Survivor's guilt threatens to keep Bryce trapped in her nightmare world unless Scarlet's love can pull her out of the darkness and back into the light. (978-1-62639-337-0)

**Soul Selecta** by Gill McKnight. Soul mates are hell to work with. (978-1-62639-338-7)

**The Revelation of Beatrice Darby** by Jean Copeland. Adolescence is complicated, but Beatrice Darby is about to discover how impossible it can seem to a lesbian coming of age in conservative 1950s New England. (978-1-62639-339-4)

**Twice Lucky** by Mardi Alexander. For firefighter Mackenzie James and Dr. Sarah Macarthur, there's suddenly a whole lot more in life to understand, to consider, to risk…someone will need to fight for her life. (978-1-62639-325-7)

**Shadow Hunt** by L.L. Raand. With young to raise and her Pack under attack, Sylvan, Alpha of the wolf Weres, takes on her greatest challenge when she determines to uncover the faceless enemies known as the Shadow Lords. A Midnight Hunters novel. (978-1-62639-326-4)

**Heart of the Game** by Rachel Spangler. A baseball writer falls for a single mom, but can she ever love anything as much as she loves the game? (978-1-62639-327-1)

**Getting Lost** by Michelle Grubb. Twenty-eight days, thirteen European countries, a tour manager fighting attraction, and an accused murderer: Stella and Phoebe's journey of a lifetime begins here. (978-1-62639-328-8)

**Prayer of the Handmaiden** by Merry Shannon. Celibate priestess Kadrian must defend the kingdom of Ithyria from a dangerous enemy and ultimately choose between her duty to the Goddess and the love of her childhood sweetheart, Erinda. (978-1-62639-329-5)